CHINESE OPERA

CHINESE OPERA

VICTOR PRICE

NEW MOURNE PRESS
2009

Published by the
New Mourne Press
178 King's Road
Belfast BT5 7EN

© Victor Price, 2009

The moral right of the author has been asserted.

ISBN: 978-0-9563216-0-2

for
Martin and Catherine, Eric and Linda,
Robin and Hugh, Jack and Sam

with special thanks to my wife Christina
who always kept the home fires burning

C   H   I

Shum Ch

PEARL RIVER
ESTUARY

LANTAU ISLAND

Siu Kau
Yi Chau

C

Tel

Shek Pik

LAM

Dumbell
Island

Foreword

Those who know Hong Kong may recognise the island I have called Dumbell as Cheung Chau, with its famous Bun Festival. This novel aims at painting an accurate portrait of the Hong Kong of the 1960s, but it *is* a novel, not a documentary; that is why I have given the place a different name.

The British colony that I experienced as a young man has become history. The Bun Festival itself has been transformed by health and safety regulations: today's scalers of the towers are kitted out like mountaineers, making the event less dangerous but also less picturesque and to my mind less Chinese.

Yet it would be a mistake to imagine that Hong Kong itself has been transformed. In spite of the changes wrought by modern technology and the transfer of power from Britain to mainland China, it still remains at a deeper level what is always was: a fragment of old China with the western world superimposed. As one of my characters puts it, 'it was Cathay, it is Hong Kong, it will be America.' The process may have moved on a little, but that is all.

Indeed if an old Hong Kong hand of 1961-62 were to be dropped into the territory today he might rub his eyes at the vast engineering feats – the bridges and tunnels built, the mountains razed to create new land – but he would quickly feel at home. Even the Europeans are still there, having adapted to the new situation. As for the Chinese, who could ever change them? They are protean, granted; but they are also timeless.

Victor Price
August 2009

I

Tzu, Tzu, Tzu

Po Lo-Nui: Ni tu shen mo, T'ai-tsu?
Ho Mu-Lei: Tzu, tzu, tzu ('Words, words, words')

So great was Verity's vexation of spirit that he stumbled after he stepped off the government launch. His front foot stopped dead, as though soldered to the ground; it was a very strange sensation.

'Damn,' he said, freeing it with a lunge. Cheung, his land assistant, puffed across to him, calling 'Oh, sir! Oh, Mr Verity!' but Verity, fearing to be touched by his plump, nervous and sweating subordinate, said 'It's nothing,' in his most clipped tones.

The object of his indignation was old Ng, who was standing on the jetty with an inane grin on his toothless face, his black samfu flapping about his ankles. 'Good morning, Mista Wei Li Ti,' he said, moving his head rapidly up and down as though he wanted to shake it off. He was a skinny old party with bones like dry sticks.

Verity refused to say good morning back; Ng ought to have had tact enough not to appear today, even though he was the chairman of the Dumbell Island Rural Committee and it was for its monthly meeting that Verity was here. But he, Verity,

had received a most disturbing letter that morning and it was
inconceivable that Ng did not know what was in it; it was
quite improper that he should be there.

'Are you sure you're all right?' blurted Cheung in an
imploring voice.

'Don't fuss, Cheung!'

'It's just that you look strange,' was the broken rejoinder.

'I'm perfectly all right,' said Verity, squaring his shoulders.

In the meantime Ng was gabbling in Cantonese. Would
the Fu Mu Kwan (or District Officer) wish him to call the
meeting early? If so, would he deign to take some
refreshment in a wine shop belonging to his, Mr Ng's, sister?
Mr Ng was ready to offer his services in whatever form the
Fu Mu Kwan might require.

'The meeting will take place at two-thirty, as arranged,'
said Verity in firm Cantonese. 'Mr Cheung and I are going for
a short walk before having lunch at the government
bungalow.'

A walk? Mr Ng would do the honours. Mr Ng knew the
island better than any man alive; he would show Mista Wei
Li Ti anything he wished. For instance temples ...

'We are not looking at temples today. Merely taking some
exercise.'

In that case Mr Ng would be their guide. He would
conduct them by a way which would gently stretch their legs
and furnish their eyes with views of the sea.

'No.'

Mr Ng protested. How could a man like the Father
Mother Officer, who had so many cares to occupy his mind,
carry in his head the geography of an insignificant place like
Dumbell?

But Verity could and did. He halted Ng with a firm

goodbye and walked off with Cheung, leaving the old man grinning and gesticulating on the praya.

It was a relief to be moving. They pushed through the warren of little streets that made up the town. A fierce heat drained the blue from the sky and turned it almost black; only an assortment of ancient awnings and broken-fingered umbrellas offered any shade. Out in the bay, high-prowed junks were floating in a sea of molten tin; in front of them a great stink rose from hundreds of dry salt fish lying on wire-netting frames, their heads swathed in paper.

Everything around them was rickety, pullulating, picturesque: furnace-hot noodle stalls, lean-to booths selling ballpoint pens and rubber plimsolls. Stringy men in blue shorts and white singlets washed to a uniform grey prowled around; from odd corners tiny transistors dispensed Cantonese opera, all falsetto shrieks and clashing cymbals. Who was it that had compared it to cats copulating on piles of dustbin lids? Damn; that was Sharkey's remark.

The town huddled on a tongue of land between two mountainous protuberances, hence the island's name. Having passed through it, Verity and Cheung emerged on the Back Beach, where a pair of golden-skinned youngsters were swimming in the polluted water. They then turned right and followed a concrete ribbon of path up the hill on the other side. Here there were cultivated plots, and creeper-laden trees, and a few white villas which urban Chinese from Hong Kong were starting to build.

'Whereabouts is it, Cheung?'

'Here, Mr Verity.'

The land assistant stopped at a cultivated plot beside some dusty trees. Green peppers and runner beans grew up crossed bamboo poles; someone had abandoned a rotting

wicker basket by the side of the path. He took a slit envelope
out of his brief case.

Verity, suddenly weary, put the question: 'Is it just a wild-
goose chase, do you think?'

Cheung's reply was an embarrassed giggle.

Verity looked round him. No sign of life, apart from a rust-
coloured chow lifting its leg against a bush. Yet everybody on
the committee must have known he would be coming here.
Why were they not on the watch to see what he would do?
He had lived all his life among Chinese; he spoke their
language fluently; yet there were times when he simply
could not fathom them. Shameless when it suited them, they
could also be exaggeratedly tactful. Perhaps their very
inscrutability was a form of communication, only his
European background prevented him from picking up the
signals. 'Let's see that letter then,' he said.

Cheung slid the offending document from its envelope. It
was written on the headed paper Verity had had so much
trouble getting for the Rural Committee, and was in
fractured English, a fact significant in itself. It called for the
resignation of chairman Ng Pak Chung as a 'person unfit to
hold public office' and the immediate holding of by-
elections to replace the four General Assembly members
drowned in last year's typhoon; when this had been done the
Council, now up to strength, could proceed to the election of
a new chairman and executive sub-committee. The list of
members making this request was headed by Ho Man, who
was Mr Ng's own vice- chairman. That was ominous.

'Let's take another look at what old Ng is supposed to
have done,' said Verity. He read aloud: 'Mr Ng Pak Chung
prevents his neighbour Mr Tsoi Kwok Fun from making a
living by denying him the use of water from a spring on his

land, although Mr Tsoi had been granted the use of such water by the previous owner, the uncle of Mr Ng.'

He expelled a lungful of air with a hiss. It was all intensely irritating. In the first place this was one those cases where there was nothing firm to lay hold of. In the second, there was the implied slight in the rejection of a chairman elected under his own aegis; for whatever the situation today there was no denying that Ng had proved to be a capable enough vice-chairman in his time. Thirdly and most annoyingly, the resolution of the problem did not even fall within his jurisdiction.

Earlier that same year, 1961, District Officers had been stripped of their authority to act as judges in civil cases. It was a logical move, because with the New Territories' population increasing every day and an entirely new city going up on reclaimed land at Tsuen Wan, they simply wouldn't be able to handle the volume of work. Verity accepted that, but it was nevertheless a wrench to relinquish his role of British-appointed mandarin ruling over a family of fractious but charming grown-up children. 'Let's look at that map,' he said firmly.

The black briefcase yielded a large-scale plan of the area, acquired from Land Registry the previous afternoon; Cheung's damp fingers had left misty marks on the celluloid surface. Handling it with distaste, Verity located their present position.

The situation was clear enough. Uphill, to the left of where they stood, was Ng's flourishing market garden with its plump beans and lettuces; downhill and to the right lay Mr Tsoi's less prosperous plot. Ng's spring bubbled up from under a little rockface at the top of his holding and came chattering down to a concrete basin beside where they stood;

but from there it did not continue into Tsoi's property as gravity would have dictated, but was diverted through a rusty pipe to end up heaven knew where.

'He certainly deprives Tsoi of water,' said Verity. 'Question is: is there anything about water rights in the titles?'

'No, sir.'

'Or has Tsoi an undertaking signed by Ng's uncle?'

Cheung wriggled in his clothes. 'Not sure, sir.'

Verity recognised the signs: Cheung knew the answer well enough but wasn't saying anything. Perhaps out of prudence: would he not have to work with both these men in the years to come?

'Do you think he has?'

Cheung giggled. 'I think maybe not.'

'What about Ho Man and the other signatories? Do they think the same way as you?'

'I think maybe yes.'

Verity sighed. 'In other words it's a put-up job. For some reason they want to get rid of Ng and they're grabbing hold of the first excuse they can think of.'

Once again Cheung wriggled inside his khaki drill shirt. Verity thought: well, now at least I understand. Yet at the same time he suspected that his land assistant had been trying to pull the wool over his eyes. He looked him directly in the eye.

'Tell me, Cheung,' he said sternly. 'What would make twelve responsible committee members want to get rid of a chairman they've worked with for so long?'

Cheung furrowed his brows. 'Maybe they think he's dishonest,' he said.

'Well, is he?'

Cheung did what he always did when confronted with a direct question: he contrived to look like a halfwit, and said nothing. Verity sighed. This also was a known situation; Cheung's reason this time was that the whole thing did not redound to the credit of the Chinese as a race. 'Put away your papers,' he said wearily. 'It's past one.'

They walked the rest of the way to the bungalow, Verity reflecting on the phenomenon that was Cheung. This ridiculous man, with his sweat and his capon's body, ought to be a fool. But he was far from that. He knew the district intimately; the villagers respected him, told him things they would never tell himself. Besides, he was a man of substance who didn't need to work for the government but did it for status. He was known to rent out rooms and bed-spaces in Kowloon tenements, and to possess a wife and a concubine who quarrelled incessantly (another sign of success).

But he offended Verity's sacerdotal concept of colonial administration; how could such an undignified man maintain the gravitas of the office?

The bungalow was a yellow-washed building with metal window bars and a flagpole on the parched lawn. Ah Shing, the departmental cook-boy, a small brown-skinned man with horn-rimmed glasses, was waiting for them at the door. 'Lunch ready, massa,' he said.

Verity was glad to sit down. It had been an exhausting morning, spent at Silvermine Bay on Lantau island, attending to a long-running demarcation dispute over some watercress beds (many a time he had found the rival claimants camped outside his office in Kowloon when he arrived in the morning). And now this Ng business, of which the worst was yet to come: the committee meeting. He felt aggrieved, unwilling to face it. This was his third Hong Kong summer on the trot; he was tired and jaded. And his home leave wasn't due until next year.

Ah Shing was afflicted with asthma but in every other respect magnificent.

Breathing noisily through his nostrils, he served up an excellent European meal. There were fresh mangoes for dessert – a small miracle for September – but then he knew they were Verity's favourite fruit.

But Verity was unable to do them justice. The bungalow smelt permanently of singed air; the windows were usually kept shut, even in hot weather, and no amount of ventilation could dispel it. The smell, he found, killed his appetite.

They clattered up the scuffed wooden staircase to the Chinese Chamber of Commerce, a long room above a restaurant on the praya with a flyblown window overlooking the harbour. The General Assembly of the Rural Committee always met there.

The entire Assembly was already in place, a score of men in samfus or cotton suits: grizzled elders whose heads might have been carved in teak, younger, stockier men with broad cheekbones and eyes that spoke intelligence, cunning, impudence even. All of them were quite sure of their status; they were the leaders of their community, not arrogant but not apologising for anything either.

When Verity and Cheung walked in they rose to their feet, smiled, spoke a greeting and sat down again. Verity sensed the underlying tension, a kind of extra alertness; but his unease was swallowed up by the spontaneous pleasure he always experienced on these occasions: he was the representative of official power, charged with looking after these people. That inspired him with affection for them, a real desire to serve them. His smile, as he went round the table shaking hands and exchanging greetings in Cantonese, was a genuine one.

Mr Ng, officious in his black silk, bustled to the door and called down the stairs, whereupon an amah in a white tunic flip-flopped up from the restaurant below with a tray full of glasses of tea. She set it on the table and shuffled off. Each glass was an amethyst column topped by an empty, steam-frosted cylinder, into which twenty snub noses were immediately plunged.

After a sip at his own Verity set it down and said 'I declare this session of the General Assembly of the Dumbell Island Rural Committee open.' He spoke in English, not out of cultural imperialism but because the islanders preferred it that way, particularly as the official English was usually broken up by jokes and banter in Cantonese. But there would be no banter today.

Cheung translated his senior's English and called the roll. The only absentees were the four men who had been drowned in Typhoon Mary.

'Shall we get down to business?' Verity suggested. 'You all have copies of the agenda: proposed Hung Lee Elementary School, election of Organising Committee for Three Mountains Festival, and Any Other Business. Shall we start with the school?'

It should have been an open and shut case. The Executive Committee, consisting of seven members of the present Assembly, had already negotiated a price for a parcel of land at the south-western corner of the island as the site for a new school, funds were available, a document of sale had even been drawn up. All that was required was the approval of the Assembly.

It soon became clear at once that it wouldn't get it. Ho Man, the Deputy Chairman and principal signatory of the letter in Cheung's briefcase, opposed it. He was a thin man with glasses too wide for his face and a prominent Adam's apple that kept up a perpetual dance as he spoke. His delivery was jerky, his expression pop-eyed, but he spoke well. His main objection was that the land they were proposing to buy was badly situated and had no water supply.

'But, Mr Ho,' said Verity in a pained voice, 'you've attended every session of the Executive Sub-Committee to date and you've never raised these points before.'

'I've been thinking things over.'

'There's piped water fifty yards away,' put in Cheung. 'You can put in an extension ... '

A murmur of protest. 'Fifty yards of new pipes?' questioned one man in a sarcastic tone of voice.

'At twenty dollars a yard!'

'Twenty-five, more likely!'

'But you know as well as I do,' said Verity in what he hoped was a soothing tone, 'that the Round Table will pay half the whole bill, pipes included.'

That brought a moment's silence into which a small man with the look of a bushbaby stuttered the words 'But what about g-g-ghosts?'

'What ghosts?' snapped Ng, suddenly taking a hand.

'The p-p-place is unlucky. There was a m-m-murder there forty years ago.'

'Fool,' hissed Ng.

'I think you'll find that it happened fifty yards away,' said Verity patiently. He had previously been briefed by Cheung.

There followed a long and bitter debate on the precise distance between the site of the murder and the plot for the school, during which it became clear that the anti-purchase, and therefore anti-Ng, faction had chosen to sit along one side of the table and the pro-Ng faction along the other. Interestingly, this division overrode old antagonisms. For example, Mr T.C. Leung and Elder Kwok were sitting beside each other, in spite of the fact that they constantly quarrelled; Leung, a rope-maker by profession, made a habit of laying out his goods on the ground outside the hovel that Kwok dignified with the name of a bean-curd factory, thus – he claimed – depriving him of business. Now the two – the burly Leung and the emaciated Kwok – were almost civil to one another.

Verity listened to this futile discussion until his patience gave out. 'This is getting us nowhere,' he said. 'Let us put it to the vote.'

'Those in favour?' called Cheung quickly. 'And against?' Hands shot up.

He announced the result. 'In favour, fourteen votes. Against, thirteen. I declare the motion ... '

But Elder Kwok was on his feet. 'I object,' he piped.

'On what grounds?' asked Verity, irritated.

'On the grounds that this meeting is four people short.'

'What four?' shrilled Ng.

'The four drowned in the typhoon.'

Verity was on the verge of saying 'Irrelevant; we have a quorum' when he realised that Cheung was making frantic signals. He hesitated.

'Maybe with new members the vote would go the other

way,' broke in Ho Man, moving his glasses up and down in rhythm with his Adam's apple.

'Maybe pigs have wings,' muttered Verity in English. Cheung translated:

'That is mere speculation.'

'This is a democratic decision,' shouted Ng, standing up and waving his arms about.

Verity silenced him. 'Order, please. You have left me with no option. I am obliged to make a ruling ... '

'If it goes against me I resign,' cried Ho Man, agitated.

'I resign! I resign!' Twelve other voices followed.

'Then no quorum,' cried Ho Man, triumphantly.

Verity felt utterly fed up with the whole business and furious with Ng for foisting it on him, however indirectly. Granting Ho Man's party a victory would be a travesty of democracy, but he could see no way out. 'Decision postponed pending by-elections,' he announced wearily.

Pandemonium ensued. Ng and his supporters vociferated loudly; Ho Man and his tried to prevent them being heard. Finally, Verity's hand re-established silence. 'Nobody has lost,' he said indignantly. 'The decision is merely postponed. – Next business.'

'Election of Organising Committee for Three Mountains Festival,' said Cheung quickly.

This, thought Verity, should be simpler. The Committee was normally re-elected year by year without opposition. Its constitution was a masterpiece of diplomacy, holding in balance the conflicting interests of the island: the clan associations, the Chamber of Commerce, the Joint Fisheries Association, the T'ung Hing Welfare Association. What could possibly go wrong?

Everything, apparently. Ng was the chairman of this

committee too, and in a matter of seconds the Assembly was involved in another bout of acrimony, with voices trying to shout each other down across the table.

Verity, gathering what energy he had, adopted a solemn, more-in-sorrow-than-in-anger tone. 'Gentlemen,' he said, I hardly need remind you that if the name of Dumbell enjoys fame beyond the confines of this colony it is because of the Three Mountains Festival. People come from far and wide to see it. It is a glorious manifestation of the traditional culture of the Chinese people. Do you seriously want to place it at risk? Let us put our rivalries aside and re-elect the Organising Committee; the reputation of this island stands or falls by our decision.'

It was useless. The Assembly was determined to disagree and disagree it did.

The issue of the Organising Committee also had to be postponed pending by-elections.

The old amah, flip-flopping her way up the stairs with fresh tea, brought a welcome truce, during which Verity contemplated the rival factions: Ng and Ho Man, Li Ho Wing of the Celebrated Elegance restaurant, Lam Ping Sung the junk-builder, Elder Kwok and T.C. Leung and all the others, sitting there with stern faces.

He tapped the table with his glass and Cheung said 'Any other business?'

Well, this was it; might as well get it over with.

To his surprise there was silence, a long drawn-out silence that made Verity wonder whether anybody was going to say anything at all. He realised that he would have to raise the taboo subject himself; perhaps that was what they were all driving at anyway. 'Very well,' he said, 'I have a point to raise myself.'

There was an intake of breath round the table. 'Pass me that letter, will you, Mr Cheung?'

He read the letter slowly in English, with Cheung translating. Ng listened impassively as he was stigmatised and called on to resign. When the reading was over a slow sigh rose from the meeting.

Verity put on a stern face. 'This letter is completely out of order,' he said. 'Mr Ng was constitutionally elected and cannot be removed from his post unless a majority of the members of this assembly wish it, which is clearly not the case.' He held his hand up to prevent any interruption. 'As for the accusation it contains, I can only advise the signatories to withdraw it. Regarding Mr Tsoi, if he has a case to plead let him put it to a court of law. It will not be tried by me ... ' His lip twitched involuntarily. 'But it will be tried fairly and objectively.'

Cheung translated again, and Verity went on. 'I have in my hand a map of the area in question. The boundaries of the two parcels of land involved are quite clear; so is their ownership. But Land Registry have no record of any claim of Mr Tsoi's to water from Mr Ng's spring.'

'Ng's uncle gave it to him!' cried several voices.

'Can you prove that, Mr Tsoi?'

'Everybody knows it,' said Tsoi sullenly.

Verity addressed the meeting at large. 'How long has Mr Ng been denying My Tsoi this water?'

No answer. Then Cheung said, quietly: 'Five years, Mr Verity. Since his uncle's death.'

'I see,' said Verity, now totally in command. 'In other words Mr Tsoi has waited five years before it occurred to him to object. Why is that, Mr Tsoi?'

Tsoi wriggled in his chair and said nothing. 'Ng is a bad

man!' shouted a grizzled old fellow who had said nothing until now.

'Indeed, sir? Then why is it that you, and all the others who have signed this letter—' He waved it in the air '—have put up with him until today? You are well aware that Mr Tsoi never had an undertaking from Mr Ng's uncle, yet you are pretending that he had. In other words you are attacking your elected chairman for nothing. – Or for some reason you are not prepared to reveal to me.'

Being so blunt was a gamble; in Verity's experience Chinese were wary of direct confrontations with authority. But this one seemed to be coming off. He looked round the circle of baffled faces and thought: Now I've got them. The time was ripe for a homily. To the Chinese villager, since time immemorial, a high-minded telling-off was the natural way to end such disputes. It was what the people of the New Territories had always expected from their Fu Mu Kwan. He took a deep breath and prepared to deliver one.

To his astonishment, an anonymous middle-aged man sitting at the far end of the table stood up and shuffled out of the room. A second followed, then a third; they were all Ho Man supporters. In a moment half the assembly members were creaking down the wooden stairs and away. Ng and his defiant party remained. It came to Verity in a flash: they knew he had no authority to judge them any more; the world would never be the same again.

'No quorum, Mista Wei Li Ti,' said Ng with a crooked grin.

Verity did the only thing he could: he declared the meeting closed.

The *Sir Cecil Clementi* drew away from the quayside and its
raucous life: the old women selling heaps of orange-yellow
squid, the idlers padding around on rubber sandals, the
coolies in cotton vests loping on mysterious errands, the stall-
holders staring incuriously at the government launch.

They chugged past the lines of black-hulled junks,
sending a bow-wave slapping against their sides, narrowly
avoiding a boat-woman poling a sampan shaped like a slice of
melon. Then they swung round the north end of the island –
yellow, rocky, strewn with great boulders – and headed east
for Hong Kong.

The view from the bows was inspiring. Looking round in
a broad arc from left to right you saw first, to the north, the
rugged mass of Lantau, then Stonecutters' Island with its
two low peaks and array of wireless masts, then, full ahead,
Kowloon, a cluster of huge cubes glittering in the rays of the
westering sun. To the right lay Hong Kong island itself with
its fringe of skyscrapers and desiccated hills gullied by the
rains of the typhoon season, barren save for one irregular
green streak, the Dairy Farm, running down its western
flank.

Between all this and the launch rode the ships that gave
the place its living.

Anchored in lines were battered little tramps of unknown
provenance, the neater cargo vessels of Maersk or the Head
Line, a white-painted schooner on an island tour, and black-
hulled lighters glued to the sides of merchantmen, each with
a wheelhouse aft and bits of old tyres hanging round its hull.
Assiduous launches flying blue ensigns with concentric

circles of yellow and white crisscrossed the harbour; and, today, for a special treat, an American aircraft-carrier was anchored out west, a floating wall with planes on top like insects with folded wings.

Four generations of Verity's family had lived in this place. His great-grandfather had come out as an army subaltern in 1879, in Pope-Hennessy's time, and stayed to import jade and silks from Canton; his son, Verity's grandfather, had been a government surveyor and given his name to Verity Path that used to climb from Boundary Street to Kowloon Peak until it was obliterated by resettlement blocks. And that son's son, Verity's father, had worked all his life with Marine Department until he retired to the colder waters of Poole Harbour.

He himself, the fourth in the line, in a sense represented its culmination, because each generation had served the community more altruistically than its predecessor and himself most altruistically of all. He was the goal towards which they had all been tending, and that gave him an almost impossible ideal to live up to – especially today when he had been rebuffed by the people he served. Cheung was chatting with the Chinese seaman whose job it was to moor and unmoor the vessel; the skipper, a jovial Yorkshireman with a beard, stood smoking at the wheel. Verity called his land assistant over.

'Do you understand what this thing is all about, Cheung?' he asked. 'This Dumbell business, I mean.'

Cheung wriggled inside his shirt. 'Oh no, Mr Verity. Indeed no.' He managed to look wary and terrified at the same time.

Verity shrugged. 'Clearly they couldn't care less about the school, or the Festival Committee, or even that stupid water.

They wanted to get at Ng personally.' Then a thought struck him. 'Or perhaps at me.'

'Oh no!' cried Cheung, horrified. 'Not at you. At Mr Ng.'

'So you do know something?'

Cheung protested his innocence. 'Not at all, Mr Verity. Not at all!'

'Well, whatever it is it must be pretty bad; I've never seen them so worked up before.' He stared gloomily at the oily water sliding past the bow of the launch. 'And now what a to-do there will be.'

It was all too painfully clear. He would make his report to the District Commissioner, who would raise the matter at the morning liaison meeting. But not before someone had given the story to the Chinese press and perhaps even to the *Kwangtung Courier*, where the governor's private secretary would read it and pass it on to H.E. There would be a debate in Legco and the elected members would have a go at the New Territories Administration ... He shook his head in annoyance. There would be no end to it.

'After by-elections everything will be all right,' said Cheung, surprisingly reassuring.

'I hope you're right. – But how on earth do we organise them?'

'I don't know. I'll look it up in the book.'

'Could you do that by tomorrow morning?'

'Oh yes, sir!' Cheung was delighted; to be asked to do extra work in the evening was a signal favour.

Verity's depression began to lift. Perhaps it wouldn't amount to much after all. Perhaps they would settle things among themselves when he, the intrusive European, wasn't present. Racial solidarity could work wonders sometimes.

They were now nosing in towards the pier through a

flotilla of sampans, bobbing indomitably, unsinkable as corks. In front of them the sheer temples of free enterprise were resplendent in the sun, standing over the life of the colony like the sampan-owners over their single oar. How reassuring they were!

Cheung watched his boss step on to the quay. He was a preposterous man of course, as only Europeans could be, with their pursuit of wraithlike ideas and their blind eye for reality. Yet the ideas, though ridiculous in themselves, were genuine and Verity believed in them with all his soul. His very sincerity gave him a ludicrous kind of dignity, like a hippopotamus.

On the way home he called in at the lounge of the Gloucester Hotel for a drink; he needed one. It was seven o'clock and dark by the time he got there, but he had rung his cook-boy Ah Lok and told him to put his dinner in the oven. He lived on the Peak, in a government quarter in Stewart Terrace. It was inconvenient for his office in Kowloon and damp ran regularly down the walls; but he liked the quiet up there.

He liked the Gloucester too, for its neutrality. You were on the seventh floor of a colonial building in the Far East but you might as well have been in the lounge of a hotel back home. There were leather bench seats, moquette armchairs and little wooden tables. The murmur of middle-aged European voices was soothing.

No sooner had he sat down than he saw Sharkey. Damn,

he muttered, and would have got up and gone had not the barman already been at his elbow waiting for his order. Resignedly, he asked for a Scotch and soda and hid his face behind a copy of the *China Mail* which he had just bought in Statue Square.

He couldn't settle to reading; Sharkey's presence kept obtruding itself. He was sitting alone at a table, quite drunk and laughing helplessly to himself. He'd known the fellow for over thirty years – ever since they'd been at Wellington in fact – and had never liked him. He was a disgrace to the school, to his country, to Verity himself. Look at him, sitting there in his crumpled suit, laughing idiotically and making patterns with his fingernail in a pool of spilled beer.

To his horror this vision lurched round, saw him, and cried boozily 'Verity! Haven't seen you since pussy was a cat ... – Oh dear, there I go, talking about pussy again.'

Heads swivelled in their direction, then turned back to their own affairs, keeping one ear cocked for fresh developments. Verity, in an agony of embarrassment, apostrophised heaven for allowing this man to follow him half way round the world, like a disreputable Siamese twin. 'I have to go in a minute,' he said stiffly.

'Ballocks! Come over here for a chat.'

He went; there would be the most appalling fuss if he didn't. Sitting down gingerly – the slopping beer was beginning to drip off the table – he noticed a second glass. 'But you've got company,' he said.

'Only Gus Donoghue. He's gone for a slash.'

'Who's Donoghue?'

'Who's Donoghue? Who's Donoghue? Donoghue's just the fastest gun in the East, that's who Donoghue is.' He tittered drunkenly to himself.

At that point the door of the Gents opened and Donoghue himself emerged: a large, craggy, handsome man with curly black hair and Celtic eyes of a fanatical blue; a ragged scar ran from the corner of his left eye to the lobe of his ear, giving him a sinister, Byronic look.

'Verity here doesn't know who you are,' said Sharkey owlishly.

Donoghue extended his right hand and said in a phoney American accent:

'Hiram C. Donoghue, First President, Trans-Asia Pipe.'

'Laid any good pipe recently?' simpered Sharkey.

Donoghue replied gravely: 'It's been a below average drilling season. My mains pressure was abnormally high until relieved by Miss Tube of 1961.'

'My tunnelling shield has practically seized up,' sighed Sharkey.

'You need an urgent blow-through. Never mind the quality, think of the length.' Sharkey gave a military salute. 'The essence of good pipe-laying is strength and regularity of thrust. Remember that and you'll not go far wrong.'

'Excellent fooling,' said Sharkey, wiping his eyes. 'But is the witching hour of eight not nigh?'

'True. See you, old sport,' said Donoghue. 'Cheerio, squire,' he added for Verity's benefit, tossed back his drink and left.

'Don't forget we're dubbing on Sunday!' Sharkey called after him. Then, to Verity: 'He dispenses pap on Hong Kong Radio tonight: namely the hit parade.' He sank back into laughter, his lips wet with beer.

Verity contemplated the small, slim figure in front of him. Above the crumpled suit and the corkscrewing tie the face was certainly striking. Its upper half was refined, even

exquisitely so: a high, delicately shaped forehead framed in
silky fair hair, poetic blue eyes under arched brows, a nose
aristocratically narrow. But under that it was almost bestial,
with thin lips curling back over forward-set teeth in an
obscene monkey's grin. In the past thirty-odd years Verity
had seen more of the simian than the angelic qualities. A
sight more.

'Poor Nigs,' Sharkey was cooing. 'Can't make me out.'

'Why must you use that silly schoolboy abbreviation? My
name is Nigel.'

'Auld lang syne, Nigs.'

'Not at all. It's in order to get on my nerves,' retorted
Verity, not without humour.

'Touché,' Sharkey conceded and tried to shape his pool of
beer into a map of Ireland. 'The Shannon estuary's the
difficult bit,' he said aloud.

'What's difficult?' asked Verity, nonplussed.

'Chastity, Nigs, chastity.'

'Why do you waste your time like that?' said Verity,
frowning.

Sharkey's voice dropped dramatically. 'I suffer from an
incurable illness.'

A stab of involuntary alarm went through Verity. Sharkey,
contrasting the other man's horrified disbelief with his
military crispness of bearing – the straight back, the long
head, the skin tanned to a milk-chocolate brown, the
greying hair and moustache – burst into a great splutter of
laughter

'You're priceless, you really are. I was referring to the
malady of this and every other century: boredom. 'Tu le
connais, lecteur, ce monstre délicat – ' He leaned forward
and hissed the words 'Hypocrite lecteur, mon semblable,

mon frère!' At which point the gas inside him escaped in a juddering belch, catching Verity full in the face.

'You look shagged, Nigs,' Sharkey went on.

'I've been doing a hard day's work,' objected Verity, dabbing his face with his handkerchief.

'Implying that I have not. – And it's quite true. The university term has not yet begun, and even if it had French is not the most popular of subjects, I rarely have more than three students to a class. In addition to which the *Kwangtung Courier* is going through a somnolent period and Hong Kong Radio won't use me – perhaps I've got halitosis and it comes across on mike. So I'm reduced to alcohol and entertaining lustful thoughts about young women.'

'You needn't elaborate,' said Verity, and prepared to get up.

But Sharkey stretched out an ancient mariner hand. 'You wouldn't desert a lonely man, would you?' he pleaded. 'Boy! Same again.'

'No please ... '

'Let's talk about old times.' Sharkey was inexorable. 'For example, that time when I cribbed your Latin unseen and old Thompson thought it was the other way round and gave you six of the best.'

'You could say it sums up our relationship.'

'Indeed. You never split on me. Took your punishment like a man. Always trying to live up to something, Nigs,' he tut-tutted.

'You should try it some time.'

'The only thing I try to live up to is girls taller than myself. Of whom there are many.'

Verity gave a small, sharp shake of the head. 'I sometimes wonder what possible satisfaction you can get from this life of yours,' he said.

Sharkey's reply was to fold his body in two, spread his fingers like claws, bare his teeth and utter a grating cry half way between a seagull's shriek and the squeal of a rusty hinge. This performance occasioned some perturbation among the denizens of the Gloucester lounge.

'What on earth ... ?' began Verity, starting to his feet again.

'It's only my warp-spasm,' said Sharkey in an offhand voice. 'Reserved for people who insist on talking about satisfaction.'

'I don't follow ... '

'The warp-spasm was devised by my ancestor Cuchullain to discomfit his adversaries.'

'Your ancestor who?'

'Cuchullain. Legendary Irish hero.'

'If he's legendary how can he be your ancestor?'

'I spoke metaphorically. – But to your previous remark. Frankly, I get very little satisfaction from it. I look at the universe and I look at myself – the relationship is to say the least of it tenuous. It's my considered opinion that the universe could get on perfectly well without me. In fact the only thing that ever gives me a thought is my own shivering little soul. So I lift the trapdoor to the underground pit it lives in and I call out: are you OK down there? What does it reply? Fuck all, Nigs. Fuck all. Les bêtes l'ont mangée.'

'You ought to change,' was Verity's lame reply.

'I agree. My shirt's disgusting. Trouble is, my amah's left me ever since I put her in the family way.'

This piece of vulgarity was too much for Verity. 'Excuse me,' he said stiffly, 'I really must go.' And he did, leaving his second whisky untouched on the table.

Sharkey, lolling over his pool of beer, blew a raspberry after him. Poor old Nigs: no sense of humour, no sex life, nothing but superannuated ideas. A sad case. Yet he had to admit that he felt a certain admiration for him.

Seven floors below, Verity's eye caught a headline he had not noticed in the *China Mail*: TWELVE BODIES WASHED UP. Standing in Des Voeux Road, he skimmed over the short article. The bodies had been discovered at Telegraph Bay, on Hong Kong Island. They were accompanied by stray planks, presumably from a junk, the implication being that these were mainland Chinese who had been trying to enter the colony illegally.

He shook his head: a horrifying story. But at least it hadn't happened in his district.

I have no boat, so can mount no expedition to an outlying island. And I will not immerse myself in the warm urine of Deepwater Bay. Ergo, thought Sharkey, I go to Whitesands.

He was sitting in a sampan in Hebe Haven with Mary Rhodes, Alec Scrymgeour and a melancholy Chinese youth called Wilson Ho. Dinghies and yachts fidgeted around them, and rusty beer cans embedded on the foreshore mud mocked the grandeur of the hills. A transistor wailed from a rickety shed, its caterwaulings punctuated by taps from a boat-builder's mallet.

Alec turned to the boatman, a toothless old Chinese with grey stubble on his chin. 'How much?' he asked, smiling his fastidious snarl-smile.

'Two dollar.'

'You come fetch us six o'clock?'

'Sik o klok.'

The man grinned and pulled his frayed rope; the outboard motor ran. They chugged sedately across to the rocks that marked the entrance of the narrow inlet: one embittered historian, one widowed lecturer in English and himself, a jolly party of middle-aged academics. The Chinese youth hardly counted; he rarely opened his mouth anyway. Sharkey, contemplating his hangover, wondered why he had come.

Once clear of the entrance they rode into a choppier sea. The boatman swung hard to port and put in at a sheltered little beach where a motor boat was anchored, with a man in flowered trunks in the act of diving from its deck. On the sand two European children played with a beach ball. Few Chinese came here.

The engine stopped; the sampan nudged the sand.

'Land ahoy!' cried Mary in her girlish voice and leapt into the water with her sandals in her hand. Scrymgeour, bespattered, brushed the drops off his shirt. 'Damn,' he said, flattening the vowel as only an Edinburgh man can.

'She's the active type,' said Sharkey.

The boatman pushed off and they carried their togs up the sloping beach: swimsuits, towels, an inflatable rubber mattress. Scrymgeour carried his cigarettes and lighter in a plastic toilet bag.

'I can't wait to take the plunge!' cried Mary. 'Oi oi,' said Sharkey meaningfully but she ignored him. Holding a towel round her shoulders with her teeth, she tugged her way out of blouse and brassiere and into the top of her two-piece. Alec had trunks on under his trousers: he was a canny man. As for the Chinese youth, he didn't swim.

Sharkey was glad to get his clothes off; it was after all his natural state. Drink and fornication had made no impression on his boyish body. He admired the clear skin, the good proportions, the lack of hair: only two silky tufts in the armpits. Not bad for a drunken whoremaster of forty, he gloated. Forty-five, amended his conscience.

He swam strongly out and dived into green glooms. It was beautiful under the water; the sun's rays wobbled through the turquoise and gold of it, and tiny fish, glimpsed out of the corner of his eye, swam by on slanting courses. He rose and dived and rose again, purifying himself; then came up for the last time and opened his eyes on a burst of glare. Spots of light danced everywhere: on the waves, on the hills beyond, on the sky. It was like looking at the world through salt crystals. 'Not bad, eh?' he called.

No reply. Alec was doing his silent breaststroke, his head craning forward like a cormorant's. Mary was hull down in the water, a resting leviathan. Both were full of their own concerns. He pinched Mary on the thigh to waken her up.

She splashed water at him and they wrestled together like children, dazzling each other with flying spray. His fingers sank into the flesh of her shoulders; his hard thighs tangled with her soft ones.

'Pax!' she cried at last. 'I'm too old for this lark.'

Scrymgeour swam up. He raised one arm, taking in the sea, the hills, the profound blue of the sky. 'This is how it was,' he intoned, 'before Homo Crapulens came along with his armies and inquisitions and shit factories.'

'At least you can't blame the Chinese,' said Mary. 'Look at Wilson. He's doing absolutely nothing.'

It was true. The young man was sitting on the beach in floppy shorts and Hawaiian shirt, his back stiff as a ramrod, reading.

'Where did you dig him up?' asked Sharkey.

'He's a student of mine. Bright but shy. Needs encouraging.'

'I suppose you expect us to do some winkling,' drawled Scrymgeour.

Mary looked at her toes, twin rows of charming little sausages peeping up from under the water, and said, 'I expect a lot more than that. I expect Liam to arrange for him to get this Lok Yuen Scholarship.'

'Helping people is against my principles.'

'We'll talk about it later,' said Mary firmly.

Scrymgeour's mind was elsewhere. 'What a pity the Chinese are taking to the beach,' he murmured. 'It's the end of Hong Kong as we know it.'

'Repulse Bay must have been like this once,' observed Sharkey, following Alec's train of thought. 'Two or three parties on the beach and not a villa in sight.'

'There would have been bathing machines.' That was Mary.

'An impressionist Deauville on the South China Sea.'

'Did I ever tell you what happened to me once in Castlepeak Bay?' enquired Alec.

'No, but you're going to.'

'It was just like today. Rocks, sand, sun, sea ... A little cove down off the road – Gemini Beach, I think. I'll not say I felt happy. But reconciled. And then I saw them.'

'Saw what?'

'Turds. Hundreds of them, bobbing gently. Turds from Tsuen Wan.' Mary pouted in discomfort. 'See what I mean? Homo Crapulens.'

They wanted to get out of the sea then, so swam back to the beach and lay down on their towels. Wilson looked up from his book and said in his precise voice 'Did you have a good swim?' His face was thin, expressionless, his brows furrowed.

'Fine,' said Sharkey. 'What's the book?'

'*Nicholas Nickleby.*'

'Do you like it?'

'The style is vigorous, plastic, tending to caricature,' said Wilson, blinking.

'You're right,' Sharkey said. There didn't seem to be any other possible comment.

Conversation having died, they stretched out in the sun with closed eyes. From further along the beach came the two children's voices, high and disembodied like the spirits of the dead.

Eventually Mary spoke. 'I didn't know you were so good a swimmer, Liam,' she said.

'My mother was an O'Donovan.'

'What on earth is that supposed to mean?' came Alec's sarcastic voice.

Sharkey opened his eyes and addressed him. 'You confirm my worst suspicions,' he said. 'You're not a real Celt; you're the worst kind of Lowland Sassenach. Real Celts know that the O'Donovans have a seal-ancestress.'

A musical sigh escaped Mary. 'I once had a Labrador dog exactly like a seal. He was the creature I loved best in the whole world.'

'Perhaps he was a seal,' drawled Scrymgeour. 'That would make him Sharkey's cousin.'

'Going back to that ancestress of yours,' said Mary in her most academic voice, 'I don't see how a man can have carnal knowledge of a seal.'

'Love will find a way.'

That was Scrymgeour. Sharkey said nothing. He had just made an embarrassing discovery; he desired carnal knowledge of Mary.

He blamed it on Verity. Why had the wretched fellow said 'You ought to change' just when he did – at the precise moment when the S.S.M. had let him down? The S.S.M., or Sharkey Standard Model, was three inches taller than himself, had pale blue eyes, long legs and windswept hair painfully fair. It suffered from agonised sexual hunger and never stayed for long, being hell-bent on pursuing its erotic Calvary; but when you happened upon it the result was ecstatic. Or had been. Only last week he had discovered a perfect specimen, a young domestic economy teacher at Belilios Girls School just out from England – perfect in appearance but, alas, far from that in performance.

Lying on the sand in a cocoon of heat, he pondered the situation: was the relative fiasco her fault or his? Was she merely damp tinder or had he failed to ignite her? He had reached the male menopause, that fateful time for all men. Some developed a taste for boys, but who ever heard of one lusting after fat middle-aged university lecturers? Was he some kind of pervert? The thought had rushed into his mind the moment after Mary's legs had twined round his own.

Hold hard though. The experience had been pleasurable enough. So perhaps his yen for a closer acquaintanceship with the said legs was not necessarily a proof that he had gone soft in the head. Mary was a large woman, granted; well-upholstered everywhere, but she was not actually fat. Her flesh had neither folds nor flabbiness in it; it didn't quiver when she moved. And move she did, vigorously; he had seen her play a fearsome game of tennis. Men had desired her in the past – after all she had had a husband – and for all he knew still did.

Could it be that this odd dilemma was his fault, not hers? Perhaps with advancing years a man's taste changed, from hard to soft as it were, from sword-like thighs and tight little breasts to something more restful and enveloping, as an ageing lion might crave a tenderer cut of antelope. Well, there was only one way of finding out: have her and see. That was precisely what he proposed to do.

She was talking to Wilson now, mothering him. 'Not too hot, are you?'

'No, Mrs Rhodes.'

'For heaven's sake, call me Mary.'

'Yes, Mrs Rhodes.'

'I don't think you really enjoy the beach.'

'It's very pleasant.'

Sharkey looked across to the young Chinese. 'Did you ever hear the one about the Englishman, the Irishman and the Scotsman?' he asked.

'No, Mr Sharkey.'

'That's funny. Neither did I.'

'Don't be a beast, Liam,' cried Mary.

'I was only trying to make him laugh.'

'Well don't.' She proceeded to lecture Wilson on the subject of Robert Browning, about whom he had to write an essay.

Scrymgeour sat up; his dugs were fleshy and slightly drooping. 'A fine place, this, for the Twilight of the Gods,' he observed.

'Here we go again,' said Sharkey sourly.

'Don't interrupt. The gods usually enjoy their twilight in foggy Nordic locations. How much more comfortable to experience it here, where the moribund flesh is at least covered with a becoming tan.'

'You've been reading Spengler again.'

'I never read anything later than Gibbon. But you don't need Spengler to know that the west is in decline. Just look at us: the ten thousand who have fetched up in this odd little appendage of China. We're all second-raters. Like you, for instance – scraping a living from a bit of lecturing here and a bit of journalism there. You wouldn't get either at home. And do you imagine Mary and I would have our cushy jobs back in England? No, we're all second-raters, cast up on this Prospero's isle, feeding off magic banquets and swigging at Trinculo's bottle.' He waved a languid but dramatic arm. 'The question is: what shall we do when the bottle runs dry?'

'We're not the west, Alec,' broke in Mary. 'The better people back home are.'

'Indeed?' retorted Scrymgeour. 'Trade unionists and Mr John Osborne and these Earwigs ... '

'Beatles.'

'All right, Beatles. But aren't they all squabbling and squealing and jigging their way to perdition? And they're not even having a good time, as we are.'

'Whereas the Chinese ... ' prompted Sharkey. He had heard the speech before.

'Whereas the Chinese will inherit the earth. And do you know why?'

'No birth control?'

'No sense of humour!' said Alec triumphantly.

Mary intervened; Wilson and she had abandoned Browning and were now listening. 'Because they work!' she cried. 'Look at Wilson here. His family lives in a resettlement block that we couldn't begin to put up with. Yet they're in clover compared with most of their people. They all chip in to keep him at university; they work and slave the way the English used to do but have forgotten – the way my old Dad did on the railways. We can't do the same; we've been spoiled by comfort. Wilson's family will inherit the earth because they deserve it.'

'I wish you joy of it, Wilson,' drawled Scrymgeour, 'but your family aren't the Chinese I was thinking of.'

'Who were you thinking of then?' said Mary.

Scrymgeour flung his arm wide towards the east, beyond Mirs Bay, in a gesture that embraced the China that lay beyond: the hundreds of millions of mysterious, disciplined, dangerous people; the communes marching out to the fields in the morning and marching back at night with martial songs on their lips. If reports were to be believed they were all tightening their belts just now; there had been two bad harvests. But what of that? The Chinese had starved before and come back before. Whatever their destiny in the years to come, they would be back in force. And then, according to the Scrymgeour philosophy, they would clean up the rest of humanity and set it to work. 'We're like greenfly,' he announced. 'Living on roses today, milked by ants tomorrow.'

Sharkey eyed Wilson as he made this speech. It must be as embarrassing for the young man to be hailed as a member of the master race by one foreign devil as to be ordered off the grass by another. But whatever his feelings, his expression did not change. The weight of melancholy that knowledge and responsibility had placed on him merely showed more burdensome; he furrowed his brows and blinked, convulsively. 'It is half past five,' he said earnestly. 'You should swim again.'

So they did. Sharkey lured Mary into a wrestling match.

She fought with abandon, unselfconsciously, indulging her
tomboy streak. Afterwards they floated side by side, she
Leviathan and he the hook wherewith to catch it.

He thought: she likes me. Because she clearly did. And
what of him – did he like her? Of course he did. You could
even say that he liked her more than anyone else, because he
liked no one. He didn't have time to like people if John
Thomas was to be properly serviced.

His mind drifted to Verity – did he like him? He would
require notice of that question. Liking hardly entered into it.
His relationship with Verity was a professional one; he was
his gadfly. The gadfly stings unemotionally, not to hurt but
because that is its job. The only emotion Verity roused in
him was an itch to get to work on him, because he certainly
needed a gadfly. Sharkey didn't hold anything against him
for being the way he was.

So, it was clear that he liked Mary more than he liked
Verity. Indeed you could probably conclude that he liked her
in absolute terms.

At six o'clock the old Chinese came and fetched them in
his boat. They were dazed with sun and sea. Scrymgeour
drove them home, climbing up from Hebe Haven to the
switchback of the Clearwater Bay Road. The Morris Minor's
windows were wide open and as they drove between the
walls of hewn yellow rock the purr of the engine
reverberated from its crumbling surfaces.

'Hong Kong,' called Mary over its noise, 'is driving home
with warm air coming through the window and dried salt on
your face.'

'Hong Kong,' said Scrymgeour, 'is listening to Richard
Strauss on the hi-fi while the amah crushes cockroaches with
her bare feet.'

'Hong Kong,' said Sharkey 'is where second-raters like us can become our true selves.'

'I do not know what Hong Kong is,' said Wilson.

They crossed the harbour on the Yaumati ferry. Wilson insisted on getting out on the Hong Kong side and taking a tram to Shaukiwan, where he lived. Sharkey was dropped at Breezy Court and Mary at her diminutive place in Conduit Road. Scrymgeour then drove to the end of Lyttleton Road and parked his car; he lived in a big house on University Path.

After supper Sharkey made his way to the Ladies' Recreation Club in search of the Belilios girl. A forlorn hope, maybe; but his need was great.

Turning into Gascoyne Road, Verity had to brake hard to avoid an ancient Chinese in a dove-grey samfu. He was white-haired and parchment-faced, and had a feathery waterfall of beard hanging from his sunken cheeks. As the car jolted to a stop he smiled ethereally and bowed.

Verity recognised him. He was General K'ou, a courtly old refugee from north China who was a well-known figure in Hong Kong. Living nobody knew where, speaking neither Cantonese nor English, he somehow survived, a vision of ancient China walking the clangorous streets of this money-grubbing town.

The District Office was a long low building. Walking down the corridor to his own suite, Verity passed doors opening on roomfuls of permit clerks, land clerks,

correspondence clerks, finance clerks, land demarcators.
Eyes dropped to their papers as he passed; stray villagers,
sitting on benches waiting to be attended to, stared at him
without special interest.

He passed through a wooden gate into the land assistants'
room – Cheung was there, fiddling with some papers – and
on into his own office.

At the desk nearest his door sat Jeffrey Wing, a smiling
young Chinese with gold-rimmed spectacles whom he had
lifted out of the unleavened mass of finance clerks and made
his private secretary, or Confidential Books as the Chinese
called it. He was boyish, quick and eager; working with
Europeans had given him a European smile, which he
smiled now.

'Good morning, Mr Verity.'

'Good morning, Jeffrey. What have we got today?'

'The District Commissioner will be calling at ten o'clock.
And I've put some files on your desk.'

'Good. Show Mr Cairns straight in when he comes. – Oh
Cheung!'

Cheung jumped to his feet, his flesh quivering. At this
hour his white shirt was still neatly creased; he hadn't had
time to sweat. 'Yes, Mr Verity?'

'Come in when I give you a buzz, will you?'

'Yes, Mr Verity.'

He closed his door behind him with an odd feeling of
relief and sat down amid the throaty roar of the air
conditioner. The files were routine enough: a row over
compensation paid to villagers losing their land to the new
Shek Pik reservoir, an application to build houses on land
reserved for agricultural purposes near Tai O, a complaint
from villagers on Peng Chau about a piggery which they said

was polluting their only source of water. When he had looked through them he rang for Cheung.

The land assistant came in, quietly twitching, but the information he was able to provide was full and to the point. The Shek Pik compensation claim was for land that actually belonged to the government; the Yap family, who were making the claim, had been cultivating it illegally. At Tai O, the application to build houses could not be granted – but what if the owner swapped it for another parcel he had further up the valley, which was derestricted?

'I suppose you've sorted out the Peng Chau business too?' said Verity with a hint of pique.

Cheung was horrified. 'Oh no, Mr Verity,' he protested. 'I just thought: maybe when P.W.D. go there next month to make harbour improvements they could put in drains for the piggery at the same time.'

'That's settled then.' Verity took a deep breath. 'Now: as you know, the D.C. is coming at ten o'clock. I'm going to have to tell him about Dumbell.'

It was true. He'd been lucky; the junk deaths at Telegraph Bay had given him a full day's grace by sucking Jack into a series of meetings, with the Executive Council and the police, following which a press release had been issued, revealing nothing but saying that everything was being done to discover the cause of this terrible tragedy, etc. But now Jack was his own man again; the music would have to be faced.

'What do you think, Cheung?' asked Verity.

Cheung looked uncomfortable; a bead of sweat appeared on his forehead. He cleared his throat. 'By-elections are no problem,' he said. 'We just have to get agreement from Exco to hold them in the four wards concerned. Then we post

notices: we give candidates fourteen days to come forward
and hold the elections fourteen days after that. – Maybe we
should get Hong Kong Law Society to supervise them. To
show they are fair.'

He had clearly done his homework, but Verity was
dissatisfied with his answer nevertheless. He tapped his desk
with his pencil and said: 'Very nice. But what I really want to
know is: what have people got against Ng? What's he been
up to?'

Cheung shifted his weight in his chair. 'I don't know, Mr
Verity.'

'Come along, man, you must have some idea. It's nothing
to do with Tsoi and the water; so what is it?'

'I don't know,' said Cheung unhappily.

'Ng's got family connections all over the island; has he
been using them to put the squeeze on somebody? Is he
involved in some racket with Ho, and has he double-crossed
him?'

'Oh no!' cried Cheung in a horrified squeak. 'Mr Ho is an
honest man.'

'I'm glad somebody is. I was beginning to think they're all
a pack of rogues.'

It was ten minutes to ten. He dismissed Cheung and
pondered the Dumbell question – quite fruitlessly – until
the buzzer sounded and the District Commissioner was
shown in.

'Morning, Jack.'

'Morning, Nigel.' Cairns took Verity's surprisingly delicate
hand in his own hairy paw. Hair was his determining factor;
he was enveloped in it. An auburn mane framed his huge
face and merged with a bristly jungle of moustache and
whisker. Hair was so thick on his legs that it held his khaki

shorts half an inch from his skin; it sprouted in fuzzy tufts on the back of his fingers. He was the exact picture of a Chinese devil with his redness, his pointed ears, his curling brows and his broad mouth rising in a diabolical grin at the corners. When they first saw him Chinese children ran away in terror, but they soon came to know him as a large friendly beast with a booming voice and a pocket full of ten cent pieces and sticky sweets.

'Damned awful thing, this,' he boomed.

Verity, taken unawares, jerked out 'I don't know what came over them!'

'They got drowned, that's what came over them.'

Verity then realised his mistake, but it was too late to do anything about it. 'I meant what happened on Dumbell,' he said lamely. 'Have you heard anything about that?'

'Of course I have. It'll sort itself out.'

'I wish I agreed.'

'Now look here, Nigel. You're not to worry and you're not to feel guilty about it. Just elect your four chaps and put it out of your mind.'

'I can't. I really must find out what Ng has done to them – it must be something very bad.'

Cairns stood up and started striding round the office. 'Listen,' he said, 'either it's not important and they'll make it up. Or it is and it's for the police. Either way it doesn't concern us.'

'I can't help feeling a certain responsibility ... '

'You must help it. Just do your job conscientiously – as you always have – and forget it. – Now about these junk deaths: do your chaps know anything about them?'

Verity was aghast. 'How could they? And how could I ever ask them?'

'Just call them in and put it to them. It might have been a junk from Dumbell after all.'

'But the bodies weren't even found in my district!'

'I know, I know. But you might just have heard something about a missing junk on Dumbell.'

'I've heard about dozens,' said Verity stiffly. 'They still haven't made up their losses from the last typhoon.'

Cairns pursed his lips. 'I see,' he said.

'Look, Jack. It's bound to be a mainland boat, and not one of ours. – Put yourself in the place of a mainland Chinese who wants to get out: is he really going to risk trying to contact people here? I don't think so. Wouldn't it be safer to look out for a willing junk-master on the spot?'

'That's the most likely thing, certainly. But you mustn't lose sight of the fact that there are Hong Kong boats doing it for money. They mostly ply across the Pearl River to the Four Districts, and you know how many links there are between those and the Colony. The police have to bear that in mind.'

'Is this what they've been saying at H.E.'s meetings?' said Verity, aggrieved.

'It's part of it.'

`Well, you tell them they're barking up the wrong tree. Everybody knows that things are hard over there; bad harvests and all that. Refugees are trying to make it to Hong Kong in all sorts of crazy ways – swimming across Mirs Bay with inner tubes round their waists or basketballs in nets tied to their necks. If you can find a junk all you've got to do is sail it here and vanish in the crowd. And if that junk happens to be unseaworthy ... '

Cairns sighed. 'I daresay you're right. But we've got to see this thing from the police point of view. If the junk happened to be one of ours they'd have to chase it up.'

'Good luck to them then,' said Verity grudgingly.

'They have a job to do, same as us. So be nice to them, Nigel; you may well find yourself seeing more of them. They're wondering about possible triad links – you know, one triad sinking another triad's boat. Ask old Cheung. He's a good chap. He may even know something and if you ask him the right way he may let you in on it.' He had talked his way to the door. 'Cheerio, old chap,' he boomed, and left.

When he had gone Verity walked up and down. He was agitated; stupidly, unnecessarily so. He hands were trembling. He found it hard to accept criticism, however oblique – and here was Jack implying that his sense of responsibility was excessive! Being an honest man, he couldn't wholly absolve himself from the charge; but dammit, his whole life had been built around the concept of duty, and when had duty ever let a man down?

He buzzed for Jeffrey and for an hour they went through a sheaf of land titles, deciding which plots needed to be visited to re-establish the boundaries. The work soothed him, though he had an underlying feeling of guilt that he wasn't doing it with Cheung. But Cheung revolted him physically, whereas Jeffrey was an attractive person, with his light bronze skin, his speaking eyes, his easy movements. Besides, the boy was highly intelligent, quick to anticipate problems and offer a solution. But, he thought, I must avoid showing him too many favours, otherwise I shall be laughed at in the office.

But he was a solitary man, and in spite of his reservations found himself confiding in the boy about Dumbell – not that Jeffrey hadn't a pretty shrewd idea of it already; indeed the whole office knew, it was their main topic of conversation. Jeffrey's reactions were discreet and sensible. He agreed that whatever Mr Ng had done it was nothing to do with Tsoi; but it must have offended people badly; otherwise they would have taken the more moderate course of boycotting Ng's shop.

'I hadn't thought of that. But he may just have got some sort of hold over them.'

'Perhaps. – Mr Verity, may I take a day's leave tomorrow?' He smiled his open, European smile.

'Of course. But why tomorrow?'

'I was thinking that maybe a private person could pick up some information. I have connections on the island. There's a Mrs Wong who is my mother's kit pai – you know, official friend, with a signed paper and everything. I could go and visit her.'

'But, Jeffrey,' said Verity, touched by the offer, 'holidays are for relaxation, not for work.'

'I can relax better on the island than at home.'

Verity didn't know what Jeffrey's home circumstances were, but could well imagine that what he said was true. 'Well,' he said, 'if you want a day off you may have one. But see that it's a real day off.'

'Thank you very much,' said the boy, beaming.

It was only after he left the office that Verity had doubts. Was what he had just done quite ethical? Was it even sensible, in view of what Cairns had said? What had Ng's conduct to do with him? But a strain of obstinacy in him made him retort: everything. These were his people after all, and he was their District Officer.

He had another motivation as well, less clearly formulated but strong nevertheless. He had run out of luck recently, and must do something about it. And everything Jeffrey touched seemed to turn out well. Why not let Jeffrey carry his luck?

The film studios stood on a height above the Clearwater Bay Road, their entrance guarded by a sentry box and a horizontal pole which Sharkey's pass caused to rise. His old Hillman entered the compound, climbing past the permanent set of the Chinese village. This was built for inside shots only and turned an assembly of laths and cardboard to the outside world, like a stage set turned inside out. The inside, invisible to him now, was plastic and plywood sprayed with a mixture of cement and sand, effective enough until it started peeling.

He drove past the main building, grey and anonymous behind its circular plot of shrubs which a little old Hakka woman was watering, her cans suspended from a pole across her shoulders. The dubbing studio was behind it; so he parked the car and walked round.

Derek Stillgoe, universally known as The Creep, was standing limply at the studio door: a tall, weedy man wearing dark glasses which he never took off, in navy shorts and knee-length white socks. 'We've been waiting for you,' he said in his toneless voice.

'Sorry. The top of my head fell off and I couldn't find it.' He was indeed suffering from hangover.

Stillgoe, Sharkey reflected, was one of those people at whose appearance everybody instinctively melts away. It wasn't just his appearance, though his complexion was bloodless, his lips slack and his body wavered like a polyp. Also, his handshake was a fistful of wet seaweed, the hand seeming to ooze out between your fingers. But he also had an air of looking at a spot six feet behind your back, an aloofness that befitted a literary man: he was the recently sacked editor of a magazine called *Lotus*, a self-appointed bridge between east and west which published discreetly adulatory articles about Chairman Mao and referred to Mount Everest as Jolmo Lungma. Nevertheless, thought Sharkey with those among his grey cells which had not been converted to broken crockery, he's the boss, he's the man who pays the dollars. 'Ready when you are,' he said.

They walked together into the studio, a small room with a glass window looking into a film theatre. A projectionist's cubicle, to which there was a talk-back, was next door.

Gus Donoghue was sprawling at the microphone table, alongside a crew-cut young man who had an air of having begun to run to seed. 'Good drilling,' said Gus.

'And up your pipe,' added the other in a Canadian accent.

'Up your own,' retorted Sharkey.

A young Eurasian on the other side of the glass flashed Sharkey a smile.

'Morning, Fergus,' mouthed Sharkey, tickled by the idea of a half-Cantonese called Fergus O'Hanlon: the seed of old Ireland scattered wide indeed.

Donoghue produced a bottle of San Miguel beer from a case on the floor beside him and wrenched the metal cap off with his teeth. 'To lubricate your vocal chords,' he said, handing it to Sharkey. 'How about you, Cappuccino?'

'Count me in too,' said the other, who also answered to Ed.

With the acrid liquid swirling in his belly, Sharkey spoke to the hitherto disregarded Stillgoe. 'What about this film then, Derek?'

Stillgoe's face twitched slightly and his colourless voice, which had the knack of coating everything it touched with a layer of dust, explained that this wasn't just the usual cheap

Japanese stuff they dubbed for the South-east Asian market; this was a private up-market venture of his own. He had acquired the English language rights, and a promise of distribution by the Shaw Brothers organisation whose studio they were now using, of a new three-film version of the Japanese classic, *The Forty-Seven Ronin.*

'Ronin in the Glonin,' suggested Ed. He was a disc-jockey like Donoghue and thought in terms of song-titles.

'A ronin is an unemployed samurai,' expained Stillgoe in a sepulchral voice.

'Nowhere to put his weapon?' asked Gus.

'Shut up,' said Sharkey. 'This happens to be the Japanese equivalent of *Hamlet.*'

Stillgoe continued. 'It starts with this noble, called Hangan ... '

'Hang Out.'

'Hang Low.'

'Wun Hung Lo, son of Hu Flung Dung.'

'Aw shit,' said Sharkey.

Stillgoe made no effort to stop this banter. The morbid sensitivity that made his face twitch at a shadow was combined with an odd detachment from whatever was going on. 'The Shogun has forced Hangan to commit suicide,' he said.

'Supremo Cuts Courtier Dead,' quipped Gus.

'Hadn't we better get on with it?' said Sharkey. Stillgoe opened his briefcase, took out sheaves of script and handed them round. He pressed the talk-back key. 'Run the first clip please.'

The unseen projectionist got to work. On the screen on the other side of the glass there appeared an assembly of berobed Japanese, their mouths moving mutely. Stillgoe started directing takes, which Fergus recorded. Each actor had to do several voices, which was par for the course in their dubbings.

The cast included Hangan and Wata-No-Suke, nobles; Moronao, villain; a heroic merchant, assorted courtiers, servants and populace. Donoghue took the lion's share of the parts. He was an actor of genuine if limited ability. Ed's speciality was funny voices; he had half a dozen of these to do. Sharkey had the fewest speeches, which was a good thing as he was an indifferent actor. His real value to Lion Rock Soundtrax Ltd was as a translator of dialogue.

They worked from scripts which had the original Japanese dialogue in Roman script, with a literal English translation on the facing page. This English was frequently garbled and always unspeakable. In some places Stillgoe had altered it but, as he said, dialogue was not his forte; he was more a free-association prose man. So it fell to Sharkey to find off-the-cuff English equivalents which fitted the lip movements. This he did well.

The dubbing process was painfully slow, prolonged as it was by beer-drinking and horseplay. Ed and Donoghue squeezed every variety of indecent pun from their lines and as a result frequently fluffed them. Occasionally Sharkey joined in the fun, but quickly became exasperated as they mangled speeches which he himself had devised.

They took lunch in a tatty canteen with painted concrete walls, alive with the banging of aluminium chairs. When Sharkey had finished he walked out alone on to the hillside among the permanent sets. He sauntered past the Forbidden City with its pond and nine-angle bridge, down the dusty village street where on weekdays peasants trotted, mandarins in brocaded gowns were borne along in litters and moustachioed warlords galloped between the papier mâché houses, scattering people right and left. There was even a wooden bridge crossing a manufactured gorge, where many an actor had been thrown over the parapet with a blood-curdling shriek, to fall into a safety net below.

Today being Sunday, everything was gloriously still. There couldn't be many film studios, Sharkey thought, which overlooked a panorama of blue sea and green islands. To the left, cradled among its hills, was Hebe Haven, where he had been the other day; distance had cured its small boats of the fidgets.

To his irritation he saw Stillgoe wandering double-jointedly up.

'Nice place,' said Sharkey.

'The sun gives me migraine.'

'Hence the glasses, I suppose.' Stillgoe nodded. 'Better not stay long then.'

But Stillgoe showed no signs of wanting to leave. He looked blankly out over the sea, seemed to ponder a moment and then announced 'We've got to do twenty-five minutes running time today.'

'That's a lot.'

'There are three films, you see. *The Death of Hangan*, *Kampei and the House Of Pleasure* and *The Forty-Seven*. Six hours all told. I contracted to dub them twenty percent cheaper than the Filipinos. Paid a big deposit: twenty thousand HK.'

Sharkey whistled. 'Where did you get that kind of money?'

'Legacy. My aunt in Melbourne died.' He blinked behind his sunglasses. 'March is the deadline. Fourteen studio bookings, alternate Sundays, a thousand bucks a time. In advance. As well as which I've got to pay the projectionist and the sound recordist and the actors. Say another twenty thousand. Total: forty-four thousand dollars. Everything I've got.'

Why this sudden loquacity? Sharkey wondered. He seemed to need to tell somebody about it. 'Bit of a gamble, eh?'

'My last throw,' said Stillgoe tonelessly.

'Christ.'

'If it comes off I make a lot of money. Then I'll do a film of my own.'

Sharkey tried to imagine a film of Stillgoe's own but failed miserably. 'What if it doesn't come off?'

'Then it's back to Square One.'

With that gnomic utterance Stillgoe wandered off again, leaving Sharkey nonplussed. What was the point of having a big scene and then playing it so limply? He pondered that question all afternoon, while a beery Donoghue fluffed and fluffed, and Ed got his voices mixed up. Even Sharkey himself realised, just before six o'clock, that he'd given the same man two different voices.

'Perhaps we'll get away with it,' opined Stillgoe, looking into vacancy.

'Perhaps we won't,' snapped Sharkey. He'd invented the damned speeches and was feeling sore.

'Who's going to notice a little thing like that?' said Donoghue with a curl of the lip.

'I'll sleep on it,' said Stillgoe.

'That all you can find to sleep on?' That was Ed.

'If I don't like it we can re-do it in a fortnight's time.'

They left it at that. Sharkey was baffled by the whole business. Here was Stillgoe needing to have twenty-five minutes in the can and they had done scarcely half of that – and what did he do about it? Sweet Fanny Adams. He stood there wincing. He almost seemed to be issuing an open invitation to wreck his whole enterprise! Sharkey didn't understand it. Still, there was one satisfactory point about it: Stillgoe had a wallet full of Hong Kong notes in his jacket pocket and paid them at the end of the session. How Gus had the nerve to take the money was beyond him.

At one minute past six the said Gus was roaring off to Kowloon with Ed in his blue Morgan. He himself gave Stillgoe a lift in the Hillman. Stillgoe asked to be dropped at Boundary Street and said he would walk from there; he didn't seem to want to have people know where he lived.

Verity sat on his balcony, his head between the wings of a rattan armchair, a glass of Johnny Walker at his elbow. In this end-of-summer heat Mount Kellet shimmered in the moonlight. An occasional car screamed up the road behind him, and from along the corridor came the wail of Cantonese story-telling on his cook-boy's transistor. In quiet intervals he could even hear the cheep of crickets.

But he was consumed by a feeling of unease. When he went to bed his sleep, never of the best, was disturbed by dreams. He was in a light, airy place, like the hills of the New Territories, when a crushing weight would suddenly descend on him, pinning him to the ground like Mars in Vulcan's net. The sensation of impotence wakened him; he lay there in discomfort until he nodded off again and the cycle repeated itself.

Finally, inevitably, the Sharkey dream would come: the re-enactment of the most shameful thing that had ever happened to him. It was his final year at Wellington; he was the captain of his house cricket team and his star batsman was none other than Liam Sharkey. They were a good team, favourites to win the inter-house trophy the final of which was due to take place the following day, a Saturday.

Then came catastrophe. The news flew round the sixth form like wildfire: Sharkey had been caught cribbing in an exam and had been given detention for the weekend. He couldn't play.

But on Saturday morning he turned up. 'I'm playing,' he said.

'You can't.'

'Why not?'

'You're on detention.'

'How do you know?'

'Everybody knows.'

'Well, everybody's wrong. It's been cancelled.' With that he gave Verity his most impudent grin.

Was he lying? Probably. But for Verity winning the inter-house trophy was a sacral thing, there wasn't time to contact the head and the rest of the team was clamouring for Sharkey to play: they wanted that cup too and, anyway, it would be a lark. Verity, unsure of himself, yielded, Sharkey made fifty and the cup was won.

But that evening Verity was summoned to the house master's study and asked the single question: 'Did you know Liam Sharkey was on detention?' He stammered, turned red and answered 'Nobody told me, sir.' With that, he was dismissed and told to wait until Monday.

The thirty-six hours until Monday morning assembly were

a nightmare. The rest of the school gave him those detached, curious looks that people reserve for the stricken. He was assailed by feelings of guilt, at least partly deserved. In assembly the head made his announcement. The inter-house trophy had been won by their opponents, on a disqualification: the actual winners of the final had fielded a disqualified player. That player, who had cut detention to play, was summarily expelled. As for the captain of the team he played for, the head had some sympathy for him but was obliged to say – with regret, because he had a good record – that he had been guilty of negligence. And now the matter was closed.

Sharkey left school publicly swigging a bottle of Bass (it was only a week till end of term anyway), but Verity fell ill and had to be fetched by his aunt in a taxi; the humiliation had been too much for him.

Even today, twenty-eight years later, he had not atoned in his own mind for this dereliction of duty. The dream kept recurring, it might be after intervals of months or even years, but he knew it would always do so. The head would tower over him in his black gown, like a great bat; and a circle of accusing faces would thunder: You knew! To escape them he would stumble between rows of chairs in an interminable assembly hall while human legs and schoolbags were stuck out to trip him. Finally he would fall, the vengeful faces would close in ... And at that point he would wake.

He woke now. It was just before six o'clock. He went to the kitchen, woke Ah Lok, who was snoring with his head on one of those earthenware cylinders the Chinese use as pillows, took an early breakfast and drove to the office.

There wasn't a soul about except an ancient crone who was mopping the floor; she gave him a toothless grin, her lips drawing back to reveal grey-pink gums.

He felt worn out, but worked doggedly at his files until ten o'clock. Then he buzzed for Jeffrey; if he'd done it any earlier he would have aroused suspicion in the others. It was a relief to see the round young face, intelligent behind its glasses, with its air of always being good-tempered.

'Tell me about your day on Dumbell,' he said.

'Thank you, Mr Verity, it was very pleasant. Very restful.' Then, as though it was an afterthought: 'People are very angry with Mr Ng.'

'Ah.'

'Did you know he was a money-lender?'

Verity's eyebrows lifted in surprise. 'No, I didn't.'

'It's often like that in these small places. Fishermen have no money and the banks won't lend them any. If they want to buy a boat they have to find somebody prepared to lend without security.'

'And that somebody is Ng?'

'Yes.'

'It's logical. But I don't understand why I hadn't heard about this before.'

'I believe Mr Cheung knows.'

Verity sidestepped the implications of Cheung knowing. 'Why should they get worked up about it just now?' he asked.

'Mrs Wong – you know, my mother's kit pai – told me that he suddenly put up the interest. From twenty-five per cent a year to thirty.'

'Was he entitled to do that?'

'The old agreements had run out.'

'Then he's legally in the right.'

'Yes, but people say he shouldn't have done it just after the typhoon. Lots of his clients lost everything then.'

Verity pondered the situation. Rapacity on Ng's part was a possible reason for the upset, but he wasn't wholly convinced. The Chinese were realists where money was concerned; the rich were expected to grind the faces of the poor. Yet that same rich man, for the sake of family honour, would allow himself to be milked of thousands to help a worthless grandson out of a scrape. So it didn't quite make sense for the islanders to get up a petition just because their chairman was too enthusiastic a usurer.

'I see you have doubts, Mr Verity,' said Jeffrey, smiling. 'So do I as a matter of fact.'

'It doesn't quite add up, does it?'

'No. But I did hear another rumour.' He lowered his voice. 'About triads.'

Verity gave a snort of displeasure. He loathed triads. Not that he didn't see how the various sordid little activities they engaged in – prostitution, drugs and protection rackets – would find a natural soil in the packed slums of places like Dumbell. It was just that he could not bear to contemplate that fact; it somehow reflected on his own administration.

'What was this rumour?' he asked with distaste.

'It's general knowledge that the Twenty-One K triad has been growing in strength in recent years, with all these refugees coming in from Kwangtung ... '

'I'd heard that.'

'Well, some say there's been trouble between it and the old T'ung – the triad the Dumbell fishermen traditionally belong to. A year or two ago the two of them burned the yellow paper, which means that they swore brotherhood and all that. But the agreement didn't last, apparently because quite a few people belong to both and the Twenty-One K wanted them for itself. The T'ung are fighting hard against

this, because they know that if it happens it's the end for
them.'

'And how does Ng fit into all this?' asked Verity wearily.

'Some say he's a big man in the Twenty-One K. – Of
course it may not be true.'

But Verity felt in his bones that it was true. There was a
look of dreary inevitability about the whole thing; the worst
was going to happen, and it was going to happen to him.

Sharkey took Mary to the Garrison Players' production of
Arms and the Man. Sergius was played by none other than
Donoghue, whose scar emphasised his Byronic appearance.
He was a reasonable actor but a lazy one, with the result that
he had to be heavily prompted.

After the show they decided that they needed some
Shanghai food, and went to the Lao Shing Hing restaurant
where they found Scrymgeour sitting with a long, thin,
gannet-like Chinese woman called Rose Leung, who was a
junior lecturer in English at Hong Kong University. 'Fancy
meeting you,' he drawled, pursing his mouth into an inverted
U. Rose stared at them through impenetrable brown eyes.

'I'm starving,' Mary announced.

They joined up and ordered a meal: cold cuts and beer to
start with (cold cuts being thin slices of chicken, brisket and
pork mixed up with prawns and vegetables). Rose, bent flat-
chested over her chopsticks, shovelled these into her mouth,
pausing only to announce that her special subject this year
was pastoral poetry.

The main courses arrived together Chinese-fashion: prawns in chilli, great white fatty balls in an orange-coloured sauce set off with diced vegetables; candied leg of pork which must have been cooking all day so tender it was, the brown-black glossy skin merging into fat that had no substance and flesh that fell into its constituent fibres at a touch; thin slices of eel, also browny-black, in an oily sauce.

They ate with gusto, as is proper in a Chinese restaurant, making a great deal of noise and scattering boiled rice on the tablecloth, discussing literature with the passionate vulgarity that their neighbours put into their talk of money. Liberal quantities of San Mig, which the waiter replaced with miraculous speed, helped matters along.

The last courses were jiao tse, the north Chinese ravioli: soft pasta bags freshly boiled with pork mince inside and served in a container like a bamboo sieve; followed by toffee-apples: segments of apple in a syrupy cladding of burnt sugar plunged to harden in a bowl of water.

Counting the beer, Sharkey worked out that the whole meal came to seventeen shillings and sixpence a head.

Stepping out into the clamorous street, with its hot smell made up of boiled cabbage, small workshops and humanity, completed the process of intoxication.

'I want to do something silly!' cried Mary.

'Me too,' warbled Sharkey (who was not as drunk as he sounded).

'Let's go for a midnight swim.'

Rose laughed like a macaw. 'I go' a bathing house at Sou' Bay. I won it in the lottery.'

'Capital,' said Alec, drawing out the vowel intolerably.

'We ge' our costume then?'

'Right.'

They flung themselves into the two cars, Mary squeezing into the front seat of the Hillman with Sharkey and Rose snapping her bony knees shut like a folding ruler in Scrymgeour's old Morris.

Lights glistened on the tramlines; the old green trams whined up and down as thronging pedestrians and hooting cars played tag with them; the life of this place never seemed to stop. Noodle stalls, lit by bare electric bulbs, were still open and hawkers padded about with little trays of sweets and cigarettes, making a living God knew how.

At Causeway Bay they flashed past the handball pitches and the statue of Queen Victoria, a dumpy throned figure with a preposterously small crown. In Wanchai the big apartment blocks gave place to older tenements with ferns and shrubs and washing growing out of their walls.

After calling at Conduit Road and Breezy Court for Mary's costume and Sharkey's own, the Hillman skirted the harbour on the natural balcony of Magazine Gap Road and Stubbs Road before turning right and making for the south coast of the island. As they dropped gently down towards Repulse Bay the precipitous hills were probed by travelling sheaves of light from cars' headlights, their positions plotted by the fixed stars of the apartment blocks. There was a lovely, broken view of mountain and sea, silky in the moonlight.

At South Bay the road petered out under a canopy of flame trees. Steps led down through a minor village of concrete huts to the little beach. Sharkey and Mary ran down these and emerged into a whispering of small waves; occasional shivering heaves ran over the sea's surface, releasing wriggling green reflections like living things.

'God but it's lovely,' sighed Mary.

'Let's get changed quickly before the others arrive.'

They did so in the lee of separate huts and left their clothes in two neat piles on Rose's doorstep, and were already wading into the water when Rose herself came down the steps like a double-jointed cormorant, Alec following along with his fastidious gait, picking his way through non-existent rubbish.

There was a marvellous coolness in the night sea. Their strokes sent waves of phosphorescence across its surface; sound was muted. Sharkey drifted into a kind of trance. He could easily have swum on, quietly and without effort, until a gentle lassitude overpowered him. The idea of sinking soundlessly into death was oddly attractive; he hardly knew whether he wished it or feared it.

A big circular raft loomed up; he hauled himself on board. Mary followed. As they got to their feet a gleaming curtain of water ran from their bodies. Mary planted herself, feet apart, a thin trickle running from between her thighs, reminding him why he was there. Scrymgeour and Rose were floating nearby.

Sharkey put his arm round Mary's shoulders in a man-to-man kind of way. 'Not bad, eh?' he said.

'Oh Liam, it's absolutely super.'

There was a yielding springiness about her flesh that he mustn't let affect him. The trout mustn't realise it was being tickled.

Mary was in romantic mood. 'With how sad steps, O Moon, thou climb'st the skies,' she recited soulfully, 'how silently and with how wan a face.'

Sharkey returned the romanticism with interest.

'The moon shines bright. In such a night as this,
When the sweet wind did gently kiss the trees
And they did make no noise, in such a night

Troilus methinks mounted the Troyan walls
And sighed his soul towards the Grecian tents
Where Cressid lay that night ... '
His arm tightened imperceptibly round her shoulders.

Mary gave a high-pitched, musical sigh. 'Oh Liam, I wish you hadn't said that.'

'Why not?'

'It was Harold's favourite passage.'

'Harold?'

'My late lamented.'

'Sorry.'

'You couldn't know. Poor bloke, he died shortly after we arrived here. He was the bursar.'

'What happened? You never told me.'

'Heart attack. He just keeled over.'

'Come in again, you two,' called Alec from the sea. 'It's fabulous. Not a turd in sight.'

Sharkey ignored the invitation. 'What's it like, Mary?' he asked, lowering his voice.

'It's bloody awful to start with. You feel so empty. Then, little by little, you get used to it.'

Pause.

'I don't want to pry, but what's it like doing without ... ? I mean, now you have it, now you don't, if you see what I mean.'

Mary looked at him in surprise, decided that his motive was friendly interest and answered: 'I wouldn't say this to many people and I don't quite know why I'm saying it to you now, but the fact is, our sex life wasn't exactly sultry. Harold was twenty years older than me to start with. But, even so, it's no fun. You feel you're no use to anybody any more.'

Sharkey assumed his wicked-squire voice. 'Darling,' he cooed, 'you can be of use to me any time you like.'

'Filthy beast,' said Mary, laughing, and pushed him into the sea.

They joined Rose and Scrymgeour and swam ashore. Once his feet were on the bottom, Sharkey bent over the water, cupped his hands and with his mouth half in and half out of the water uttered a ululating seal-bark.

'That's the O'Donovan coming out,' commented Alec.

Rose, her swimsuit draped limply on her bony body, wandered off along the beach. 'What do you drag that awful woman around for?' Sharkey whispered to him.

'As a decoy,' replied Alec enigmatically.

'No secrets!' called Mary, just out of earshot.

They all lay on their towels on the cool sand, a position which called forth Scrymgeour's prophetic strain. 'History,' he declared, 'will regard us as a last generation of fortunate idlers, inmates of a modern Pompeii before the lava came.'

'Defeatist sod,' said Mary with conviction. Rose laughed harshly; it was a pleasure to hear Europeans disagreeing with each other. 'You're forever pronouncing funeral orations over the body of the West. I can't imagine why.'

'Because, my dear Mary, we are as a fruit that is rotten within.'

'Speak for yourself,' put in Sharkey. 'I've never felt better in my life.'

'Just think of the Roman Empire. It looked in good shape too, what with senators dining off nightingales' tongues and chilling their wine with ice carried by relays of runners from the Alps, doling out free bread to the plebs and lashings of money to the Praetorian guard. But all the time, over the horizon, there were these blond men with huge biceps and a total contempt for death.'

'Not many of those around today.'

'Tut-tut. When will you learn that when history repeats
itself – which it does all the time – it does so in a different
form? Our modern Goths and Vandals are small, fine-boned
Orientals with big brains and endless stamina. And their
contempt is not for death but for life. Isn't that so, Rose dear?'

Rose laughed, marvellously cacophonous. She was having
a wonderful time.

'Alec,' said Sharkey, 'you bore me. I prefer to be a seal.'
He stood up, tucked in his elbows and flapped his forearms.
'Arf arf!' he cried, waddling in a tight circle. 'The call of the
male seal seeking its mate.'

'Who is its mate?' asked Mary.

'You are.' He made a sudden leap and flung his arms round
her, crying 'My seal mate!' They fell together on the sand;
but she was a big strong girl and sent him sprawling with a
push. He dived rugby-fashion and caught hold of her heels,
but she shook him off with a kick that made him bury his
nose in the sand.

'Oh my God, what have I done?' Mary drew in her breath,
appalled at her own strength.

'Woman, you'll pay for this!' Sharkey rose in mock wrath.
But she got up and made a break for, it, shrieking with
amused terror. Thirty yards down the beach he caught up
with her and pulled her down; they were on the other side of
a jutting rock, out of sight of the others. 'Got you!' he cried.

They wrestled on the sand, Mary giggling breathlessly. But
he was using all his strength now, gaining the upper hand.

'Stop, Liam,' she panted. 'Pax! I surrender ... '

'Expect no mercy from me.' He pinned her down on her
back, covering her big thighs with his wiry ones. 'Now you're
my prisoner.'

Her laughter became less sure of itself. 'Come on, Liam,

I'm as fond of a joke as the next person, but it's time we got back to the others.'

'Oh no, it's not!'

'Oh yes it is.'

'Oh no it's not.'

The true situation began to dawn on her. 'Please stop,' she said in a small voice.

His only answer was to turn a pair of glittering eyes on her, to lame her will. He put one hand on her midriff and tried to slide it under the waistband of her two-piece.

'No, Liam, no!' Her voice was indignant now.

At that point he uttered a groan of lust; something in her size compared with his, a sense of being a small demented insect crawling over a mountain, intoxicated him. He shoved the hand further down and cupped her pubic hair.

That broke the spell. Mary hit him with her joined fists full in the chest, making him fall back winded. 'You bastard,' she said and lay there panting.

'I'm not a bastard,' he said, genuinely hurt.

'You are! Making a set at me like that, after four years when I might as well have been the sideboard.' She started to sniff. 'Damn, I haven't got a hankie.'

'Neither have I ... Oh Mary, can't you see I want you something awful? I haven't had such a horn for years.'

'I suppose you think that's a compliment. Well, as far as I'm concerned you can take your horn or whatever you call it somewhere else. It's come to the wrong address.'

He raised one fist as though to smash it into the sand, then thought the better of it and said, in as reasonable a voice as he could muster: 'But it makes no sense, Mary. We're both free, white, twenty-one and vaccinated. We can do what we like. And you'd enjoy it, you know you would.'

'A therapeutic lay for the old lady, is that your idea?' she said bitterly. 'And what am I supposed to do? Give three cheers and throw my knickers away? Well, I won't.'

'Jesus fucking Christ,' muttered Sharkey between his teeth.

'Don't swear. And show me a little respect for a change.'

'Respect? You want respect? I respect you something shocking. I respect you like my own mother.'

'Now I'm his mother,' she wailed.

'Bugger and damn,' groaned Sharkey.

There was a pause while Mary wiped her eyes. Then she sniffed: 'I just don't know what you want from me.'

'Want?' He almost shouted in exasperation. 'I want to fuck you till your arse drops off, and then fuck you some more. Do I make myself plain?'

'Common, I'd say. If that's all you want, go to those dolly girls of yours.'

'I'm a changed man. I've gone off dolly girls. I want you.'

'Tell that one to the Marines.' She looked at him reproachfully. 'Why did you have to say those things, Liam? It was lovely before. We were pals. Now you've gone and spoiled it.' She stood up. 'I'm going back to the others,' she said.

'You can't. You're weeping all over the place.'

'Whose fault is that?'

'Have a dip. It'll clean you up.'

'That's the first considerate thing you've said this evening.' She waded into the phosphorescent water and splashed her face. Sharkey followed her, the coolness enveloping his privates and freezing desire. They swam back to the others in a broad arc.

'What have you two been up to?' snarled Scrymgeour when they appeared.

'What do you think?' challenged Sharkey.

'Lots of things. You were behind that rock long enough.'

Rose laughed harshly. 'Too long!' she shrieked, shaking with mirth.

Too bloody long, Sharkey mentally agreed. And Mary would have said amen to that.

The Triads Society Bureau was in an old building off D'Aguilar Street. It stood on a steep slope and, viewed from the side, its base was more or less triangular. Above that rose alternating bands of brick and yellow-painted concrete that disappeared under overhanging eaves. The inspiration was more or less Florentine.

A neat policeman showed Verity into Joe Miners's office, a large old-fashioned room with a roof fan crunching away, setting the papers on the wall fluttering: official notices, pages torn from illustrated magazines, group photographs of policemen in uniform, the Miners family on the beach at Stanley.

Joe himself, a small tubby man with a pipe that had just gone out, was sitting at a littered desk with his hand in a buff envelope. 'Come in, Nigel,' he said in a Lancashire accent.

'Morning, Joe.'

'What can I do for you?'

'I was just wondering,' said Verity cautiously, 'have you got anything on triads on Dumbell Island?'

Joe fumbled for his Swan Vestas and relit the pipe, sucking vigorously until his head was aureoled in blue smoke. 'You scared it was Dumbell chaps that bumped off those blokes at Telegraph Bay?' He gave a beatific grin.

'Certainly not. There's not a scrap of evidence linking the two,' said Verity stiffly. 'I'm interested in relations between the T'ung and the Twenty-One K – why are they at each others' throats?'

'So they're at each other's throats, are they? You know more about it than I do.' Miners gave him a sly look.

'Come on, Joe.' Even Verity realised that he was being made fun of.

'All right, I'll tell you. – But first, take a look at these.' He removed his hand from the envelope and pushed it across to Verity.

It contained a sheaf of coloured photographs that looked vaguely familiar. The top one was of a scowling man in a red dressing gown with a shoe on one foot and a sandal on the other; he had a strange headdress consisting of a broad band of red material with knots sticking out of it like horns and held, crossed over his chest, a sword and a triangular yellow pennant. 'Ah,' said Verity, 'isn't that one of the triad photos you used in your lecture?'

'Somebody must have been paying attention,' said Miners, smiling cherubically. He held his now smoking pipe three inches from his mouth so that a thread of spittle quivered between it and his lower lip. 'Take a look at the others too, will you?'

Verity leafed though the other photos; they were all along the same lines.

'Fierce looking, aren't they?' said Miners. 'But don't worry; I haven't joined. It's just my chaps dressed up.'

'I remember some of these,' said Verity. 'But why are you showing me them now?'

Miners pushed the pictures around the table with the mouthpiece of his pipe; the little filament of spittle snapped. 'I'm doing a book,' he said proudly. 'For the government.' He mused for a moment, then the pipe stem stabbed a man in a black gown and white belt, with a red band tied round his head and knotted on the middle of his forehead, leaving the ends to trail as low as his knees. 'That's the one to look out for,' he said, almost voluptuously.

Verity examined the photograph. 'Isn't that a so-called red pole official?'

'Spot on. Leader of the fighting section. They've got a couple of those on Dumbell.'

'In a small place like that? I don't believe it!'

'Take my word for it. The T''ung has one. So has the Twenty-One K.' He pushed across another picture, this time of a man in a black gown with the belt tied differently and the knot placed to the left side of his head. 'Here's your intellectual,' he said admiringly.

Verity examined the man. 'Pak Tsz Sin official,' he said. 'Responsible for planning and rituals.'

'I can see you really did listen,' rejoined Miners. Then, an expert expatiating on his subject, he leaned across his desk as though imparting an eternal truth, 'You see, Nigel, it all depends on the position of the knot. This bloke for example has it over his right ear.' He stabbed with the pipe again.

'He's a messenger, isn't he? A Cho Hai official.'

'Well done!' A trickle of smoke filtered from the bowl of the pipe. 'Now what can I tell you about the T''ung and the Twenty-One K?'

Verity spread his fingers wide. 'Just what's going on between them?'

Miners leaned back in his chair. 'Well,' he said, 'the

T'ung's a bit of a toothless lion. Been around too long. The Twenty-One K is taking over from it, little by little. That's what's going on.'

Verity gave a cautious nod. 'I'd heard something like that.'

'Trouble is, its methods aren't of the gentlest.'

'In what way?'

'Beatings up. Murder threats. Maybe even more than threats.'

'I've never heard of anything like that. Not on Dumbell anyway.'

'They'd take care not to tell you.'

'But surely somebody in the office would get to know?'

Miners puffed reflectively. 'Old Cheung perhaps, yes.'

Verity was vexed. Why, when people wanted to praise anyone in his office, did it always have to be Cheung? If Cheung was so omniscient why hadn't he shared his knowledge with his District Officer? Even a tyro like Jeffrey showed a higher sense of loyalty than that. 'How do you know all this?' he said.

'Informers. There's no lack of half-starved hawkers and noodle sellers, you know. The triads put the squeeze on them and they don't like it. So they pass on little titbits to us. For five or ten dollars a time.' He shook his head sadly, his untidy grey locks flying in the breeze from the fan. 'Poor blighters, it's a fortune to some of them.'

Verity risked the approach direct. 'What made you think I was afraid this Telegraph Bay business had a Dumbell connection?'

Joe's pipe had obeyed the main rule of its being: it had gone out again. He knocked the slab of dottle, like a pellet of singed peat, into a glass ashtray beautified by a picture of Blackpool tower. 'Look,' he said, 'it's just one of our lines of enquiry. Has to be. You see, we're pretty sure the Twenty-One K specialises in smuggling people in from the mainland. – Among other things, of course,' he added with a boyish grin. 'And they tend to operate from outlying islands, like Dumbell.'

'You mean it might have been one of their junks that sank?'

'Or one of the T'ung's they pulled the plug on.'

'But that's horrible!' Verity shuddered.

'These are pretty tough chaps. As a matter of fact, Nigel, one of our contacts says your Mr Ng is a big man in the Twenty-One K. – Of course it may just be a rumour,' he added, seeing Verity take on a pained look. 'If we paid attention to everything we hear the whole blessed colony would be in jug.'

Verity suddenly felt tired, an increasingly regular occurrence with him these days. What Joe had just said, chiming in as it did with what Jeffrey had discovered, depressed him. He sat mute while Joe, seemingly oblivious of his mood, explained a further batch of photographs: triad hand-signs with the fingers extended or tucked in in various ways, pennants and seals, even a series of weird, rather repulsive ceremonies.

He was strong on the symbolism of it all. 'White Paper Fan officials – you know, Pak Tsz Sin – have a number, 415, allocated to them. But you mustn't think of that solely as four hundred and fifteen; it can be any combination of its digits. For example, multiply four by one-five and you get sixty. Add another four, representing the worldwide triad fraternity, and that gives you sixty-four, the square of eight. And eight is Pat Kwa, the Eight Diagrams of the Emperor Fuh Teh (he's the fellow who devised the Chinese script). –

Amazing, isn't it? Quite ordinary blokes carry all that stuff around in their heads.' He shook his own head. 'All that intelligence wasted on petty crime.'

'I don't like the idea of worldwide fraternity,' said Verity with a shiver.

'Me neither. The triads are pretty fragmented since the old days, of course, when they were a unified society fighting the Manchus. We've been hitting them hard. But I'd be worried if they managed to pick themselves up off the floor and moved into the old country. Our flatfoots wouldn't know how to cope.' He grinned beatifically. 'They'd have to call in chaps like me.'

'What's the significance of the name Twenty-One K?' wondered Verity.

Miners refilled his pipe from a large rubberised pouch. 'Well,' he said, 'they're really a Kuomintang organisation, quasi-official you might say. Set up to fight the communists. Twenty-One is the number of the house in Po Wah Road, Canton, that was their headquarters. After 1949 they skipped over the border and degenerated into a kind of Mafia, as all these societies tend to do. They cleaned up the local triads, including a big one in Sham Shui Po, and to celebrate the fact added K to their name. K standing for karat, because karat gold is harder than the local variety. – Symbolism again, Nigel.'

'And you think Ng is one of these karat-hard men?'

'Oh, no,' said Miners, putting on a scandalised expression. 'I never speculate. I wait till I get hard evidence.' He fell to perusing his photographs again. 'Can't help admiring the buggers in a way,' he said. Triads were his vocation.

Sharkey was so put out by the events of South Bay (when
had he ever failed when in serious pursuit of a woman?) that
he set himself a virility test: he seduced Donoghue's titular
mistress. She was a tall, cool Swede called Ulla and he got
her by a trick.

She was something to do with Volvo cars, and well-heeled.
To celebrate her birthday – which one was not clear -- she
gave a party, one of those slinky affairs in which white-coated
waiters from Jimmy's Kitchen served beef Stroganoff about
eleven o'clock and the air was resonant with Ella Fitzgerald
on the hi-fi. The guest list included a minor film star passing
through and a South American nightclub dancer who
specialised in making a pair of tassels attached to the nipples
of her brassière revolve, one clockwise, one anti-clockwise.

Sharkey, who knew that Gus could not stay the night (he
had an assignation with a quite different lady) hid in the
lavatory and when the flat was empty of all save Ulla
emerged, crying 'Surprise, surprise!' The Swede, giving a
detached Nordic smile, accepted his ploy in the spirit in
which it was intended; she probably knew what Gus was up
to anyway.

The experience was quite pleasant but meant that he did
not get home until dawn. When he woke it was past eleven
and the sun was luminous on his green curtains. He opened
them on a stupendous view: the harbour with its many craft,
the yellow gullied hills beyond Kowloon, the urban areas
thrusting up their skyscraper fingers. It inspired him with
daily indifference.

From the steady undertow of city noises a series of regular

thuds emerged; they were taking down an old Chinese house
in front of his flat. Armies of coolies swarmed over the aged
shell, chipping at walls and chimney stacks with little
hammers. The regular thuds came from a team of three who
were using sledgehammers to punch a hole through the flat
concrete roof. Their movements were perfectly synchronised
as though the hammers were attached by strings: as the first
crashed down the second was pulled sideways from the point
it was about to hit, and the third raised high, ready to drop in
turn. Down, sideways, up; down, sideways, up: an apparatus
of trained muscle that could apparently go on all day. And
with each stroke breadcrumbs of cement flew from the
irregular hole and lengths of rusty steel were uncovered.

Meanwhile a circle of little women dressed in dusty black,
their wide hats scalloped with fringes, sat tap-tapping bricks
released from wall and chimney with hammer and chisel,
returning each to its pristine state before sending it sliding
down a wooden chute to another of their tribe who piled the
new-old bricks into stacks.

Here was work, and with a vengeance! Watching it,
Sharkey wondered whether it could have any possible
relevance to Mary. His crude initial gambit had sent her
galloping off; how could he possibly lure her back? Perhaps
through work, he thought; he would work for his lady love.
She was an engine-driver's daughter; she must value work.

Then again: she was warm-hearted and prone to
performing good deeds, especially for Chinese. Why should
he not do likewise? There was a ready-made Chinese handy
in the shape of Wilson Ho and, now that he remembered, she
had said she wanted him to help her get Wilson the Lok
Yuen scholarship. Very well, he would do that. He would
approach Lok Yuen himself, who was a well-known

millionaire, and before you could say knife he would have swung it.

He got up and showered. As he soaped his crotch he wondered: why am I doing this? Why am I bothering? Provided he was discreet Ulla remained available, and there were plenty of others where she came from. Why persist in pursuing this large lady of forty?

Put it down to curiosity on John Thomas's part. Yes you, he said, his hands full of suds and private parts. Been up some strange orifices in your time, haven't you? Once a male anus, but that was only an experiment. Tried it once didn't like it, as the bishop said to the actress. He held up his disreputable member and looked at it: circumcised in babyhood, blunt in repose, a faded purple like a whisky-drinker's conk. But how different, old jack-cock, when you're poised for entry ... ! Quelle est la différence entre un homme et une femme? La différence entre. We put our spare baggage in them, they have a gap to fill. We have building bricks over, they are unfinished. Our troubles come from over-endowment, theirs from under.

But all this was beside the point. John Thomas was anxious for a change, granted. But was it not also true that he, Liam Sharkey, wanted one too? He wanted not so much a new kind of lay as someone who could lie back after the business was over and make intelligent conversation. That much he could admit to himself; what he half-knowingly suppressed was his hankering for simple companionship. The veteran of so many campaigns needed somebody nice to come home to.

He knew Lok Yuen's daughter-in-law Diana. She ran a pop request programme in Cantonese on Hong Kong Radio. The youngsters who wrote in to her under their Chinese names reappeared in Donoghue's English-language programme as Elvis Wong or Cliff Chung. He remembered from his own broadcasting days – that was before he called the Head of Programmes a brainless goon – that Diana's recording day was Tuesday, late in the afternoon. So the following Tuesday he loitered with intent in Connaught Road, outside the radio building. It was six o'clock; the westering sun was blinding over Green Island, giving the skyscrapers long violet shadows. In due course Diana emerged.

'Why Liam!' she said with an alluring smile. She had a provocative wiggle and her cheongsam was split to halfway up the thigh, revealing creamy skin the colour of white chocolate.

'Diana, darling. Just the girl I wanted to see.'

'Ooh lovely,' she mewed, touching him gently on the forearm. 'What exactly did you have in mind?'

'When I look at you I've only one thing in mind. But apart from that I'd like a word with your father-in-law.'

She gave him a suspicious look – what was he after? – then melted into sweetness again. 'Why not come home with me now?'

He gave her his randy ferret look, which involved baring his simian teeth; she responded with another alluring smile. What they both knew was that he had a hold over her. He had once caught her shivering and naked in Donoghue's bathroom when her family thought she was recording a programme. He hadn't split on her but she knew he always could. That occasion, by the way, had brought an incidental discovery: namely that her provocative, un-Chinese bosom was a thing of art, not of nature.

They walked over to the waste ground behind HMS

Tamar, to his car. A stringy Chinese in blue shorts ran a perfunctory cloth over his windscreen and was rewarded by a dollar tip: when you're with a millionaire's daughter-in-law you can't afford to look mean.

'Where to?' he asked when they were inside.

'140 Stubbs Road.'

He drove up the Peak in the growing dusk. It was rush hour; he was one of a line of metal bugs crawling up the spine of the dragon. When they'd lost the Peak traffic at Magazine Gap he pulled into a lay-by, braked, put his hand on Diana's thigh and said: 'To hell with business. What I really want is a good shag.'

'Naughty boy,' she said with a silvery laugh and removed the hand. A lorry, climbing slowly towards them, blinded them with its lights. 'There's a time and a place for everything. As you'll see. – It's the next house on the left.'

He drove down a steep concrete drive and parked in front of a big old Chinese house. 'Blow the horn,' ordered Diana; he obeyed.

The front door opened and a middle-aged amah with a put-upon expression appeared. 'Welcome home, missy,' she said in Cantonese.

'Is master in?' said Diana in a voice suddenly hard.

'No, missy.'

'And my husband?'

'No, missy.'

'When are they coming back?'

'They telephone. Say come back quarter to seven.'

Diana looked at her watch. 'Hm. Twenty minutes. – Whisky. Soda. At once,' she snapped at the amah, who scurried off. 'Well, Liam, how about it?'

Sharkey was examining his surroundings: an odd mixture

of east and west, with camphor wood chests and a Sung painting on a scroll (the inevitable philosopher in the mountains playing what looked like a zither beside an impossibly gnarled pear tree) next to European armchairs and a glass-topped table bearing a streamlined telephone. 'Well what, my poppet?' he said.

'What you were saying in the car.'

'About your father-in-law? I'll wait ... '

'Not that.' She touched his arm again, this time gently digging her nails in.

The amah returned with a tray of drinks and offered to give Sharkey's whisky a splash of soda.

'Go away and don't come back,' said Diana curtly. The amah put down her tray and scuttled out.

'You don't mean now?' said Sharkey in disbelief.

'Why not? We've got twenty minutes.'

The hairs at the back of Sharkey's neck stood on end. 'But where ... ?'

'On the floor. Where did you think?'

A wave of lust and terror swept over Sharkey. He grabbed the back of her dress and pulled the long zip down; she slipped her arms out of it and undid his trouser belt. Somehow he struggled out of his underpants while she kicked her knickers off. She pulled him down on top of her and he penetrated her; she was moist and ready for him.

She made love with cool ferocity, determined to get the maximum physical pleasure for herself. He came to a massive climax, too early. 'Don't stop!' she cried angrily. By some miracle he managed to continue until she had her orgasm, an in-turned shudder in which he had no part to play.

'Sorry I was so quick,' he said, panting.

'At least you kept going. – Ah Tai!'

Sharkey made a panic-stricken grab for his underpants.

'Don't be a fool. She knows better than to say anything.' The terrorised old amah came in again. 'Take that dress away and bring me my blue one. And clean that stain on the carpet.' Diana walked regally into the next room, clad only in a brassière which was undone at the back and riding up over her shallow breasts, and carrying her briefs in her hand. For the first time in at least twenty years Sharkey felt himself blush, an unstoppable ocean swell that engulfed him to the roots of his hair.

He was zipping up his flies when Ah Tai came back with a blue dress which she draped over the back of an armchair; she then fetched a damp cloth and wiped clean the stain he had caused: millions of little spermatozoa, each capable of making a man.

'Now clear off,' said Diana coming in fresh and unperturbed in bra and knickers. She poured herself into the blue dress, pulled on her stiletto-heeled shoes and looked disapprovingly at Sharkey.

'Silly Europeans with your pink faces,' she said. 'You can't hide a thing. – Drink up that whisky.'

He gulped the drink down: at that very moment the noise of a revving engine was heard in the drive and a car headlight swept across the window. Ah Tai flip-flopped to the front door. He became aware of a crawling itchiness in his privates: what wouldn't he do for a wash!

Lok Yuen came in with a rush: a powerful body in a well-cut suit, broad, short, pyknic, with cropped hair and a face glittering with gold: gold spectacles, a row of gold teeth. Following behind was a sad-looking young man whose limbs wobbled as he walked. This poor creature had the double misfortune of being the millionaire's son and Diana's husband.

'Puh my bliefcase in study, Eugene,' ordered Lok in a baritone voice which was vigorous without resonance. His son obeyed.

Diana, who had wriggled to her feet, planted a coy kiss on her father-in-law's cheek. 'This is Mr Sharkey from the University,' she said. 'He would like a word with you, father.'

'That's right, sir,' said Sharkey in his best humorous-public-schoolboy voice, a ploy that usually went down well with the Chinese.

'Ah Tai, whisky! – Sih down, Mista Sha'ee. Now wha' dis all abou'?' The millionaire was a sore destroyer of consonants.

'Well, sir,' said Sharkey, surreptitiously scratching his privates from inside his pocket, 'it's about the Lok Yuen scholarship.'

Lok barked with surprise; he had clearly not expected such triviality. But Sharkey ploughed manfully on. 'The situation is this, sir. The Committee – that is, Professor Scrymgeour and Mrs Rhodes – think they have the man you want. A man fit to be the first of a new race of executives capable of moving freely in the world of culture as well as that of industry. – We all know,' he added winningly, 'how many deals are made in the social rather than the business context.'

Lok rotated the ellipse of whisky in his glass, looked through it and said: 'He speak Freng?'

Sharkey was nonplussed. 'French?' he queried. His scrotum was shrinking as it dried, a maddening sensation.

'Yea. Freng.'

'The Committee wasn't aware ... I mean they thought English would be sufficient.'

'Gotta ha Freng too. Blitain gonna join Common Mahkeh. I wanna man can go Blussel, Pa'is, Hamburg, speak Freng.'

Sharkey thought as quickly as his physical discomfort would let him. 'He's learning the language, sir. He could be fluent by the end of the academic year.'

'O.K. He do.' The millionaire laughed loudly, denoting authority rather than amusement.

Jesus Christ, thought Sharkey, now I'm committed to teaching this bloody man French! It was appalling how far one miserable little good deed could take you.

Eugene came back in, minus the briefcase. 'Young peo'le too sof today,' said Lok, observing him dispassionately. 'Have ting too easy.'

'Would you have me starve just to show I can run the business?' said Eugene, who might be down but was definitely not out.

'Where dat whisky?' called Lok. 'Ah Tai!'

The amah returned, drink-laden. 'You wan some mo, Mista Sha'ee? Or maybe you ha' enough awready.'

'I can manage another,' said Sharkey stoutly.

Whereupon the old amah poured him a glass, aimed her siphon at it and let fly. Unfortunately a spasm of nervousness overcame her and she squirted the jet of soda water on to his trousers. While she was retiring in shame and confusion Diana, uttering a silvery scream, produced a lace handkerchief (Irish linen by the look of it) and rubbed his leg some three inches from the organ which had just pleasured her.

Conversation resumed. 'This place on the uh and uh,' said the millionaire. 'Industrial base glow twenty-fi' pessent peh yeeah. Ekpor' uh all de time. Plastih flower, tehtile, you name ih. Need men speak English, Freng, talk guvvama, play golf. Tha' why I give money. Want one every yeeah.'

'Very generous of you,' smarmed Sharkey, downing his whisky in desperation; a swarm of tiny biting insects was intent on devouring his scrotum.

'You geh me guy speak Freng nek summer, he get skolarshih, O.K.?' Lok thrust out a powerful hand; Sharkey was dismissed. He left to the cooing tones of Diana saying 'Father, you certainly know how to make up your mind.'

He drove to Breezy Court with his flies open and ran himself a bath, which brought blessed relief. Ah Hoy made him pommes de terre rissolées, of which he was particularly fond. He had a date with the Belilios girl that evening but rang to cancel it, feeling smugly virtuous.

'But why?' she asked tearfully.

'Lok Yuen scholarship,' he replied elliptically, and put down the receiver.

Dumbell's by-elections were held in early November. As all four wards were in the little town itself they made do with a single polling station, in the Chamber of Commerce. The independent presiding officer, supplied by the Law Society, was a young barrister just out from England; he was fair and rangy, with the look of a rowing blue. Ng, in a black silk samfu, sat to one side of him, full of impertinent banter; on the other was Ho Man, his chair constantly shifting with protesting squeaks on the floor, his Adam's apple jumping up and down like a cardiograph reading.

Verity and Cheung called in during the morning to observe the voting. Occasional men, in suits or in coolie's rig of white singlet and navy shorts, dropped their folded ballots into the slot of a large wooden box. Verity was shocked by the impudence of Ng.

'He really has a cheek,' he protested. 'Especially when you think he's in grave danger of losing his position.'

Cheung moved uncomfortably in his damp shirt. 'Mr Ng is a very powerful man,' he said.

'What do you mean by that?'

'A lot of people won't want to go against him.'

'You've never said that before!'

'Just an opinion, Mr Verity,' said Cheung.

'But for heaven's sake, they were all against him at that meeting. Calling him a bad man and insisting we hold this election. How can they possibly vote for him now?'

'Sometimes strange things happen,' was the infuriating reply.

It was a relief to be on a mountainside in Lantau that same afternoon, even though his lunch had left him with heartburn and his limbs were vaguely aching. He mustn't be getting enough exercise.

He was with a sour-faced man from Public Works Department called Tattersall, investigating a claim by the villagers of Tai Long Wan Tsuen that the ancillary works of the Shek Pik reservoir had caused their water supply to dry up.

The great dam was in the valley beneath them, a shallow wall of earth coped with stone that sloped southwards towards the sea a quarter of a mile away. Behind it the valley was already half-flooded. The huge curving scars left by the earth-moving equipment had almost disappeared and in some places the muddy water had already started to creep up still intact green slopes. Here and there the roofless gable of a house broke the surface.

'These people are a pack of liars,' said Tattersall.

'They say you didn't stick to the agreement.'

'But that's absurd! We're a government department.'

'You should take their complaint as a compliment. In the old days nobody would have dared. Across the border they called New Territories people China's spoiled children.'

Tattersall snorted. 'It's all a lot of nonsense.'

Verity stopped, the better to make his case. 'It's quite simple,' he said. 'You're bringing in water from all the surrounding valleys to feed the dam; you've riddled the hillsides with culverts and tunnels. One of these cuts across their stream. You say you made free passage for the water underneath and they say you didn't ... '

'Of course we did!'

'Maybe so, but their water supply has dried up just the same.'

'Have any of them been up to look?'

'Oh no!'

'Why on earth not?' Tattersall's neck swelled like a turkey's.

Verity, exercising extreme patience, replied 'Because they're afraid. The mountain is a dragon and dragons don't like people gouging holes in their backs.'

'What childish nonsense!'

Verity ignored the remark. He stepped aside, took his binoculars from their case and looked down at the village, crowded with its patchwork of rice-paddies into a pocket-handkerchief of coastal plain. The dykes, or bunds, that separated the paddies and permitted flooding, were dry now; this was the time of the second harvest.

The village women were gathering in the crop. They stood, legs apart, under big hats like black dinner plates with valences, and with quick movements caught the tufts of ripe grain in their left hands and sliced them off with billhooks. One appeared to be laughing (no sound reached him), uncovering a convex upper gum and teeth planted awry. Another was cross-eyed. A third, older than the other two, had a remarkable face: a regular triangle of bronze. Her eyes and mouth were slits, her lips parted over even teeth, the skin pitted, also like old bronze. Just a peasant woman, this, one who had never had any idea of making herself attractive yet was supremely attractive all the same.

Tattersall had climbed on impatiently; Verity put away his binoculars and laboured after him. They reached the culvert, a broad cement channel three feet wide that went snaking along the contour of the hill.

'There you are,' said the P.W.D. man triumphantly. 'I told you so.' He pointed to a neatly stepped passage under the concrete where it crossed the course of a stream. At this season the little watercourse was reduced to a trickle but they immediately saw that below the culvert there was no water at all.

'What the hell ... !' said Tattersall, turning red.

They soon discovered what had happened. The summer rains had loosened a boulder which had rolled neatly into the passage, almost blocking it. The stream itself completed the job with the earth and pebbles it carried down. Now, instead of passing underneath, the water flowed into a natural little dam which drained back into the culvert and in due course into Shek Pik, whence at some future date it would be pumped across the harbour to flush somebody's toilet in Hong Kong or Kowloon.

'Silly buggers,' said Tattersall, chastened. 'If only they'd had the sense to come up and see.'

'Shall we move it?'

With a deal of grunting and sweating they rolled the stone away and dislodged the rubble around it. The little thread of water resumed its habitual course; in five minutes' time the first refreshing tinkle would be heard in the village.

Directly under the boulder they found the skeleton of a grass snake which the fall of the stone had trapped by the tail and condemned to death by starvation. The bones were incredibly fine, like the ribs of a tiny accordion.

'Poor bastard,' said Tattersall, who was not devoid of finer feelings.

'A victim of progress, you could say.'

Having done their good deed, they scrambled down the slope again. It was exhausting work, constantly reining themselves in under the blazing sun. When they levelled off at the bottom Verity's body was still under the impression that it was going downhill. His centre of gravity remaining slightly in front of him, he had to keep running after it. He staggered a few steps and fell, grazing the palms of his hands.

'Silly of me. I've got so unfit.'

The village women, still toiling in their tiny fields, saluted them without breaking their rhythm. Work, it seemed, was a reflex with them, the natural condition of their existence. Labouring for their families here, or for the community across the border, who could ever break them of the habit?

Cheung rang Verity at Stewart Terrace that evening with the results of the by-elections. Ng's candidates had won all four seats. It was back to bloody square one, thought Verity savagely.

In the Mary business Sharkey was exercising a self-restraint that was positively heroic, considering that his professional vanity had been injured: the irresistible seducer had been resisted, and by the least considered of his victims! Unrest entered his soul, and there would be no getting rid of it until he had vanquished her. He found himself thinking more about this campaign than about any he'd had for years, and because he was an intelligent man he thought to some purpose.

He realised that he must keep away from Mary and let the news of his good deeds percolate through to her. Absence, he reflected, either makes the heart grow fonder or it doesn't. In Mary's case he was prepared to put his money on the former; she was a warm-hearted woman and, he was pretty sure, liked him. Besides, must she not be fantasising – however scornfully her conscious mind rejected it – about the possibility of achieving, even at this late hour, Romance?

So he kept out of her way, contacted Wilson and started French lessons with him, leaving it to the young man himself to pass on the news. And when term started he had his reward.

He was walking up the big stone staircase at the main University entrance and met her coming down. He was wearing his best dove-grey suit and his Dior tie with the interlocking blue patterns, a combination chosen to stress his youth and freshness, even – if that was not too crass a piece of effrontery – his innocence. 'Hello, Mary' he called gaily. 'Long time no see.'

She made a circular movement with her toe on the stone

step and said in a high-pitched voice 'Hello, Liam. As you
say it's been ages.'

'I've had lectures to prepare. You know me, always leaving
things to the last minute.'

She was wearing a neat green dress and had, he thought,
lost weight. She was also wearing lipstick. He allowed her to
see that he had noticed these things.

'What's your timetable like?' she asked in a close approach
to their old pally tone.

'Not so bad for a dogsbody like me. Some eighteenth
century stuff and the usual proses and unseens. Not very
arduous. My biggest class consists of four students.'

'I say, Liam,' she suddenly jerked out.

'Yes?'

'It's decent of you to look after Wilson.'

'Aw shucks, it's nothing.'

'It's not nothing. It means a lot to him. And his people
have no money, you know.'

'I know.'

There was something quizzical about the way he said it
that made her blurt out 'You're not making him pay, are you?'

His answer was to hunch his shoulders, flap his arms and,
thrusting his head forward, bare his teeth and make his eyes
pop. This performance was accompanied by an eldritch
screech; it was Warp Spasm Number Two.

Mary let out a yelp and her hand went to her bosom
where, for some reason, it clutched her amber brooch. Some
Chinese students at the top of the steps were set chattering
like starlings. Flushing, she said 'You are a sod, Liam.'

'Just the reverse, my dear. Anyway I was only practising.
And I'm not making Wilson pay.' It was a good note to end
on, he thought: what woman does not feel a certain

fascination for a man who is unpredictable and a little frightening?

He seemed to be right. They started going out together again. He took her to the film of *The World of Suzie Wong*, where they laughed in all the wrong places, and to the Hong Kong Stage Club's production of *Five-Finger Exercise*, which didn't impress them.

On the Double Tenth, when the colony came out in a rash of Kuomintang flags, they drove to the New Territories with Scrymgeour and Rose. Above Tsuen Wan, where brand new blocks housed a quarter of a million people who were somewhere else mere months ago, they climbed Route Twisk to the water splash, past squatter huts and patches of cultivation, past banana trees and stray clumps of bamboo. To the right rose Tai Mo Shan with its round dome and wireless mast; to the left were superb vistas of mountain and sea; but then such views were the small change of Hong Kong.

They left the car by the road, walked up the brawling little river and lowered themselves into the pouring water, settling their behinds gingerly on the uneven brown rock. The sensation of coolness was delicious.

'To think we're rationed to two hours a day of this stuff,' said Alec, flinging handfuls of spray in the air.

'Bless the amahs,' said Mary fervently. 'They make sure the roof tank is kept full.' A small waterfall was battering her shoulders, voluptuously. Rose gave her discordant laugh.

During these bathing-suit sessions Sharkey contrived to touch Mary's bare flesh and then draw back, hinting at physical things without actually stating them. And sometimes Mary would touch him back, almost without realising it, a look of puzzlement in her big blue eyes. On such occasions he hardly knew whether to exult or feel ashamed of himself, because did he not have Ulla, and the Belilios girl, and whatever casual conquests came along, while she had nobody? He half wished his ploy would fail: poor bitch, she didn't stand much of a chance.

A strange two-layered dialogue had developed between them. On the surface was the academic talk: the learned jokes and chit-chat, the pseudo-philosophic pseudo-discussion, full of pseudo-tentative pseudo-modesty. But under that was a subtext as subtle as perfume and as pervasive, in which two nervous systems spoke on behalf of two bodies: one spoiled and satiated yet curiously unsatisfied, the other inured to hunger by long abstinence but now protesting that abstinence was not its natural state. Oh the pity of it, Iago!

Sharkey could hardy guess what was going on in Mary's mind, but his own was in a perpetual low fever, its temperature hovering a degree above normal. He was split down the middle: one half the familiar randy baboon, the other a decent if hypocritical chap who dishes out French lessons for free. How long could he keep it up? And what happened if the decent chap won out in the end?

He decided on shock tactics and bought Mary an ivory carving. It was of a fisherman in a loose dress gathered at the waist; a broad straw hat with a hole where the crown should be hung down his back. He had a feathery beard and black hair swept up into a bun on the top of his head, and was holding a fish in one hand and a bamboo pole twined with rope in the other. The thing was exquisitely carved; Mary's mouth opened when he presented it to her.

'Liam! What do you think you're doing?'

'Giving you a carving.'

'What for?'

'For that little table in your drawing room. It needs something to set it off.'

'Don't be infuriating. I didn't mean it that way.'

'What way did you mean it?'

'Oh what's the use?' Mary gave up and kissed him, holding him by the shoulders; her lips were tense and trembling as they touched his.

Scrymgeour noticed this ornament and soon discovered where it came from. 'Getting chivalrous in our old age, aren't we?' he observed with all the moral frost of Morningside.

Unfortunately Mary's dehumidifier was too strong; it split the fisherman's rosewood base. Mary was red-faced with embarrassment, which Sharkey laughed off. 'For heaven's sake, sweetie, we'll get another. Cat Street is full of them.'

'Antiques specially run up for the occasion,' commented Alec. They were dining at Mary's; her amah, Ah Yee, was banging saucepans in the kitchen.

'Not all of them,' said Sharkey. 'There are old ones too.'

'I remember once looking at a T''ang horse,' said Scrymgeour meditatively, 'and wondering whether I could afford it. I happened to look though a crack in the place's floorboards and saw half a dozen little men running them up for the tourist market.'

'They didn't run up my fisherman,' said Mary stoutly.

'He's from the mainland and there's a certificate to prove it,' said Sharkey.

'Maybe they ran that up too.' That was Alec again.

'Oh phoo,' said Mary.

The day after this conversation Sharkey and Mary went to Cat Street to buy a new base. They parked the Hillman beside the Hop Yat church, a hideous piece of Chinese

Gothic, coloured pink and cream, and walked down Ladder Street, a kind of open-air staircase lined with junk sellers and their wares. A colony of incredibly thin cats loped around; Mary tried to fondle one but it was too quick for her. A man in a singlet and baggy shorts was carving a piece of wood with a chopper; he looked the very picture of despondency.

Further down, Ladder Street became Cat Street; they found an authentic-looking base there without difficulty and turned to walk back up again. As they crossed Hollywood Road they saw a tall, gaunt, stringy woman with a crazy glint in her eye emerge from the Chinese temple there, a fantastically shaped building all multicoloured tiles; she wore the amah's uniform of white overshirt and black trousers and walked past them unseeing.

'Good heavens, it's Ah Yee,' exclaimed Sharkey.

'So it is,' said Mary and marvelled as the jerky figure, carrying a basket full of potatoes and red peppers, disappeared into the crowd.

'What's got into her?' said Sharkey. 'She never even noticed us.'

'I'm worried about her,' sighed Mary. 'She's been upset these last days.'

'She was making a terrible row in the kitchen last night,' Sharkey remembered.

'That's one of the signs. Another is the cheese. – You know how cheese disgusts the Chinese. Well, when Ah Yee is in a good mood she lays cheeses out properly on the plate. But when she's out of sorts she just piles them on top of each other and dumps them on the table.'

'Have you spoken to her?'

'She wouldn't say anything. Chinese women never learned how to complain.'

'Unhappiness doesn't exist, eh? An ideal philosophical state.'

'Not if you're in it. It also means that happiness doesn't exist either. Life just consists of endurance. – Come along now.'

'Where to?'

'After her. I'm going to make her talk.'

They fetched the Hillman, waited for ten minutes to give Ah Yee time to settle down, then drove to Mary's diminutive flat in Conduit Road: a two-room affair with waist-high concrete balconies like snipers' positions. As Mary turned the key in the front door they could hear something being chopped up with a meat-cleaver. The sound was unnecessarily loud.

'Ah Yee!'

'Ya, missee!'

'Come in here for a minute.'

The amah came in, sleeves rolled up, hair pulled together in a bun.

'Sit down,' said Mary.

'Oh no, missee!' She sounded scandalised.

'Don't be silly,' said Mary in her most commonsensical voice. Putting an arm round the amah, she forcibly seated her on an armchair, where she sat as stiff as a guardsman, then sat down herself.

'Something's wrong, Ah Yee. I know it. – Tell me what you were doing at the temple today.'

'Me say player, missee.'

'A prayer? Why?'

'Me go often.'

'But this time there was something special, wasn't there?'

'Oh no, missee.'

At this point the dialogue entered a repeating groove until the amah, jumping sideways out of her chair, cried: 'Me put meat in oven.'

'Come back when you've finished,' Mary called after her.

While she was away Sharkey and Mary debated how on earth to get her to open up. Sharkey finally had an idea he thought worth trying. When Ah Yee returned, five minutes later, she was amazed to be greeted in fluent Cantonese by this man whom she privately thought of as Small Foreign Devil With Wicked Mouth; how was she to know that he was an expert linguist who had seduced women in at least half-a-dozen languages?

'Ah Yee,' he said in his most impressive voice, 'it's about your brother in China, is it not?' This was an astute guess. Mary and he knew that her husband was dead and that she had no children; in addition she had no money worries that either knew of. But they'd seen her huge bevy of brothers and sisters in a wedding photograph she'd brought back from her last New Year's visit to Kwangtung: a dozen Chinese, anonymous in boiler suits. It must concern one of these, and more likely a brother, sisters being creatures of no importance.

The amah gulped; a stern, difficult tear welled up in her eye. Little by little, in pidgin English and Cantonese, her story came out: a story like many another in this day and age.

She was Elder Sister in a family of twelve. Her father, a cooking-oil salesman, had married twice; the youngest child,

Yee's favourite brother Fan Fan, was twenty years younger than she.

The arrival of the Japanese in the 'thirties scattered the family. Two brothers joined the Kuomintang, a third emigrated to Singapore. A pair of sisters settled in Cholon, the Chinese quarter of Saigon, and became amahs like herself. She took Fan Fan, who was six years old at the time, with her to Hong Kong and looked after him there right through the Japanese occupation, a time when many thousands died of starvation. Life improved in 1945, with the return of the British. She got a good job and was putting Fan Fan though the Diocesan Boys School.

The bombshell came in 1947, when he was sixteen. The amah from the flat above brought her a letter written on a page torn from an exercise book. The writing was Fan Fan's and it read as follows: 'When you get this I shall be on the other side of the border. I am joining the People's Liberation Army to fight for a new China. We shall come to Hong Kong and drive the foreigners out. I am sorry for doing it this way, but you will be proud of me one day.'

The new China was duly created, but the only people to come to Hong Kong were a million refugees. As for Fan Fan, he was directed to a commune in the south of Kwangtung, where he was put to work in the labour brigade, tilling the soil and feeding the animals. As a member of a tainted class – his father was a merchant and his own heroic decision for the communists counted for nothing – he could expect no better. The maths and English he'd learned at D.B.S. were of no use to him now.

It turned out too that he was a spoiled boy. He criticised the brigade's working methods and was dubbed a counter-revolutionary. They put him on the night-soil carts that plied between the commune and a neighbouring town, along with a former landowner who was in even worse case than himself: many of the peasants had formerly been his tenants. This man was supposed to be observing the four withs: living with the masses, eating with the masses, working with the masses and discussing with the masses. This boiled down to pulling the night-soil cart by day and suffering argument and recrimination in the evening, a process which he as a hardened adult was better able to bear than Fan Fan.

It was in the town that the boy met the mysterious man who called himself Sin Fung, or Vanguard. He was resting under a tree with the noisome cart beside him, waiting to pick up the day' consignment, when a coolie in shorts and singlet sat down beside him and offered him a cigarette. As they smoked the man said in a low voice 'You have a sister in Hong Kong.' Fan Fan made no reply; there were agents provocateurs everywhere.

Then the man whispered Yee's name and address and said: 'I will carry a letter to her. – One, free. After that you pay.'

'Come to this place tomorrow,' said Fan Fan and got up. While pushing the cart back to the commune he thought the whole thing over. He was permitted to write to his sister but the letters were severely censored. The only way to get uncensored messages to Yee – and perhaps even organise his escape – was to find a reliable private contact; perhaps Vanguard was that man.

He composed an innocuous missive, writing on an old paper bag. Nothing in it would cause him trouble if the man turned out to be a double agent, but it contained two key sentences: 'Did you remember to pay the messenger?' and 'Is Uncle Yuen still of the same opinion?' The first was to test the man's honesty, the second an oblique reference to the possibility of getting out of China, because in the days before he ran away his Uncle Yuen in Singapore had wanted to take him into his business.

About three weeks later Sin Fung had turned up again, this time with a letter in a crumpled envelope. The hand was undoubtedly Yee's; she said she had paid nothing and that Uncle Yuen had not changed his mind; far from it, he was even more convinced than before, and she agreed with him.

A regular correspondence ensued, with Sin Fung as the postman. Brother and sister agreed that Fan Fan should first seek the right to emigrate through legal channels. So, when she was in China the following New Year, to attend another brother's wedding – the one at which the photograph Mary and Sharkey had seen was taken – Yee travelled to the commune and told the secretary of the administrative committee that her brother wished to emigrate to Singapore, where he had an uncle, she herself would be the financial guarantor.

The result was three months of humiliating interrogation for Fan Fan, following which his application was turned down. After that Vanguard visited Yee in Hong Kong and asked her whether she would be prepared to pay to have her brother smuggled out. She said she would and handed over the sum asked for, all paid from her own resources because by now the Singapore uncle had no desire to take on so unreliable a young man as Fan Fan. That had happened in July; Fan Fan was to be smuggled out at the earliest opportunity.

Weeks passed and nothing happened. Ah Yee feared that she had been swindled and would never see her money again, but one day the previous week she had got a message asking her to meet Sin Fung in their usual place, a public space between two resettlement blocks at Shaukiwan.

There the man told her, with a degree of embarrassment, that something had gone wrong but he didn't know what. Fan Fan was to have been taken out by junk in early August, but all trace of the boat concerned had vanished. What about the one that had sunk? shrieked Ah Yee. Might her poor brother not have been one of those bodies washed up at Telegraph Bay? Sin Fung admitted that he did not know. But, an honest rogue as rogues go, he promised to do what he could to find out, and to help Fan Fan if he was still alive. Yee had paid her money and was entitled to a fair deal.

That was the situation at the moment. Ah Yee had no idea whether Fan Fan was alive or dead, inside China or out. 'Me dunno how find out, missee.' Her voice was hectoring in its grief; she was a tense woman and emotion didn't take the easy way out.

'So that's why you were at the temple,' said Sharkey.

'Me burn joss stick. Pay money for player.'

'But Ah Yee,' said Mary gently, 'you're not a believer.'

'Maybe Fan Fan dead, missee. Must say player.' She turned a reproachful stare on her employer.

'Do you need any ... money?'

'No missee,' said the amah proudly. 'Me pay ten thousand dollar. No need money.'

Sharkey whistled. Ten thousand HK! Why, that represented about three years' wages for her. Who but a Chinese would have done it?

'How can we help, Liam?' cried Mary, waving her hands impotently.

'No wolly, missee. Sin Fung find out.'

'But I do worry! And we will help. But how, Liam?'

'By contacting this Sin Fung, I suppose. I can't think of any other way.' He spoke cautiously; he felt himself being trapped into Good Works again and didn't like the sensation. Virtue seemed to be taking him over progressively, like a wasting disease.

'Of course! We'll do that,' cried Mary, buoyant with relief. Ah Yee seemed to cheer up too, though Sharkey couldn't for the life of him see why. Perhaps it was just the feeling that she wasn't on her own.

'I don't know about you, but I could use a drink,' he said.

'Me too,' said Mary. She produced the Johnny Walker from her rosewood sideboard and they drank two large snorts. 'That's better,' she sighed. 'My guts are starting to unknot again.'

But the relaxation of her muscles released a small fluttering creature in her nasal cavity. Picking up Ah Yee's wedding photograph, she found the sight of all these stiff, decent, inarticulate, put-upon people too much for her. She suddenly started to blub.

'What's the matter?' cried Sharkey in alarm.

'I ... don't know. Life, I suppose.'

'No use weeping about it. It's incurable.'

'I know. I just can't help it. Poor buggers, what have they done to deserve it?'

'What has anybody? – No, disregard that remark. Get it out of your system.'

'Oh Liam,' she sobbed. 'You can be so nice when you want to!' She collapsed on his shoulder, copiously wetting the lapel of his jacket.

'There, there.' He soothed her, but inside him alarm bells were ringing again. What had he let himself in for this time, chasing some mysterious Chink? It was ludicrous. But all the time the generous flesh he was doing it for was draped round his neck and smelled, he realised, slightly of musk. Musk was not good for the will, being exciting and calming at the same time. Besides, it was being aided and abetted by an insidious little advocate inside himself pleading the cause of weakness, of letting your bone go with the dog. He had kept that little sod at bay all his life: was he going to give in to it now? No bloody fear.

But the irony of the situation struck him too. Just when Mary was ripe for the picking his own defences were starting to wobble. He had an incongruous vision of their two citadels crumbling simultaneously, two hermit crabs shivering there without a shell between them. What a feast for any passing predator!

On November 1st the *Kwangtung Courier* ran an editorial in heavy print; the subject was the junk deaths. 'Six weeks have passed,' it thundered, 'since twelve bodies were washed up on the west coast of Hong Kong island. Six weeks during which the Royal Hong Kong Police has not made a single satisfactory statement. How long must the citizens of this Colony wait before the perpetrators of this dastardly act are brought to book?'

The following morning the paper printed a response to this blast from the Commissioner of Police himself. He queried the assumption that the bodies necessarily had any connection with Hong Kong at all. 'The known pattern of currents in the Pearl River estuary is quite capable of bringing bodies here from long distances.' Considering the state of need at present prevailing in mainland China, he concluded: 'What is more likely than that these bodies belong to a group of unfortunates who were attempting illegal entry into the Colony in a boat that was not seaworthy?' Nevertheless strenuous investigations were going on into all sea-going activities in the Colony's waters, etc., etc.

There followed a burst of correspondence in which some writers endorsed the police view and others did not. Mr N.T. Chow – a noted scribe and the only Chinese ever to sign letters with his real name – called the twenty dead 'martyrs to that cause of Freedom which this Colony, however imperfectly, maintains as a beacon to six hundred million fellow-Chinese.' In opposition to whom a more sceptical writer – unnamed – posited 'some profit-minded gentleman from Cheung Chau or Aberdeen having a difference of opinion with some other acolyte of the capitalist system, who then sinks his boat by way of discussion.' This letter Verity found particularly annoying; it would not have surprised him if Sharkey had been the author.

Another man whose teeth it set on edge was Inspector Dashwood, who the following morning, in the Commissoner's absence, found himself in the chair at the Police Liaison Meeting. As the man in charge of the case he felt himself particularly vulnerable. 'Damned little jumped-up nobodies!' he fumed, meaning journalists. He was a sandy-haired, ferret-faced man with a high idea of his own importance.

'Sounds a reasonable enough assumption to me,' commented Joe Miners drily, his pipe billowing. 'How far have you got anyway?'

Dashwood waved a folder in the air; some of its pages had been flagged with paper spills pinned to their top right-hand corners.

'We've taken in excess of one hundred statements. From Yaumati and Aberdeen and Tai O and Dumbell.'

'That's a lot of literature,' said Joe.

Dashwood ignored the provocation. 'It's a difficult case,' he said, somewhat loftily. 'Evidence is hard to come by.'

Verity, who was also present, deputising for Jack Cairns, was basically on Joe's side, but fretted at this evidence of departmental in-fighting, while Anderson, the man from Chinese Affairs, sat placidly listening. He was big, broad-faced and glabrous and though he mightn't look it was fluent in Mandarin, Cantonese and three other Chinese dialects.

Dashwood started reading from his flagged statements 'From Choi Kwok Fun, junk-master, domiciled in Tai O. He was drinking with friends in a wine shop in Kennedy Town one day last September when he heard two men talking at a neighbouring table. 'You were lucky all those people drowned,' one of them said. 'If any of them had got away he would have had a fine tale to tell.' He was convinced the man was referring to the deaths at Telegraph Bay. He would not be able to identify either man.'

'Surprise, surprise,' said Joe, pipe-smoke leaking from his open mouth.

'And here's another,' said Dashwood, opening his file at another flag. 'Kwan Shui Hing, street hawker, domiciled An Lok Street, Dumbell Island. A regular informant of ours, by the way. – About 25th September he was approached by someone he refused to name for protection money, of which an instalment was due. As they talked a third man came up and said 'You'll be giving that to me from now on. Might as well start now.' The first man said a dirty thing about the other man's mother, whereupon the other replied: 'You be careful or we'll do to you what we did to those junk people.''

'Hm,' said Joe, whose pipe had gone out again. Scraping out the dottle, he said: 'You're getting warm. Those sound like our friends Wong and Lim.'

'Wong and Lim?' echoed Dashwood, startled.

'That's right. Wong Au Nai, small shopkeeper, lives in one of those little streets behind the praya. He's a Red Pole – fighter official to you – with the T'ung. The other is Lim Sik Fuk, does the same job with the Twenty-One K. Tough eggs, both of them. – Know them at all, Nigel?'

'No,' Verity had to admit. 'But how do you know about them?'

'Usual source: hawkers. 'Course it's all off the record; nobody would ever testify. All the same I reckon I could give you a pretty accurate list of the junior members of both triads – the Grass Sandals and Red Poles and White Paper Fans – on the island. Good blokes, those hawkers. Of course they never get to see the bigger fry. *They* could be anybody. Maybe some of our leading citizens; maybe even working for Government.' He gave Dashwood an impish look. 'Perhaps even some of your chaps.'

'If that's a joke it's in very bad taste.'

Miners turned to Verity. 'Perhaps even some of yours, Nigel – Old Cheung, say.'

The idea of old Cheung being in the pay of the triads was too much for the meeting; everybody burst out laughing. Even Anderson let a slow smile spread over his broad features.

'I suppose it's possible,' said Verity, for whom the whole thing was far from being a joke. 'What I can't understand is: why bother? Dumbell is a poor place; there's not a lot to be made there.'

Joe's eyes shone; here was a golden opportunity to

expound his private doctrine. 'What people don't understand,' he said, 'is that triads are impoverished organisations. You don't get fat on screwing twenty bucks from the odd hawker. That's why they're so keen to get into the smuggling racket – they get a thousand dollars a head for that. And if ever they break into the really lucrative heroin markets, like the States and Europe, then we'll have trouble. But for now, they're just gangsters functioning at subsistence level.'

'A thousand dollars a head,' murmured Dashwood, impressed in spite of himself. 'That's the kind of money to attract the Big Men.'

A hush fell, as the Big Men were contemplated. Because Big Men, as Joe had indicated, were commonly thought to be behind all triad activity. No one knew who they were of course, but it was enough for a Chinese millionaire to get himself elected to Legco, or start a commercial radio station, for someone to opine that he was really a Big Man in triads, making pots of money from drug smuggling.

Joe broke the spell. 'I've no idea who the Big Men might be,' he said, 'but I do know that the only way to get at them is to keep chasing the little ones.'

With that the meeting got down to practical business. Dashwood, on behalf of the Commissioner, proposed that a show be put on in the outer islands, and this was accepted. Inspectors would be sent on a fact-finding tour and the sub-stations at Cheung Chau, Dumbell and Silvermines Bay would have their establishments increased by one constable each.

Precisely nothing came from all this. Even the press campaign died of inertia. And, at last, the bodies which had been washed ashore at Telegraph Bay all those weeks ago

were released from the morgue and buried at Aberdeen
cemetery to a great wailing of pipas.

⌒

Sharkey ran into Stillgoe one lunchtime at the Cricket Club.
'Hello,' he said. 'I shouldn't have thought this was your
scene.'

'Nor I yours.' Through his dark glasses Stillgoe gazed
mournfully out over the most expensive square of grass in
the world.

'It's not, as a matter of fact. But we're here, so why not
have a drink?'

They sipped their San Migs in the balmy autumn
sunshine, sitting on chairs overlooking the broad flight of
steps which ran down to the hallowed, if desiccated, turf.
Behind them the lunchtime fauna of barristers and import-
export men was indulging in its daily swill. Youngsters with
blond down on their cheeks shouted 'Boy!' with self-
conscious insouciance, and the impassive old waiters glided
over to take their orders.

'What are you doing here anyway?' asked Sharkey.

'Just hanging around.' Stillgoe's face twitched. There was
something at once limp and hypersensitive about him; he
seemed to be permanently recoiling from blows that never
came. The mere contact of the air made him wince. In
addition to which, Sharkey observed, he was so
unprepossessing that he stirred up your sadistic instincts; you
kept wanting to stick pins in him.

'Where are you living now?' he asked.

'Kowloon side.'

'Whereabouts?'

'Behind the Park Hotel.' The words came out with extreme reluctance.

'You got a flat?'

After a pause: 'It's not exactly mine.'

'Whose is it?'

'Ed's. I share with him.'

'Then it's Ed's.'

'Not exactly.'

'Whose is it, for Christ's sake?'

Word by word he extracted the story. A jazz combo, the Bradbrook Trio, had come out to play at the Princess Garden night club. Unfortunately Bradbrook himself (who was the double-bass player) stepped under a bus and was killed. The others couldn't find a suitable replacement in time and had had to go back to the UK. Unfortunately they had paid the rental of a flat for six months in advance and the owner refused to cancel the contract. So they passed it on to Ed, who had interviewed them on their arrival and become something of a boon companion.

'So you're fixed up till the lease runs out,' said Sharkey.

'Yes.'

'When's that?'

'Next March.'

About the same time as he hopes to finish the dubbing, thought Sharkey and said aloud 'What will you do after that?'

'I'll get by.'

A few more beers (which Sharkey paid for as Stillgoe wasn't a member and couldn't sign chits) loosened the other man's tongue. Sharkey was favoured with the story of his life. It was a tale of genuine but ridiculous vicissitudes. Stillgoe's was an existence dedicated to art, and art's response had been to kick him firmly in the teeth. Apparently even Destiny found something irritating about him.

His father, a night watchman in Stoke on Trent, had burned to death. Fire broke out in the department store in which he worked; running to raise the alarm, he tripped and fell, knocking himself unconscious against a counter. He perished in the ladies' underwear department.

After her husband's demise his mother emigrated to Australia and married a labourer from Sydney. The young Stillgoe went to school in that city and discovered his vocation for things artistic. He published verse in the school magazine and, later, at Sydney University, wrote and produced a play about Ned Kelly. His text introduced the word 'fuck' to the Australian amateur stage, and he was sent down.

There followed a number of casual jobs, including work on a cattle station and getting lost in the outback, and culminating in the role of deckhand on a cargo vessel on the Singapore run. His fellow sailors gave him a torrid time and threw the unfinished manuscript of his epic poem *Botany Bay* into the sea. 'That's for behaving like a bloody sheila,' they said.

At Singapore he left the ship and things began to look up. He got occasional journalistic work for the *Straits Times* and had just moved on to Hong Kong, when the great news came: his aunt in England had left him money. With it he proposed making a film, a personal version of the Burke and Wills story.

'Why that? You're not even an Aussie,' said Sharkey.

'It's a great subject,' said Stillgoe gloomily. 'They travel to a place where life and death are the same thing: the red desert at the heart of experience.' He blinked painfully in the sunlight.

Sharkey thought: you wouldn't last five minutes there yourself, but was impressed by the choice of subject. He whistled with surprise, even admiration. 'I take it the money wasn't quite enough – which is why you're dubbing the *Ronin*.'

Stillgoe nodded. 'The legacy pays for them and they make enough to set up Burke and Wills.'

Very nice in theory, but Sharkey had grave doubts about the practice. Because the dubbing was getting seriously behind schedule. At the moment, for example, they were labouring over a brothel scene involving Okaru, the wife of the retainer Kampei, who had been sold into prostitution by her father-in-law.

Okaru was being played by Annabel Letterby, a girl with the crazy slenderness of a model and a beautiful vapid face who wore her black hair on top of her head in a lacquered beehive. She worked as an announcer in Hong Kong Radio. Sharkey had sniffed around her in the past but rejected her on grounds of invincible stupidity. She had a husband who was rumoured to be even thicker than herself, but as he was an army officer stationed somewhere beyond Castlepeak no one had ever been able to verify the fact.

'That father-in-law knew what he was at,' said Donoghue roguishly. 'If this Okaru was anything like Annabel the men would be queuing up three deep.'

'Naughty naughty,' replied Annabel, pleased. To keep on the right side of her you had to pretend to be in a state of sexual excitement over her without expecting her to do anything about it. She smiled at Gus, gracious as a duchess.

'Let's get back to the bloody film,' said Sharkey, exasperated. 'We're in a whorehouse, remember ... '

'I was preparing myself psychologically,' said Gus.

'Well, stop it.'

'Just like you have?' asked Gus pointedly.

'Don't believe everything you hear. – Now, Annabel, you're supposed to be half cut. And, Gus, you're a decent chap pretending to be dissolute. It'll be hard work for you.'

'Jealousy will get you nowhere.'

'Come off it, will you? I'm trying to sort out this bloody scene. Annabel, you're coming down a ladder and Gus is standing at the bottom.'

'I never stood at a bottom in my life.'

'Shut up and read. I need to see your lip movements.' He called to the projectionist. 'Roll 'em!'

A twittering Okaru appeared at the brothel window, while Yuranosuke (played by Gus) stood on the street below, holding a ladder. Annabel and Gus then read their lines, in the literal translation provided by the film company.

OKARU. I am afraid of your ladder. It feels strangely dangerous.

'Don't worry. He'll be gentle with you,' commented Ed.

YURANOSUKE. You are past the age for feeling frightened. You could come down three rungs at a time and still not open any fresh wounds.

'Work that one out,' said Ed.

OKARU. It's like being on a boat.

YURANOSUKE. I can see your little boat god from here. Haha.

'He must have X-ray eyes.'

OKARU. Tut tut.

YURANOSUKE. I'm admiring the autumn moon over Lake T''ung T''ing.

'No you're not. You're admiring her fanny.'

OKARU. I refuse to come down if you talk like that.

YURANOSUKE. If you do I shall climb the ladder and deflower you.

'Beautifully put. You should try it on a bar girl.'

OKARU. Your language is disgusting.

YURANOSUKE. Anyone would think you were a virgo intacta! If you do not be quiet I shall make love to you from the rear.

At this point Ed dissolved in laughter and Gus, taking care to make it decorous, seized Annabel from behind, buried his nose under her left ear and whispered in a Charles Boyer voice: 'My darrrling ... '

'You'll mess up my hair,' complained Annabel, otherwise unmoved.

'You shouldn't lacquer it,' said Donoghue, who was getting his face scratched. 'It's bad for it.'

Annabel craned her head round: at last a serious subject. 'Only some lacquers,' she said earnestly. 'The hard ones; and I never use those.'

This wisdom was lost on Gus, who suddenly bellowed: 'Beer! I need beer!' and bit the cap off a bottle of San Mig. As he put it to his head his scar, catching the light, glinted lividly.

It took Sharkey half an hour to invent plausible English dialogue for this scene, and even then he could do nothing about its uncontrolled, macabre quality for European ears. Fortunately it would mostly be heard by Asiatics.

Somehow they managed to complete the scene that day, but didn't even start the key one in which Kampei, thinking he has killed his father, commits hara-kiri, so impressing the ronin that they admit him to their league in extremis. Still,

Gus had probably drunk too much beer to be able to handle his dying speech: 'How thankful I am that my father's death and my wife's becoming a prostitute have not been in vain!', following which he cuts his belly, pulls out his entrails and presses them to the scroll containing the ronins' names.

All afternoon Stillgoe had stood there saying nothing, his eyes invisible behind the sunglasses and only the working of his features betraying that something was going on in his head. He made no complaints about the wasted time and paid his actors without a murmur. Decidedly there was something uncanny about the man, Sharkey thought.

The necromancers had fixed on November 28th as the most propitious day for the removal of the village of Ying Pun lock, stock and barrel to the new city of Tsuen Wan. The village was now a sad little cluster of houses stripped even of the wood in their roofs and waiting for the Shek Pik waters to come and engulf them.

Cairns and Verity were the guests of honour at the propitiation ceremony and official luncheon to mark their transfer, and sailed to Lantau together in the *Sir Cecil Clementi*; Cheung and another land assistant called Cordeiro, a round-faced Eurasian with pebble-lensed glasses, had gone on ahead of them. It was a typical autumn day: blue sky, warm sun, dry air. The necromancers had chosen well.

'End of a long haul, what?' said Cairns, basking in the sunny weather like a large animal.

'Three years, yes. But I must say I don't care for their choice. Would you choose to live in Tsuen Wan?'

The hull of the launch sliced the glittering sea, scattering spray on to the windscreen. Cairns gave his booming laugh and said: 'I daresay it would have been nicer for paternalist romantics like ourselves if they'd chosen to build another village just like the old one, picturesque and impoverished, somewhere in the Territories.'

'They'd have been happier,' Verity insisted. 'They'd have had continuity. Whereas in Tsuen Wan ... '

'Not exactly the New Jerusalem, I agree. Still, it's the future.'

'Who says so?' cried Verity bitterly.

'Everybody does.'

'Then everybody's wrong. – Anyway who is everybody? A bunch of self-appointed experts sitting in air-conditioned offices drawing large salaries. What do people like that know about anything?'

'Not a lot, I'll grant you. Trouble is – as we've been saying all along – these people have made their choice. They're getting what they wanted.'

To Verity's mind that was the most depressing thing about it. He stared out over the water, unseeing. Poor chap, thought Cairns, he doesn't look at all well; but of course nobody could ever tell him. So he gazed out over the side himself.

What he saw was Silvermines Bay, which the rays of the morning sun had transformed into a habitation fit for the gods. The green mountains, falling in irregular rushes to the sea, sparkled as on the first day of creation.

They landed at Cheung Sha Wan, where the local constable greeted them with a grin and a salute. A young English inspector took them to Shek Pik in his car.

As they breasted the slope the valley opened before them: the new dam with its muddy lake building up behind it, and to the right the village, teetering on the water's very edge. All its house doors opened on emptiness, because the inhabitants' worldly goods were in an ancient landing craft drawn up on the beach under the dam: a huge abandoned shoe-box with one end hanging open.

Beside the houses a mat-shed had been set up. The locals were standing round it in their black samfus, like shiny insects. There was a Land Rover too, in which sat the site manager of the construction company and the master of the landing craft, sharing a cigarette.

'Looks like quite a party,' said Cairns, getting out of the car.

Verity, through a slight feeling of nausea – his breakfast had disagreed with him – examined the villagers critically. They would do; his little flock wouldn't let him down. They'd show Jack what a real district was. Meanwhile Cairns was humming under his breath, thinking: could be worse. Mind you in my day ...

A round-bellied little Chinese was bowing and beaming in greeting. His chin boasted an enormous wart that trailed half a dozen filmy hairs.

'Mr Lim!' said Cairns heartily and shook him by the hand. Verity did likewise. Then Mr Lim, who was the heung cheung, or village headman, launched into a speech of welcome.

When he had finished Cairns clapped him on the shoulder and plied him with questions in faultless Cantonese: 'How many grandchildren do you have now? Fourteen, is it? You're a fortunate man. – And I see old Mrs Kwok is dead, may her soul rest in peace. – What good compensation you got for that

bottom field of yours, by the way. – Mind you, I had my
doubts about those boundary marks of yours, but no matter;
it's all over now; you've got your money and nobody can take
it away from you ... '

They laughed together and the villagers laughed with
them, delighted. Verity found it hard to suppress a feeling of
jealousy. Jack was simply too good at his job. A man shouldn't
be blessed with a memory like that, or have so easy a manner
with people; it wasn't fair.

Nevertheless he joined in the conversation, doing his best.
The notables bobbed up and down, chattering like rooks,
while their womenfolk quacked with laughter and their
children giggled behind their hands. Then a pair of Taoist
priests in red cloaks and black caps who had been lounging
round the fringes of the group suddenly banged on a gong; a
pipa, that bell-mouthed Chinese clarinet, uttered its
plangent wail.

'Propitiation ceremony start now,' called Mr Lim.

Everyone turned to face the mat-shed under the roof of
which stood a spavined table bearing the images of Tien
Hou, the Queen of Heaven, and some deity peculiar to the
village. Both had been bright red and green in their time,
but now what colour remained had taken refuge in their
cracks and hollows. The women lit joss sticks and set them
in bowls of sand in front of them; then the ceremony
began.

It was a perfunctory affair; this was a poor village. While
the nasal chanting was going on Verity's attention wandered.
One man was picking his nose. Another was cuffing a child's
ear. A third was shambling up to the altar with a joss stick in
his hand. As he watched them he suddenly felt his eyes blur.
A numbness invaded his brain and, to his horror, he realised

that his body was affected too. He tried to move his foot but could not. He was as stiff as a plank of wood.

But this was absurd, absurd! The priests intoned, the gong banged, somebody hawked and spat – and it all came to him as if through a layer of cotton wool.

Slowly the fit passed, leaving him with shaking knees. He thought, in amazement: why I'm sick, really sick. A wave of hatred blew through him, for all who were thoughtless and active and in command of their bodies as he was not. It was a shameful thought; he shook his head doggedly, refusing it.

But there were things he could not refuse, not any more: his curious paralysis on the praya on Dumbell, his fall coming down this very hill the other day, not to mention an assortment of recent aches and pains and sudden indigestions. There was no denying it; he was ill, genuinely ill, in the way that calls for thermometers and hospital wards, for doctors and nurses in white coats.

As he struggled out of this personal morass the ceremony ended. His legs started functioning again; he was able to follow the others to a long table set up in the open beside the abandoned houses. Little white bowls glinted on it; paper napkins stirred in the breeze. Beside it there was a makeshift kitchen, rigged up out of four poles and a length of jute sacking like an outdoor privy; inside, two cooks presided over an array of pots and pans from which emerged Chinese cooking smells which for once nauseated him.

Cairns was walking in front of him with the village children crowding round him, trying to touch him. He caught one little boy up and rubbed him against his whiskers; the child shrieked with fear and pleasure. 'That'll bring you good luck,' he boomed in Cantonese and distributed boiled sweets among the disappointed.

As they took their places at the table Verity remembered with drugged horror that he would have to make a speech. Fortunately Jack came first. In a moment he had the village in the palm of his hand, making them laugh with in-jokes, or referring obliquely to things in which they took pride: Lim's son's success at the Tung Wah College, for instance.

While the heung cheung was replying Verity struggled to put his thoughts in order and when the time came was able to string a few commonplaces together without actually disgracing himself. But all the time a disembodied voice was whispering in his ear: you are a sick man.

He sat down to polite applause. There were three other speeches after his, including a good one from a sweating Cheung. Then the meal was served. In the general clamour no one noticed his lack of appetite. At last it was over. After the final bowl of rice the company rose abruptly, Chinese fashion, and left the table.

But the day's activities were far from finished. The villagers would carry their gods in procession to the landing craft, board it themselves and be transported to Tsuen Wan. It was now half past two; given two hours to get themselves on board and another two to reach their destination (with Cheung and Cordeiro in attendance), they could be in their new homes at sunset. And might the Lord have mercy on their souls.

Cairns and Verity were able to go immediately; for Verity it was a relief to be in the launch again.

'Well, that's that,' said Jack, fetching a great breath.

'There's a terrible sadness about it, I find,' said Verity despondently. His crisis was over but had left him with aching joints and an undertow of bitterness in his mind.

'It doesn't do to get too attached, Nigel.'

'You seem to be more aware of the dangers than I am.'

'I've brought up a family, you know.' There was no answer to that, not from a barren man like himself. Jack went on: 'Lim was in high old form, don't you think?'

'Wait till he wakens up in Tsuen Wan,' said Verity grimly.

'I suspect you're right. His authority will last about a fortnight. By then the villagers will have learned to ignore him.'

'And the poor battered old gods will be on the junk-heap.'

'They won't be the first.'

'I wish it didn't have to happen, Jack!' cried Verity in a spurt of anguish. 'I really do.'

Cairns clapped him on the shoulder. 'Take it easy, old chap. I can't rub *you* against my whiskers, you know.' He boomed with laughter.

In a while they went forward and stood on the deck with the wind plucking at their clothes. It was half past three. They were level with Sunshine Island, with its privately run settlement for the treatment of drug addicts. Hei Ling Chau, the leper island, was off the port quarter and beyond that lay Peng Chau, which had smoke rising from its tiny, crowded fishing village. To the east of it were two uninhabited islands. Jack drew attention to the first of these. 'That's Siu Kau Yi Chau. Know what happened there during the war?'

Verity shook his head.

'It's one of those uninhabited places where the Japanese left people to die. There's still supposed to be bones lying around. The Chinese won't go near it.'

Verity shuddered. Abandoned there, waiting impotently for the end! *Absit omen* ... But for whom was the omen intended, for those unfortunate villagers who would be chugging past here in a couple of hours' time, or for someone nearer home? Was his own end inside him right now, trying to gnaw its way out?

He straightened his back, and with an act of will banished the thought.

Wilson Ho was a learning machine. He would sit attentive as Sharkey expounded the basics of French grammar and then write out the translation exercises in his Americanised hand, full of long loops. There was rarely a mistake. And when he had learned a thing he never forgot it.

As a Cantonese he had difficulty with some aspects of the pronunciation; for example, his nasals always included a 'g' sound, 'ong' for 'on'. But he was able to use French from the beginning. And that Sharkey found odd, because he gave no indication of possessing intuition, a 'feel' for the language. By abstract intelligence alone he was able to conjure up things that should have been beyond him, as a blind man might reconstitute sight.

It was impossible to lure him into making a personal statement. 'Do you like French?' Sharkey asked him one day.

'It is a very useful language.'

'I know. But do you like it?'

'It is very logical.'

'That's what I told you. But does it appeal to you personally?'

'I am very happy to be learning it.'

At that point Sharkey gave up. Had the young man been lobotomised? Had all human emotion been excised from his brain with a scalpel? What did it matter anyway? He learned fast; that was the main thing.

The lessons usually took place in Sharkey's room at the University, but on occasion the two of them had to go the Ho family home, to take tea.

The Ho's lived in a resettlement block in Shaukiwan, and it was politic to go there by tram, in order not to embarrass them with the affluence of a car. One day early in December they were doing just that. They boarded the swaying old vehicle at Bonham Road. The conductor, seated on his little wooden bench behind a chipped green metal table, handed them their tickets with a grin. The other passengers – coolie women in black, briefcase-carrying clerks in open-necked shirts, young wives with one child in a sling on their backs and another inside – grinned too: a rich foreign devil using public transport must be eccentric.

They got seats at H.M.S. Tamar; for the rest of the journey Sharkey watched the unique and fascinating Chinese world go by. Wilson was looking out the window too, but unseeing; his eyes blinked behind his tortoiseshell glasses.

.They got out in an area of crumbling arcaded buildings with ferns growing out of their walls and rusty metal windows open wide – all that was left of the old city. Behind these stood the great concrete resettlement blocks, like dominoes placed on their edges. There was also a still-unrazed patch of shacks and lean-to shops, and beyond that again a squatter township, climbing the hillside – there are always hills in Hong Kong – like the cells of a chaotic beehive.

Walls of wood and canvas, rickety wooden poles sticking out from the roofs, frayed rope holding everything together: it was a life-sized Mikado game humanised by washing and flower pots set on precarious ledges. The wonder was how neatly turned out the people emerging from it were.

'We go to Block Four,' said Wilson impassively.

They walked between two of the great cliff-faces. Each had parallel balconies running its length, giving it the air of a multi-storey car park if it were not for the jungle of organic life that it contained: pot plants, caged birds, laundry like the petals of gaudy flowers.

There were no lifts; they had to walk up a dank concrete stairway. Coming down to meet them were all kinds of people, even one exquisite girl in a white cheongsam who could have stepped out of the pages of a fashion magazine. God knows how she does it, thought Sharkey with an admiration almost innocent of sexual desire.

He took a deep breath before turning the old mechanical bell at the apartment door: good, decent people tended to be heavy going.

The door opened on a room in which seven human beings disputed ownership with articles of furniture. Wilson's father ushered Sharkey to the best chair in the house (his own) and kept saying 'Please sit down. Please sit down.' He was a small nervous man who worked as a clerk in the Taikoo dockyard. His wife, a squat woman with a face like a frog's, said in Cantonese: 'Come in. We shall have some tea.' Sharkey's reply 'Please don't bother on my account' was also in that language; but Mr Ho felt it incumbent on himself to speak English, and did so.

'Sit down. Sit down. It is good of you to assist my son,' he said.

'It's a pleasure.'

The other occupants of the room were three little girls, a middle-aged woman (presumably an aunt) and a wizened crone who was clearly the grandmother.

'Wilson is a very good pupil,' volunteered Sharkey. While this was being translated into Cantonese he stole a glance into the flat's only other room (apart from a tiny kitchen which also served as a bathroom); this contained a double bed and three bunks one above the other in a metal frame. A quick calculation showed that the two older women and Wilson somehow found a place to doss down in the room he was now in. There was no visible lavatory; clearly they all used the outdoor wooden cubicles he had noticed downstairs.

His praise of Wilson provoked a volley of exclamations in everyone except the praised one himself. His aunt called him a good boy; his little sisters tittered. Sharkey felt hot under the collar; he was being cast in the role of a good man, a benefactor.

'I bring tea,' Mrs Ho announced.

'Not on my account, please ... '

'Oh yes. She bring it,' said Mr Ho, coughing nervously.

'Perhaps we should wait for Mrs Rhodes,' said Wilson.

'Mrs Rhodes? Is she coming?'

'Oh yes.'

'She come fetch embroidery my sister make. She like embroidered handkerchief.'

'I told her you were coming,' said Wilson in his neutral voice. 'She said she might as well fetch them today, then you could go home together.'

'Good idea,' said Sharkey. Well, I'll be damned, he thought; she's following me. He was being followed by a large lady of forty! But it would be a pleasure to see her just the same, quite apart from the relief she would bring. He also rather admired her cheek: it takes one rogue to appreciate another.

One of the little girls suddenly blurted out: 'Speak French for us!' and hid in confusion behind her sisters. The three ladies clacked in unison: how typical of the young, such bad manners!

Sharkey said: 'Nai Yeung is better than me.' (Nai Yeung being Wilson's Chinese name). But this was hotly denied. Mr Ho shook his head and said 'They are naughty girls. Always laugh at my son when he talks French.'

So Sharkey recited for them a La Fontaine fable about a cat called Raminagrobus; he had a recording of it by Gérard Philippe. He rolled the animal's name round his tongue, villainously dramatic. It brought the house down; even the crone tee-hee'd, showing her toothless gums.

At this point there was a discreet knock at the door and Mr Ho admitted Mary. She was in a flowered blue dress and looked flushed after the climb. 'Hullo,' she said off-handedly to Sharkey. 'Fancy meeting you here.'

He observed her narrowly: was there any sign of embarrassment or irony? None; she was a better dissembler than he gave her credit for.

Mrs Ho then fetched the tea, along with a plate of European-style cakes, purchased for the occasion. Dry, but of course he ate them with relish.

'I hear you're doing well,' said Mary to Wilson.

'He is indeed,' said Sharkey.

This fascinating subject was returned to with greedy interest. When it had been exhausted the aunt produced a crumpled piece of brown paper which she unfolded to reveal Mary's handkerchiefs: white cotton, finely embroidered.

'How lovely they are!' she cried, passing one to Sharkey. He admired and passed it back, observing as he did so that she had trimmed another pound or two off her weight.

'Been playing some tennis lately?' he asked casually.

'Well, yes ... ' she began, confused.

This exchange, when translated, provoked an orgy of admiration: what a wonderful thing it must be to play this difficult game so well! 'But I don't play all that well,' said Mary, embarrassed. But of course they knew she did; there was no way they could be persuaded of the opposite.

As they waded through this verbal morass Sharkey reflected on the penance the company of good and worthy people could be: if only they didn't always have to try and say the right thing! An hour or two with an amusing villain like Donoghue would be a blessed relief.

But they got away at last, and he found himself standing, alone with Mary, in the late autumn Hong Kong sunshine. It was the first time they'd been together since they'd discovered Ah Yee's secret, and to his surprise he found himself at a psychological disadvantage. Was he dispirited by the vision of the Ho family, or had the physical tone resulting from tennis kept Mary fresher?

What to do? His centre was crumbling; his wings in retreat. Very well; like Marshal Foch he would attack.

'Madam,' he said, putting on his humorous face, 'I suspect you've been following me.'

'Sir, you're no gentleman to say so.'

'And you're no lady for pointing it out.'

'That makes us evens.'

They laughed. 'How about a drink in the Repulse Bay Hotel then? I could use one.'

'I'm on.'

'Damn!' He suddenly remembered. 'I didn't bring my car.'

'I've got mine.'

He took her bare arm and steered her in the direction she indicated. Walking made the arm move up and down under his hand. It was a highly desirable arm, he reflected, and rather a confident one today. He didn't quite know how to feel about that.

Suddenly she planted a kiss on his cheek and said 'That's for being a good boy.'

'What, me? A good boy? You must be joking.'

'I'm not joking. I'm saying thank you. For being so nice to Wilson and his family.' She paused for a moment, then went on: 'For being so nice to yourself. For allowing yourself to be nice.'

She really did have the upper hand today, he thought with mingled alarm and admiration. This new coolness baffled him.

'Now look here, Mrs Rhodes,' he said, moving to the attack again. 'Nobody calls Liam Sharkey nice with impunity. If you want to know what he's really like there's only one place for it – bed.'

'Oh, phoo! You'd think bed was the only place that existed.'

'Well, isn't it?' he cried in mock-indignation. 'What else is there, for God's sake?' Then, suddenly, the unconscious humour of the situation struck him. He looked around him, taking in the resettlement blocks, the countless Chinese coming and going. 'Funny place to have a big scene,' he said.

'You admit it is a big scene then?'

'You cunning old bag!' This time the indignation was genuine, so genuine that she smiled in spite of herself.

They looked at each other and, simultaneously, burst out laughing.

'Pax?' said Mary finally.

'All right, pax. – But listen, I do need to know your intentions. Are you or are you not going to go to bed with me?'

There was a pause.

'To tell you the truth, Liam, I don't know.' She wrinkled her nose. 'I've been rather cross with you, you see.'

'With me?' He threw wide his arms in disbelief. 'How could anyone be cross with me?'

'Quite easily. – You see, you keep getting me wrong. You classify me as a kind of elderly Madame de Tourvel who has to be seduced by a trick. It doesn't seem to occur to you that I might be perfectly willing to go to bed with you – because I like you. Out of good fellowship.' She took a deep breath. 'It also hasn't occurred to you that I may have done so with one or two others ... '

'Who are they?' he cried wrathfully. 'I'll slaughter them.'

'Nobody you know, Liam. Anyway it was before your time. Afterwards I let myself go a bit and got no offers. Until yours, I mean.' She looked at him with innocent puzzlement. 'And that's the other problem. I just don't understand why you seem to want me.'

'I'll show you. In bed.'

'Who said anything about bed?'

'You did. – Purely out of good fellowship, of course.'

'All right. I concede that. I suppose I've granted the possibility. But if you ever imagine you've seduced me against my will, if I ever see the slightest trace of triumphalism in you, I'll drop you like a hot brick. – Will you settle for that?'

At that moment Sharkey would. He was even beginning to wonder whether Mary hadn't fallen in love with him (otherwise why think of Madame de Tourvel?), when, about twenty yards away, he noticed an ancient Chinese gently fall over and measure his length on the ground.

Mary heard his intake of breath, followed his gaze and saw an old man lying prone, with two companions in attitudes of distress: a small bird-like Chinese with a round face shot through with wrinkles, and a large European dressed in a Russian mouzhik's blouse belted at the waist. The small one was waving his arms helplessly, while the European plunged his hands into his beard, a great bush of white hairs somewhat stained by tobacco.

'Do something, Liam,' she cried.

Sharkey ran over to the little group, calling in Cantonese 'Can I help you?'

The small round-faced man raised his eyebrows and spread the fingers of both hands wide, denoting incomprehension; incredibly, he spoke no Cantonese. The European, clearly one of the colony's White Russians, boomed in English: 'Can somebody find a doctor?'

'I'll go,' cried Mary and rushed off in search of a telephone box.

Sharkey went down on his knees and, ever so gently, undid the cloth knots on the front of the fallen man's jacket; he was frail and old, with a parchment face and a wispy beard like a waterfall in a Sung painting. Suddenly he recognised him: it was General K'ou, a distinguished resident and a minor celebrity in his way; the *Courier* had run articles on him.

By now people had come running across the open space and were standing in a rough circle, waiting to see what the foreign devil would do. Sharkey, shaking with nerves, put an ear to the general's chest; to his relief he detected the tiny, fluttering beat of his heart. 'He's alive,' he said.

Mary came back, agitated, calling: 'I can't find a phone box anywhere!'

'Do not distress yourself, madam,' said the Russian. 'He will be all right now. He is prone to fainting fits.' The words issued from the depths of his chest like the rumble of distant thunder.

At that point General K'ou opened his eyes – infinitely old, infinitely wise, infinitely tired eyes – took in the world, these strangers, the whole incomprehensible scene, and said something in a voice as faint as a cat's.

'He wishes to express his regret at having inconvenienced the company,' translated the Russian.

The general then tried to get up but failed and fell back again. Mary uttered a little yelp and fanned his face with one of Aunt Ho's handkerchiefs. From his supine position the old man made little gestures of thanks and apology. The crowd, seeing he was not going to die, began to drift away.

'Are you sure he won't need a doctor?' asked Sharkey, supporting the old man's wren-like body.

'Oh yes,' boomed the Russian. 'But if you would be so good as to help us get him home ... '

'Where's that?'

'Just over there.' The Russian waved a lordly hand.

They got the general to his feet, Sharkey and the Russian supporting him on either side, and made their slow way across the open space. The Russian emitted a strong odour of Balkan tobacco. Mary and the round-faced man followed behind, smiling inanely at one another, perfectly incapable of communicating.

They were heading for the jumble of rickety shacks on the

still uncleared land. A narrow passage led to what was the complex's central street; they turned left into it and stopped at a house distinguished from its fellows by a roof made entirely from old seventy-eight gramophone records that overlapped each other like the scales of an armadillo (where on earth had those come from?); a strip of tarpaulin, stretched over the ridge of the roof, kept the rain out.

There was a single room inside, with a bare earth floor. Three coloured towels hung from rusty nails; there were three bed-platforms, three tottering chairs and an old deal table overflowing with piles of tattered Chinese books.

Sharkey and the Russian laid out the general on one of the beds, from which vantage point he smiled courteously on one and all and said something in Mandarin. 'We sleep on faggots and wake to the taste of wormwood,' translated the Russian. 'A saying of the exiled King K'ou Ch'ien of the kingdom of Yüeh, with whom my friend shares a name.'

Sharkey then introduced Mary and himself, whereupon the Russian presented the round-faced one as Mr Teng. As for himself: 'Anastas Trofimovitch Chernikov,' he said, with a sweeping bow.

'The Russian restaurant!' cried Mary impulsively.

'Indeed. It belongs to my brother. I, having artistic instincts, am as a child in commercial matters. But I do him some service, principally as a doorman, and so survive.'

Mr Teng started rummaging in a drawer of the table and pronounced a sentence containing the word tsai; he was proposing to make tea. He boiled water in a kettle powered by an unsafe-looking plug, and in a moment they were gratefully sipping the yellow liquid. The general had recovered sufficiently to be able to sit up.

Chernikov told them the story of his three friends: K'ou,

Teng and the man to whom the third bed belonged, a Mr Li. All three had had to flee Peking in 1949, when the communists took over. K'ou was then a brigadier-general in the Kuomintang; he was of a good family and a considerable Confucian scholar. Teng was Professor of History at Peking University. And the absent Mr Li came from a long line of imperial civil servants and had been himself a civil servant with the republic.

Mr Li was by far the richest of the three. He spoke some Cantonese and had found a job as turnstile-keeper on the Star Ferry, where he earned thirty-five dollars – just over two pounds – a week. The others made their living by placing occasional essays in the press – written Chinese being the same everywhere – at twenty dollars per thousand words: about an eighth of what the *Courier* paid Sharkey – and by giving Mandarin lessons.

'Of course,' said Chernikov, 'it is a disadvantage that my friends speak no Cantonese. They can communicate with their pupils only through writing.'

'Can't they learn the language?' Mary enquired.

'Dear me, no. They regard that dialect as a vulgar corruption of the Chinese tongue.'

Sharkey, somewhat to his surprise, found himself asking 'Could the general teach me?'

Chernikov translated, and the general inclined his head. He would be honoured to give Mr Sha Ki lessons, but how?

Sharkey explained that he possessed a manual of Gwoyü from which he could read simple sentences which the general could correct; as for the writing he had learned a couple of hundred Kanji characters when he was studying Japanese.

The general bowed again; he would be delighted to

instruct Sharkey free of charge. Sharkey politely replied that
such a thing was impossible. There followed a three-way
discussion in which the old man was persuaded to accept
twenty-five dollars an hour. Another five minutes fixed the
date and time of the first lesson, and Mary and he were able
to leave.

When they emerged from the warren of shacks it was five
o'clock; a westering sun was wedged between two
skyscrapers, far away over Kennedy Town.

'Now,' said Mary, 'where were we?'

'You were just about to go to bed with me.'

'No, I wasn't. We were going to have a drink in Repulse
Bay.'

'That was earlier on.'

'Persistent, aren't you?' By her grin he knew she wasn't
really cross.

'I'm like a ferret,' he said. 'When I get my teeth into
somebody the jaws lock. They're in you right now.' He
lowered his voice dramatically. 'When I'm finished with you,
my girl, they'll be able to fry eggs on your bum.'

Mary gave a great splutter of laughter. 'You're priceless,
Liam, really you are!'

'I am not priceless. I am a wicked and dangerous man.'

'You're a big silly. – I mean you're a little silly.' She ruffled
his hair.

He pounded his temples with his fists. 'I've never been so
insulted in my life.' He gazed mutely at the heavens. 'I hope
you're enjoying it up there!'

'You know something, Liam? You're basically a nice
person. You can't bear people to think so, of course, but it's
true just the same. Look at the way you behaved with old
K'ou – ordering those lessons and all.'

Sharkey was not at all sure why he had done that – perhaps he had been stampeded into it by the revelation of the general's poverty, by Mary's presence, by the amount of milk of human kindness that was circulating just then. He said nothing of that however; he assumed a querulous tone and protested: 'I want to learn Mandarin. It suits me.'

'There you go again!' They were at her car now. 'If you like,' Mary said hesitantly, 'we can have that drink at my place.'

'Whee!' said he, giving her a lustful look.

She started the engine and nosed the car out into the rush-hour traffic. 'Don't jump to conclusions, though.'

'Now wait a minute, young woman. In my etiquette book that kind of invitation always means one thing.'

She wrinkled her nose. 'Not in mine. At least, not necessarily. So let's wait and see, shall we?'

He had to be satisfied with that and was so, more or less. After a couple of glasses of Scotch, a good meal and close physical presence he ought to be able to swing it.

When they appeared Ah Yee put her head round the kitchen door and said: 'Phone call for massa. They try everywhere. I take number, say you ring back.' She pointed to a torn piece of paper lying beside the telephone.

Sharkey looked at it, did not recognise the number, and rang. And immediately regretted it; the voice at the other end of the line was that of Teddy Broome, features editor of the *Courier*.

'Thanks a million for ringing,' he heard. 'You've saved my life.'

That was ominous; saving people's lives was usually inconvenient.

'They've found a heroin factory.' Teddy's voice was high-pitched and had the gargling quality of an inferior English tenor.

'Indeed.'

'You've missed the press conference but you can still catch the visit to the house. We'll hold a couple of columns for you.'

'Teddy,' said Sharkey in a hard-edged voice, 'the last time we met you were a features man, not a reporter.'

'Oh, didn't I tell you? The news editor's slipped a disc. I'm standing in for him.'

'Delighted to hear it. So why don't you just get one of your staff boys to do the story?'

'There's nobody available. Honest.'

'Pity. Because I'm not available either.'

A throaty wail came down the line. 'But you've got to be, old boy! Otherwise I'm in the shit. Up to me bally neck.' His voice became more pressing. 'Look, Liam, there's good dough in it. We plan a major series on drugs. If you do this piece you can do the lot. I promise you.'

'Why not do it yourself?' said Sharkey with asperity.

'I can't, old boy. No transport. You know how I pranged the Merc at the Macau Grand Prix. I was leading, too, till I ran out of road at Reservoir Bend. – So it's got to be you, Liam.'

Sharkey fumed inwardly. It was a fair cop, and Teddy knew it. A choosy freelance soon became a hungry freelance. 'Where is this sodding place?' he grated.

'Good chap,' cried Teddy with a counter-tenor yelp. 'I won't forget this, honest I won't. It's up Route Twisk, just after the water splash. Big house on the left.'

'That's bloody miles away!'

'I can't help that, can I? – Show your press card, by the way. They're expecting you.'

'You bugger! You even gave them my name ... '

Broome let out a wail of contrition. 'What else could I do, old man? I was in it, up to the neck. Had to give some bally name.'

Sharkey slammed down the phone, shouted 'Jesus fucking Christ!' and stamped around the room making warp-spasms in all directions.

'Poor boy,' said Mary, but without warmth. How ugly he was when he was behaving like this! She was quite put out.

'Thanks for nothing. You'd think we hadn't anything planned for tonight.'

'Maybe we didn't have ... '

'Shit, shit, shit!'

The repetition of the swear-word was too much for Mary. 'Stop it, Liam,' she said decisively. 'You're acting like a spoiled child. I can't get over the difference in you in the last five minutes. – Go and do your work like a reasonable man.'

Sharkey ground his teeth. 'That's all I need, a sermon!'

'Somebody's got to show some sense around here. Otherwise we're going to have a row. Can't you see that?'

He could see it all right. So when she took him by the elbow he allowed her to pilot him out of the flat. 'I'll come back when I've finished. It won't be all that late,' he suggested.

'No, Liam. We'll leave things for today. It'll be better that way.' She gave him a peck on the cheek and closed the door on him.

As he went down the stairs – she lived on the second floor – he swore at her, at Teddy, most of all at himself. By a momentary flash of temper he had spoiled everything, had lost all the ground he'd worked so hard to gain.

Inside the door Mary sniffed to herself. She felt hurt, let

down. There was more of the unregenerate Adam in him than she'd reckoned with: that monkey mouth of his, which had well-nigh disappeared (being largely caused by tension in the facial muscles) was back with a vengeance. How she hated it! How she longed for the bitterness that underlay it to be soothed away by common sense and affection! But the day when that happened – if it ever did – was further away than she'd thought.

And what if it never did come? In that case she was going to be badly hurt – perhaps even more than she had been by Harold's death.

The attendant at the Yaumati car ferry, nautical in sailor-suit and white cap, waved him straight on board; the big door clanged shut behind him. Well, that was a stroke of luck if you like; another one was the fact that the endless procession of earth-carrying lorries usually to be met on the Laichikok Road had dried up; the drivers had finished for the day.

The Hillman climbed out of Kowloon. Night was gathering, but Sharkey could still see how the friable rock-faces on either side of the road had weathered like Cheddar cheese. Concrete nullahs ran obliquely down their steep slopes.

He drove down the big hill to Tsuen Wan, switching on his headlights as he did, then turned right uphill past the water splash – as he had done with Mary and the others just a few days ago – to where a big modern bungalow stood. There was no mistaking the place; there were lights everywhere, a constable was posted at the end of the drive and half a dozen police cars were parked at odd angles, like scattered dominoes.

He left his own car by the roadside and showed his press card to the constable.

'Solly, no can come in.'

Sharkey, who was in no mood to be trifled with, snapped 'Take me to your inspector.'

The constable considered his request for a moment, then turned on his heel and said: 'Follow me please.'

They walked up towards the house. Light was streaming from every window; men kept walking in and out the front door, some uniformed, some not. One of these turned out to be a man he knew, Inspector Borland of Narcotics Bureau, a large, senatorial-looking fellow with a broad face and a high colour; something about him suggested an ancient, drunken baby.

'Ah, Sharkey,' he said in a cooing public-school voice. 'We've been expecting you. – Thank you, constable.' The policeman peeled off an impeccable salute and returned to his post.

The still was in the bathroom, which was swarming with people getting in each other's way: photographers taking pictures with flashbulbs, a fingerprint man dusting square yards of surfaces with white powder, reporters from the Chinese press scribbling their characters in little notebooks.

Taking out his own notepad, Sharkey examined the makeshift apparatus: a stainless steel dixie and an oil drum standing on planks laid across the bathtub; rubber tubes snaking everywhere, one of them emptying into the lavatory, where presumably the unwanted residue was flushed away. A cat's cradle of electric flexes powered the whole thing.

A police sergeant was explaining, in English then in Cantonese, that this makeshift apparatus refined morphine, smuggled in from Macau, to heroin one tenth its volume. He removed a piece of crumpled aluminium foil from a plastic tray and revealed a pile of white granules, like icing sugar. Sharkey mechanically licked the end of his finger and stretched it out towards them, wanting to know what they tasted like.

'I shouldn't, old man,' admonished Borland. 'There's a million dollars' worth there.'

When the sergeant had finished the reporters and photographers rushed out in a body (as pressmen always do), leaving Sharkey alone with Borland, who handed him a press pack with basic information: a quarter of a million addicts in the colony, each spending a thousand dollars HK a year; the basic methods of smoking the stuff – on silver paper with a lit candle underneath, inhaling the plume of smoke through a length of bamboo ('Chasing the dragon') or through a matchbox cover ('Playing the mouth organ'). Useful material for the series Teddy had promised him.

On the present incident Borland told him they'd had a tip-off (in drugs stories you generally did, although no one could ever find out where it came from). When they raided the premises they'd found nobody there, not even the small fry. Perhaps they'd been tipped off too, but by somebody else.

'I can't get over the fact that people are prepared to spend as much as a thousand bucks a year on the habit,' said Sharkey. 'Where do they get their hands on that kind of money?'

'They steal it, or turn pushers,' replied Borland. 'There's nothing else they can do.'

'What a bloody life!' said Sharkey with conviction.

'If you lived in a bed-space and hadn't enough to eat you'd be looking for an escape yourself.'

That was true enough. Even today he felt the need for one; so he stopped off at Kowloon for a Chinese meal. He chose the Shamrock restaurant ('strikin' a blow for oul Oireland' he called it) and drafted his piece on the table beside him. Then he crossed the harbour and typed out the story (ten slips it made) in the gloomy old *Courier* building in Wyndham Street; the place was as dark as a vault and practically empty of people at this hour.

When he came out, about 11.30, Hong Kong's night life was in full swing. Milling thousands were still on their dogged, slack-kneed Cantonese trot in pursuit of pleasure. A sudden impulse – anything to kill the sense of human misery aroused by the heroin factory – drove him to turn the car's head towards Macdonnell Road and the Belilios girl.

An uneasy sense of guilt made him almost glad that she proved as unresponsive as ever. That evened things up between Mary and himself, he reckoned sardonically. It was his punishment, just as sleeping with the girl at all had been hers.

There was no question of Verity seeing a doctor. In the first place the Veritys were born to service and brought up in the stoic school; he would go on while he could still stand up. In the second, he surely wasn't as ill as all that, and in any case he had home leave coming up in six months' time, in June 1962. He would soldier on until then, and see a doctor in England.

There were third and fourth places too, but he did not

dwell on them. The third was his instinctive distrust of the human body, which turned any physical weakness into a moral stigma as well. And the fourth was his hatred of handing over his books and his office to a third party, as always happened when he took his home leave; to allow strange eyes to peer into his affairs and perhaps criticise his methods any earlier than next June was not to be contemplated.

So he did soldier on, and his illness – whatever it was – progressed so slowly that he was almost unaware of it, except when he had one of his strange fits of paralysis, and those he schooled himself to live with.

It was the small things he found hardest to bear; for example Cheung's physical presence, which disgusted him. So he delegated much of his office work to the land assistant and took Jeffrey Wing on most of his trips to his district. He announced this as a matter of career development.

They went together to Peng Chau and Lantau, to the resettled villagers in Tsuen Wan (who were already acquiring the casual effrontery of townees), above all to Dumbell where the boy's local knowledge came in handy. And on Dumbell the amazing, unsettling thing was that there was no trace of the recent disturbance. The Committee, strengthened by its four new members, functioned as though nothing had happened. There was no mention of Mr Tsoi's water, or of ghosts; and the purchase of the site for the new school went through on the nod.

In mid-December Jeffrey and he put in an appearance at the first meeting of the reconstituted Organising Committee of the Three Mountains Festival, which was held as usual in the Chinese Chamber of Commerce; the same old amah flip-flopped up the stairs with her glasses of tea. The cast list was almost identical with that of the previous committee, and indeed of the Rural Committee itself. The ubiquitous Ng was in the chair, and the most notable addition was the restaurant owner Mr Li Ho Wing, a twinkling, bonhomous man of sixty with white hair and gold-rimmed spectacles. The most notable absentee was Elder Kwok, still a committee member but for some reason not present today.

Ng kicked off with his usual speech: the world fame which the island had acquired through its festival, the fact that it would, as usual, last three days and involve the by now famous procession, numerous religious ceremonies, the decoration of the streets with floral arches and the non-stop performance of Cantonese opera.

And of course the celebrated bun mountains, from which the festival took its name. Ng described these, although everyone knew what they were: hollow bamboo towers sixty feet high, to which were attached thousands of yellowish buns, each stamped with a pink character so that the finished tower looked like a huge pink corn-on-the-cob. The climax of the festival came when, at a given signal, the young men of the island swarmed up the towers and tried to pick off the buns, which conferred good luck according to their height above the ground; acquiring the top bun was a cast-iron guarantee of good fortune for the year to come.

Ng perorated: 'Ours is a community which lives off fish, prawns and other animals of the sea. Let us as usual expiate the wrong we do these small creatures, and let us do so in a more magnificent style than ever.'

There was polite applause, and Ho Man rose to speak. Everyone knew what he would say; he would offer an alternative view of the origins of the festival, as he did every year. 'Far be it from me to question the opinion of our distinguished chairman,' he said, his Adam's apple bobbing like a yo-yo, 'but is it not a known fact that our festival had its beginnings in the discovery of human remains on this island more than a hundred years ago? It was to placate the ghosts of these unfortunates that the Three Mountains Festival was instituted. We are concerned with the ghosts not of fish but of men. That is why, for three days, we eat only vegetarian food, with the solitary exception of the oyster, which as you know has no soul.'

More polite applause, and Verity could only wonder how quietly the allusion to the dead bodies had passed off. It was as if a stone had been thrown into a calm pool; there had been a great splashing but now the waters had closed again, leaving no trace. Yet the stone must still be there.

The meeting then proceeded to business. The date would be fixed, ostensibly by the casting of lots before the image of Pak Ti, the Spirit of the North, but actually according to when a well-known Cantonese opera troupe, the Brothers Of The Pear Orchard, happened to be free. That turned out to be, Chinese style, some time between the first and tenth days of the fourth moon; when the lots were actually cast the dates fixed on were 7th to 9th May, European style.

On finance, the committee ageed to increase its budget by five percent over 1961. The discussion then moved on to the organisation of the procession. Mr Li, because of his catering experience, and possibly because as a new member he had not had time to antagonise anybody, was put in charge. And all agreed that it should take its traditional form: the gods of Dumbell first (the Spirit of the North; the four images of T'ien Hau – the Queen of Heaven – all accompanied by unicorns, coloured banners, and Chiu Chau drums and gongs).

After that would come the contributions of the street

associations: lion dances, gymnastic displays – and, most important of all, the floats.

These were the real subject of the meeting, and a feature of the Three Mountains Festival which was in Verity's experience as unique as it claimed to be.

They illustrated moral themes in a style based on defiance of gravity: small children would wobble along the streets of Dumbell, hovering in mid-air perhaps ten feet from the ground (supported by metal rods under their clothes, but it would bring bad luck to mention that), in illustration of moral themes. For example a small boy, rouged and silken-clad, would appear to be balancing on one toe, ballet-fashion, on the tip of a gigantic mahjongg chip, which was supported in turn by a monster pack of cards standing on a roulette wheel; this depicted the Evils of Gambling.

Some of the themes were from Chinese legend, for example the white monkey helping Hsuan Tsang find the Buddhist scriptures, or the fable of the kingfisher and the oyster: a kingfisher attacks an open oyster, which snaps shut; a passing fisherman puts both in his net. A small, aboriginal-looking man explained: 'Fisherman stand with net on arm. Girl with two fans represent oyster. Fans close over foot of boy, who is bird.'

There were contemporary themes too, such as Misfortunes of Chinese Girl Who Marries A Foreign Devil (discussion of this was in no way inhibited by Verity's presence). The guiding theme of the most important tableau had just been decided on ('Perils of Drug Addiction') when the old amah's sandals were heard slapping on the stairway. She flung the door open unceremoniously and cried 'Elder Kwok has been killed!'

General confusion. Men vociferated, struggled to their

feet, tried to find their way to the door. Verity experienced a pang of anguish: was it somehow his fault? Fortunately the local police sergeant, following in the amah's wake, was already taking the stairs two at a time. 'Don't be alarmed,' he called over the hubbub. 'Elder Kwok is alive. He was attacked, but only injured.'

Verity's relief left him gasping, helpless. In jumping to his feet he had knocked over his chair; his wits were so scattered that he made no attempt to pick it up. Then he heard Jeffrey Wing's quiet voice in his ear: 'Hadn't we better go and see him, sir?'

That galvanised him. 'Where is the Elder?' he asked the sergeant in his most authoritative voice.

'At factory. Doctor with him. Take him Hong Kong side next ferry, half an hour.'

'Good. We have time to go and see him.'

The sergeant coughed discreetly. 'I must ask question.'

'Don't bother us now!' snapped old Ng. But the sergeant insisted, apologetic though firm. It emerged that no one knew why the Elder had not been at the meeting, but he had been heard saying that he was going to see his son, Kwok Siu Hung, a pig-keeper from Chi Ma Hang, that same morning. He clearly hadn't gone there; he had been found lying beside his own bean-curd factory.

'At what time?' asked Verity.

'Ten thirty-five a.m.'

In broad daylight then; that was daring.

'Where is Kwok now?' snapped Ng.

'In factory.'

'Good. I declare this meeting adjourned.' And Ng, his samfu flapping round his scrawny shanks, led the way down the stairs.

The bean-curd factory was a wooden shack with a corrugated-iron roof and a drunken chimney held precariously upright by three rusty wires. Its owner being temporarily disabled, Mr T. C. Leung's ropes had spread over the pavement in front of it; the committee members, plus Verity and Jeffrey, kept getting their feet entangled in them.

Inside it was sordid and chaotic. A single electric bulb, lit even in the middle of the day, revealed cobwebs, empty bottles and rusty tin cans amid which stood a huge stone grinder and attendant motor, along with a sawdust-burning stove to which the crazy chimney belonged. Three grinning Hakka women presided over piles of trays containing square wooden grids for shaping the curd.

A rickety door at the back led to a shed containing a chemical lavatory and a plank bed on which Elder Kwok was lying, his head swathed in bandages. A Chinese doctor – a small, nervous man with a habit of swallowing his saliva – was in attendance.

Ng pushed his way in first and said, unnecessarily loudly, 'This is a bad thing, Elder Kwok.'

No reply, apart from a low groan.

'How is he?' Verity asked the doctor.

'Badly bruised. He probably has concussion. I have ordered an x-ray from the Queen Mary Hospital in Hong Kong.'

'Can't they do it here?' The doctor shook his head.

They all looked at the Elder, who continued groaning. Then, as it became clear that nothing more was going to happen, they filed back out through the factory, where the three Hakka women were still working (could anything stop a Chinese from working?) on to the little street, where a small knot of onlookers had gathered.

'Can we be of further assistance?' Verity asked the sergeant.

'No, sir. We shall come to you if we need any help.'

Jeffrey and he escaped to the bungalow for lunch. It was not a cheerful meal. Verity's limbs were aching from too much standing and a general stiffness had invaded his stomach, killing his appetite.

'What do you make of all this?' he asked the young man, pushing aside his plate.

'It worries me.'

'Who on earth could have done it, and why?'

The young man gave him a concerned look, as though anxious about his peace of mind, and finally said: 'I think it may be part of this triad business.'

'You may be right. But where does that leave us? Elder Kwok originally voted against Ng – does that make him a member of one triad and Ng of another?'

'It is possible. Did you notice how unsympathetic Mr Ng was to the Elder just now?'

'I did. And I can quite believe that Ng may have some sort of triad connection. – But Elder Kwok? Surely not, Jeffrey. I've always particularly liked him.'

After a moment's hesitation Jeffrey said: 'Pardon my presumption, but I have always found that human beings do not come ... how do you say it in English? ... all of a piece. The good have some bad in them, and the bad some good.'

'That's true,' said Verity, wearily. 'So we'll jump to no conclusions.'

Ah Shing came in to take away the dishes. When he had finished Verity said, somewhat ruefully: 'Well, let's not waste our time this way. As people keep telling me, triads are police business, not ours.'

'Excuse me, Mr Verity, but may I say something?'

'Of course.'

'Our concern is the welfare of the people in this district, and that welfare is affected by crime and violence. To that extent triad activity does concern us. With our local knowledge it is possible for us to pick up pieces of information that would never reach the police. Is it not our duty to to pass such information on?'

'Indeed it is. To people like Joe Miners.'

'Miners?'

'Yes. The inspector in charge of the Triads Bureau. Don't you know him?'

Jeffrey shook his head.

'He's a little man with a pipe. Knows everything there is to be known about triads.'

With that they abandoned the subject. But the conversation had been important; it had impressed on Verity's mind the maturity of judgment Jeffrey had shown. And not only that; he had an intuition, together with a diplomatic sense, which allowed him to confirm you in a decision you were just about to make yourself. So why feel guilty about sometimes preferring him to Cheung? Was not the boy's career well worth promoting?

Alec Scrymgeour gave a party on the last day of term; as it was the third time he had done it, it was regarded as traditional. The fact was, he had to do something with his barrack of a house – a huge structure on University Path –

which came with the job. Built in brick to shoulder level and in cream-washed cement above that, it was attached to a mirror image of itself and could therefore be regarded as a superior form of semi-detached.

Both houses had square stone pillars and wide balconies on both floors; both could have housed twenty people, which was perhaps the retinue expected of a professor at the time they were built. In Scrymgeour's case all he could muster was himself, his cook-boy Ah Fun and Ah Fun's mother Ah Fah, who spent her time wandering through the empty rooms, dusting.

Sharkey and Mary were walking along University Path. Ahead of them the old house blazed with lights at every window; they could see human figures on the balconies and paper decorations inside. It was a fine evening: warm but with a freshness in the air, the last expression of the Hong Kong autumn. They had been stoking up on Johnny Walker.

'Are you compos?' Mary asked with a giggle.

'As a judge,' said Sharkey loftily.

'Me too.'

'Watch it, my girl. Some nasty man will take advantage.'

The house was perched six feet up, behind a stone retaining wall like an Inca terrace, with the front door up some steps to the side. At the top Ah Fah let them in; they walked into the drawing room, where people were standing about with glasses in their hands.

Scrymgeour detached himself from a group of young Chinese whom Sharkey recognised as history students, came over to them and said 'Salutations' with all the warmth of a Writer to the Signet greeting a client charged with indecent exposure.

'*Salut,*' said Sharkey. 'May Saint Patrick and the Blessed Oliver Plunkett be with you.'

'Why?'

'Why not?' was the answer.

'Nice party,' said Mary, waving a hand at the flitting groups.

'Hope so. Enjoy yourselves, my children.' And Scrymgeour turned away to greet another guest, none other than Teddy Broome. Ah Fun, a small man with bulging eyes and adenoids, offered a tray with drinks; Sharkey and Mary each took a whisky.

Having said hello to his host, Teddy came across to them, calling 'Greetings' in his strangulated voice. He had a small toothbrush moustache like an inverted V and a mouth puckered p like a duck's arse about to excrete. Add to that tightly-waved black hair close to the head and an air of vague good nature and you had Teddy.

'Greetings,' responded Sharkey. 'Haven't run into you for weeks.'

'Ouch. Don't use that expression. Not after Macau.'

'How's the car?'

'It's a heap.'

'And yourself? I see no plaster?'

'I did have one. On the elbow – they took it off today. This is my coming-out party, yuck-yuck-yuck.'

'What actually happened?' asked Mary politely.

'I was overtaking old Jimmy Chang and ran out of road. Saloon car race, you know. I was in the Merc and Jimmy was driving that Volvo of his.'

'Tell us more,' put in Sharkey. 'I'm sure you're dying to.'

'Well, I was on the straight trying to take him but the bally old bend came up too soon. Tried to slot in in front of him but my rear bumper caught his wing. Pair of us went cartwheeling like a couple of biscuit tins. Ended up against a tree, ker-plonk. End of Merc, but yours truly stepped out without a scratch. Apart from the cracked elbow, of course. Old Jimmy was OK too. – I say, Liam, should have mentioned it earlier, but I liked that drug piece of yours.'

'I always try to give satisfaction. As the actress said to the bishop.'

'As the patrol leader said to the scoutmaster, what?'

'As the Holy Spirit said to the Virgin Mary.'

'Who's calling me a virgin?' cried Mary belligerently. Her tone was a matter of satisfaction to Sharkey, who was acting tipsy in order to make her drink more. He was determined to make a major push tonight.

They circulated, past Rose who was deep in conversation with a pink young man with a downy blond beard, unknown to Sharkey, towards McPhee, an earnest engineering lecturer who was telling Diana Lok about a spear head he'd just picked up on Peng Chau; Fergus O'Hanlon was in moody attendance.

'Hello, Fergus. I didn't know you knew Alec,' said Sharkey.

'I dubbed some tapes for him once.'

Mary resisted the temptation to run her hand over Fergus's hair, which was like a black scrubbing brush. 'Tapes?' she asked. 'I didn't think Alec had musical interests.'

'They were speech actually. Some Frenchman. By the name of Jenner, or Jennet, or something like that. I didn't understand a word of them.'

Hm, thought Sharkey. Then, changing the subject abruptly: 'I thought of you the other day, Fergus. We met a man who lives in a house with a roof made entirely of gramophone records.'

'General K'ou, was it? I gave him those.'

'Did you then!' cried Mary, delighted.

'Oh, yes. Nice old man, though we can't say anything to each other.'

'Where did the records come from?' asked Sharkey, curious.

'Old Hong Kong Radio stock, seventy-eights just replaced by LPs. We're supposed to paint them with size so that nobody can use them again, and then throw them out. I painted them all right but I didn't see why I should throw them out. Had a better use for them.'

'Good for you,' said Mary and succeeded in giving his hair a glancing caress. But Fergus's attention was now on Diana, who to the accompaniment of much wiggling was quizzing McPhee on matters archaeological, and perhaps getting more than she had bargained for.

'Did you know that the Chinese only came here as late as the third century?' he was saying. 'There were people here before them who left rock inscriptions on Lantau that date back to before the birth of Christ. Unfortunately nobody has ever been able to decipher them.'

'Oh, Mr McPhee, you're so clever ... '

'Nonsense, my dear, but I get so tired of Europeans who say there's nothing to do in Hong Kong when all they need to do is look around them ... '

Sharkey and Mary separated. He talked business with Teddy, and noted down two fresh commissions in his new 1962 diary (a present from Mary). The party, he observed, was beginning to draw and give off a low roar, like a furnace. All good parties did.

With the roar there usually came an irresponsible feeling of dizziness which in its early stages was delightful. He was

savouring this sensation when he found himself looking
down the front of Rose Leung's dress; this revealed the fact
that her chest was not only flat, it was hollow. The downy-
bearded young man with whom she was in conversation was
holding forth to her about French literature, from which he
realised that this was a colleague: the new, highly thought-of
French lecturer who had been appointed during the summer
but had claimed that he couldn't possibly start before the
New Year. Now he was here; name of Julian Massingbird.

'The Carte du Tendre,' this Massingbird was saying,
'represents the troubadour idea of love as strained through
the Cartesian distrust of passion.' He sipped delicately at his
gin and tonic.

'Aark,' uttered Rose, presumably in approbation.

'Love is equated with tenderness, as you can see. Nothing
elemental here.' The small Vandyke beard moved prettily as
he spoke. 'There are three different Tendres, each situated
on its own river: Tendre-sur-Inclination, Tendre-sur-
Reconnaissance, Tendre-sur-Estime. – You understand these
terms, do you not? – Now to reach the first of these
destinations you sail straight down the river of Inclination;
which is fast-flowing and can easily sweep you on into the
Mer Dangereuse.'

Rose went 'Aark' again. She was evidently familiar with
the perils of tumultuous love.

'Tendre-sur-Reconnaissance,' fluted Massingbird, 'is an
altogether more sober destination. You reach it via stops like
Petits Soins, Assiduité and Empressement – you understand
these French terms, do you not?'

'I understand all ri.'

Sharkey's ears began to sing, and it was not he effect of
the whisky.

'Of course the Tendre that really counted in the seventeenth century was Tendre-sur-Estime. You reach that by way of the social graces – Jolis Vers, Billets Doux and the like – followed by a display of the great qualities, such as Sincerité, Probité, Générosité. If you go off course you can end up in the Lac d'Indifférence; otherwise you proceed through Exactitude, Respect and Bonté to Tendre itself. – A pretty conceit, don't you think? And interesting to compare with Donne and the Metaphysicals, who pre-dated it by two or three decades.' He crooked his little finger and took another sip of his gin.

Sharkey's head cleared. He decided on war to the knife, but later, friend, later.

Mary had gone out on to the balcony. In the garden under her a breeze rustled in the leaves of a magnolia tree; through its branches she could see a million-dollar view of Hong Kong harbour. A long sigh escaped her.

'Oh,' said someone, starting up from the shadows.

'Oh,' she repeated, then laughed. 'Must have thought I was Juliet. Oh Romeo, Romeo, wherefore art thou Romeo?'

'Actually I'm Fergus.'

'Of course you are.' She resisted the urge to caress the lavatory brush of his hair. 'But what are you doing out here?'

'I don't care for parties.'

'Try alcohol. It helps.'

'It makes me morose.'

'I don't believe it. You look good-natured enough to me.'

'Nice of you to say so, Mrs Rhodes.'

'Why did you come if you don't like parties?' she asked in her forthright way.

'I didn't want to disappoint Professor Scrymgeour.'

'Of course; you dubbed that stuff for him. You're an engineer, aren't you? With Hong Kong Radio?'

'Yes. I'm a freelance.'

'More money that way?'

'Less.'

'Why do you do it then?' She took a great breath of the cool air.

'Because I'm a Eurasian.'

'I'd rather guessed that.' The moonlight, falling on his head, revealed a series of nascent cows-licks; perhaps that was why he kept his hair short.

'I don't get on well in big organisations,' he said wistfully. 'I can't get the big jobs because I'm not a European, and the Chinese don't like me because I'm not really Chinese.'

'That's rotten!'

Ah Fah, doing her rounds, arrived with drinks. Mary took another whisky, Fergus an orange juice.

He told her about his family. O'Hanlon had been a corporal in the Royal Engineers, who vanished when he was small, his mother Chinese. 'A secretary, not a bar girl.'

'You should jolly well tackle those radio people. Make sure you get your rights.'

Fergus shrugged. 'I've nothing to complain about. Nobody discriminates against me. I just don't get certain jobs.'

'It's a shame,' said Mary, but with less conviction than usual. The night was balmy, and she had knocked back that last glass too quickly. She felt her head rotating slowly, like a large planet. Inside the house a gong banged. Good; that meant grub.

Ah Fun and his mother had wheeled in trolleys with containers full of hot cannelloni and beef Stroganoff, and there were piles of plates, forks and spoons on a table beside them; they all crowded round and helped themselves, before finding seats wherever they could, mostly on raffia mats against the walls. They applied themselves to the serious business of eating.

It was when the room was full of lying, crouching, sitting bodies, all trying to ingest food, that Sharkey noticed Donoghue and Ed, obviously gatecrashing; their noses were deep in Stroganoff. He made his way over to them and said 'I didn't know you were a friend of Alec's, Gus.'

'I'm not. But I'm not prejudiced. – What's the pussy like here?'

'We've really come to lay some pipe,' explained Ed. 'If we can find any.'

While people ate things began to flag. The furnace roar abated as food soaked up the alcohol. The noise level slackened; you could actually hear the Modern Jazz Quartet on the hi-fi. Then dirty plates were exchanged for clean ones; savoury dishes for French cheeses (just in off the *Cambodge*) and fruit salad. More wine was drunk, sending the noise level up again.

Finally Ah Fun and Ah Fah wheeled in two more trolleys, one with bottles of chilled champagne, all frosted from the fridge, the other with a Christmas pudding and cake, brandy butter and mince pies.

At that point catastrophe struck. Ah Fah's trolley was a folding one and a little unsteady on its wheels. It snagged some obstacle, suddenly collapsed and sent its contents rolling on the floor.

That was the signal for the party to go crazy. 'Tallyho!' cried Donoghue, falling to his knees and shovelling the mince pies back on their plate. Then an idea came to him; he tossed one to Ed, who lobbed it over Mary's head at Sharkey; he did the sensible thing and ate it. Most of the others were devoured that way too, but a few were crushed underfoot, to general hilarity.

To much popping and fizzing Ah Fun, giving his mother dark looks, helped Scrymgeour to open the champagne bottles and pour out their contents, manfully restoring the situation. Everyone in the room was hysterical with laughter, Teddy's strangulated tenor riding over all.

'Please serve the pudding, Ah Fah,' called Alec. 'And by the way, where is the cake?'

'Oh, massa,' called the old amah, aghast, 'me no findee cake!'

There was a further roar of laughter. The fact that a Christmas cake had gone missing was the funniest thing anyone had ever heard of. Somebody shouted 'Hunt the cake!'

Whereupon Teddy grabbed Rose by the waist and danced her out of the room, chanting 'I came, I saw, I conga!' Someone caught hold of his waist, another linked on, and in a moment the entire company was snaking through the house, upstairs and down, chanting the conga, ostensibly in search of the cake.

They returned in a few minutes, hot and dishevelled, polished off the pudding and brandy butter, and emptied the champagne glasses which Ah Fun, labouring to restore face, had replenished at the speed of light.

While they were all guzzling Sharkey sidled up to Massingbird and said: I presume you've heard of the Carte du Con?'

'I beg your pardon?' responded the downy-faced one, startled.

'It's reputed to be the joint work of Hemingway and Scott Fitzgerald when they lived in Paris in the twenties but I doubt if their French was up to it.'

'I don't really ... ' Massingbird opened his rosy little mouth to say something, but Sharkey was inexorable.

'Con is like Tendre,' he went on, 'in that there are three of them. – In actual fact there are a lot more, but seen one seen 'em all, I always say. The most uncomplicated of them is Con-sur-Accord, where you just bash on and the devil take the hindmost. But, like Inclination, Accord is a swift-flowing river and you can easily be swept away into the Slough of Detumescence via Surexcitation and Ejaculatio Praecox.

'We twentieth century people tend to distrust anything as straightforward as that. Our map offers two alternatives, Con-sur-Dollar and Con-sur-Flagellation, which reflect our fascination with capitalistic and authoritarian values.'

Seeing the little duck's arse of a mouth about to open again, he pressed on. 'The road to Con-sur-Dollar leads though Short Time and Payment-on-the-Nail, and if you're not careful you can end up in Ballocks-en-Capilotade or Chancre-sur-Scrotum. As for Con-sur-Flagellation ... '

'I prefer not to hear about that,' said Massingbird, who had found his voice at last.

'That's lucky, because I haven't thought it up yet,' replied Sharkey. Then, observing Rose craning her neck to have a better view of the fun, he seized her by the shoulders and shouted 'Rape!'

Donoghue had materialised beside him. 'Impossible, squire' he said coldly. 'Confucius he say: no such thing as rape. Lady with skirts up run faster than gentleman with trousers down.'

'She's raping me, you big oaf!'

'Well then, when rape inevitable, lie back and enjoy it.'
He examined Rose more closely. 'In this case I am prepared
to reconsider.'

He took himself off. Sharkey was pondering the question
of who had won this exchange when Mary – who had been
on the balcony again – returned, discovered that dancing had
started, spotted Wilson Ho and claimed him as a partner.

'It's time for me to go home, Mrs Rhodes.' It was indeed
well on towards midnight.

'Nonsense, Wilson. Put your arm round me.' She waltzed
him out into the middle of the room; the hi-fi was now
playing Johann Strauss. She was pleasantly tipsy, having in
her own opinion handled her drink very well: she had
managed to stay on the crest of the wave, neither falling back
nor tipping over the other side.

Wilson danced like a Chinese Pinocchio, all wooden limbs
and no strings to hold him down. 'Let yourself go!' she said,
wrapping her arms around him in motherly fashion and
humming the immortal Johann. But nothing could unfurrow
that gloomy brow.

As for herself, the movement of dancing slowly raised her
level of intoxication; perhaps her drinking had not been so
judicious after all. In a kind of haze she was aware that
Wilson was leaving, along with the other Chinese students,
leaving the serious business of dissipation to those past
masters, the Europeans. She went over the crest. Not in her
case into maudlin pugnacity; rather she shed what remained
of her stray clouts of inhibition and became the essential
Mary, a jolly North Country lass, as sunnily disposed as a
barmaid. She thought in a confused way: maybe this is how
I'd have been without the education.

She was dancing with Sharkey now. Dancing had

developed into random pawing, but she made no objection; the swear words and the monkey mouth were forgotten.

He nuzzled her ferret-like behind the ear, whispering 'You're a lovely lump of woman, Mary.'

'You're right there, lad,' she answered in broad Lancashire, laughing; then clamped her two arms together, trapping him between them.

'Ow!' he cried in mock indignation.

What might have happened next would never be known. Donoghue, who happened to be dancing close to them with Diana Lok, suddenly did the same as Mary and crushed the Chinese girl in his arms. He followed this up by bringing his mouth down brutally on hers. She screamed, mincingly to begin with, then in earnest as she realised he was hurting her. Whereupon he opened his arms with a disdainful look.

'Pig,' hissed Diana.

'Tart.'

At that moment Donoghue felt a hand take him by the biceps, turned round and saw Fergus O'Hanlon, who was fairly spluttering with rage.

'Let her go!' cried Fergus.

'I have let her go,' said Donoghue scornfully.

'You bastard!' cried the little Eurasian, aiming a puny fist at him. Donoghue, who had been a boxer in his national service days, parried it easily.

'Come off it, Fergus. You're getting on my nerves.'

'Don't think I'm afraid of you, because I'm not.' He was game all right, if a tad ridiculous, thought Sharkey, admiring Fergus in spite of himself.

At that point Diana turned on her would-be protector. 'Go away. You're making a scene,' she snapped.

'I will not go away. I love you.'

'You love me?' Diana was dumbfounded. 'How dare you!'
She turned on her heel and walked out, leaving both men
standing. Fergus felt a wave of humiliation rising behind his
eyes, but he was used to that. As for Donoghue, he gave a
quick bark of laughter and allowed Ed, who had suddenly
materialised, to take him by the arm.

'Come on, Gus,' said Ed, 'the pussy here's the worst I've
seen in months.' He dragged him away.

'That's a nasty man,' said Mary to Sharkey.

'No doubt about it. Mind you, he was almost chivalrous
with Fergus there. He could have knocked him into the
middle of next week.'

'He can keep his chivalry as far as I'm concerned. – How
about another drink?'

As the fumes of alcohol rose the incident was forgotten.
Things became hilarious again. Dancing was abandoned in
favour of Truth Or Consequences, in the course of which
Scrymgeour had to stand on one foot and make a noise like a
flamingo. No one had ever heard s flamingo's cry, so his
eldritch screech was accepted.

Then a chemistry lecturer's wife, a fluffy blonde just a
little over the hill, had to remove her panties. She did so,
adroitly enough, under her dress and flourished the desired
garment in the air. Whereupon Teddy Broome, who couldn't
see why a good idea shouldn't be used twice, grabbed hold of
it, shrilled 'Hunt the panties!' and ran off. In a moment they
were all after him, eventually catching him only to discover
that he had already hidden it. Drawers and cupboards were
emptied, bedclothes were flung on the floor; everything was
breathless and ecstatic.

Mary, caught up in the excitement, giggled helplessly.
Then Sharkey started crawling among everybody's feet,

crying 'I'm the three little piggies – all three of them!' She got down and crawled beside him while both snuffled at the tops of their voices.

People were flinging open doors everywhere, looking for the panties. Sharkey, on his feet again and somehow separated from Mary, threw open a door himself. It turned out to be the upstairs lavatory. Inside he was astonished to find Donoghue, sitting on the throne with his trousers round his ankles and biting into the missing Christmas cake.

'So that's where it went!' cried Sharkey.

'Bugger off or I'll shit on you,' countered Donoghue.

'I'll say one thing for you, Gus. You have the gift of repartee.'

Donoghue then broke off a large piece of the cake, dropped it in the lavatory pan between his knees and intoned: 'Double, double, toilet trouble.'

'Where the hell's the rest of it?'

'Rocked in the cradle of the deep,' sang Donoghue. 'I've flushed it down the bogs.' He then slammed the door shut in Sharkey's face.

No one saw Ed or him leave, but when Scrymgeour had seen his guests off, an hour or so later, they had gone.

Only Sharkey and Mary were left. Mary's ears were ringing but she didn't want to go home. 'I don't want to go home,' she intoned.

'Stay then,' said Alec. 'I'm having another drink. I've been so busy attending to your sordid little wants that I haven't had time to get properly drunk.'

'No more for me or I'll puke,' said Mary, making herself comfortable on an armchair while a bleary Ah Fun brought whisky for the two men. Sharkey stationed himself beside a

flowerpot and surreptitiously poured his into it. Tonight was
the night, dammit.

They made owlish conversation about current affairs:
the Berlin crisis, the fire at the Hong Kong Products
exhibition, the Indians marching into Goa (a terrible blow,
this, for the Hong Kong Portuguese), famine in China.
Then, as Alec slowly became drunk and Sharkey
pretended, the talk became more surrealistic. Sharkey
mentioned the fact that he knew a man whose sole point of
pride was that he had slept with a girl who had slept with
Dylan Thomas.

'Did it make him a poet?' snarled Scrymgeour, settling
himself on the settee.

'Or Welsh?' put in Mary, sitting up and taking notice.
Sharkey shook his head to both questions.

'Here, Ah Fun, I'll have that whisky after all,' said Mary.

Sharkey pondered. 'If you laid all of Dylan's mistresses
end to end,' he wondered, 'how far do you think they would
stretch?'

'Depends which end you're thinking of,' said Scrymgeour,
yawning.

'And that in turn depends on how you define the ends of
a body,' said Sharkey. 'The fingers and toes? Or the head and
bum?'

'God but men are disgusting!' cried Mary, looking
heavenward.

But Alec and Sharkey insisted on discussing the point,
Sharkey maintaining that in one sense the front end of a
woman might be regarded as the tips of her nipples.

'See what I mean?' said Mary, addressing the gods again.

'Tits,' pronounced Scrymgeour, 'are of no account.
They're mostly water anyway.'

'Mine are of great account,' said Mary, offended. She flung her bosom out towards him. 'Are those of no account?'

Scrymgeour examined her anatomy with a weary eye. 'I would be prepared to wager,' he said, 'that they don't weigh more than a pound and a half apiece.'

'The cheek of it! – We'll see about that. – Ah Fun!' The cook-boy put a bleary head round the kitchen door. 'Bring the kitchen scales please.'

Ah Fun obliged, his face betraying not the slightest flicker of curiosity. When he had gone, Scrymgeour said: 'Now you will realise the truth of my statement.' He stretched himself out luxuriously.

'Right then,' said Mary, tipsily determined. Putting the scales on the floor, she stood over them on hands and knees, like the she-wolf of Rome, then lowered one of her breasts into the pan. The needle wavered, before stopping at two pounds and eleven ounces. 'There you are,' she cried in triumph.

'You were leaning into it with your body,' said Scrymgeour, regretting that he had ever raised the subject.

'I was not!'

'Better take your blouse off, so he can see,' said Sharkey helpfully. Mary did so, revealing a white brassiere with capacious cups. The breast, weighed again, sent the needle up to two pounds and eight ounces.

'I don't see how that can be accurate,' said Sharkey, scratching his head. 'The thing can't fall freely, if you see what I mean. The bra creates tensions.'

Mary had the bit between her teeth now. 'Very well,' she declared. 'I'll take it off.'

'We can hardly ask you to do that,' said Sharkey .

'Oh for heaven's sake, Liam! What age do you think I am? I know all about the birds and the bees.'

He allowed himself to be persuaded. 'All right, if you insist. But you only need to lower one of them into the pan. Independently of the ribcage. Sort of floating. – Can you manage that?'

'Of course I can.'

Her bra was half off already; a couple of seconds more and the job was complete. Her breasts were large but shapely, with delicately pink nipples which he found oddly touching. She lowered one of them into the pan, gingerly. 'Ow, it's chilly!' she cried. The needle, after some wavering, settled at two pounds and nine ounces.

'There you are, Alec,' crowed Mary. A snore from the settee announced that Scrymgeour was taking no further interest in the proceedings.

'You've won,' said Sharkey, putting an arm round her in a man-to-man way.

'I jolly well have!' She twisted her head round towards him, accepting his congratulations. He kissed her on the mouth.

'Steady on, Liam ... !'

She was sketching a protest when she felt his hand on her thigh, under the skirt. In a moment he was caressing her through her knickers.

Realising the true situation, she felt a pang of alarm while at the same time longing for the caress to continue. 'No, Liam, no,' she said, uncertainly.

'Yes, Mary, yes.'

'But Alec ... ?'

'Dead to the world.'

It was true; Scrymgeour was out for the count, his nose pointing skywards.

She pleaded: 'I'm too old. Don't rouse me again ... ' But he closed her mouth with another kiss, a long, exploring one. All the breath left her body; she opened herself to him.

There was a good deal of panting and pulling at clothes. In a moment her knickers were off and he had heaved himself on top of her; then he was inside. Her pelvis was reassuringly broad, steadying him. He sank slightly – alarmingly because he was not used to it – into her flesh.

They came quickly to their climax. Then Mary's head cleared; she looked up at him strangely: was it enquiry? Or was it reproach? What had he done to her? And what would come of it? He had to find the right thing to say.

As she looked up at him he was touched with sudden pity; he saw her as she must have been when she was a child, tomboyish but vulnerable. He reached out and touched her cheek, whispering 'Dearest Mary.'

She pulled his head down to her with a little cry; they lay there, perfectly silent; perhaps they even slept for a while.

At any rate time passed, after which they got to their feet, picked their way through the débris of the party, let themselves out of the house and walked along University Path and Lyttleton Road to his flat in Breezy Court. The night was calm; an orange haze hung over the city.

Back in the house Scrymgeour still slept. About the middle of the night he shuffled to his room, collapsed on the bed and fell into a rhythmic snoring. Behind the kitchen, Ah Fun and his mother had long since stretched themselves out on their plank beds, their heads on those odd little china cylinders like upturned sugar bowls, and were sleeping dreamlessly

II

The Year of the Tiger

The Fat Shan was an old, stately, stand-up kind of vessel that made the daily trip from Hong Kong to Macau; on Christmas Eve it transported Sharkey and Mary to the Portuguese colony with dignity, if not speed.

The weather had turned cool, and they sat in the lounge drinking coffee; neither felt like spirits and it was too cold for beer. A racket of pop music came over the loudspeaker system. They were the only Europeans on board. Chinese family groups sat chattering at the other tables, with crew-cut children in wadded blue jackets gazing at the foreign devils with liquid eyes. One solitary, brown-skinned man with scattered bristles of moustache was deep in the sports pages of the *Wah Kiu Yat Po*.

They passed Green Island and sailed between Lantau and Dumbell. On Lantau the scar of the new road snaked along the precipitous coast; on Dumbell a smoke haze lay over the clamorous little town on its isthmus. Past the tip of the big island the sea changed from blue to green: this was the Pearl River estuary. Their passports were collected.

They watched high-pooped fishing junks sailing on unknown errands.

'Maybe those bodies that were washed up in the summer came from one of these,' said Mary.

'What on earth made you think of that?' asked Sharkey.

'I don't know. But isn't it awful how quickly we forget disasters?'

There was the essential Mary, he thought: warmth combined with impulsiveness. Her love-making was like that too; they had spent most of the time since Alec's party in bed, so he knew.

His amah, who had the nautical-sounding name of Ah Hoy, was used to these sessions that made a nonsense of day and night, but she had been surprised and concerned when this new partner turned out not to be a long-legged blonde but a sensible-looking lady of generous proportions, past the first flush of youth. That smacked not of a mistress, but of a potential wife.

Sharkey was surprised at himself too. In the past, sex had always been for him a clash of slim bodies and hard thighs, a tough sensuality that broke both partners on the wheel. He called it the Mask Of Pain. With his sharp-boned dolly girls he had often been driven to shriek out obscenities at the supreme moment.

That was not the case with Mary, though she gave him as much sexual pleasure as any of them. He was, he reflected, more likely to cry out 'Mamma!' at the critical moment, like a lost little Oedipus returning to the womb that had borne him.

As for Mary, he was her little boy, a masterful, dangerous little boy-genius with Machiavellian skills. He released in her an untapped talent for sensuality; she was bewildered by her own shamelessness. And with the shamelessness came a tempest of feeling that left her liable to laugh or cry at a trifle. Underneath, she was rather frightened.

To his surprise he was able to find the tact to reassure her. But his underlying feeling was wariness. He was like one of those youthful delinquents in Boy's Town: the nice young priest had tempted him to virtue, had given him a moral wash and haircut; superficially he had capitulated. But underneath, in some private part of himself, the flag of independence still flew. He was giving virtue a serious trial, but he reserved the right to throw it over if he felt like it. Did Mary realise that? Perhaps, but she gave no sign. Perhaps that was her private reservation.

Macau appeared out of the sea, a series of low bushy hills set with pastel-coloured buildings. As they approached the sea changed colour again, the green turning to brown. They sailed alongside a breakwater, a line of sea-slubbered stones; then the Fat Shan nosed its way round the colony's southernmost point, past the praya with its banyan trees and handsome, colour-washed buildings set on little heights, and into the narrow inner harbour. Two gunboats were permanently anchored there; reversing the stereotypes, the Chinese one was a battered old sardine tin, the Portuguese one spanking new.

They found themselves in a creek of filthy brown water a quarter of a mile wide. To the left, the mysterious landscape of China and its lean-bellied people. To the right, the cheerful squalor of Macau's waterfront, a chaos of junks and sampans and landing-stages built on slimy wooden piles. The ship edged its way up this channel, reversed its engines and shuddered to a stop, stirring the muddy water into circular patterns. A Chinese sailor threw a rope across to a colleague, who looped it round a bollard. Then the ship's winch turned, pulling it taut; it twanged on a low-frequency note and sent a shower of silver droplets flying. They had arrived.

The passengers, Sharkey and Mary among them, shuffled down the gangplank into a dun-coloured building with peeling shutters: the custom-house. A notice on the wall read FAVOR DE ESPERAR. Sharkey, wilfully misconstruing, grinned and said: 'Difficult, but I try.'

Once through customs, and with their passports returned, they engaged a trishaw ridden by a small ascetic-looking man with calf muscles like whipcord. He pedalled them back the way they had come, along the waterfront with its dusty little shops, each with a long Venetian blind hanging from its balcony and fastened with string to the kerb below, round the southern point of the island to the praya. The twisted old banyan trees, they noted, grew straight out of the patched macadam. The tide was out, making the inner bay an expanse of gleaming mud. There was a Venice-like smell in the air, part sea-water, part sewage.

The trishaw man stopped at a little children's playground and said 'I no can go further', pointing to their destination, the Belavista hotel, which was perched on an eminence above the road. They paid him off and lugged their bags up the steep little road that lead to it.

Choosing it had been another of Sharkey's good ideas. It was a picturesque but decrepit colonial-style building, green and white in colour, with rusty stains down its sides from overflowing pipes. It had been built as a rest home for French officers fighting colonial wars in Indo-China and was spurned by most Hong Kong residents because the service was so bad. But when he had suggested it Mary clapped her hands with delight; she knew and loved it.

They checked in and were taken to a cavernous room with
an ancient ceiling-mounted fan in place of air-conditioning
(but at this time of year they would need no air-conditioning
anyway).

Mary walked over to the balcony, admired the view, and
spoke: 'The Belavista, like the true church, is built upon a
rock.' But Sharkey was in no mood for biblical quotations.
He embraced her from behind, cupping her breasts in his
hands. 'Enough of this badinage,' he hissed. 'Get your
clothes off.'

'But, Liam! We haven't even unpacked.'

'Submit, woman.' She submitted.

Afterwards, lying on the bed beside him, she didn't know
whether she was deliriously happy or endlessly miserable.
Was this sudden conquest of her a thinly disguised rape, or a
thrilling but legitimate courtship, à la Clarke Gable? She
only knew that the seeds of happiness were in her, if only he
would tend them properly. Please, please, let him tend them
properly.

After resting they showered (together – who in his right
mind wants to shower alone?) and went out to view the town.
Mary wore her parka with the fur-fringed hood and Sharkey
an old crombie overcoat, fished up from the bottom of his
suitcase, officially blue but now tinged green with age. 'The
relics of oul dacency,' he called it.

They wandered through the crumbling streets, not caring
where they went. There seemed to be nobody about, but
then Macau, in spite of its quarter-million population, was
always like that. The houses looked as though they would
fall down if you breathed on them, but kept stubbornly
standing.

They walked up to the Chinese border with its yellow

gate. A detail of Mozambiquan soldiers with red fezzes grinned across at their Chinese counterparts, small, unsmiling men in khaki caps with red stars. Then they went up the little tree-clad hill to Camoens's grotto. A lean-faced bronze bust of the poet stood on a pedestal inside a kind of granite dolmen; a pair of feathery little palms grew out of its base.

'Poet in a cleft stick,' said Mary, thinking of how he had clung grimly to the manuscript of *The Lusiads* in the shipwreck.

'Right place for him,' observed Sharkey. 'It's supposed to produce better art.'

At that moment a distinguished-looking elderly man, standing nearby, hawked vigorously and expelled a gobbet of greenish phlegm. A glutinous, adenoidal quality in his performance struck a chord in them; they looked at each other simultaneously and said 'Ah Yee! – Snap!'

That made them laugh until Mary, stricken with remorse, confessed: 'I feel guilty about leaving her, Liam.'

'Don't,' retorted Sharkey. 'You're doing her a favour, by relieving her of what takes up most of her time, namely looking after you. She can beaver away at finding her brother as much as she likes. – As for you and me, we've tried everything; we've spoken to those Chinese journalists, to the Ho family, even to General K'ou. And where has it got us? Precisely nowhere. None of them knows anything about this Vanguard person.' He shrugged his shoulders. 'If you ask me we've heard the last of him. And of Fan Fan too.'

'Don't say that!' Mary wailed. But she felt in her bones that he was right. Even Ah Yee seemed to have given up on her brother and, with the infinite Chinese capacity for putting up with things, was stoically getting on with her life.

They didn't even know whether she'd been back to the temple.

Turning sadly to Sharkey, she rested her head on his shoulder (bending over to do so, of course). He stroked her cheek and said 'There's nothing we can do, love. Absolutely nothing.'

They went back to the hotel to freshen up, before going out to dine at the Fat Siu Lau restaurant, near the centre of Macau's gridiron of streets. Their table was in an upstairs room and had a dazzling white cloth, as well as a copper spittoon like a chamber pot on the floor beside it. The house speciality, which both of them knew from previous visits, was roast pigeon; with it they drank a bottle of red vinho verde, mildly fermenting and the colour of purple ink.

Sharkey paid with clean Hong Kong dollars and got some remarkable notes back as change: Macau dollars which had been issued before the second world war and were held together now only by human grease. Symbolic of the place, he thought.

Walking back to the hotel pleasantly fuddled, they were struck by the silence of Macau, what a splendid antidote it was to its big neighbour across the Pearl River. A few wraith-like figures flitted along the streets. The lighting was anaemic. One or two clapped-out American limousines were the only motor traffic; but they, and the muted transistor wails and rumble of mahjongg from behind distant shutters, merely enhanced the silence.

The two of them sat down on the praya wall. The incoming tide, sending tiny waves to sigh against the pebbles, loosened their tongues. They told each other the story of their lives.

Sam Rhodes, Mary's father, had been one of a dying breed,

all calm assurance outside and granite integrity underneath. He was a driver of steam trains and as such enjoyed genuine status among his working-class neighbours. Politically he was a man of the left – that was automatic; the bookcase in his front room was full of volumes from the Thinker's Library, and his newspaper was the *Daily Herald*. But he thought things out for himself; for example he disapproved of that socialist mantra, redistribution. It might be good for those who gave but it was bad for those who received; it weakened their moral fibre.

Esther, his wife, was physically very like Mary but psychologically a woman of her time: a model working-class wife, supportive, self-effacing, level-headed. Where Mary got the brains and determination that took her to grammar school and Cambridge she didn't know. But she did know that these were the very qualities that made it inevitable that she would grow away from her parents.

'We working-class kids who won scholarships were just as much refugees as the Chinese trying to get into Hong Kong today,' she said. 'More so, even. Because we also have the guilt. I had to grow away from them, I knew that, but I still haven't got over it and never will. What makes it worse is the fact that they were so understanding; they took it so well. Ordinary people often have such wisdom.'

'Maybe they weren't so ordinary. – Where are they now?'

'Dead. Dad had a heart attack quite young, when I was in my twenties. Mum slipped away a couple of years ago, when I was here. Discreet till the last, didn't want to cause any trouble.' She sighed. 'You know, Liam, the frightful thing is that I feel ready to come back to them now. Years too late.'

She wiped her eyes with her handkerchief, but there was pleasure in these memories too. She felt obscurely that every moment you spent thinking of the dead brought them back to life, gave them a tiny sliver of immortality.

Sharkey's story could hardly have been more different. He came from a family where eccentricity took the place of affection, the kind of parents who, in one final kick of energy, sometimes give birth to a genius. It didn't do so in this case; he himself was that final kick.

Born in Armoy House, North Antrim, only son of Hector Sharkey, Esquire, a youthful friend of Roger Casement and sharer of some of his political ideas, believer in a notional Celtic Commonwealth uniting all Irish, Scots, Welsh and Manx (he hadn't got round to thinking of the Gallegos or the Cornishmen). 'If you liked him you called him a visionary; if you didn't, you said he was crazy.'

Physically Hector was a stocky man with a shiny bald head. He always carried a rolled umbrella, which he used as an offensive weapon: he would poke it in the ground to emphasise a point, he would swing it by the handle round his head to the manifest danger of bystanders, he would jab you in the ribs with it when he was excited. His voice was high-pitched and braying, with the timbre of a Bach trumpet. 'The locals used to say: "Man dear, you could hear oul Hector in the next townlan'."'

He stomped round the countryside between Bushmills and Ballycastle trying to convert people to his views. If you questioned his advocacy of the Irish language he would say: 'It's perfectly simple, dear boy. We can be Irish-speaking in a generation. We old folks can learn it from our children.'

His wife Celia, Sharkey's mother, was as passive as he was active. She spent her time painting, or what she defined as such. Actually she was a copyist; she would copy anything from a Raphael print to a postcard of Fair Head. 'The house used to be full of her pictures. Where they've gone since the nuns bought it I don't know.' Sharkey got his slight build from her; but a more important legacy was the feeling that nobody really wanted him. 'Run along, Liam,' she'd say, 'can't you see I'm busy?' In adolescence, when he had found out about the facts of life, he wondered how such a pair had ever managed to conceive him.

'When she shooed me away I would trail along to him, but he would just lecture me about politics; God, how I came to hate that Celtic Commonwealth! – It was a great relief to both of them, I think, when I was away at school – Rockport in County Down, and then Wellington.'

'Why Liam, you were deprived of love!' exclaimed Mary. 'That explains a lot.' And ruffled his hair.

His response was an impish grin. 'I think I was put on earth to redress the family balance. They were all spirit and no flesh; I'm the other way round. You could call me nature's little compensation.'

'Oh, phoo! Stop playing the hard man. It doesn't fool me.'

He told her about his forebears. 'The first Hector, the Colonel, was a soldier. He fought at the Boyne in 1690 and, in the Williamite settlement afterwards, was made a grant of most of the land between Fair Head and the Bush river. That was the high point in the family history; after that it was downhill all the way. What with mismanagement, gambling and too strong a taste for the product of the local distillery, they kept having to sell off bits of the land. Where other families were expansionist, they were contractionist. Finally, in 1932, the house itself had to go. The old man sold it to a Catholic order of nuns; it's now an Assumptionist convent.' He grinned again. 'Neat bit of irony, isn't it? The house I grew up in is now a place where sex is banned.'

'What happened to your parents?'

'Oh, they retired to a cottage in Dalkey – doesn't everybody in Ireland? But honour where honour is due, the old man did the decent thing by me. I'd just finished at Wellington and he put enough of the loot into a trust fund to see me through Oxford – Worcester College, it was.'

'Maybe he loved you after all,' said Mary, ever charitable.

'Maybe so,' conceded Sharkey. 'But to tell you the truth, by that time I was a lost soul. I didn't care any more. – I blame the Irish climate for that.'

'How on earth do you make that out?'

'I'll tell you if you promise not to interrupt.'

She gave him a push. 'Rotten so-and-so! But I promise.'

'Right then. – It's because of the damp, which has a double effect. It saps the will and, more important, it spreads a haze over everything. Now intellectual hazes promote dreaminess, and dreaminess promotes imagination. And imagination, I'm sure you'll agree, is a highly dangerous phenomenon: it enables you to compare things as they are with things as they ought to be. In young Liam's case that led to a preference for the latter; in other words he cried for the moon. He cried first for his mother's affection and was sent packing. Later, at boarding school, he longed for a different kind of love, and what did he get? Buggery ... '

'How disgusting!'

'I know, I know. But it turned out to be a salutary process. It put paid to the crying for the moon. It made me a realist.'

His face, she noted, hardened at this point; the monkey mouth returned momentarily. But today she could forgive him. She looked at him round-eyed and said: 'Good heavens, Liam, you've never come out with anything like that before.'

'And probably won't ever again.' He shrugged again and

said: 'Lucky Mary. You were better off with the railway engines.'

They fell silent; there didn't seem to be any more to say. So they walked back to the hotel, said 'Boa noite' to the night porter in the vestibule, and went to bed. Lying there side by side, each thought about what the other had said. Then, imperceptibly, they fell asleep.

Wakening, Mary perceived a high ceiling with stucco mouldings. Where on earth was she? Then she remembered: the dear old Belavista! Sharkey was still asleep, his nose buried in the sheet beside her.

She felt a lift of the spirit. Progress had been made; he had revealed more of himself than ever before. And now the holiday was really beginning (this never happened until you had spent the first night away). She slid out of bed with a feeling of expectation and walked across the dusty carpet to the bath cubicle. The water, she knew, would run cold and brown until, after a couple of minutes, it would splutter itself into warm life; but what of that? You didn't stay at the Belavista for the comfort.

The tempest in the water pipes wakened Sharkey, and they were soon soaping each other in the shower. 'No sex just now, Liam,' she admonished; they completed their shower in an air of comical abstinence.

They breakfasted off cardboard cornflakes, dried-egg omelette, slithery bacon, leather toast and ground-acorn coffee, all of which added to their good humour. Through the

dining room window they could see woolly clouds clinging to
a low hill with a lighthouse on it, and lifting slowly from the
island of Taipa. A church bell rang somewhere, and was
answered by another. Bells were always ringing in Catholic
Macau.

They decided to visit the old East India Company
graveyard. 'And why? Because it represents the pre-history
of Hong Kong,' said Mary.

It was situated behind a yellow wall; they rang the bell,
and a small boy opened for them. Inside, they found
themelves in an oasis of stillness; trees, birds, flowers and old
tombstones were the setting for a little Anglican chapel,
bedded a little off-centre like a pearl in an oyster. It was
freshly swept and smelt of pitch-pine pews and carbolic soap;
it might have been in England.

There was something innocent and unworldly about the
graves: the moss-green obelisks, the chipped stone slabs, the
carved urns and scrolls. The painter George Chinnery lay
there, and a Churchill, and dozens of young men from
England and Holland and Germany who had come to this
fever-ridden place years before Hong Kong existed to make
their fortune, and found death instead.

While they were looking at the tombstone of a Holsteiner
who had died in 1807 the bell rang and someone came in;
they paid no attention because Mary was wondering aloud
why so many people found graveyards calming. 'You'd think
they'd run away screaming,' she said.

'Some children do,' said Sharkey, thinking of himself.
'They suddenly realise that they're going to die themselves.'

'I've never realised it,' announced Mary. 'Not emotionally
anyway. It doesn't frighten me in the least.'

'Lucky you.' He sounded genuinely envious.

Mary tossed her head. 'If you're scared of death why toss your life away then? That's what you were doing, wasn't it?'

'Because it's the only way to save it. By throwing it away you kid yourself you've got an endless supply. Like the man who lights his cigar with a five pound note to persuade himself he's a millionaire.'

'Very plausible, I don't think,' snorted Mary.

The other visitor had worked his way closer now and was standing with his back to them, examining the Churchill grave. It was a back familiar to Sharkey, military of aspect but sadly stooped today. 'How are you, Nigel?' he said.

'Why Liam! Good to see you. – I'm well.'

'Do you know Mary Rhodes?'

Presentations made, Sharkey said to Verity: 'What brings you here, if I may ask?'

'Just a break. I could be doing with one.'

'They work you hard in that job of yours.'

'They do.'

Mary, surreptitiously examining this new acquaintance, saw a tanned, long-headed, military-looking man with cropped grey hair and a little moustache; a man of rigid posture which he was finding difficult to maintain, as though he was collapsing from the inside. He alarmed her.

He was turning to her now. 'Did I hear you talking about death, Mrs Rhodes?'

'Well, yes ... '

'Right place for it, wouldn't you say?' put in Sharkey, trying to sound jolly.

But Verity was looking into Mary's eyes with pained concentration. 'I couldn't help overhearing your question,' he said. 'About why these places inspire feelings of calm. Is it perhaps the calm of arrival, after the labours of the journey?'

There was something uncanny about the way he said this, but she hid her concern. 'Do you mean: After life's fitful fever he sleeps well?'

'Yes, something like that.' He looked around him, taking in the whole cemetery at a glance. 'Do they sleep well, these people? Most of them were failures after all.'

'Neither well nor badly. They're just dead. They don't feel anything,' put in Sharkey.

'I wonder. Perhaps even the dead are sentient in their way. – My father doesn't want to have himself cremated. A priest from the Bo Lin monastery convinced him that the body suffers pain from the flames and must be allowed to ... break down naturally, if you see what I mean. I must say I find the idea distasteful.'

'Aren't we getting a bit morbid?' said Sharkey, feeling distinctly jumpy.

'I'm sorry.' Verity straightened his back. 'Anyway I really must go.'

Mary sensed his loneliness. 'Come and have lunch with us,' she said. 'We're having African chicken at the Pousada.'

'Alas, I cannot. I leave on the twelve o'clock boat.'

'Can't you wait till tomorrow?'

'I'm afraid not. They keep me pretty busy.'

'Well, at least come up to São Paulo with us. There's plenty of time for that.'

'If it's not an imposition ... '

'Of course not,' said Mary.

The church of São Paulo had burned down in the seventeenth century, leaving only a baroque black façade standing; since then it had defied everything the weather could throw at it. They came up to it from the rear, by streets almost totally deserted, the pavements more broken than any

Sharkey had ever seen. Where the nave had been was now a paved area; they walked across it and round one end of the façade, to stand on the broad flight of steps on the other side.

'I love this place,' sighed Mary.

'You imperialists are all the same; you're fascinated by decay,' said Sharkey provocatively.

'Who's an imperialist?'

'You are. You thrill to the romance of empire.'

'Maybe. But I don't approve of it.'

'I am both fascinated and approving,' said Verity with the ghost of a smile.

A few days ago Sharkey would have devised some gibe in answer to this; today he merely said: 'In your case it's in the family.'

They looked across to where some children were flying Chinese kites from the remains of an old square fort: a green-stained keep and very little else.

At last Verity spoke. 'What changes will they see before they die? On top of the ones we've seen already.' He reflected for a moment. 'Some of us have tried to preserve the old China we took over. I'll not deny that there was an initial period of rapine and exploitation. But after that most of us governed honourably enough. Unfortunately, like the Spaniards in South America, we brought in sickness on our clothes.'

'Sickness?' queried Mary.

'The sickness of modern life. – What have I personally done with the fragment of old China entrusted to me? I don't quite know. I've done my best, I suppose, but every day another piece of it is subverted to urban use. Every day a dozen or so families leave my district for the inferno of Tsuen Wan. The sickness is catching.'

'It's not fatal though,' said Mary in her most businesslike tone.

'It infects everything I live for. And there it is.' He pointed to the mean little cluster of souvenir stalls lying in wait for them at the bottom of the stairs. Then, almost to himself: 'There's a stench of decomposition from the world I love. Every evening the night soil lorries head for the New Territories – to fertilise the fields, they say. But how horrible that we should do that by spreading our own waste products over the old China! I can't get the stench of ... well, human excrement ... out of my nostrils.'

Mary and Sharkey looked at each other in alarm, but Verity didn't seem to notice. Then Sharkey said off-handedly: 'What's the use of worrying about the way the world wags, Nigel? Every generation thinks things are going to the dogs. They haven't gone yet.'

Verity gave him a ghostly smile. 'And I thought I was the optimist and you the pessimist. It looks as though we shall have to reconsider.'

They moved off down the steps, ignoring the expectant stall-holders, and walked together to the jetty, where Verity boarded the ferry; it was the Tai Loy today, a newer, whiter boat than the Fat Shan.

He was in a curious, exalted frame of mind, perhaps even a little mad. It couldn't just be Sharkey's unexpected consideration, though that was part of it. No, it was the temporary escape, in agreeable company, from the horrible preoccupations that haunted him these days. And, sure enough, once he was sitting alone in the ship's saloon they came stealthily back.

He had never cared for the body anyway; he regarded it as a repulsive but necessary machine, to be ignored when it was

functioning properly and repaired with all speed when it
wasn't. It wasn't now. Some debilitating bug was at work in
it, and the code he lived by prevented him from setting the
repair process in motion. That was why he couldn't ignore it;
his mind kept coming back to it.

Even in normal circumstances bodily reality was a trial.
You had to break off some important business to squat on a
wooden board with a hole in the middle, like an obscene
picture frame, and squeeze out a slack and stinking black
pudding. Or turn away from some glorious view to
disentangle that absurd frilled sausage from your flies and
squirt out a scalding liquid which polluted everything it
touched.

But how much worse things were now! The very fibres of
his body, fibres he was normally unaware of, were breaking
down slowly; the mucuses were distilling a loathsome jelly,
the tissues staggering under the impact of some organism
ripping through them like chain-shot.

It sometimes felt as if his blood was on fire. Last night in
the hotel, for instance, his heartburn woke him up. He felt
hot acid being pumped through his veins: a tearing, rushing
sensation; he could practically hear the roar of it. At other
times, when the attack was milder, it was as though shoals of
little stinging creatures were wriggling though his vascular
system.

Worst of all was the tremor. It had happened three or four
times now, the right hand and right foot together. And just
the other day, in Gascoyne Road, while he was sitting at his
desk drafting a memo on duck-raising, his hand suddenly
shook so much that he had to drop his pen. Then, by some
freak, his right foot decided to shake in unison with it till the
toe of his shoe beat a tattoo on the desk-leg. It was horrible,

grotesque! And sitting there in the Tai Loy, while the ship's siren gave a mighty honk to signalise departure, he honestly couldn't see an end to it.

Moving away from the landing stage, Mary and Sharkey looked at each other in alarm. 'The man's ill,' said Mary. 'He must see a doctor.'

'He won't. He'll play Horatius and keep the bridge till the bitter end.'

'There must be something we can do for him.'

'He'll never accept help.'

'Damn,' said Mary. 'Damn, damn, damn. Things like this simply shouldn't happen.' She turned to Sharkey. 'At least,' she said, 'we can keep an eye on him.'

Sharkey made a face. 'Along with Ah Yee and Wilson and General K'ou? Old Uncle Tom Cobley and all?'

'Yes, Liam.' Her voice was firm.

Sharkey sighed. 'At least I was nice to him. First time ever, poor sod.'

But Verity's gloomy apparition soon faded from their minds. They slipped into a tourist routine: Sun Yat Sen's house, a little zoo with peacocks in cages, the Leal Senado with its discreet little garden and exquisite azulejo tiles.

They ate every day in the Long Kei restaurant, opposite the senate building in the main square and under the accusing eye of General Mosquito ('The less warlike a nation,' Sharkey declared, 'the fiercer its statues.') In the afternoon they read on their balcony; he succeeded in finishing Proust, a task that had hung over him for twenty years. Time was refound, definitively.

One evening, out of curiosity, they went to the big Central Hotel, Macau's vice centre. The building was relatively new but was already dilapidated. Its big neon sign was a red rectangle with a vertical stroke through it, meaning 'middle'. The same character appeared in the name of China herself, but this was a Middle Kingdom with a difference, the realm of *l'homme moyen sensuel* whom it kept supplied with whores and gambling tables. Strange to think that when the bleary-eyed pleasure-seekers were falling into bed here, the Spartans across the border were marching out with shouldered tools and the name of the Great Helmsman on their lips, to toil in the wintry paddies.

They found, on one of the middle floors, a gambling table which fascinated and repelled them. The game was fantan, and a few enormous specimens of homo americanicus were risking their dollars on it.

A wizened old woman would spread a pile of pearl buttons on the green baize then, with a kind of conductor's baton, keep dividing it into halves, discarding one half each time. As the pile diminished people betted on how many would be left when the process was finished. It was dreary but hypnotic, carried out in almost total silence. And when it was over the whole thing started again, the relentless old hand dividing, dividing, dividing. Mary found herself thinking of Coleridge's Life-In-Death.

While they were bending over this lugubrious ritual they heard a low voice, somewhere close to them, saying something. What was it? Could it have been 'Fan Fan not dead, he send letter'?

It could, it was! Sharkey spun round to see who this mysterious informant might be, and was aware of a medium-sized man disappearing from the room. He made out a head of sleek black hair, a crumpled suit of white ducks and a pair of tan and white winkle-picker shoes; no more.

He leapt to his feet and shouldered his way past the

huge Americans, trying to catch the man up. But the doorway was blocked by a group of new arrivals. He got clear of these as best he could and ran out into the street; there was no one there.

⌒

In the course of his duties Verity visited Dumbell about once every ten days; the rest of his time was taken up with paper-work, receiving petitioners, liaison meetings and visits to other parts of his scattered empire: Lantau, Cheung Chau, Mirs Bay and the Sai Kung peninsula.

But since the attack on Elder Kwok there had been an increasing police presence on the island. Dashwood of Special Branch, and even Joe Miners, were often there, operating from the Chinese Chamber or Commerce, where a procession of police constables, witnesses and informers would clatter up and down the wooden stairs.

When Verity was also on the island it became accepted practice for them all to lunch off Ah Shing's cottage pie in the Adminstration bungalow. Cheung or Jeffrey Wing might be of the party too, depending on which of them Verity had brought along (he made it Jeffrey as often as he dared).

One day near the end of January the luncheon party consisted of Miners, Jeffrey and himself. Verity was in reasonable shape, for once. The burning tightness he had felt in his muscles all through the Christmas period had eased; he felt a cautious buoyancy, like a convalescent venturing out for the first time.

When they had finished eating Joe filled his pipe

elaborately, lit up and said 'Dashwood thinks we're getting somewhere. At last.'

Verity was mildly surprised. Joe, he knew, delighted in saying indiscreet things, and had frequently done so in Cheung's presence – but wasn't Jeffrey a little junior for that? He took liberties himself, of course, but that was different; he knew Jeffrey so much better than Joe did.

Miners continued blithely: 'We're getting more information in these days.'

'About who attacked poor old Kwok?' enquired Verity.

'About all kinds of things. Some drug caches even. Minor stuff, of course, a few ounces here and there; the Narcotics boys say they mostly come from that house up Route Twisk they raided a few days ago. Not my pigeon, of course, but I get to hear things myself. About triads, naturally.'

'Anything of interest to me?'

Joe drew arabesques in the air with his pipe-stem. 'I wouldn't be free to tell you if there was. Not yet anyway. – We have our own informers, of course. I call them our old faithfuls. But there's been a new development recently: anonymous phone calls. Usually putting the finger on one of the triads. Where Dumbell's concerned – I can see the question coming! – that means either the T'ung or the Twenty-One K.'

'Both? Not just one of them?' queried Verity.

'Far from it. These people are nothing if not even-handed.' He sucked at his pipe, which was going out again. 'Both of them, quite indiscriminately.'

'You said: putting the finger. Any important names so far?'

'Bless you, no. Only small fry. Minor officials, people like that. But Dashwood thinks we may be able to run a few of them in before long.'

'May I ask a question?' ventured Jeffrey.

'Go ahead, lad.'

'You'll have to bring forward evidence, won't you?'

'Only too true.'

'Will you be able to?'

'Shrewd fellow!' Miners resuscitated the pipe with a deal of puffing and said: 'It'll be the usual story. We'll get them on membership of an illegal organisation, the beak will fine them a hundred bucks and it'll be bye-bye birdie.'

'Is it worth it?' asked Verity in distaste. He would have preferred to draw a veil over the whole business.

'It's a game, Nigel. We've got to play it like everybody else. We can't just sit on our backsides doing nothing.' He took another puff. 'At least it keeps the lads alert.'

Verity sighed. 'Going back to Dumbell. If it's true that Ng is Twenty-One K, doesn't that make poor old Kwok a T'ung?'

'Nigel, your guess is as good as mine. Or as young Jeffrey's here.'

He took the pipe from his mouth and smiled his cherubic smile, the long filament of spittle glinting in the wintry sun.

On the way back to Hong Kong in the launch Verity and Jeffrey discussed what he had said.

'What did you make of all that?' asked Verity. His voice was weary; he could feel the stiffness returning to his joints. Only a hint as yet, but he had come to recognise the signs.

'It seems a little ... defeatist, if I may say so. I was wondering if there was anything I could do to help.'

'How do you mean?'

He pointed back to the island. 'I could talk to people back there. Listen to gossip, that kind of thing.'

'I don't think that's a good idea,' said Verity uncertainly.

'But it's almost my second home. Everybody knows me. Nobody would think anything of it ... '

'Listen, Jeffrey,' said Verity, making a big effort. 'As a government official you mustn't compromise yourself. And as a friend of mine you mustn't put yourself at risk. Promise me that.'

The boy's face flushed with pleasure, particularly when Verity referred to their friendship. 'I promise,' he said.

Reassured, Verity looked through the launch's windscreen at the twin bow-waves, sparkling in the January sunshine. Then, as his eyes wandered, his stomach suddenly lurched: they were passing the sinister little islet that Cairns had told him about, which he couldn't help thinking of as the Isle of the Dead. It too sparkled in the winter sun, but coldly, with a deadly chill.

His thoughts locked on to it, involuntarily. And to his horror his eyes followed suit. His stare was glued to it; it was a full minute before he could wrench it away.

Sharkey and Mary were welcomed back to the Conduit Road flat by a jubilant Ah Yee. 'Missee! Massa! I get letter!' she cried, waving a flimsy envelope that had not quite the strength to be blue in colour.

Mary embraced her. 'Is it from Fan Fan?'

'Yes, missee. He no dead. He all right.' Her glaring eyes were almost sinister in joy; she grimaced convulsively and her catarrh broke out in sharp snorts, like a pneumatic drill. 'He not on boat, missee. You look. Look, massa.'

The envelope contained a sheet of grubby, tea-stained paper torn from a school exercise book, with Chinese characters inscribed by a blunt pencil. 'Fan Fan write!' said Ah Yee proudly.

'Perhaps we could sit down first,' suggested Sharkey; they were still standing in the little hall.

'Oh missee, I solly! You come in, sit down. I get drink.' She rushed across to Mary's drinks cabinet.

They put down their bags in the bedroom and returned to the living-room to examine the letter while Ah Yee banged with her bottles. The characters were scribbled any old way. 'I can't make anything of it,' confessed Sharkey.

'I bling gin-tonic! I bling whiskee!' cried Ah Yee. She was as good as her word.

Mary sat her down forcibly in a chair and said to her: 'We can't read this; Ah Yee. You'll have to tell us.'

It took a good hour to get the story out of her. Nothing could induce her to speak Cantonese; only the language of her missee could match the importance of the event. Finally, they pieced together the story.

The letter merely said: 'I am well. The boat had to turn back. They caught me and sent me back to the commune. I got two months detention and then they put me back on my usual work.' There was no signature, but Ah Yee knew the writing.

The rest had been fleshed out by no less a man than Sin Fung, who had brought the letter personally to Ah Yee's kitchen door. She had told him that her missee was in Macau, before he disappeared as mysteriously as he came. From her description it was clear that he was the same glossy-haired man who had spoken to them in the Central Hotel.

Fan Fan, once the money for his escape had been paid,

had been told to make his way to a village called Wun Tsuen
in the Four Districts, an area on the west coast of the Pearl
River estuary. That sounded simple enough but was in fact
the most difficult part of the whole enterprise.

He had to slip away from the commune at night, carrying
enough food to keep him going for two days. He reached the
city of Canton during that first night and waited until dawn,
in order to be able to make his way through the built-up area
by day, when there would be thousands of other pedestrians
doing the same. That meant spending an exhausting day on
foot, nibbling the piece of boiled cabbage and the few grains
of rice he had managed to bring with him. He dared not stop.

He was lucky; nobody challenged him. He timed his
departure from the south-western suburbs of the city to
coincide with nightfall and, dropping with fatigue, walked on
southwards during the second night. When dawn was
breaking he crept into a clump of bamboos and slept.

He was near Wun Tsuen now, he knew. So, about five
o'clock in the evening, he left his bamboos, making sure
there was no one to see him, and headed east towards the
sea. Wun Tsuen was a fishing village and there, at dusk, by
the waterfront, precisely as arranged, he fell in with that
same shiny-haired man who had accosted him beside his
night-soil cart. Without a word the two of them headed south
along the coast until they reached a sheltered cove where he
could see a pair of boats with masked lights edging in
towards the shore. Perhaps a hundred nervous people were
waiting to board.

They were ancient fishing junks, each with a master and a
crew of three. The waiting refugees shuffled on board,
making as little noise as possible. Fan Fan, as the last to
arrive, was in the second boat. Both were overloaded and low

in the water, but it was a calm night. The only thing he worried about was being intercepted by one of the Chinese gunboats which patrolled the estuary.

His fellow refugees, like himself, were almost too tired to feel fear. As the junks nosed their way into deeper water and time passed Fan Fan fell into a half-sleep with his chin in his hands.

He woke to the sensation of a bright light shining in his eyes, blinding him. Around him people were chattering in alarm. His heart sank; the worst thing had happened. But the crew were curiously unconcerned.

There was a sudden whoosh and a scream of displaced air, followed by a dull clang; a shell passed overhead. Everybody started screaming; somewhere a baby wailed.

'Shut up! You're not dead yet,' shouted the junk-master scornfully.

The light continued to blind them, preventing them from seeing anything of the craft from which it came. But it was getting closer and closer, to within a few yards. An indistinct message came from it, shouted over a loud hailer. Nobody could make out the words.

'What was that? What was that?' they all cried. The only reply was a sudden, brutal rattle of machine-gun fire, which left them screaming. Then they realised, to their astonishment, that the bullets were passing overhead. How could anybody miss at that range?

The searchlight slid off them and focussed, not on their companion boat but on the empty sea behind it. Another burst of machine-gun fire came; then the light beam snapped off and the patrol-boat, quite inexplicably, sheered off and roared away, so close that Fan Fan could smell the diesel fuel from its exhaust.

The two junks sailed slowly on, the refugees holding their breath, hardly daring to trust their luck. Finally one man had the courage to ask: 'What does it all mean?'

A crew member eyed them pityingly. 'They've been paid,' he said. 'What did you think it meant?'

That provoked an eruption of talk and laughter that took a long time to subside. The two boats sailed triumphantly on through the dark.

Just before dawn, when the excitement had died down and the decks were strewn with sleeping bodies, another vessel loomed up out of the paling eastern sky; it was before the first red streaks had appeared.

This turned out to be a junk like their own; nobody paid attention. But it held its course directly towards their leading boat and would not be deflected, even when the crew started shouting. The junk-master, swearing, was forced to reverse his engine and heave to; whereupon the strange junk swung round in a neat semi-circle and came up alongside him. 'Who are you? What do you want?' he shouted.

Fan Fan, watching from the other boat, could see half a dozen men crouching by the intruder's gunwale, holding in their hands long poles with objects like pineapples at their ends. At a command they swung these out against their companion junk's timbers, there were simultaneous orange flashes and small, unimpressive pops: the pineapples were hand grenades.

There was pandemonium aboard. Fan Fan could hear the screams of injured men and women and see, against the lightening sky, water pouring into the stricken junk. Overcrowded as it was, it settled, turned slowly turtle and pitched its cargo of human beings into the sea.

Meanwhile their own junk-master had opened his throttle

to make a dash for safety; they could see their attackers arming a new set of poles.

An eerie slow-motion chase began. The other junk was scarcely faster than they were, perhaps only by a knot. But as their old boat laboured along they could see they were being gained on. The eastern sky was now blazing red; soon they would be visible for miles around. If they could hold the attackers off for perhaps five minutes more they would be safe. Everyone was on tenterhooks; could they possibly make it? Fan Fan felt a wave of hatred against these people who were trying to kill him: what had he ever done to harm them?

One moment the attacking junk was getting closer and closer; the next it sheered off unexpectedly and headed at full speed towards the south-east, and Hong Kong. So that was where it came from! The refugees were jubilant; they were going to live after all. The question was: what would their own junk do with them?

The answer came soon enough. It headed south-west towards the nearest piece of land, which could only be communist China. It was populous, cultivated: rice paddies and fish-ponds all crocheted together by snaking bunds. Their escape attempt was going to fail, that was clear; but at least they would live to try again another day.

But how could the crew land them on such a populated coast? They didn't. The master approached as close as he dared to the shore, then the crew threw them overboard, one by one. The water came up only as far as their shoulders; they were able to struggle to dry land. As far as Fan Fan could see no one was drowned; there was even a small baby who bobbed his way shorewards on his father's shoulders.

He decided that it was vital to distance himself from the others, and from the sea. So, exhausted and starving as he was, he trudged inland until a detachment of the People's Liberation Army picked him up.

'Where do you think you're going?' they questioned him.

He tried to look as stupid as possible. 'I don't know,' he said. 'I was running away.'

'Why?'

'I'm hungry.'

They looked at each other as if to say: like all the others, and asked him where he came from. He told them.

'But that's miles away!'

He grinned inanely. He was ragged, and stupid, and clearly a person of no importance. So they put him in a lorry and sent him back to the commune. And there the authorities contented themselves with putting him in a cell for three weeks and forcing him to make a routine confession of harbouring counter-revolutionary thoughts. He was made to recant, soundly berated and then put straight back on the night-soil cart, where his services were required. And there he was still.

In her jubilation Ah Yee made them a vast steak-and-kidney pie. It would have been pointless to ask her to cook Chinese. On triumphal occasions like this only European food would do, and in her mind steak-and-kidney had somehow become identified with the British Empire.

So it was with full stomachs that they broached a subject which was acquiring some urgency: what to do about their two establishments. Sharkey was for staying as they were for the present.

'But it's wasteful,' protested Mary, all her housewifely instincts coming out.

'Don't burn your boats. You hardly know me; I'm middle-aged, set in my ways and extremely selfish.'

'No more than I am. We'll simply have to adjust.'

'Don't overestimate our ability to do that.'

'Now listen, Liam,' said Mary firmly, 'I'm not going to play the bachelor girl you come up to see every time you feel like a shag.'

'I'm not suggesting you do. But think of the amahs. They'll never agree to live together. So wouldn't it be better to keep both flats going, with duplicate toothbrushes and the rest?'

Mary reflected. 'You have a point there.'

'Just so long as we spend our nights in Breezy Court,' said Sharkey with a grin.

'Why?'

'Better equipped for fornication. It has a double bed.'

'Horrible man. But I agree.'

'We can eat more often here though. Ah Yee's a better cook than Ah Hoy.'

So they began a nomadic life, using both flats. Both wondered how long it would last. The two amahs hated it; eventually one of them would give notice. Probably Ah Hoy, Sharkey thought, because Ah Yee and Mary were genuinely friends and the amah was touchingly grateful for the interest her employer showed in Fan Fan.

They knew they were merely postponing a decision, but Sharkey had another, less avowable reason for doing so: why shut the cage door before you have to?

As for Mary, she was aware of the dangers but willing to put up with them. She loved Sharkey and was a little frightened of him; she longed to have him to herself, but was shrewd enough to realise that if you want to keep a man you have to give him a long leash.

Elder Kwok, being a man of nearly eighty, had been making a slow recovery but was doing well now, in mid-January; the time was more than ripe for Verity to pay him an official visit.

'May I come too, Mr Verity?' asked Jeffrey.

'You don't have to, you know. Mr Cheung has already been to see him, but then he's known him for fifteen years.'

'I'd quite like to go just the same.'

'Come along then,' said Verity, secretly pleased. Sitting by the bedside of a man with whom you can exchange only the rigid formulae of etiquette was no picnic, not even for him.

The weather had turned cool, blowy and damp; rather like England, in fact. The Peak was shrouded in great billowing clouds; driving down from Stewart's Terrace in the mornings he had to keep his headlights on as far as the top of Garden Road. It was that kind of day when he and Jeffrey went to Pokfulam, to the hospital; but it was late in the afternoon and the humidity, which was at least ninety percent, was putting smudged haloes round the street lamps.

They found the Elder in a long brown-painted ward, sitting up in his metal bed on a mattress at least a foot thick. His peaked little body scarcely raised a crease in the coverlet and his stringy neck poked out of flannel pyjamas seemingly held upright by their own starch. With the big plaster on the side of his head (his bandages had been removed), his pale face and wispy beard, he looked frail but distinguished.

'Mr Verity! This is an honour,' he said in Cantonese and held out a paper-thin hand.

Verity took it gently. 'How are you, Elder?' he asked.

'Very well. Apart from some noises in the ears.'

'I'm glad to hear it. – You know my assistant, Jeffrey Wing?'

The Elder nodded briefly towards the young man, and proceeded to ignore him.

'Who's looking after you?'

'Dr O'Young. A very clever man.' Kwok fingered his plaster as though seeking confirmation of his opinion there. 'Soon I shall be allowed to go home.'

He then asked for news of Dumbell. It was a ritual question because, as Verity was aware, he knew at least as much about it as the district officer himself. But proprieties had to be observed. So Verity told him about the activities of the Rural Committee and the Three Mountains Festival Organising Committee and all the rest. Had the junks sunk in Typhoon Mary been replaced? inquired Kwok. And were the authorities still issuing dry rations? Again Verity gave full and courteous replies.

Then it was his own turn to put the questions. He asked about the attack on Kwok, although he already knew the answer, having read the Elder's testimony to the police. But it was the old man's turn to appear in an interesting light.

He told how he had been about to set off to Chi Ma Hang to give his son's pigs their swill when he noticed how Mr T. C. Leung's ropes were encroaching in a most blatant manner on his ground space. He had been bending over to push them aside with his foot when he felt a blinding blow to the side of his head; he had no idea where it came from.

'This happened about the middle of the morning?'

'Yes, Fu Mu Kwan.'

'And you didn't see anyone?'

'No, sir.'

'And the neighbours – did they notice anybody?'

'No, Fu Mu Kwan.'

'That sounds strange. Don't you agree, Jeffrey?'

Jeffrey turned to the Elder and asked politely: 'No one saw anything at all?'

Kwok didn't as much as look in his direction. He directed his eyes deliberately towards Verity and said: 'Nobody saw anything.'

Verity concealed his annoyance; why, this was pure snobbery! Yet they had the cheek to call us class-ridden!

The conversation flagged. Verity was wondering whether he had allowed his feelings to show too plainly when a group of people entered the ward and made for Elder Kwok's bed. Ho Man was one of them; he was accompanied by an earnest young Chinese and ... ? Why yes, it was Mrs Rhodes, whom he had met in Macau.

'Why, Mrs Rhodes!' he said. 'I'm very glad to see you again.'

'So am I. But call me Mary, please.'

'As long as you agree to call me Nigel ... '

'Done!'

Verity then looked towards the young Chinese. 'My nephew, Ho Nai Yeung – Wilson Ho in English,' explained Ho Man with a jump of the larynx.

Wilson blinked, shook hands with Verity, then his eyes swivelled of their own volition in Jeffrey's direction.

'Hello, Wilson,' said Jeffrey quickly. 'We were at the Diocesan Boys' School together,' he explained.

Mary examined the strange young man in a motherly way. He was a hidden fragment of Wilson's life, and there weren't many of those around. 'So you were both at DBS, were you?' she said.

The strange young man smiled, winningly. 'Wilson was

the star of the class,' he said. 'I was miles behind him.'

Wilson's only comment was to clear his throat, a brusque bark.

'Come on, don't be bearish,' said Mary. 'Tell us all about it.'

Wilson knitted his brows and made a statement: 'Jeffrey is doing himself an injustice. He was strong in English and history. We have not seen each other for approximately three years.' He relapsed into silence.

Elder Kwok then had to repeat, for Ho Man's benefit, the narrative he had delivered to Verity. Mary, hot with indignation, cried: 'It's absolutely incredible that such violence is allowed to happen!'

Verity, touched on the quick, responded: 'The authorities can't be everywhere, you know ... '

Damn. She could have bitten her tongue out: what a fool, not to realise that he would take it personally. Trying to make amends, she cried: 'I know, I know! Worse things happen in other places. Like these dreadful people who sink junks with illegal immigrants on board ... '

A tense silence fell. She realised she'd put her foot in it good and proper – but in what way? Casting round for a way out of the embarrassment, she said: 'Did you know they did it by exploding hand-grenades against them?'

Now she'd really put the cat among the pigeons; with growing panic she cursed herself for not keeping a closer guard on her tongue. If she didn't watch out she'd be blabbing Ah Yee's secret and they'd all end up in gaol.

Verity, looking pale, asked: 'Who told you this, Mrs Rhodes?' And Jeffrey added: 'If you can remember please inform the police.'

Crestfallen, she said: 'I'm sorry. I was just trying to impress. It's staffroom gossip, that's all. I was speaking out of turn.'

The tension slowly dissipated. But she felt more was required. She said contritely: 'I'm very sorry. I should have known better, repeating old wives' tales.'

Her intervention had created an awkwardness that refused to go away. It was a relief when Wilson suddenly said: 'We must be going now, Mrs Rhodes.'

'Of course, Wilson,' she blurted, as though they had a pressing engagement. She took Wilson's arm, Wilson took Ho Man's, and together the three of them left the ward, muttering embarrassed goodbyes.

She suddenly thought: if only Liam had been here! The streak of childish impulsiveness in her had landed her in hot water. She'd never have given way to it in his presence; he was streetwise, you had to think before you spoke when he was there. She really needed to have him around.

Back in the ward Verity had his own troubles. What could Kwok and he say to each other now? He needed to get away, especially as he could feel the muscles of his knee-joints starting to shrink over the bone; in a few minutes the upper and lower legs would be welded together and he'd be unable to move – how to explain that away?

Fortunately a smiling, brown-skinned Chinese in a white coat materialised; a pair of gold molars glittered behind his upper incisors. 'Excuse me please,' he said. 'I am Doctor O'Young. I need to examine this patient.'

'Of course. We were just going.'

So Jeffrey and he made their escape. As they left the ward, Verity's knees slowly seizing up, they observed the doctor flashing a small torch in the Elder's eye, smiling with relentless bonhomie.

Early in February Chinese New Year placed a semi-colon in everybody's life. It had been preceded as usual by the firecracker days. In the evening there was a feu de joie of exploding bangers that rolled round the natural amphitheatre of the harbour; by day you might be walking in the street when there would be an ear-splitting crack under your feet and a Chinese youth would lope off with a grin on his face and the glazed eyes of a drunk man. It was not alcohol that intoxicated him, just New Year.

Mary, who was a devotee of Chinese traditional culture, found all this rather jolly; most other Europeans, Sharkey included, hated it.

There was nothing they could do about it. Their servants collected their two months' pay – the Hong Kong year having thirteen months – put their belongings in airline bags or cloth bundles and went off to spend the holiday with their families. Often that meant crossing the border; the Kowloon station, a sedate little brick building with a clock tower, heaved with good-natured masses, shoving and shouting and shouldering their way on board the trains. The Lo Wu border crossing, normally an austere place, was almost cheerful as the hordes bustled through. Immigration formalities went by the board.

The Europeans were left alone to face a three-day ordeal of cooking and washing up for themselves. Scrymgeour, whose professor's salary made him a wealthy man, checked into the Repulse Bay Hotel and had the place's speciality, flambé Morello cherries, for dessert every evening. Mary cooked Sharkey black puddings,

which he pronounced excellent, and a Chinese concoction
of her own featuring shredded beef and green peppers,
which he pronounced even better. Verity, amid the roar of
dehumidifiers in Stewart Terrace, lived off tinned tuna fish
and ravioli.

At midnight, to a firecracker fortissimo, the Year of the
Tiger was ushered in. Ships in the harbour sounded their
sirens; Europeans clinked their glasses, wished each other a
happy new year, drank copiously and staggered off to beds
they had forgotten to make the previous morning.

Wherever there were Chinese, children bowed to their
parents and were given lucky money. The inner courtyards
of houses were strewn with sesame seeds and sprigs of fir and
cypress, which were then set on fire to represent the passing
of the Year of the Ox. Lamps were lit at the shrine of the
Kitchen God (who had gone off on a Celestial Visit, thus
celebrating the holiday himself). House doors were locked
and sealed; and at five in the morning, an hour at which
Scrymgeour was still snoring in his hotel room, the
householders unlocked them, spoke words of good omen and
burned paper representations of the gods, to the bursting of
yet more crackers.

Then every occupant of the house bowed three times to
its own family gods and ancestral tablets, and – in southern
China at least – a bowl of rice was placed on the altar,
together with flowers, cypress sprigs and ten pairs of
chopsticks. That done, the Year of the Tiger could be said to
have arrived, definitively.

Mary explained to Sharkey the significance of the tiger in
Chinese mythology. 'He's the king of the land beasts as the
dragon is king of the water beasts. If a tiger eats you he
enslaves your spirit. So watch out.'

'I'm not looking forward to a year that has an animal like that for its emblem.'

'There are compensations. Tigers are expert at chasing demons.'

'That's something, I suppose.'

And so the New Year came in: a year of power and violence, of the masculine principle which the tiger wears in the character of wang in the four stripes on his forehead. Perhaps there'd be demon-chasing too, thought Mary. She hoped so, because there always were demons to chase.

Verity's demons were those that assail lonely men. They had been getting worse with the years and the only way to fight them, he found, was to go into his empty office and work at his files. He got a lot done that way, but sometimes a shiver would run down his spine at the feeling of utter solitude he had, the absence of every human being but himself.

He remembered how before the war Chinese children were made to wear suits of tiger clothes to protect them from baneful influences. These consisted of striped yellow jackets, caps with furry ears and tiger-shoes, which had bewhiskered heads in front and tails at the back.

He was not the most imaginative of men but he couldn't help wishing he had such a suit himself.

Shortly after New Year, in cold, clinging weather, Inspector Dashwood's men made their arrests. The event was something of a damp squib as only two people were involved; one of these was from the T'ung and the other from the Twenty-One K. Their names were Wong Au Nai and Lim Sik Fuk; Verity remembered how Joe Miners had mentioned both of them months before, and was impressed with his expertise.

It was a relief to him that something, however insignificant, had happened. As his body grew weaker his sensitivity to criticism had increased; this event would at least eliminate one cause for reproach.

The trial was held in Hong Kong's tiny neo-classical courthouse in Statue Square. Fog blanketed the harbour, ships called to each other with mournful siren-blasts like large sad beasts in pain.

Among the evidence presented was triad paraphernalia. The constables had seized from Lim Sik Fuk a red robe with a spider's web embroidered across the belly, a red pennant with a serrated yellow edge and a large curved sword legally classified as an offensive weapon. Wong Au Nai had the same minus the sword, which neatly encapsulated the difference between the Twenty-One K and the T'ung.

There was, for once, clear evidence of intimidation. Wong had been rash enough to commit to paper a demand for money presented to a tray-hawker and seal it with the official triad chop; he was given six months in gaol. As for Lim, a stall-holder had agreed to testify against him but when he took the stand his courage failed him and he said nothing. So Lim got off with the statutory hundred dollar fine for being in possession of an offensive weapon.

When the trial was over Verity and Miners stood for a few moments on the courthouse steps discussing it. Joe was filling his pipe, and Verity was looking out over the forest of parking meters and car roofs in the square towards the flat low wall of the Star Ferry concourse, the bulbous façade of the Hong Kong Club and, behind that again, the building site for the new City Hall: a concrete cliff behind bamboo-and-raffia scaffolding whose crazy lines made it look unsafe. Only when this had come down would the clean geometry emerge.

'Strange business, that stall-holder who wouldn't talk,' said Verity.

'Not so strange as the fact that he agreed to do so in the first place,' said Joe, puffing mightily.

'But the tray-hawker spoke up all right ... '

'Only against the T'ung. A dying organisation. Twenty-One K is a different kettle of fish.'

'I see what you mean,' conceded Verity. 'Will he be all right, do you think?' he went on, concerned.

'For a couple of months, maybe.' Miners's voice was sombre. 'They'll let him sweat it out. Make his life a misery. Then they'll strike.'

'But that's horrible!'

'Triads are horrible.' Joe took the pipe from his mouth but the filament of spittle didn't let it wander far. 'And there's bugger all we can do about it!'

Verity had never heard him so passionate before.

☞

One afternoon when Sharkey was gazing into Gande Price's window, wondering whether he could afford a case of Pouilly-Fuissé, a voice whispered in his ear: 'Don't worry, squire. It may never happen.'

'Hello, Gus,' he said without enthusiasm.

'You look glum.'

'I'm just off to Fanling to do a piece on some young Australian golfers. They're playing in the Hong Kong Open. Isn't that enough to make anybody look glum?'

'When do you finish?'

'Dunno. Late.'

'Not too late, I hope. I was going to invite you to a stag-do.'

'Stag-do?' The unregenerate part of Sharkey perked up.

'Yeah. Rita's doing a strip. And we've got some blue films. Come along if you can make it.'

It was a quarter to twelve before he parked the Hillman outside the Wanchai restaurant Donoghue had mentioned but he decided to look in just the same. Mary wasn't expecting him until after midnight.

The party was in an upstairs room; by the time he arrived everybody was drunk. The show was just finishing; Rita was divesting herself of her G-string and planting a triumphant foot on the torso of a guest who had passed out on the floor. In this heroic attitude she presented the assembled company with a grandstand view of her silky black triangle, glossy as a spaniel's pelt. Her thrown-back shoulders lent her breasts a spurious resilience.

Good old Rita, thought Sharkey, game to the end. Still waging a lone battle against mammary droop.

'Greetings, old man,' said a high, gargling voice: Teddy Broome. 'Tank up.'

A waiter handed Sharkey a San Mig, which he downed in a long draught. He looked around the room, which was carpeted and plushy, with red-painted walls decorated with geometric patterns in silver. There was a projector at one end, now being packed up; at the other a Chinese in a gold lamé suit was playing selections from South Pacific on the piano.

'I see it's all over,' said Sharkey. 'What have I missed?'

'Two Japanese girls with a rubber prick,' replied Teddy.

'Live or on film?'

'On film.'

'I've seen it.'

'Also a negro, a Filipino girl and a goat.'

'Where exactly was the goat?'

'In pole position, yuk-yuk-yuk.'

'Ouch,' said Sharkey. 'Waiter, another beer!'

As he drank Ed appeared. 'Hi, Liam. Long time no see. What are you doing these days?'

'Same as usual – brain surgery.' He raised a palsied hand; it was a routine he had with Ed.

Donoghue now appeared – a dangerous-looking, half-cut Donoghue who said lazily: 'So you were able to make it after all.'

'How are you making out these days?' continued Ed. His voice was full of professional concern, as though he were Sharkey's doctor.

'Liam seems to have retired from the pipe-laying business,' put in Donoghue.

'Please!' retorted Sharkey. 'Some things are sacred.' He turned quickly to Teddy; anxious to change the subject. 'What price motor sport?' he asked.

'Firing on all cylinders,' was the response. 'Old Walter has imported a one and a half litre Lotus. Proper racing job; for Macau. He's giving me a spin in her tomorrow.' His moustache twitched in anticipation.

While Teddy descanted on the new Lotus, Donoghue and

Ed drifted away. Two or three beers later they were back. The room had half-emptied.

'Hey fellas,' called Ed. 'What say we go round to the Princess Garden? They've got new girls there. We could get fixed up easy.'

Sharkey, now fuddled, was tempted but had the strength of mind to say 'No dice. I've had a long day. Besides, I've got a headache.'

'Hey, man, that's what mummy says to daddy when she doesn't want to do it!'

'Maybe Liam wants to go home to mummy,' said Donoghue icily. Sharkey recognised the danger signals; he had seen Gus like this before, just before he beat up three American sailors in a waterfront bar. He'd better watch his step or he'd end up in a fight which he couldn't possibly win.

'Shut up, Gus,' cried Ed. 'This is supposed to be a party.' In spite of his lifestyle he was essentially an innocent.

But Gus was not going to shut up. 'Got a headache, Liam? Must be getting old; can't make it with the younger generation any more. That's why you've shacked up with granny.'

'Hey, Steady on, Gus!' yelped Teddy, another would-be peace-maker.

Sharkey flushed. Watching his step had become irrelevant – God damn it, he had some shreds of pride left! He took Gus by the shirt-front and said 'You're an ignorant slob. If somebody gave you a whole wit you'd still only be a half-wit.'

The next thing he knew a fist had exploded in his face. His jaw was stricken with sudden numbness. Things moved fast and confusedly; the world spun around him and didn't right itself until he found himself back in his car, which Teddy was driving.

'Whass going on?' he asked thickly.

'I'm taking you home,' said Teddy.

'Where's your own bus?'

'Ed's bringing it. Come on; got to get you to bed.'

Sharkey touched his mouth, gingerly; his lower lip was the size of a hen's egg. 'Christ almighty,' he moaned.

'Bit of a lump, what?'

'Bloody right. What the hell will I look like tomorrow?' .

'Don't worry, it'll go down.'

They were climbing the steep incline of Breezy Path. Broome turned the car sharply into the entrance and parked it in Sharkey's garage space. He helped his passenger out, deposited him in the lift and pressed the button for the eighth floor. 'Got to go, old man,' he said. 'Ed's picking me up in the street below. – Don't think too badly of Gus, though; he was as pissed as arse-holes.' With that he vanished.

Sharkey was struggling to get his key into the lock when the door opened of its own accord. Mary was standing there in her dressing gown, looking concerned.

'I told you not to wait up,' he growled, forcing the words past his swollen lip.

She said helplessly: 'What's going on, Liam?'

The worry on her face made him suddenly furious. 'Don't ask,' he slurred. 'We'll talk tomorrow.'

She clearly couldn't make out what he was saying. 'But, Liam ... ,' she began.

'Liam nothing!' he spluttered. 'Go to bed. I said we'll talk tomorrow.'

She stepped back as though afraid he would hit her. He made unsteadily for the bathroom to sponge his aching jaw

The following morning he surfaced to awareness of an injured lip and Mary sitting up in bed beside him with puzzlement written large on her face.

'We must have a heart-to-heart,' she said firmly.

'My jaw hurts,' he groaned.

'No matter about that. We must talk.'

He clenched his fist; she saw it and bridled. 'Don't be impossible!' she cried.

'I need a pee,' he said. It was true; he had drunk a lot of beer. But he also wanted to give himself time to think.

He peed sitting down. The pan in his bathroom was so low that aiming a jet at it in his present condition would have been to court disaster. So he sat there emptying his bladder and staring self-pityingly in the mirror at the great blue bruise, by now yellowing round the edges, on his lip. Was this the face of a man who deserved to be hen-pecked?

He washed his hands and returned to the bedroom. Mary, lying stiffly on the bed, said: 'Come on then. Tell me what happened?'

'Donoghue hit me.'

'I hope you hit him back!'

'I didn't have time.'

'What made him do a thing like that?'

'He was plastered.'

Mary, aggrieved by his lack of communication, got out of bed and started looking for her clothes. 'Whatever you do don't tell me,' she said sarcastically. 'I know my place.'

'For Christ's sake don't nag!' he retorted.

'And don't you be a bastard.'

'Snap.'

Mary, thoroughly angry now, said: 'Correction. Don't be a little bastard – a little, ferret-faced bastard.'

'If I'm little you're large. Barrage balloon! Porker!'

There was a pause. Mary turned pale. 'This is in earnest, I see.' She had taken off her nightdress and was standing there naked with her panties in her hand, looking hurt.

The sight brought him to his senses. 'I'm sorry,' he muttered. 'I am a bastard. To tell you the truth, I don't know why you bother with me. You could get better than me any day.'

'Hadn't you better tell me about it?' she suggested, partly mollified, and put her underclothes on.

'It was like this. Donoghue invited me to a stag-do ... '

'Oh no!'

'I'm afraid so. But the show was over by the time I arrived. Then we had a couple of drinks and he started needling me. About shacking up with granny, as he called it. I told him where to get off, and he hit me. Teddy Broome got me home.'

Mary thought for a moment. 'Right,' she said. 'But what I'd like to know is: did you not want to tell me this out of consideration or because you were ashamed of going to the stag-do in the first place?'

'A bit of both, I think.'

'Hm. – I suppose I should be grateful that you disagreed with Donoghue in the first place. – That is, if you really did.'

Jesus Christ,' said Sharkey wearily.

'Don't blaspheme.'

'We're heading for a pointless row. Isn't that enough to make anybody blaspheme?'

'Let me make one thing clear,' said Mary with a residue of

bitterness, 'you don't have to stay with me unless you want to. There must be dozens of little tarts who would be only too willing to minister to your wants. And they'd be much better in bed than I am.'

Sharkey knew when a major effort was called for. He said: 'Let's get things straight, Mary. You're a lovely sexy woman. Yes, you are. – And I'm not just talking about your physical attributes; you've got it up here too.' He tapped his temple with his forefinger. 'And please don't credit that prat Lawrence when he rabbits on about sex-in-the-head. The head's the main theatre of activity.'

'I tend to agree with that,' said Mary, reflectively.

'Good. We're in agreement then: D.H. Lawrence is, in every sense of the word, a useless prick.'

Mary burst out in a great splutter of laughter. 'You're utterly revolting, Liam, but you do have the gift of the gab. It must be the Irish in you.'

He grinned back at her. 'Is it pax then?'

'All right. Pax.'

'And I'm sorry I called you names.'

'I started it, remember?' she said ruefully. 'But I did mean what I said about not staying with me unless you wanted to.'

As she stood there in her panties like a big schoolgirl he was touched by genuine feeling. He kissed her pink nipples one by one and said: 'Now how about dressing? Ah Hoy will be getting impatient about breakfast.'

So they breakfasted. And as they ate Sharkey reflected on what had just happened. Every successfully negotiated row, he concluded, created an additional bond between people. He had little experience of long-term relationships, but that was how they seemed to work. In his own case the only discordant notes were Donoghue's fist and, above all, what

Donoghue had said. They hung in Sharkey's flesh like poisoned darts. The question was: how strong would the poison be?

They were returning to Hong Kong after a day spent on Lantau. 'I meant to tell you,' said Jeffrey. 'It was probably information I gave that led to the arrest of Wong.'

'What?' Verity was startled. He added, sternly, 'You mustn't put yourself in danger, Jeffrey; I told you so before.' The thought of somehow losing the boy filled him with alarm.

Jeffrey smiled; a ray of afternoon sunshine glinted on his spectacles. 'Oh, there was no danger, Mr Verity. It all happened by chance. Shall I tell you about it?'

'I shall be disappointed if you don't.'

'Well, I happened to be buying lucky money for New Year from a hawker, when some boys came along and made mock of him. "Look out or Grass Sandal will get you," they were saying, "and its not lucky money he's after." He chased them off saying something about a man not being able to make his living nowadays. "Just let them wait," he said, "I know who they are. I know how to put a stop to their monkey tricks." What could I do then but tell him he must report anything he knew to the police? I took him along to the nearest sub-station and made him report the boys as neighbours and friends of a certain Wong Au Nai; if they paid a visit to where he lived they might find something interesting. So they did, and found the papers and the sword hidden under a mattress.'

Verity shivered. 'That was public-spirited of you, Jeffrey,' he said, 'but these are dangerous things to get mixed up in. Dumbell is a very small place.'

'Don't worry, Mr Verity. I didn't actually go into the sub-station myself. I told the hawker that if I discovered he hadn't reported the incident I would be forced to report him.'

'Well, at least you've been shrewd,' said Verity, 'but for God's sake don't ever do it again.'

He shuddered involuntarily. A frightening vision had just occurred to him: of Jeffrey dead, Jeffrey struck down by some triad thug, lying in his own blood. It came with horrifying distinctness, but then the idea of death had been running in his mind for weeks now. He simply couldn't shake it off.

As chance would have it they were sailing past that damned islet at the time. No wonder the accursed skull-and-bones was rattling!

'Is something wrong, Mr Verity?' Jeffrey's nose wrinkled with concern.

'Of course not!' he barked, the old, peppery Verity reasserting himself He regretted it immediately. 'I'm sorry, Jeffrey,' he said. 'It was nothing.'

The boy nodded understandingly, but clearly didn't believe him. And as that low, yellow silhouette loomed up he felt a sudden need to confide in him.

'Do you see that island?' he said.

'Which one do you mean?'

'The one on the port bow there. It's called Siu Kau Yi Chau.'

Jeffrey's eyes narrowed. 'Indeed? I never heard of it before.'

'It's an evil place, Jeffrey.'

The boy looked at him with concern, making him hesitate: would he think him crazy? Perhaps he was a little crazy; this obsession of his was surely not quite sane.

But he had to talk. 'Something dreadful happened there during the war,' he said.

'What was that?'

'The Japanese marooned people there. Left them without food or water, to die.'

Jeffrey made a face. 'That was indeed an evil thing.'

'I ... I can't get my mind off what their last moments must have been. Did they go mad and attack each other? Did they turn cannibal? And how did the final survivor feel, dying there with decaying bodies – maybe even half-eaten ones – all round him?'

There was a moment's silence before he went on.

'The authorities had the place cleaned up after the war. They buried all the human remains they could find, but I'm told you can still happen on the odd human bone.'

As Jeffrey looked at the islet, daunted but not afraid, Verity suddenly realised what he must do. He must play the man, the sore must be lanced. He had hardly the strength to do it on his own, and in the company of indifferent, perhaps scornful people it would be quite impossible. But along with a discreet, understanding person like Jeffrey – that was something different altogether.

'Let's stop the launch and land there,' he said firmly.

The boy's reaction was unexpected. 'Oh, no, Mr Verity! Please do not!' His voice was sharp, and he was pale under his golden burnish.

'What's the matter, Jeffrey?' he asked.

'Wouldn't there be ghosts?' faltered the boy.

'You're not afraid of them, are you?'

Jeffrey nodded, shamefaced. 'We all are,' he said. 'No matter how we've been educated.'

Verity's resolve melted. 'I'm sorry,' he said. 'I should have realised.' He looked again at the islet; it had won this time, the bastard.

'Please don't talk about going to places like that, Mr Verity,' Jeffrey was saying, his colour slowly returning.

'Of course not, if you don't like it. It's just that ... it's better sometimes to face up to the things you fear.'

'Not ghosts, Mr Verity.' He managed a smile.

'Don't worry. I shan't go there now.'

They sailed on until the islet faded behind. Verity was in an odd frame of mind. He was disappointed, of course; the sore remained unlanced. But an unavowed part of him was relieved. The demons were hell to live with, but at least they were familiar, they were his own. Might not the blank horror of their absence be even worse?

Looking across at Jeffrey, he felt closer to him than ever. They were a pair, the two of them, each with his secret irrational fear. Weaknesses, he reflected, were like the hooked atoms of Epicurus; our flawed human affections could never gain hold on the smooth surface of perfection.

Sharkey went once a week to General K'ou's shack in Shaukiwan. Sometimes Mr Teng was there too and, as his Mandarin improved, he was able to exchange polite greetings with him. But Mr Li rarely appeared; he often worked double shifts at the Star Ferry.

The General gave him access to an ancient China, now vanished. He marvelled how the old man and Teng were able to reel off thousands of lines of Confucius, Mencius and the poets, their voices full of ceremonious relish. What a poor figure he himself would have cut had he been asked to do the same in English! The only texts he knew by heart were those he had been given as school impositions, like Hamlet's soliloquy or the *Ode To A Nightingale.*

Not that K'ou had any illusions about the relevance of this age-old discipline. He pointed out, with sad courtesy, that in the contemporary world it had about as much relevance as those Greek and Latin tags the Victorians used to bandy about. The ancient culture was like an Egyptian mummy, he said; there was a real man inside the linen wrappings, but he was dead.

One day Chernikov was present too, and Sharkey was able to ask him about things he hadn't understood because of his imperfect Mandarin. 'These men are not to be envied,' said the Russian in his rumbling voice. 'This place is entirely foreign to them and they have no home left to go to.'

'Isn't it the same for you?'

'Not at all. We Russians can go anywhere in western Europe without really leaving home. The cultures are similar and the languages easy to learn. Imagine yourself set down in the middle of China with no England to go back to – that's how it is for the General.'

'But this is Hong Kong. He's in China.'

'Not his China. This is a commercial city that doesn't value the classics. All it cares for is money.' His voice vibrated disapproval; Sharkey hid a smile but it was a sympathetic one.

'And even if he had free passage across the border,'

Chernikov went on, 'what would he find? A shattered culture; the classics undermined, even the script simplified. Can you imagine a communist government in London which has rewritten Shakespeare in terms of *The East Is Red* and pulped the original editions? That is the way things are tending.' He took Sharkey's arm to emphasise his point. 'The universities are being purged of the past. Only abroad do a few scholars pore over the old texts.'

All this had been said in English. The General, who had been sitting with his hands in his lap, asked politely what they had been talking about. The Russian and he had a long conversation in Mandarin, which Sharkey could not wholly follow, then the Russian explained in English.

'General K'ou wishes you to know that even now he is not without hope. He envisages a future in which the West takes an ever greater interest in things Chinese. Gradually the Chinese culture permeates its own, more materialist values. Then, at some time in the distant future, it will hand that culture back to the Chinese. The wheel will come full circle.'

What a lovely, preposterous dream it was! And what pride these Chinese had! Even when they were down and out they still believed their culture would dominate the world. Sharkey looked at the frail figure of the General, whom he himself had once rescued, and hardly knew whether to feel admiration or amazement.

Meanwhile the General himself was pointing to a scroll on the wall and saying something to Chernikov. The Russian, smiling and nodding, said: 'He wants me to tell you a story. About his namesake, King K'ou Ch'ien, who, as you may remember, was captured by his rival, the King of Wu.

'That was not the end of the story. After three years of captivity the king of Wu released him and allowed him to return to his own country of Yuëh. To express his gratitude he sent the king of Wu a special gift: the most beautiful concubine in the land. The king of Wu became so infatuated with her that he neglected the task of governing; whereupon our king, K'ou Ch'ien, marched in at the head of an army. Where he had once lain in captivity he now reigned.'

Sharkey laughed. 'I don't quite know why, but that's a very Chinese story!'

'"It is indeed.'

'Does the concubine represent Chinese culture? And is the west the king of Wu?'

The Russian laughed uproariously, but did not answer. Instead he pointed to the scroll and read the text inscribed on it. 'It is from Confucius,' he said, 'and reads as follows: "With coarse rice to eat, with water to drink, with my bent arm for a pillow, I nevertheless feel joy".'

The K'ou clan had clearly not changed much over the centuries.

Interestingly, the General was acquainted with the Wilson's father and visited his flat from time to time. Wilson's father spoke a few words of Mandarin; when the General and he were at loss for a word they would scribble the character for it on a piece of paper.

'These people have a very hard life,' said the old man, shaking his head sadly.

'Do you think so?' said Sharkey, surprised. 'Aren't they better off than most people here?'

The General was not disposed to grant this point. 'They are very unfortunate,' he murmured.

Sharkey realised that their deprivation, in K'ou's eyes, was the fact that they did not speak Mandarin.

As a privileged European Verity was granted a glimpse behind the scenes at the preparations for the Three Mountains Festival. It was still only February, and the event was nearly three months away. But as Mr Ng, importantly if toothlessly, said: 'We work at Festival all year. Festival is Dumbell Island.'

He took the District Officer on a tour of the assorted dusty sheds where the Residents' Associations and Mutual Aid Societies and Sports Clubs of Dumbell were preparing their coloured banners and gymnastic displays and tableaux. He also showed him the four shrines of the Queen of Heaven, which had acquired a fresh coat of red paint.

To be allowed to see the tableaux in preparation was a signal honour. 'You no see this before,' said Ng, ushering him into a big wooden hut. The lazy-eyed Mr Lam was waiting at the door to do the honours.

'At last I discover how miracles are performed,' said Verity in Cantonese. The half-dozen workmen standing around in shorts and singlets grinned with pleasure.

The theme of this particular float was Drugs Are A Self-Killer. Mr Lam showed him an assemblage of aluminium rods, all shaped and welded together, that would have graced a contemporary art gallery. He demonstrated how this could be inserted under a child's clothes, run up the leg and chest and arm, then on along the leg of a second child, who would then appear to be standing on the first child's hand.

'How will they be dressed?' asked Verity.

'I think you wait till festival,' replied Lam with a burst of laughter.

To visit the next tableau they had to shuffle their way along the praya, past sniffing dogs and shuffling people, with the ubiquitous smell of dried salt fish in their nostrils.

'When do you start building the bun towers?' enquired Verity.

'Not till April. Plenty time.'

'Provided you can all agree till then ... '

'We all agree. Very friendly place here.'

'You've had no disagreements since the by-elections then?'

'Oh no, Fu Mu Kuan. Everybody friends here.'

At that point Verity heard, maybe twenty yards away, a short sharp pop, then another. Everybody started shouting and running about in confusion; out of the general ruck one figure emerged, running harder than all the others. He might have had the hounds of hell after him; he ran and twisted so crazily, cannoning off passers-by and finally disappearing down a side-street. The one thing Verity noticed about him was that he had unusually glossy hair.

'What on earth is going on?' he shouted. Ng was screaming like a madman; no sense could be got out of him. He would have to do something on his own.

Instinct took over; he squared his shoulders. He was a white man, a person in authority, on whom it was incumbent to set an example. This damned debility of his might have diminished him. but by heaven he wasn't going to let it grind him down. 'Let me through, please,' he called out in Cantonese, and walked purposefully in the direction the shots had come from.

A knot of people was standing round two blood-stained bundles lying on the ground, talking urgently in Cantonese; the abruptness of the language made it sound as though they were quarrelling. The first bundle, a man in a crumpled suit, was very still; the other, an elderly woman selling squid he had noticed on the way there, was conscious but bleeding through her black samfu.

'Send for the police,' Verity ordered.

'Police coming, sir,' replied a chorus of voices. And indeed, at that moment, a wiry little constable with a revolver holster almost as big as himself came up. He took one look at the two victims and said: 'Send for a doctor.' Someone on the edge of the crowd ran off.

The man in the suit being clearly dead, Verity concentrated on the woman, who didn't seem to be in immediate danger. 'You'll be all right,' he said reassuringly.

She grinned gamely in reply but must have lost a fair amount of blood because the pupils of her eyes rolled up under the lids. Something would have to be done, and quickly.

'Who are you, sir?' enquired the constable, producing a handkerchief and trying to stem the woman's flow of blood.

'Sorry. I should have told you. I am the District Officer for this island.'

'Thank you for helping.'

The constable and he rolled up the woman's sleeve and examined her upper arm: blood was coming from a wound in it in little spurts. 'This could be dangerous,' said Verity. 'Will somebody get me a stick please? Any kind of stick.' He ripped off his shirt and started tearing it into strips, to make a tourniquet.

Old Ng was flapping around, protesting to one and all at the Fu Mu Kuan's being exposed to such indignity.

Verity ignored him. 'A stick, I said!' he called out more urgently; the old man's antics were making him angry. 'A stick or a broom-handle, anything!'

Someone rushed out of a nearby hardware store and handed him a frying pan. It was incongruous but it would do. His shirt was already round the old woman's arm in a makeshift bandage; he slipped the pan handle under it and started turning. It was thankless work; the pan itself kept getting in the way, banging against her ribs and the knees of the bystanders.

'Keep back, please,' ordered the constable.

'Keep back!' shrieked Ng, vituperating wildly.

Verity kept doggedly to his task. He had just managed to stop the flow of blood when the doctor arrived: a small man with protruding teeth. He took over immediately, sending someone off to the first aid post for a stretcher and, as if as an afterthought, calling for a blanket to be thrown over the dead man. Five minutes gone, thought Verity, and he's forgotten already.

The constable was now questioning the bystanders. 'Did anyone see who fired the shots?'

'There were two of them ... '

'No, three!'

'The third one was running away. The other two were firing at him.'

'Why did they shoot this man and woman then?'

'They were in the way.'

'You mean they were innocent bystanders?'

There was a chorus of affirmation. Verity, bare to the waist, his tanned body boasting a few grizzled chest-hairs, was able to confirm some of these statements. 'There certainly was a man running away; I saw him. He went down that street over there.' He pointed. 'I didn't see his attackers at all.'

'They ran back the way they came,' said a voice. A chorus of other voices shouted agreement.

'Did no one try to follow them?' asked the constable, looking up from his notebook.

'Follow men with guns?! Who do you think we are?' Laughter, mixed with indignation.

At this point Ng, who had been padding up and down like a caged lion, started yelling at them. 'Cowards! Sons of whores! You let them get away!'

'Did anyone recognise them?' interposed Verity, hoping to calm him down.

'Of course they didn't!' shrilled Ng. 'What local man would bring such disgrace on us? They'll have come from Hong Kong.' Mutterings of approval; nothing better could be expected of people who came from there.

Verity turned to the constable. 'Will you be wanting statements from my friend and myself?'

'No, sir. You were not direct witnesses. Thank you for your help.'

So they were able to go. Verity picked up his bush jacket from where he had thrown it to take off his shirt. His wallet was still there, intact, in the inside pocket. All honour to the people of Dumbell, he thought.

Ng was still muttering to himself like a man demented. 'What a disgrace! And in front of the Father Mother Officer too! We are shamed in the eyes of the world.'

His vehemence was surprising to Verity; had the old man lost face as badly as that? Then a thought struck him. Wasn't the Dumbell festival supposed to stand for repentance and reconciliation? And might the gods now forsake it? Perhaps that was Ng's worry. He said: 'All this isn't going to affect the festival, is it?'

Ng stared at him with undisguised astonishment. 'Mista Wei Li Ti,' he said with scarcely disguised scorn, 'the

Dumbell Festival is known all over the world.'

Only when he was alone in the *Sir Cecil Clementi* did Verity's body catch up with his mind. A man had been killed within yards of him, in daylight, and in his own district! And he himself had done things he no longer thought himself physically capable of.

A wave of tiredness and nausea engulfed him. He was on the verge of vomiting; his teeth chattered, his knees shook. He had to clench his jaw and jam his legs against a bulkhead, otherwise he could not have held his body still.

Back on dry land, he had to leave his car in its parking space – he was quite incapable of driving – and take a taxi back to Stewart Terrace.

About then the news that the dubbing of *The Forty-Seven Ronin* had folded reached Sharkey. He was almost glad of it. He was deluged with contracts from the *Kwangtung Courier*, including more from Teddy Broome's drugs series. It was getting more and more difficult to fit them in with his university work.

He was just finishing his eleven o'clock tutorial, looking forward to a coffee in the staff common room, when the phone rang. It was for him. Teddy again, telling him about the dubbing and in the same breath asking him to dash across to the Peninsula hotel and interview a passing Hollywood film star. He grabbed a sandwich and ran.

Interviewing film actors was a cinch; you asked them about their latest film and how they liked Hong Kong and that was that. So two o'clock found him back in Pokfulam for his two o'clock lecture on Montesquieu. After that he drove down to the Courier office and got the star's file out of the morgue. He had just finished writing up his piece, about half past five, when Teddy appeared, waddling along like an apologetic duck. 'Inspector Borland's waiting for you, old boy. At Police HQ. Hope you don't mind.'

Sharkey did mind. 'For Christ's sake, Teddy, what is it this time?'

'Drugs again.'

'But I'm shagged. Can't it wait for another day?'

It couldn't, and he couldn't say no. So it was in a mutinous frame of mind that he found himself sitting in the police Landrover, bowling along Boundary Street to an unspecified destination.

It wasn't just that he was tired. He was also hungry, and the Chinese urban smell mingled with petrol fumes made him feel sick. As well as that, his bruised mouth had not completely healed, and the spiritual hurt of it was still with him.

'I'm taking you to an arrest,' said Inspector Borland in his mellifluous voice.

'Didn't know you could forecast these things,' muttered Sharkey between his teeth.

'Some you can. You'll see what I mean in a minute.'

The neon signs were just lighting up. They drove in a cocoon of traffic-noise, with occasional snatches of Chinese music from transistor radios riding over it. Kai Tak airport loomed up, with an airliner passing overhead in a thunderous roar that made one's teeth shake. It was so low that Sharkey imagined its undercarriage whisking lines of washing from the tenement roofs.

They turned left into a tangle of ramshackle tenements and tumbledown houses with saplings growing out of the walls: this was Kowloon City, an enclave that had been left out of the treaty by which Britain leased the New Territories and consequently – in theory at least – still under the jurisdiction of mainland China. That did not prevent the Hong Kong Police from exercising occasional authority there.

The car stopped at a small local sub-station where they picked up a detachment consisting of a sergeant, five spick-and-span constables and a photographer in a van and drove a couple of hundred yards down an ill-lit street. 'This is where we get out,' said Borland.

They entered a crumbling house by a non-existent door; there were fading Chinese characters running down the jambs. A fetid corridor led to the back entrance and a piece of waste ground dotted with wooden shacks. One or two Chinese, walking in the half-light, turned incurious faces towards them and looked away; what was a police raid more or less to them?

The sergeant walked up to one of these shacks. 'Open up. It's the police,' he said, pushing the door open with his elbow.

Absolutely nothing happened. There was neither noise not movement. Sharkey felt a prickling at the nape of his neck. They all went inside: silence, and darkness, suddenly punctuated by an explosion of phosphorescent brightness: the photographer had used his flash.

A terrible scene was etched on Sharkey's memory. Dirt, rubble, torn raffia mats with men sitting or lying on them, inhaling smoke through hollow bamboos. Spectral men, so thin you wondered if they would ever be able to stagger to their feet again. A woman with her arms folded across her breast, like a cross-bones. A man lying beside her with a blue line round his nostrils. Tattered clothes hanging from nails, like obscene flowers.

As the dark descended again Sharkey heard his own voice almost shrieking: 'For Christ's sake, why don't they move?'

'They're past that,' came Borland's voice.

A second flash. This time Sharkey was able to take in the wider scene. A table with a litter of cardboard boxes, loose matches and a sheet of silver paper. A grimy metal mug covered with a film of dust: it must have stood there unregarded for weeks. And, by the table, three more men, frozen in the act of picking white granules from an old biscuit tin.

Borland and the sergeant switched on torches. At last one of the three at the table moved. His skin was pulled intolerably tight over his cheek bones; his cropped hair seemed too vigorous for the rest of him. Sharkey had never seen such blank eyes.

'God, but it's terrible,' he said.

'This is the reality of it,' responded Borland, giving an order in Cantonese.

His men closed in to make their arrests. They moved with great gentleness, as if they were hospital attendants dealing with very old men. They helped them to their feet, quietly disentangling them from the clobber of the shack. The air was filled with the smell of heroin.

Sharkey had always regarded himself as pretty tough, but now fear squeezed his entrails. This was real vice, this was real evil. What did a self-dramatising little shit like himself, who thought himself a fine Byronic devil because he'd been to bed with a few women, know about it? He felt both disgusted and humbled.

The addicts were led away with shuffling steps, like pensioners on an outing. He shuddered.

'You feeling all right?' asked Borland.

'I think so.'

'At any rate it's a story for you.'

That was true; there was work to be done here, work that would keep the dreadful vision at bay. He pulled out his reporter's notepad and was soon jotting things down in his personal longhand: how they got the tip-off, the estimated importance of the ring they had uncovered, the possibility of it leading to something bigger.

'This is off the record, of course,' said Borland. 'But if we thought it would lead to something bigger we would have let them carry on for a bit.'

Sharkey's pencil stood poised. 'And where do their supplies come from?'

'You're a holy terror for asking awkward questions! This is off the record too, but a lot of chains lead back to Western Districts. Trouble is, they go cold there. We can't trace them any further.'

He was flattered by Borland's confidence. It came about because they were both Wellington men, he knew. Not long ago he would have made mock of that fact; but in the face of what he had seen today there wasn't much occasion for mockery.

The press raised a great hullabaloo over what the *Kwangtung Courier* called the Dumbell Slaying. For once, though, Verity

was spared much of the embarrassment because of the
decisive way he had acted. The newspapers, both in English
and Chinese, praised him for taking charge of affairs so
promptly; he even enjoyed the dubious honour of having his
photograph printed.

But his subconscious did not echo these plaudits. He was
plagued by a long recurring dream that had its starting point
in the crowds that swirled round the praya that day. He
would be among the jostling mass of human beings,
oppressed by a sense of doom but unable to move because of
his condition. Then the shooting would take place as he
remembered it, but with an unsuspected consequence: a
hundred Chinese fingers pointed at himself as the assassin.

His knees were unlocked as if by magic; he ran for his life.
All around him were rows of hostile men with arms
outstretched, like enormous tentacles. He avoided them
somehow and reached the jetty; the government launch was
there waiting.

'Come this way!' cried a voice which he recognised as
Jeffrey's; he threw himself on board. Jeffrey was at the helm,
his glasses glinting underneath a Marine Department
peaked cap.

They carved their way through the flotilla of sampans
which bobbed in their wash and found themselves in the
open sea. 'Where are you taking me?' he asked, concerned.

'Where you've always wanted to go,' said Jeffrey, smiling a
broad, trust-inviting smile. Verity smiled back, in relief, and
closed his eyes. But his sense of doom persisted.

At last the launch glided alongside a small concrete jetty,
choked with tendrils of green seaweed. He stumbled on to
the land and stood half-terrified and half astonished. The
launch sped away.

He was in the place he feared most on earth, that sinister little island. What was he to do? Panic-stricken, he made for high ground, dragging his reluctant body up the island's low spine.

On the other side, there was a wide crater that was moving with some kind of life. Focussing his eyes on it, he saw to his horror that it was full of great white worms, like grave worms in medieval pictures. Their coils slithered over one another in a sea of white slime.

He knew with total certainty that if ever one of these tentacles were to touch him he was doomed. And of course it would happen; nothing could prevent it! Trying to turn round, he thrust his foot against the ground. It froze there, exactly as it had on that first morning on Dumbell.

He was falling, a slow, hieratical fall that brought him with horrifying inevitability into the lake of slime. One leprous tentacle flicked out, touched his cheek and slipped off. He sobbed with relief. But he kept sinking, deeper and deeper until the giant worms were around him in a baleful circle. A second tentacle slapped his face, covering it with a glue-like smear. Finally they were all upon him, about to engulf him ...

At that point consciousness, recognising that he had taken all he could bear, returned with a prolonged roaring rush, like an underground train in a tunnel.

Verity was not a man to attach much significance to dreams, but he soon realised that what he had fallen into was his own diseased body.

Lok Yuen must have had a highly efficient social secretary because Mary and Sharkey kept getting invitations: to parties and weddings and christenings (the Lok family were Christians), to dinners and beach barbecues. Rightly judging them to be official courtesies and no more, they turned them all down.

Then, one day in March, identical cards with embossed lettering and gold edges arrived. Wilson got one too. These were meant to be taken seriously.

They were invitations to the Loks' private box at the races; so, on the appointed day, the three of them found themselves standing outside the great concrete cliff that was the main stand of the Hong Kong Jockey Club's racecourse at Happy Valley. The narrow road was jammed with people, racing being the favourite sport of the Chinese.

A lift took them to an upper floor, where a long curving corridor presented a row of mahogany doors, each with a number and a name card in a brass frame. Racing had not yet begun; a crowd of Hong Kong's influential citizens was sauntering up and down: florid Europeans with their scraggy wives, small Chinese in Ascot wear with dove-grey toppers perched on their heads like thimbles on nutmegs.

The Loks were already assembled: the millionaire, glittering with gold from teeth and spectacles; his son Eugene and Diana; his young wife Edith, who had recently replaced Eugene's mother and whom Sharkey had never met before. Standing with their backs to the door, looking out over the racecourse, were two familiar figures, Scrymgeour and Rose.

'Alec!' cried Mary, putting her hand to her mouth, 'I'd completely forgotten about you!'

'I'd noticed, darling,' drawled Scrymgeour, 'but then you've had other things on your mind.' Rose smiled wolfishly.

'Why Liam!' mewed Diana, wiggling across to them. 'And Mrs Rhodes,' she added as an afterthought.

'Hello Diana,' said Sharkey, concealing a sudden pang of lust inspired by the area of thigh she was showing through the slit in her daffodil cheongsam; she looked good enough to eat, without pepper or salt.

'Come and say hello, Eugene,' called Diana imperiously. Her husband raised his eyes from his race-card and walked bonelessly across to them. They shook hands with him, Sharkey with distaste, Mary with a suppressed desire to straighten his tie and generally smarten him up.

'Shampeng!' called the millionaire, clasping his hands above his head like a victorious heavyweight. 'You too, young man,' he added, to Wilson, who was standing, blinking and forgotten, at the door of the box.

'Let me introduce you,' said Mary, swinging into action. 'Mr Lok, this is Wilson Ho.'

'Wilson who?'

'Wilson Ho.'

'Dunno him.'

'Wilson is the young man we have proposed for the Lok Yuen Scholarship,' Sharkey slid in dexterously.

'Oh yeah? – Didn't know he was coming.' He turned to the young man. 'You speak Freng now?'

'I am making reasonable progress,' said Wilson, his brow furrowed in concentration.

'I'm his teacher,' said Sharkey, 'and I can assure you that he's doing very well. – Wilson, recite some of that poem we were reading yesterday.'

Wilson cleared his throat and read the first four lines of Baudelaire's 'Albatros'.

'Very ni',' said the millionaire. 'Anything in it bou' tehtile?'

The arrival of a white-jacketed waiter with the champagne removed the necessity for an answer. Sharkey took a glass, nodded to Mrs Lok and drank to her health. She responded with a gracious smile.

She was an apparition in bronze and gold, a small, exquisitely proportioned doll with a helmet of lacquered hair. The cut of her cheongsam was even more expensive than Diana's, a fact which caused the latter visible distress. It was clear that the two ladies did not appreciate one another.

Sharkey had a sudden inspiration. 'Haven't I seen you somewhere before, Mrs Lok? In a film, for instance? I'm thinking of *The Dream of the Red Chamber*?'

Edith gave a little laugh; she was flattered. 'Oh that was a long time ago,' she said.

'I must beg to differ with you there,' said Sharkey gallantly. It had been no more than three years ago; he knew, because he had dubbed the film in question. If she wanted to push it further back in time that was her concern.

She moved away to talk to her husband. What a creation she was! He could have written her whole history out of his head. Bred up by a dragon of a mother, she would have lived in a block of flats beside the film studio inhabited solely by her kind, her virginity guarded over like the crown jewels until she should have landed a wealthy husband. Like her colleagues and rivals she was designed with middle-aged men in mind: child-doll-concubines with whom a man could imagine he was making love to his own daughter. Sharkey put it down as a good mark to himself that he did not feel any attraction to her. Unlike Diana – nothing of the child-bride in her!

There was a knock at the door and a tanned, powerfully-built Englishman of sixty came in. He had abundant Persil-white hair and a clipped moustache.

'Why, Rodja!' cried Lok. 'Come in plea. – You know everboh here?' He introduced his guests, naming them all correctly, and presented the visitor: 'Rodja Bulstro.'

Sharkey perked up. This was Roger Bulstrode, the current representative of the great compradore house, Bulstrode and Squire, which had existed since the time of the Opium War; some even believed that the Opium War had been fought on its behalf. Sharkey looked at him more closely. He exuded the mana of power, like a successful politician; his hair shone, his tan glowed, he looked as though he had been dipped in mildly phosphorescent paint.

'Have a dring,' said Lok, pressing a glass of champagne into his hand. 'Bottom up!'

Bulstrode clapped him on the back with his free hand. 'You old rogue,' he cried, 'what are you on today?'

'You li'e to know, eh?'

'I'd like to know a lot of things.'

'How 'bou dat new mercerise cotton we bling ou' nek year?' Lok gave him a crafty grin.

'Exactly!' Bulstrode guffawed, and punched Lok gently on the biceps.

'You can find ouh abou' dat any time you li'e. Jus' fik us up with dose sales ou'lehs in England.'

'You old villain! You know as well as I do that those stores all have their own suppliers. They don't want Orientex shirts on their shelves.'

'Oh, oh!' cried Lok in delighted horror. 'He even know name!'

'You bet I know the name.'

Lok looked at him archly. 'Maybe we do deal diffren way,' he said. 'We impor' through Denmark, Norway, some place li'e that. Cloth only, you see? Den make up some place like Lancashire, where loh of women ouh of work, come cheap. We knock other supplier on head.'

'You'll be breaking the law next!' exclaimed Bulstrode, tossing off his champagne. Both men laughed noisily. 'Now to serious matters. What about these ponies?'

Lok put on an earnest face. 'Nothing ver' goo today. Maybe Viking, third race. I know Chow, he own him. Say horse comin' on well.'

'Nothing in the first?'

'Fray not.'

'I'll just have to follow my hunch then.'

'Whah's that?'

Bulstrode wagged his finger. 'Wouldn't you like to know?' he said and departed.

When the door was well closed the millionaire spoke to his son. 'Eugene, go down puh five tousan dollar Sunseh Boulevard.'

Eugene collected the cash, plus the smaller bets of the others, and went.

'Oh father,' simpered Diana, 'you knew something after all.'

'I always know someting.' His gold teeth glittered triumphantly.

'Why didn't you tell Mr Bulstrode?' asked Edith shrewishly; she couldn't stand Diana's mincing ways with her husband.

'Business is business.' He laughed abruptly.

Eugene returned and the serious business of horse-racing began. For Sharkey it was merely boring; for Mary it was a penance. She stared moodily out through the plate-glass window to the rocky hills beyond, all bristling with high-rise apartment blocks. At ground level in Happy Valley itself, the great horseshoe of the track enclosed a chequerboard of football pitches, scuffed and yellow from overuse. In the spectator area thousands of people scurried about on unknown errands. What on earth were they all doing? What a bloody awful place, what bloody awful people.

They objectified the side of the Chinese people she deplored: namely their lack of talent for leisure. They seemed incapable of using freedom as a restorative activity in which the will was relaxed. They worked all day with corrosive ambition and when work was over they showered the money they had earned on horses or mistresses, always under the lash of material things – like that middle-aged couple she knew who sat all day in a wholesale meat store near Central Market. They were wealthy, they could easily have paid somebody else to do it. But they feared leisure; they had no idea of what to do with it if they had it.

To allay her boredom she placed a few bets. She lost on Wall Of China in the first, she lost on Petrarch in the second and Li Po on the third. By teatime she had also lost on Sun Yat Sen on the fourth she could hold her tongue no longer. 'I thought cricket was bad,' she declared, 'but this is far worse. And you lose your money.'

'I jus win tree tousan dollar,' said Lok, laughing triumphantly.

Scrymgeour then paraded his theory about the role of four-footed animals in history. So long as they were regarded as something to ride, eat or extract work from, a civilisation was healthy. But the moment they were treated as pets or racing machines it was doomed. 'Just look at Constantinople,' he said.

'They had chariot races as early as the Roman republic,' Sharkey objected – distractedly, because at that moment Diana was crossing her legs.

'That was training for battle,' countered Scrymgeour.

'A doubtful proposition,' sniffed Sharkey. Diana's legs on the other hand were a proposition about which there was no doubt whatsoever.

By now Lok was sending Wilson down to the bookie's with the bets; he had mentally incorporated the young man into his organisation. Eugene, relieved of this duty, regarded the newcomer with ironic sympathy.

Meanwhile Sharkey was making a decision. He had been a good boy for so long! He had been faithful to his Mary for three months now. He had suffered assault and battery on her behalf. He had played the good Samaritan in the Fan Fan business, and tutored Wilson for her sake. He had also been badly shaken by what he had seen in the heroin den. And it was precisely while he was in this state of mind that Diana had decided to dispense sexuality like a milkmaid, by the bucketful. Would it be all that reprehensible to take a little holiday from these stresses and strains, and – not to mince words – shag the arse off her? Surely not. It would merely be a holiday; and what were holidays but little time-outs from which one returns refreshed?

Lok was meanwhile quizzing Wilson in a bantering, mildly sadistic manner. 'You wanna work for me; I gotta know whah you know,' he said. 'You know other ting as well as Freng?'

Wilson swallowed. 'I have studied English literature, with History and Latin as subsidiary subjects.'

'La'in? Whah dis La'in? Some kind scien mebbe?'

'Latin is the language spoken by the ancient Romans.'

'Roman! What de hell you study dat kin' stuff for?'

'My dear sir,' broke in Scrymgeour, 'Latin enables one to study the history of the Roman Empire, an institution second only in importance to that of ancient China.'

Lok, who wouldn't have given a dud cent for all the Sons of Heaven put together, merely grunted. 'You know some'ting 'bou trade?' he asked.

Wilson cleared his throat and said primly: 'The present terms of trade are advantageous to Hong Kong provided that outlets can be found in overseas markets and a technological lead is maintained over other industrialised countries in South-East Asia, such as Singapore, Taiwan and Korea. However diversification away from textiles is to be desired.' It was a straight quote from the editorial of the *Far Eastern Economic Review*: Wilson had a superb memory. .

Lok was both impressed and alarmed. 'Whah you say 'bou tehtile? I make more tehtile than anybody else.'

'I said diversification was to be desired. Plastics and small consumer goods seem to be indicated.'

Lok grunted. 'Mebbe dat not so bad idea. Maybe we doin' dat anyway. But we got mercerise process, knock de head off ever'body in markeh.' He slapped Wilson roughly on the back. 'Mebbe dis La'in not so bad idea after all. You go on, learn mo' Freng. You be awri.'

It was a triumph. Even Mary, dazed with champagne and boredom, rejoiced and Diana turned the slit in her cheongsam towards the favoured young man: you never could tell, he might end up important. As for Rose, she gave her macaw's laugh and said to Mary: 'You watch out, Diana steal all your boyfriends.'

Mary didn't care. She longed to go home. The last race was about to start and she didn't want to be caught up in the stampede to get away. 'Sorry, but I must be off,' she said to Lok Yuen. 'But thanks for a lovely party.' She suppressed a tell-tale yawn.

Diana looked at her watch and uttered a tiny scream. 'I must go too. I have to be at Kow Hoo's at five.'

'But surely they have your measurements,' offered her husband mildly.

'Don't be silly, Eugene. With shoes you must always insist on a fitting.'

'Ever'body go then? You leave me all alone?' said the millionaire in mock-plaint. But the prospect hardly seemed to upset him.

'And I'm supposed to be seeing Teddy Broome at the paper,' said Sharkey.

Thus the door of opportunity swung open. Wilson took the tram to Shaukiwan, and Scrymgeour gave Mary and Rose a lift home. Sharkey found himself alone in the Hillman, with the evening before him.

He gave Diana ten minutes' start, drove to Kow Hoo's and parked in Hennessy Road. His monkey-self had taken command; he rubbed his hands at the prospect of what was going to happen. It would be a glorious, therapeutic shag, the shag to end shags. He would drop on Diana like a horse-fly; when he'd finished with her you'd be able to fry eggs on her.

She came out of the shop with a parcel in her hand. Her

walk was purposeful, even mannish: no trace of little mannerisms here. She stared straight through the Hillman as she went past.

The window was wound down. Sharkey addressed her in his wicked-squire voice. 'Where are you going to, my pretty maid?'

'Liam,' she squealed, reverting to her public persona. 'What are you doing here?'

'Seducing you.'

'Naughty, naughty,' she simpered.

'Get in,' he said, holding the car door open.

'Where are you going?'

'Wherever you please.'

'In that case all right.' She gave a pretty little shrug and got in.

The Hillman's front seat made a marvellous job of exposing her thighs. He slipped his left hand under her cheongsam.

'Wicked man,' admonished Diana and put her hand on his; the net effect was not to remove it but to keep it where it was. 'Now you can't drive,' she said archly.

'I'm happy as I am.'

She made a little moue and released the hand. 'Anyway,' she added, 'we can't go to my place. They'll all be back.'

He hadn't thought of that. 'Where the bloody hell can we go then?' he said crossly.

'Not much of a seducer, are you? Can't even think of a place to go.' She slid his hand up and down her thigh, perhaps hoping to give him inspiration.

'Your bloody family are always in,' he grumbled.

'Ah,' said Diana. 'Now I remember. They're going out later. For eight o'clock.'

His spirits rose. 'Right! At five past you and I will be in the door like a pair of shite-hawks. In the meantime, how about dinner?'

'I'm supposed to be seeing a girlfriend.'

'Put her off.'

He drove her to the Szechuan restaurant in Wellington Street, having some idea that the spicy food would make her randy. There she telephoned her friend and cancelled their date.

He enjoyed the food, but the conversation was boring in the extreme, consisting as it did mostly of mechanical sexual innuendo. He was reminded of those snatched conversations he used to have with grammar school girls thirty years ago. No doubt about it, women like Diana were made for a casual bash, anything more would be too boring. Still, the bash would be all right. He drank rather more beer than he intended.

At a quarter past eight – families out on dinner dates are not always on time – they were driving up Magazine Gap Road. The policeman in his little pagoda, seeing their winking direction light, waved them down Stubbs Road.

The house was dark when they parked, apart from a pale glimmer from the servants' quarters at the back. The old amah, hearing the house door open, appeared; Diana gave her a glare, and she vanished.

'Where now?' whispered Sharkey, exploring her dress with his hands. He even gave her falsies a squeeze, out of pure fellowship.

'My bedroom.'

She led the way up the stairs to a contemporary room with a candlewick bedspread and expensive-looking white furniture. One wall was dominated by a floor-to-ceiling mirror.

Sharkey whistled. 'Do the spectators have to pay?'

'We are the spectators,' said Diana, stretching luxuriously. She put down her parcel of new shoes, kicked off her old ones and undressed, throwing back her shoulders to make her small breasts taut and inviting. 'Well, what are you waiting for?' she said.

Sharkey tore his clothes off in his turn and stood there, small, lean and wiry, with a semi-tumescent John Thomas hanging like a donkey's yard, at the angle of a trailed lance.

They grappled in the standing position and kissed messily. Then Diana lay on the bed with one knee raised and a hard lustful look in her eye.

He fell on the bed beside her; they thrashed about on the candlewick, which dug into their bodies in lumpy lines. He got to work on her, squeezing, stroking, titillating, mumbling with his mouth on her shoulders and neck. It was all a little too hectic, because he had made a humiliating discovery: John Thomas remained stubbornly at half-cock. Nothing he did seemed to make him stand up straight.

Diana, self-absorbed and oblivious of the problem, cried out: 'Now!' and hoisted herself on top of him, where she started thrusting downwards with her pelvis. Crossing his fingers for luck, he tried to penetrate her, but John Thomas buckled like dozed rubber. 'Play with me a bit,' he urged her. 'I haven't risen to the occasion yet.'

A shadow of uncertainty entered Diana's head, but her small manicured hand moved his foreskin up and down, without ascertainable effect. She increased her tempo.

'Ow!' yelled Sharkey, suddenly doubling up. It was a crude deception, but it worked.

'What on earth is wrong with you?' she asked.

'You've hit me on the knackers,' he moaned. 'It's agony.'

'I hardly touched you!'

'You hit me just the same.'

'For goodness' sake, Liam. I was trying to make you stand.'

'I tell you, my balls hurt. You've got the kick of a mule.'

She gave him a hard look. 'You flatter so delightfully,' she said.

'Can't you understand, you silly cow?' he exclaimed. 'My balls are sore.'

The spurt of feigned anger seemed to convince her. 'I'm sorry,' she said. 'I didn't mean it.'

'A blow in the testicles gives a man nausea,' he declared primly. 'The penis contracts until the pain has gone.'

'How long does that take?' she asked, with asperity.

'A quarter of an hour or so.'

'I can't wait that long. I'm worked up.'

'I'll give you a hand job.'

She bridled. 'No second-class goods please.'

'What shall I do then?' he asked angrily. 'Ring for a friend?'

'Maybe it wouldn't be a bad idea,' she said, clearly not believing him any more. She stood up and looked at herself approvingly in the mirror. 'Heaven knows, it's not that you lack incentive.' She turned away.

'Hey, wait a minute,' he called in alarm. 'I'm not finished yet.'

'Oh yes you are.'

'We'll try again tomorrow. I'll be my old self, you'll see.'

'That wasn't so brilliant either, was it?' She started to dress.

'Shit, shit, shit!' he cried, exasperated. He jumped to his feet and started pacing the room, till the sight of John

Thomas in the mirror brought him to a halt. He kicked his clothes into a corner, out of its range, and flung them on.

'I'm going,' he declared with what dignity he could muster. 'I'll find my own way out.'

'Poor little Liam,' she called after him. 'This looks like bye-bye.'

He sat in the car for a few moments without switching on the ignition, in total confusion. The humiliation of the fiasco sent waves of hot blood into his cheeks. He hadn't known anything like this since adolescence, thirty years before.

His tumultuous feelings – shame, fury, bafflement – made him start the car convulsively and swing it out into Stubbs Road. He roared at full speed along the winding road, half tempted to drive straight at the little wall to his right and send the car crashing down the slope: crazy, but a kind of solution. Still, he was not the stuff suicides are made of; he quickly cooled off and slowed down. His teeth were chattering in his head, but at least he was in control.

Where to now? Breezy Court was an uninviting prospect, even though Mary wouldn't be there, having opted for Conduit Road, where her books were, to prepare a lecture. How about the bar of the Gloucester hotel and a few quick-style Scotches? That didn't appeal either. A line from *The Tempest* floated into his head: A turn or two I'll walk, to still my beating mind. Beating mind indeed! And where better to still it than South Bay?

Fifteen minutes later he had parked the Hillman under the flame trees and run down between the concrete beach houses on to that serene strand. A warm breeze, the first harbinger of spring, caressed his sinful cheek. The little waves sighed. The moon, that old magician, was conjuring up glints of quicksilver from the surface of the sea. But not for him.

His mind was still beating, mainly with resentment against Mary. Yes, Mary! Because, whatever her intentions, wasn't she really to blame? She had unmanned him spiritually, and that had gelded him physically. In the moment of humiliation he had tried to persuade himself that it was the mirror's fault, but that that was nonsense. In the good old days he could have copulated in the shop-window of Selfridges, and under floodlights. John Thomas would have towered heavenwards like a great purple howitzer.

After a few lengths of the beach he realised that he wasn't going to regain his calm, but at least his mind was made up. He would break with Mary the following morning and rejoin the wolf-pack. The wolf-pack was hard and unforgiving, granted, but it was a man's world, a world of strength, not weakness. It was his world. – Firm in this resolve he drove back to Breezy Court.

There was a light on in the flat. Could Mary be there after all? Well, if she was they'd have it out this evening. No point in waiting till tomorrow.

The living room was dark but for a sliver of light from under the bathroom door.

'Is that you, Liam?' came her voice.

His resolve wavered. 'Yes, it's me. What are you doing here?'

'There's been a crisis. Come in and I'll tell you about it.'

He crossed the living room and walked along the little corridor leading to the bathroom. What could the crisis be? He opened the door and saw Mary lying back luxuriously in the bath, cocooned in foam.

'Ah Hoy's left you,' she said. 'She walked out today without giving notice.'

'So that's what it's about!'

'Yes. Ah Yee told me when I got home. So I brought her round here; she's in the kitchen just now. We can let her stay till we get things sorted out.' She lay back in her foam. 'Ooh, this is lovely! After those bloody horses.'

Her body was almost completely submerged; only the tops of her breasts were clear. Sharkey reached out automatically and stroked them.

'Bliss,' sighed Mary, closing her eyes.

At that moment something unexpected happened: John Thomas hardened. A groan of surprise and relief escaped Sharkey. Mary, alarmed at the sound, opened her eyes, saw the state of affairs and closed them again. He moved his hand, shirt-sleeve and all, down her body to between her legs and caressed her there.

'God but that's wonderful, Liam,' sighed Mary. 'Absolutely wonderful.'

Still stroking her, he threw off his clothes (the second time that day) and climbed into the bath beside her. Her soapy limbs slid round him. His own body was half cold, half hot, a thrilling combination. John Thomas dived into the water, then moved from its relative harshness into the warm emollience of Mary.

He used all his art to bring her to a shivering climax before spouting mightily himself. Their movements had thrashed away some of the foam; he saw the little silver thread of sperm spurt unsteadily into the water and sink.

'Darling,' moaned Mary, pulling his head down on to her wet bosom. 'I love you, you know.'

'I love you too.' It might even be true. At the very least he felt gratitude to her, and wasn't gratitude a stage on the journey to love – Tendre-sur-Reconnaissance?

Mary's love was genuine enough, though. 'Now that

you're here I might as well wash you,' she said tenderly. He lay back and let it happen. Having assumed the initiative, she continued in the same vein. She laid him out carefully on the bed and made love to him a second time, giving him every ounce of pleasure she was capable of. When they were both drained a wonderful drowsiness came over him, such as he had not felt since childhood (and only rarely then).

Mary turned on her left side and pulled his body round hers, the fronts of his knees in the back of hers, his right arm round her stomach; he was just big enough to manage it. And then they slept.

At the beginning of April the events in Dumbell were pushed out of Verity's mind by the huge fact that had been slowly forcing itself into people's consciousness: famine in China, and the subsequent breakdown in authority.

In tens, then in hundreds, finally in thousands, refugees made for Hong Kong and Macau. They came on foot and splashed across the Shumchun river (the border with communist China); they ventured on to the Pearl River in sampans; they tied inflated bladders round their necks and swam across Mirs Bay.

Immigration Officers were instructed to return them to where they had come from – when they could catch them. But they were soon arriving in such numbers that the police and the army were drafted in to help. Constables who had been investigating the praya slaying, as well as the extra one allocated to Dumbell after the trial of Wong

Au Nai and Lim Sik Fuk, were taken away and posted on the border.

The Legislative Council debated the situation; the elected members protested against what it called 'these inhuman decisions,' namely the deportations. In response the government referred critics to the Immigration (Control and Offences) Ordinance of 1958 and pointed out that, at three and a half millions, the population of the Colony was two millions greater than in 1949; how many more people could it absorb?

Then six hundred peasants from the Yim Tin People's Commune, just north-east of Shataukok, attempted a mass escape but were intercepted and fired on by border guards; ten persons were killed and many more injured. This sent a shockwave through the Hong Kong Chinese; a number of clan associations petitioned the government not to send defectors back to what they claimed would be certain death.

Then Dumbell became indirectly involved. Six young refugees who came ashore on Ping Chau island in Mirs Bay claimed that they had relatives on the island, and the Rural Committee – at one at least on this – sent a delegation to Gascoyne Road to petition the government to let them stay. It failed.

As a result of all this Verity's office was deluged with procedural instructions regarding the apprehension and deportation of illegal refugees. He was going through some of these with Cheung and Jeffrey Wing when his buzzer went and Joe Miners was announced.

Instinctively, without thinking, he gathered up the papers and handed them in a pile to Cheung, saying 'Please go over these, Mr Cheung, and report back to me.' Only when this was done did he realise that he had treated the Land Officer as though he was junior to Jeffrey; but it was too late to do anything about it. Cheung, pink under his perspiration, was already out of the office and Joe was standing at the door. 'Come in, Joe,' he said miserably. 'Do you mind leaving us, Jeffrey?'

'No need. No need at all,' said Miners, waving his pipe airily. 'Just thought I'd tell you something. No reason why the young man shouldn't hear it too.'

'Stay, Jeffrey,' said Verity weakly. The insult to Cheung was now compounded; he'd pay for it later. But things couldn't be much worse than they were already.

Joe registered the fact that his pipe had gone out. He took a clasp knife from his pocket and attacked the bowl with it. 'How are things on Dumbell?' he asked.

'I hardly know. Nobody's paying any attention to it these days.'

'We are. – Your Rural Committee still getting on?'

'I think so. You saw how they sent us that delegation the other day?'

'Oh yes.' Joe scraped a tarry dottle from the pipe and deposited it in Verity's ashtray, after which he pulled a pipe-cleaner though the stem with great vigour. 'They never cease to amaze me, those blokes,' he said.

'How do you mean?'

'Well, here they are all pulling together like the Eton boat and I know for a fact that they're all involved in this Sin Fung business.'

'Sin Fung?' queried Verity.

'That's right: Vanguard. The chap who went galloping past you, the one they were trying to bump off. We don't know his real name, but he's a T'ung man. Organises illegal immigration out of China – or did till the Twenty-One K sank his boat. You remember how those bodies were washed up at Telegraph Bay?'

Verity was hardly likely to forget it; the event had been haunting him these last six months.

Meanwhile Miners tapped his teeth with the mouthpiece of his briar and lit up. While the smoke was billowing he spoke again. 'We've got a pretty shrewd idea of who tried to kill him, by the way. And who tipped us off about it.'

'That's good news, isn't it?' said Verity, confused.

'Oh yes. And surprise, surprise, they're both members of your Rural Committee!' Joe grinned, waving the pipe stem in the air as though he were applying paint.

'Let me try to work this out,' said Verity doggedly. 'You say the assassination attempt was organised by a Twenty-One K man, and that a T"ung man told you about it. And both were members of my Rural Committee.'

'That's about it,' said Joe, smiling beatifically.

'May I speak, Mr Miners?' said Jeffrey politely. He had been silent until then. 'As I remember it, you get most of your information from telephone calls. But do you have any hard evidence?'

'Bright lad,' said Joe approvingly. 'As a matter of fact we do.'

'You'll be making arrests then?'

'Not at once. I'm in favour of waiting for a bit, letting things mature. You never know what surprising people might swim into your net.' He stood up. 'Well,' he said, 'I must toddle. See you soon.' And he was off.

Verity felt relieved. He wasn't feeling at all well today, and when you're like that even exciting things become a burden. He lay back in his chair and said, 'You may think this selfish, Jeffrey, but I almost hope that when they do make an arrest it will be after I've gone on home leave.'

'When do you go, Mr Verity?'

'First of June. Passage booked on the *Chusan*. I don't care for air travel.'

He longed for England, its coolness and silence, as a thirsty man longs for water. Some of his colleagues in government became so used to the heat that they spent their long leave in other hot places – in Bali, or Greece, or the South Pacific – but he wasn't one of them. Yet he had been born in Hong Kong and they had not! It must be a question of loyalty.

'I'd very much like to see England myself one day,' said Jeffrey.

'Why not do so then?'

'I'd be lost, Mr Verity. I've never been anywhere but Hong Kong.'

'You could do it at a time when I'm there. I could show you round a bit.'

'Oh Mr Verity!' Jeffrey was round-eyed, with surprise or delight or both.

A momentary vision of himself showing this sympathetic young man round the high places of England rose up in Verity's mind, only to be dispelled by the thought of Cheung – ridiculous, humiliated Cheung – sitting at his desk in the next room. 'Of course it may not be practical,' he said gloomily.

'It was most kind of you even to think of it,' said Jeffrey warmly. Then, in a more neutral tone: 'Why do you think Inspector Miners told you what he did?' he asked. 'We're not the police, after all.'

Verity dragged his thoughts back to the matter in hand. 'You know my reputation,' he said with a melancholy smile. 'Too conscientious for my own good.'

Jeffrey would have protested, but he waved the protest

away. 'I take things too much to heart; my friends, in their kindness, sometimes try to soften the blow for me.' He lowered his voice. 'To tell you the truth, Jeffrey, I appreciate their good intentions but sometimes find them humiliating.'

He lowered his eyes to a bulky instruction on the desk in front of him, one he had missed when gathering up the papers for Cheung. It was entitled *Illegal Refugees: Arrest And Deportation.*

A change had taken place in the balance of power between Sharkey and Mary. He was in a curious state of mind. She had saved him from the worst humiliation he had known and he was profoundly grateful for that. It had also made him subtly dependent on her. He felt edgy when she wasn't around and acquired a taste for spending quiet evenings with her, doing nothing in particular, maybe reading or listening to the hi-fi. He needed her presence.

At the same time her little habits irritated him. One evening they were listening to a recording of *Trovatore*. Mary adored Verdi but, particularly in the loud parts, would prowl round the room humming the big tune and conducting an imaginary orchestra. 'Wonderful stuff,' she would cry.

'I prefer the quiet bits,' was his guarded reply.

'But, Liam, can't you see that the quiet bits are what they are because of the loud bits?' This was a valid point of view; but she didn't seem to realise that it wasn't the loud bits he objected to but her reaction to them.

Yet no sooner had he articulated this thought than he felt

ashamed of it. He had recently read *The Desert Fathers* by Helen Waddell and wondered whether he wasn't in the pre-conversion state as experienced by these worthies, hating God the most a split second before accepting Him. The notion of Liam Sharkey surrendering to the deity was absurd enough to make him laugh; but if he thought of Mary not as a divine personage but as the embodiment of the decency principle, what he dubbed the Necessity for Good Behaviour, the idea was not so absurd as all that.

Now that they were together most of the time she made cautious moves towards introducing reforms. He had untidy habits, such as reading several books at the same time and leaving them open at the last page he had read, one on top of the other. Many of them were subsequently abandoned as boring and never finished; the flat was full of odd little piles of books, like upside-down pagodas.

Mary would approach one of these and ask, in her most diplomatic voice, 'Liam, are you still interested in these?'

'Of course I am.'

'Let's have a look. – Stendhal: *De L'Amour. Poetic Gems* by William McGonagall. Tolstoy's *Resurrection*, open at page 153. When did you last look at any of these?'

'Oh, I don't know. About six months ago,' he said offhandedly.

'You'll never look at them again.'

'Hey, don't disturb them like that! I'm reading them.'

'I'm just putting markers in,' said Mary. And she was. She had prepared dozens of paper spills and slipped one into each book before putting it back on the shelf. 'Now, isn't that much nicer?' she said, ruffling his hair.

'No,' he said in his most curmudgeonly tone. But he also put his arm round her, tacitly conceding her point.

This was the state of affairs between them when they found a strange postcard in his little metal post-box in the foyer. It read: I'd like it to be you. D.S.

'Who on earth is that?' asked Mary.

'No idea. But the handwriting's familiar.'

'Not a lady's hand, I'm glad to see.'

'Grrr.'

'What's the address on it?'

'Seventeen Macdonnell Road.' The Belilios girl, now deserted and tearful, lived at number thirty-five; apart from her he knew no one there. Then it came to him. 'It's Derek Stillgoe. I remember his writing from the film scripts.'

'I'd like it to be you. What can that mean?'

'God knows. He's a weird one.'

'His film has definitely folded?'

'Oh yes.' He shivered involuntarily. 'I'm going to have to go there, Mary.'

'We are.'

'No. Not you.'

'I'm free at eleven,' said Mary firmly, 'and I'm going.'

Sharkey made no further objection. Small fingers of disquiet were squeezing at his stomach; he would be glad to have her with him.

Seventeen Macdonnell Road turned out to be an old four-storey building with flaking yellow paint. Stillgoe's flat – if he was indeed the occupant – was a minuscule affair on the landing between the first and second floors. A visiting card was attached to the door by a drawing pin; it read Derek Stillgoe, Film Producer.

Sharkey took a deep breath and pressed the bell; it gave a low grinding ring as though the battery had run down. There was no answer, so he rang again. And a third time.

'Doesn't look like he's at home,' he said brightly. 'Shall we go?'

Mary shook her head and gave the door a speculative push. It yielded slightly. She pushed again, harder this time; it yielded again. 'For some reason it's left on the snib. But there's something heavy inside keeping it closed. – Give it a heave, will you, Liam?'

He put his shoulder to the door, making it move some more. 'I can see what's holding it,' he said. 'It's a chest of drawers.'

A further shove from the two of them and the gap was wide enough for a man to squeeze through. 'Come on,' said Mary. 'We're taking a look.'

'Me first then,' said Sharkey unenthusiastically.

'After all my hard work? No fear.'

Suddenly angered by the uncanny element in the situation, he retorted: 'No. Me first and that's that.' He wriggled through the opening and vanished into the room, but a moment later came back through the opening like a cork expelled from a bottle. He was white as a sheet.

'What is it, darling?' cried Mary, alarmed.

'The bugger's done himself in, that's what!'

'Good heavens.' Mary took a deep breath. 'I'd better take a look.'

'No! For Christ's sake no! It's a mess in there.'

'Women are for cleaning up messes,' said Mary quietly. She rolled up her sleeves like a housewife about to scrub the floor. 'Here we go.'

'No, Mary!' he cried wildly. 'I forbid you … '

She took him by the elbows and said, quite gently, 'Get stuffed, Liam. I'm going in. If you want you can come with me.' She pushed her way into the darkened room, leaving him to follow.

It was more of a cubby-hole than a room. A pair of dusty green curtains was drawn, making it difficult to see anything in spite of the bright sunshine outside. But she made out a plain oak bed and a small bedside table strewn with dog-eared paperbacks.

By far the most interesting object was a human figure sitting tailor-fashion on the floor between the bed and the wall with its head slumped forward. Its attitude suggested sleep, but as your eyes became accustomed to the light you could make out the stain of dried blood discolouring the front of its T-shirt and its blue jeans almost to the knee. This had overflowed into a rusty pool on the wood-block floor. The sight had Sharkey retching, but it was too early in the day for him to have anything to throw up.

'Easy, love,' said Mary and took his hand in one of hers. With the other she leaned forward, as though to touch the corpse.

'Don't!'

'All right; if it worries you.' Instead, she leaned forward and inspected the dead man's stomach – without switching on the light; it would have been unthinkable to do that. 'He's committed hara-kiri,' she said dispassionately. 'I can see the handle of a knife.'

'Jesus!' His voice came out like a shriek. He sat down abruptly on the bed, to prevent himself fainting.

'It must have happened yesterday,' said Mary. 'He probably posted that card and then come back here to do it.'

'How do you know?' faltered Sharkey.

'No smell.' She bent down to look again. 'That's strange. He seems to have pulled some of his guts out.'

'Oh no!' By an act of will he followed Mary's glance and discerned a yard or so of greyish intestine snaking out from

Stillgoe's belly; his left hand held a gory piece of paper which had dried to the texture of excrement.

'A rum do,' said Mary.

'He's done a Kampei,' said Sharkey hollowly.

'Kampei? Who's Kampei?'

'A character in the film. He's of humble origin and is only admitted to the league of ronin when he commits suicide and pulls out his entrails.' He gagged for a moment at the thought. 'Then he ... presses a piece of paper to them. Like signing in his own blood.' The speech left him exhausted.

'Poor sod,' said Mary. 'He must have thought himself unworthy or something.'

'Unless he'd planned the whole thing from the start,' said Sharkey savagely.

'Don't be hard,' said Mary mildly. 'He's to be pitied after all.' She looked round the room. 'Is there a phone here, do you think?'

'No chance. You could never get through to the bugger.'

'One of us will have to go and find a policeman then,' said Mary decisively.

'You go. I'll stay here.' His voice faltered as he said it.

'No, Liam,' she replied gently. 'This is woman's work. Besides, you can run faster than I can.'

There was no point in trying to fight her; she was completely in the ascendant. Besides, his legs had already taken him as far as the door. 'Just promise me you won't touch him,' he said.

'I promise.'

'I'll be as quick as I can!'

In a moment he was out of the room, then out of the house, running into a blinding, glorious burst of sunshine that burned up the images of death. He stood there in it for a moment, taking it in. Then he ran to the Peak Tram terminal as if his life depended on it.

The Chinese constable stationed there listened to his story politely and telephoned C.I.D. Within five minutes a small roly-poly Welshman with hair so black you could see the shadow of its roots under his scalp drove up; he had a Chinese constable in the back. 'Protheroe's the name,' he said. 'Just call me Idwal.'

'It's in Macdonnell Road ... ' Sharkey began.

'Right. Hop in.'

They found Mary sitting quietly on the bed with her hands folded in her lap. How amazing she was!

The Welshman cast a critical eye on the dead Stillgoe and whistled. 'Don't get many like that, boy!' he said. Turning to Mary: 'You're the cool one then.'

She smiled. 'What's there to worry about? He's harmless, poor devil.'

Sharkey shuddered. 'That's what you say. He gives me the creeps.'

'But look at him, Liam! He's not real. He's like something out of Madame Tussaud's.'

'Should have been a nurse, bach,' said Protheroe admiringly. His Welsh accent had got stronger; he was clearly one of those Celts who behave like stage stereotypes because the English find that easier to understand.

'The hole in his belly's real enough,' muttered Sharkey.

'Don't look at it then,' said Mary. 'What do we do now, inspector?'

'Come down to Wyndham Street and answer a few questions. The constable will keep an eye on things here till Forensic arrive.'

'Oh, I almost forgot,' said Mary. 'There's something here

for you, Liam. I found it under the pillow.' She produced a loose-leaf file with a sheet of paper clipped to it.

Sharkey glanced at the paper: it seemed to be a letter, addressed to himself. He then flicked through the file. No doubt about what that was: the script of the Burke and Wills film, entitled *The Red Heart*. A cursive look through it showed indications of settings, camera-shots, snatches of surprisingly terse dialogue.

'That's odd,' he said, 'he's put it in a Hong Kong Government file. Wonder where he picked that up.'

'Let's have a look then,' said Protheroe, stretching out a hand. Sharkey gave him the folder, with the sheet of paper still attached. He examined both and said: 'They're government property all right. Better leave them with me; I'll see you get them back after the inquest.'

Sharkey had no objections. His curiosity was no match for the eerie feelings Stillgoe always aroused in him, particularly now that his dead body was squatting on the floor not six feet away.

'OK,' he said, and they left. The constable pulled the door of the flat shut and took up his station outside, impassive as Stillgoe himself.

☙

Sharkey never thought he would long for a commission from the *Kwangtung Courier* as passionately as a Saharan traveller longs for an oasis. But it was so, and there weren't any.

He had given lunch a miss and struggled through his two o'clock translation class. And now was back in Breezy Court with nothing to take his mind off what he had just seen. If only Mary was there! But she wasn't; she had lectures all afternoon.

His mind was in turmoil. His blood ran hot and cold. He sweated under his clothes every time he thought of that slumped figure with its pink-grey gut and stains of blood like obscene excrement (which he did every five seconds or so). He had never been brought face to face with death so brutally. Here was what he now recognised as the central issue of his life, and he was having his nose rubbed in it. For what was all his feverish womanising over the years but a frantic – and doomed – attempt to escape death?

He was terror-stricken. He admitted that. But must he not find some way to fight that terror? Other people did and even overcame it – or at least learned to live with it. He must do the same.

The question was: how? How did quite ordinary people manage it? He had no idea. But one thing was clear: they were all braver, or less cowardly, than Liam Sharkey.

With that realisation a wave of shame swept over him, shame at the antics of this despicable insect, this species of jumping flea that would be pathetic if it were not so ridiculous, for ever keeping up its demented motum perpetuum to avoid being cracked between the nails of fate.

Disgusted with himself, he ran from room to room, muttering, cursing, swearing. Ah Yee, observing him though the glass panel in the kitchen door, concluded that Massa was sick, grabbed a basket, shouted 'I go shop!' and left.

He continued his running, almost by reflex, but there was no escaping what he was running from, namely himself. He thought wildly: what in God's name am I to do? Follow Stillgoe's example and put an end to it? That would be lending himself too much importance. He simply wasn't worth dying for.

How about just vanishing? He was tempted to take the first plane to New Zealand and settle there. It was an upright, dull country, just the place to start living a blameless life. But wouldn't the disreputable vision of Liam Sharkey follow him even there, tied to his coat like Yeats's tin can to a dog's tail?

In his agitation he had been opening and closing books without taking in their contents; there was no comfort in them. The one in his hand at the moment, for instance: what of it? He read the title: *Analects of Confucius*. Oh yes, the little blue Oxford Classic he'd bought second hand in London years ago and never opened.

It fell open now, of its own accord. He glanced distractedly over a short passage:

> Virtue is the denial of self and response to what is right and proper. Deny yourself for one day and respond to the right and proper, and everyone will accord you virtuous.

No doubt, but who on God's earth had the strength to deny himself for a whole day? O hard sentence!

His eye moved down the page to what looked like a prose poem As he read it he experienced a pang of recognition:

> 'May I beg for the main features?' asked Yen Yüan.
> The Master answered:
> 'When wrong and improper, do not look.
> When wrong and improper, do not listen.
> When wrong and improper, do not speak.
> When wrong and improper, do not move.
> 'Though I am not clever,' said Yen Yüan, 'permit me to carry out these precepts.'

'Wrong and improper' – who had ever been more so than himself? Who had ever had a greater need to follow Yen Yüan's example?

A sudden gulping sob broke from him, followed by another and then another. He fell on the bed, wracked by convulsive hiccups that tore their way out of him without bringing relief. These had eased into harsh, masculine tears when he became aware that a key was being turned in the front door.

'Anybody there?' came Mary's voice. She had cancelled her final lecture and come home early.

Sharkey was on the verge of panic; would she see him in his weakness? He didn't want it to happen, but didn't have the strength to prevent it.

She walked into the bedroom, saw what was happening and ran over to him. 'Oh Liam! Oh my love!' she cried, putting her arms round him.

He let his head fall on her shoulder; she was warmth and comfort, and he needed her. She uttered inarticulate little cries, stroked his head and kissed him, letting all her unruly generosity pour over him.

He clung to her, letting his sobs play themselves out, and as he did so a realisation came to him. This was how humankind coped with death; indeed it was the only way we poor forked creatures have. You could neither fight it nor deny it; only set up a positive balance against it, a human capital to draw on in times of need. If he had known love in childhood he would have instinctively been aware of that. But he had not; he was the veriest neophyte in the ways of emotion.

Well, it was one lesson at least: Good Behaviour (or if you preferred fancy words, Virtue) was a necessity and Love the only bastion against death. A useful lesson to see him through middle age and what followed.

The only problem was that he felt he didn't deserve to know it, let alone to take advantage of it. Mary had been his teacher, but what had he to give her in return? Nothing; absolutely nothing.

But, just as he had found the right words to say on another occasion, she found the right ones now.

She looked him full in the face and, with tears standing in her eyes, said in a strong Lancashire accent: 'Ee lad, tha'll never know how much I dreaded losing thee!' And buried her head in his shoulder.

When Ah Yee returned from her shopping she found them asleep together on top of the bed. She put away her purchases without the habitual crashing and banging: let them sleep on, she thought. They seemed to need it.

Verity was trying to take in a government directive on pig-rearing when Cheung came in, carrying a pile of folders. Expecting these to be put in his in-tray, Verity paid no attention.

But Cheung kept standing there. He coughed. He fidgeted. He rubbed his left calf against his right knee, scratching it. He clearly had something on his mind.

'What is it, Cheung?' Verity asked.

'Just files, Mr Verity.'

'Put them in the in-tray if you please.'

Cheung obeyed, went to the door, hesitated, then came back again. 'Mr Verity,' he said.

'Yes?'

'There is a new instruction about the apprehension of illegal immigrants. Reports must be made up in triplicate and sent to Immigration Department, GOC Land Forces, and the Commissioner of Police.'

'I am aware of that.'

Cheung coughed again. 'Mr Verity. Mr Wing is on leave today.'

'He has the day off, yes.'

'Mr Wing is rising in the service.'

Verity spread his hands on his desk, palms upward, and said 'Jeffrey is a Clerk, Class Two. He has been a Clerk, Class Two for a year and a half. I don't call that rising in the service.'

'Mr Wing has the District Officer's ear.'

So that was it. Verity looked at Cheung – familiar, exasperating Cheung with his perspiration, his capon's body, his air of generalised unease – and wondered whether it wasn't the contrast that made him incline to Jeffrey; Jeffrey was youth, charm, discretion – who wouldn't prefer those qualities?

He said firmly: 'Jeffrey Wing sometimes accompanies me on trips inside the District. So do you. I talk to him, but I also talk to you. Indeed as my land officer you have my ear to a much greater extent than he has. – That of course does not prevent him from being a promising young man, with a fine career ahead of him.'

Cheung mopped his face with his handkerchief, twisted it as though to wring it out, and finally said 'Mr Verity let him stay when Inspector Miners was here the other day.'

The reproach was just. 'I did,' Verity admitted, 'and after I'd asked you to leave. It was thoughtless of me, and I apologise.'

He couldn't say fairer than that, could he? But Cheung didn't seem to be satisfied. He screwed himself up to it and spoke again. 'It may be that the other clerks are laughing at me,' he said. 'It may be that they are saying among themselves: "This young buck is the coming man and Cheung's days are over." It may be that I shall lose my authority over them.'

'I am very sorry, Cheung. I shall see that it doesn't happen again.'

'I also ask myself,' the land assistant continued, 'is this Inspector Miners a discreet man?'

'You know he's not,' replied Verity irritably. 'He loves making provocative statements. He's not discreet at all.'

'I fear he may talk about police affairs to unauthorised persons.'

'Meaning Jeffrey, I suppose.' Verity was in grave danger of losing his temper. 'Jeffrey Wing is not an unauthorised person,' he said, controlling himself. 'Nor are you. Nor am I. – If Inspector Miners chooses to make confidential statements to any of us then that is his concern. I daresay he knows whom he can trust. – Thank you, Cheung. You may go.'

The land assistant went, carrying his little pot belly before him. Was he satisfied? Probably not. But Verity was beyond caring; he was too annoyed by the implications of what the man had said. Did he seriously think that Jeffrey would go around blabbing about his work to all and sundry? The idea was absurd.

He lay back in his chair, exhausted. How wearisome life was! An endless succession of vexations: deaths, accusations, even dreams – how much more of it could he take?

Two months to go before his home leave; roll on June. Perhaps there would be respite in England. Maybe he'd even go and see a doctor there. Correction: he would go and see a doctor there, a nice, tweedy, pipe-smoking English doctor, not somebody like that Dr O'Young at the Queen Mary. Still they did say O'Young was a good man – should he give him a try nevertheless? No; he had sworn to stay at his post and he would do so. Back in England he would have ceased being a government official with his duty to do; he would be a civilian. He could see any doctor he liked then.

But roll on England, all the same. He was tired of these sudden rigidities of limb, these bouts of unshiftable constipation. Even these bad dreams.

Sharkey and Mary gave evidence at Stillgoe's inquest.

It turned out that he had not been the official tenant of the flat in Macdonnell Road; that was a night-club dancer from Australia called Jenny Gumbo (she worked under the name of Julie Laverne). Appearing in heavy mascara, with a thatch of blonde hair which Mary swore had dark roots, she testified that she had lent the place to Stillgoe while she was in Manila on an engagement. Her regular job was at the Princess Garden night-club, but for the three weeks in question she had leave because it was featuring a singing star from England.

When the coroner asked her if her relationship with Stillgoe had been a close one she said: 'Hell, no! His mum was a friend of mine.'

The verdict was quickly arrived at: death by suicide. Thus Derek Stillgoe, who had occupied a very small space in the universe, now occupied none at all. A sister of his, also domiciled in Adelaide, was adjudged to have inherited his belongings, with one exception: a folder with a sheet of paper attached; which was now the property of Liam Sharkey.

Mary and he went down to the courthouse to collect it. Against all the odds it was beginning to loom large in their imaginations. Mary in particular had glanced over it while waiting in Stillgoe's flat, and had been impressed. The text was spare and economical on the page, a sequence of terse scenes pared down to their essentials, depicting a pair of doomed figures in a burning landscape, along with the occasional bleached silhouette of a gum tree. Mysterious black men faded in and out of the picture.

Sharkey's impression of the text, though more fragmentary than Mary's, agreed with it. He was faced with the shaming thought that Stillgoe, whom no one had taken seriously in life, might have been a more substantial figure than he realised.

A Chinese clerk took Stillgoe's possessions from a locker and laid them out on the desk in front of him. They consisted of two sweat shirts, one pair of navy shorts and one of long white ducks, socks, cotton briefs and a pair of down-at-heel shoes. They made a little pile on top of which sat Stillgoe's dark glasses. Sharkey tried them on and discovered that they had no magnification; they must have been worn solely to protect the owner's eyes from the light.

'None of these are mine,' he said. 'Haven't you got any papers?'

The clerk looked in the locker again and produced a transparent plastic bag. The contents were a couple of unpaid bills, a cheque book consisting mainly of stubs, a bank statement showing that the account holder had withdrawn his last thousand dollars on the last day of February (Sharkey, who had been paid two hundred of them, was stricken with retrospective guilt).

These, and the sheet of paper with his name on it. But there was no folder attached.

Mary explained to the clerk what was missing, the man made a detailed telephone call and said: 'I'm sorry, sir. It appears to be missing. I shall have it looked into.'

They'd have to wait then, but at least there was the sheet of paper. They drove back to Breezy Court and read it. It turned out to be a sort of art poétique.

TO THE RED HEART: A JOURNEY

In a world of objects where does truth lie?
At the red heart only.
Maxims for the journey:
Renounce.
Endure.

The red heart simplifies. By reducing possibilities it enlarges possibility.

It draws concentration to a point.
A point, having no dimensions, is intensely hot:
The red heart scorches.

Rules for an art of concentration:
No unnecessary pictures.
No unnecessary words.
No self.

The message is not the medium; the message transcends the medium.

An art fit for the rifleman's knapsack
The times being unheroic, heroes are ridiculous.
Accept this.
The first stage is to be laughed at.
The second stage is to renounce.
The third stage is to suffer.

Despair is clinker left by the flames of concentration;
reject it.

The ways are three.
The way of the samurai: scorn.
The way of the philosopher: control.
The way of the explorer: the red heart.

Give me the courage to do what must be done.
Give me the patience to suffer what must be suffered.
If it should please the divine sense of humour that I
succeed, so be it.
If not, not.
Amen.

Sharkey whistled; Mary was left wide-eyed. 'What do you
make of it?' she asked.

'I wish I knew.'

'Was he a genius, or a charlatan, or both?'

'A man of talent at any rate. – To think that for us his
writing was an embarrassing joke!' His voice was rueful.

Mary dabbed at her eyes with a handkerchief. 'Poor devil,'
she sniffed. 'Everybody despising him – it's awful.'

'We didn't despise him so much as write him off. – Maybe
that's even worse.'

'He must have been lonely. That's what I find so sad.'

She had a quiet weep over Stillgoe and, having done so,
returned to the business of living. As for Sharkey, he was

exercised for a day or so by a hidden resemblance: who was it the man reminded him of? With his ridiculous, old-fashioned heroism – a heroism that refused to accept itself as heroic; his antediluvian sense of mission? Of course; mutatis mutandis, it was Nigel Verity. The one difference was the implied death-wish. He just hoped Nigel didn't have that too.

They were both increasingly curious about the film script – had Stillgoe managed, even in part, to realise his ambitions?

A few days later he received a letter from Inspector Protheroe on headed notepaper. It read:

Dear Mr Sharkey,
Concerning the effects of the late Derek Stillgoe, I regret to inform you that the Hong Kong government folder containing the typescript which is the subject of your enquiry has been inadvertently destroyed. It was mistakenly included with a batch of similar documents intended for the shredder.

As the typescript it contained was your property I can only express my deep regret that this accident occurred and formulate the hope that any loss involved is not irreparable.

Yours, etc.,
Idwal Protheroe, Inspector.

One Sunday in mid-April Cairns invited Verity to a junk-picnic. It was an idyllic morning. The District Officer drove

round the western end of Hong Kong island – shivering only
as the car passed Telegraph Bay – to Aberdeen.

The village, whose night-time persona was one of fairy
lights and floating restaurants, presented a different picture
– clamorous, dusty and cheerfully rank – by day. Hundreds of
junks and sampans were moored in the channel between it
and the island of Ap Li Chau: some clinging to each other by
the bows like wooden splinters that have floated together in
a pail, some anchored line abreast in straggling rows, with
other craft bustling up and down the channels between
them. Here and there a circle of junks was moored to a single
buoy, the awnings of their poops to the outside: great ragged
flowers drifting on the greasy water.

On the landward side, new concrete buildings were going
up everywhere. The Chinese cemetery on the hill behind
the village rose in tiers like a step pyramid.

This was workaday Aberdeen; Verity's goal was just
beyond it: the yacht marina. Here there was another city of
boats, this time designed with pleasure in mind: dinghies,
power-boats, motorised junks, all painted and shipshape, the
toys of the affluent.

As Verity drove up he saw Jack Cairns standing beside a
wood-and-canvas shack swarmed around by a gaggle of
brown-skinned children. 'Nigel! Good to see you,' he called.
'Park your car over there.'

Verity did so, and walked over to where Cairns was
standing by the waterside. From inside the shack a Chinese
woman, cooking, sent clouds of smoke billowing out from
under the edges of the canvas roof.

A tanned, bow-legged little man came running up a set of
slimy steps from the sea. Cairns put a fatherly arm round his
shoulders and said: 'This is Ah Ngau.'

'Glad to meet you,' responded Verity.

'Ah Ngau is a very enterprising man,' said Cairns in Cantonese. 'He realised that there was money to be made from looking after the boats of the idle rich. Now he's coming down with money – aren't you, Ah Ngau?'

Ah Ngau laughed, his white teeth gleaming in his brown face. 'I am a very poor man. Everybody knows that.'

He called to one of his progeny, a wiry girl of twelve who was the pilot of a flat-topped craft like a floating tray. She edged this vessel over to the jetty, controlling the outboard motor with skill. Verity and Cairns picked their way down the slippery steps, boarded the flat-top (which bobbed alarmingly under their weight) and were conveyed to Cairns's own boat, a small motorised junk called Foo Pah, or Amber.

'Come on board,' called a large, comfortable woman who was already installed there. 'Do some work for a change.'

'So this is how we're going to be treated!' cried Cairns, in high good humour.

'Good morning, Lilian,' said Verity.

'Morning, Nigel.'

'Now,' said Cairns, 'what's gone wrong? We ought to be ready to go.'

'The engine won't start.'

'Again? Engines always have something wrong with them.' He went into the cabin, lifted a trap-door to uncover a diesel motor and started tinkering with it.

'May I help?' Verity asked.

'You can wash the deck down if you like,' said Lilian, handing him a bucket of fresh water and a chamois leather. 'But go easy on the water. We'll need some for when we get back.'

While he washed – hiding the effort it cost him – she

sponged down the superstructure. Cairns, perspiring in the cabin, boomed: 'I don't know why we bother with these things. They get dirty while they're in harbour and you have to wash them. Then you take them out and the brine attacks them; you have to wash them again. And half the time the engine dies on you. Call them pleasure boats!' But he couldn't hide the fact that he was enjoying himself.

He soon had the engine running; they cast off and headed for the overlapping breakwaters that marked the marina's entrance. Then they steered south-west, round the tip of Ap Li Chau, towards Picnic Bay on Lamma island. Cairns stood, massive and hairy-legged, at the wheel, clad in floppy British shorts and a Hawaiian shirt. Lilian and Verity shared the bench under a canvas awning translucent with sunshine; her calm motherliness relaxed him.

They dropped anchor a hundred yards from a little beach; there were only two other boats there, far enough off not to disturb them.

They lazed the rest of the morning away. The sun, reflected from the sea, made small rippling patterns on the underside of the awning, like watered silk.

Lilian produced knitting, explaining that she had a grandchild coming back in England, while the men reminisced about their early days in the New Territories Administration.

Cairns's career was not typical. He had been a village boy from Buckinghamshire who got himself a grammar school education and won a scholarship to Oxford. He came to Hong Kong as a government cadet, but opted out of the power game in favour of the N.T.A. 'I'd learned the requisite two thousand words of Cantonese, you see, and wanted to learn more.'

This move was deplored by his contemporaries, one of who told him 'Go for Secretariat, Jack, and you'll end up a big man.' At which Cairns had pointed to his girth, laughed and said: 'I'm a big man already.' He couldn't, he said, bear the thought of polishing a chair with the seat of his pants for the next thirty years.

Verity was in nostalgic mood. 'Unlike you, Jack,' he said, 'I was always intended for government service. The family's been here for four generations.'

'I know, Verity Path. I was sorry to see it go.'

Luckily for him, he had been at home finishing a law degree when the war broke out. He was with Auchinleck in the western desert when the Japanese occupation came. His parents were both interned in Stanley. His mother died of it. His father survived but didn't want to see Hong Kong again and retired to the family house in Dorset instead. 'I missed the horror, of course. For me the Administration was a home from home.'

Cairns mused. 'Those were good days, Nigel,' he said. 'We were land officers together, remember? You at Tai Po and me at Sai Kung. That's when I wrote my book on Hong Kong butterflies. If only I had time for that sort of thing now!.'

'Seems you've ended up polishing that chair after all.'

'Touché!'

There was a pause, then Verity said: 'I sometimes wonder what I'd have done if I'd stayed in England. Can you see me as a City man, commuting to Waterloo? Or a country solicitor, playing golf on Sundays and buttering up the local bigwigs?'

'Oh, it mightn't have been as bad as all that,' said Cairns unexpectedly.

Verity didn't agree. He had slipped unconsciously into his habitual daydream, a kind of unspoken poem in which he

figured as a man destined to guide other men, and with so
sure a touch that he ruled by acclamation. It was a balm he
sometimes needed to apply to a soul injured by the baseness
of experienced reality. The balm was flowing now, under the
influence of this large benign man who was his boss..

'Come on,' said Cairns, breaking off and standing up.
'Let's have a dip while Lilian gets the grub ready.'

They went forward to the cabin and changed into their
trunks. Cairns had a strong male smell, the kind that calms
fractious children. He dived over the rail, making a mighty
splash. Verity lowered himself over the side and stepped
slowly down the ladder into the sea.

'Splendid, what?' called Cairns, doing a water-churning
crawl.

'Wonderful,' Verity assented, floating on his back.
Weightlessness restored his old flexibility; he suddenly felt
younger. He risked a gentle breast-stroke, swam in a circle
and then returned to the junk. Lilian was busy unwrapping
sandwiches from oiled paper and setting up cans of beer. He
grinned up at her through the water-dazzle.

Still feeling good, he hauled himself up the ladder. Jack
followed. In a moment they were dripping over the deck that
he had just washed down.

'For heaven's sake dry yourselves,' grumbled Lilian and
passed them two big soft towels.

Verity, patting his skin dry, looked across to the green,
scrub-dotted landscape of Lamma and then in the opposite
direction towards the gullied hills behind Aberdeen, scored
by water-courses and strewn with apartment blocks like great
dominoes set on end. Between the two a fishing junk, bow
down, was heading west. God but he loved this place!

'Fall to, lads,' said Lilian, and they obeyed. Even Verity

had a passable appetite; he applied himself to the chicken sandwiches and sipped at his San Mig.

When they had finished the two men went on to the deck, spread their towels and settled down to bask. Lilian stayed in the cabin. 'I flake easily,' she said.

After a period of silence Cairns leaned forward confidentially and said: 'Pardon my mentioning it, Nigel, but is something bothering you?'

'Bothering me? Of course not. Why do you ask?'

'You look off colour.'

Verity's euphoria started to deflate. 'I've never felt better,' he said.

'Forget it then. I'm just being silly.' Cairns lay back and closed his eyes.

But Verity wasn't going to forget it. Speaking in a whisper so that Lilian couldn't hear, he said: 'Isn't my work up to scratch?'

Cairns opened his eyes again, genuinely surprised. 'Of course not, old boy,' he whispered back. 'Your district runs like clockwork. You don't need me to tell you that.'

'Why do you think there's something bothering me then?' Verity's voice had acquired a querulous edge.

'Like I said, you look off colour.'

'I'm perfectly all right!'

'How many summers have you had on the trot?'

'Three.'

'There you are then; that's one too many. You need a spell in England.'

'My batteries do need recharging, I'll grant you that,' said Verity grudgingly. 'But I've got home leave coming in six weeks' time.'

There was another pause. In for a penny, in for a pound,

thought Cairns. 'Do you mind my giving you a piece of advice?' he said.

Verity shook his head.

'See a doctor.'

'But I'm all right! I can see a doctor in England if I want.' He was speaking louder now, but Lilian pretended not to hear.

'No, Nigel,' said Cairns firmly. 'I'd like you to see one now. In fact I've taken the liberty of making an appointment for you. – You can always cancel if you don't like it.'

A wave of bitterness swept over Verity; he could not bring himself to say a word.

Cairns went on with gentle insistence: 'Have you ever thought of early retirement? With your length of service you'd have a jolly good pension. And when your health improved you could always make a fresh start.'

Verity's mortification was complete. So that was what it was all about! The picnic, the joviality, everything. All just to give him the boot. – Oh he didn't doubt that Jack's concern for his health was genuine; he knew himself that he wasn't in good shape. But to be sent packing like this! What a liability he must have become to the service!

The moment was deeply embarrassing. With some idea of laughing it off Verity got to his feet and proclaimed in a voice full of ghastly gaiety: 'Anyone for a swim?' He walked over to the ladder. At that precise moment the familiar sensation of giddiness came over him; he felt his centre of gravity jerking forward. His body had perforce to follow. He fell inelegantly into the water.

Lilian opened her eyes. 'Man overboard!' she cried with studied unconcern. Verity surfaced, his hair plastered to his head. 'My foot slipped,' he called with a wan smile.

As for Cairns, all he could do was pretend nothing had happened. But under his massive calm he was racked with pity and exasperation: the man really was impossible! But in a moment his annoyance had melted; he was left with a profound feeling of sadness. What wretched tricks life got up to – particularly when it discovered someone who hadn't the strength to stand up to them.

The flood of illegal immigrants was drawing most of the police resources of Hong Kong to the land frontier with China, but there was still plenty of work to do in other areas. One day at the end of April Joe Miners and Borland of Narcotics found themselves on Dumbell, and it wasn't to see the preparations for the Three Mountains Festival.

As they boarded the *Sir Cecil Clementi* to return to Hong Kong the Chinese helmsman informed them that he had been instructed to make a stop at Silvermines Bay on Lantau island, to pick up Mr Verity of the New Territories Administration; did they mind?

Of course they didn't. Indeed Joe was glad of it. He hadn't seen Verity for a couple of weeks but had heard alarming reports of his state of health. He would be glad to see for himself.

So Verity duly came aboard. 'Inspector Borland – good to see you!' he said. 'And Joe – what brings you here?'

Miners replied, watching him surreptitiously as he made his stiff-legged way to the bench and sat down. He was indeed a pitiful sight. His back was bent, his gait that of an old man. Worst of all, there was a frightening rigidity about him; even the eyes seemed locked into an unseeing stare. He was clearly at the end of his tether.

What on earth was he doing working? Joe put it down to his inborn stubbornness, being unaware of what had happened. In fact Verity was determined not to see that damned doctor, who had probably been briefed to certify him unfit, so that they could put pressure on him to take early retirement. He simply wasn't going to play ball. He was going to carry on to the bitter end and depart for England when the time came, not before. Beyond that he set himself no goals as he didn't know whether he'd be able to. Thank God he was still able to make coherent conversation though.

Joe watched him sit down and said in an offhand voice: 'Had a hard day, Nigel?'

Verity's locked eyes swivelled in his direction. 'Boundary dispute,' he said gruffly. 'You know how I hate them. – What were you doing on Dumbell?'

'The usual.'

Verity nodded, a painful spectacle. 'That Telegraph Bay business drags on, doesn't it?' he said.

'It wasn't so much that today.' Joe held up a hand as though calling for silence, ascertained that the rush of water past the launch's side prevented the Chinese helmsman from hearing, and said: 'The focus has changed.'

'In what way?'

'We're less interested in people-smuggling at the moment – they're smuggling themselves these days, aren't they? It's more about narcotics.' He waved his pipe in Borland's direction. 'Hence Arthur's presence.'

In his senatorial voice Borland enlarged on what Joe had said. 'You see,' he said, 'the K have always been a drug-based operation essentially; it's where the money is. Smuggling people into the colony was always a sideline – indeed it's not long since they and the T'ung made an agreement. The K were to stick to drugs and the T'ung to people.'

Verity's face twitched. 'Why did the K sink that T'ung boat then?'

'A good question. – Ng became the K's top man in Dumbell. He had big ideas. He wanted to get rid of the T'ung altogether, so he welshed on the agreement and sank their boat.'

'A tough customer, old Ng,' said Joe, almost admiringly.

'Do you have evidence for that?' asked Verity stiffly.

'Not yet,' Borland admitted. 'They're all too scared to testify. And too weak to hit back.'

'Is it all right if I tell Nigel what the situation is as of now?' Miners asked.

'Of course. I don't imagine he's going to rush off and tell old Ng!'

'Right then,' said Joe. 'Nigel: you know the general situation. Opium in its raw state arrives in Macau, where they refine it to morphine. The morphine is smuggled into Hong Kong in small consignments, by junk, and in Hong Kong it's refined further, into heroin (which has only one ninetieth the volume of the original opium). The refining takes place all over the shop – remember that Twenty-One K place we raided up Route Twisk? The lads keep moving on, trying to stay one step ahead of us.

'Once the dope is in the form of heroin it's practically impossible to trace; they can put thousands of dollars worth in an attaché case and take it on the Star Ferry if they feel like it.'

Joe's pipe had gone out. He was groping in his pocket for

his clasp knife when he realised how abnormally tense Verity's attention had become. He went on.

'Arthur will bear me out here: we're pretty certain that the K has become more ambitious. They're refining much more of the stuff than they used to, probably with the American market in mind (they've got connections in places like San Francisco). What we have to work out is: how do they get the heroin out of HK?'

Borland cleared his throat and said: 'Perhaps I should take over here, Joe. Our thinking is that they get it to an outlying island like Dumbell, which has hundreds of boats and is difficult to monitor. It's put on one of them and transferred to some freighter outside territorial waters.

'The problem is that as far as we can make out Dumbell is clean as a whisker. We've got plain clothes men on the ferries, we spot-check as many junks as we're able, and we find nothing. Absolutely nothing.'

Miners butted in. 'Perhaps Arthur should have explained that we've traced a lot of the Twenty-One K heroin to the western districts of Hong Kong island, especially Kennedy Town. Now Dumbell lies almost opposite Kennedy Town; you'd expect it to go to there. But it's Persil-white; we haven't found a thing. You'd almost think they know where we were going to look.'

'Baffling,' observed Borland mournfully. 'It's as though the stuff disappeared into a hole in the ground.'

Silence fell. The launch ploughed steadily on. Having called at Silvermines Bay, it was heading east through the Adamasta Channel, further north than the usual route from Dumbell. Its course brought it close to the islet of Siu Kau Yi Chau.

Verity was showing signs of agitation. His eyes were

locked on the little islet. Now, at four-thirty in the afternoon,
the westering sun, shining from over his shoulder, struck a
momentary gleam from an outcrop of rock at the summit, a
brief illumination which flared into incandescence in his
mind.

He took Joe's arm. 'I think I know where it is,' he said
hoarsely.

'Where what is?' Joe was baffled.

'The heroin.' Verity pointed a trembling finger towards
the islet. 'There,' he said.

'That little place?' put in Borland in polite disbelief.
'Nobody ever goes there.'

'Precisely,' said Verity.

'But the Chinese think it's haunted!'

'All the more reason.'

Borland, nonplussed, turned to Miners. 'What do you
think, Joe?' he asked.

Miners gave him an odd look, like a dog that has picked up
a new and intriguing scent. 'It's just a hunch, of course,' he
said, 'but it's worth trying.'

'But isn't it time we were getting back ... ?'

'It wouldn't do any harm to take a look.' Joe walked over
to the helmsman. 'Is it possible to land here?' he asked. The
man looked at him in some alarm. 'Don't worry; you can stay
on board. We'd just like to stretch our legs.'

The man took a chart from his cupboard, consulted it and
said: 'There is a jetty marked, sir.'

'Good. Make for it, will you?'

It turned out to be a slab of crumbling concrete with grass
and weeds growing out of it. Were there any signs of recent
use? Impossible to say. The helmsman laid the launch
expertly alongside, and the three of them disembarked.

Verity had half expected to see the hollow full of worms he had dreamt of, and was relieved that it wasn't there. He was in an odd, disembodied state of mind, as though inside and outside himself at the same time. He was like a pair of communicating jars – the kind you see in lab experiments – one containing reason and sanity, the other what he hardly dared name madness, but rather irrationality. As the level of one rose, the level of the other fell.

He shivered. Perhaps he was on the verge of losing his reason. But no, he told himself; he was just exhausted through pain and lack of sleep. He forced himself to think logically, to walk along examining the ground.

Miners seemed to be enjoying himself. In his creased shirt, khaki shorts and knee-length socks he looked like a schoolboy let out of school, a schoolboy with grey hair and a pipe – perhaps the victim of a spell which had given him a head thirty years older than the rest of him. As for Borland, his big body was labouring over the rough terrain; he was here under protest.

In Verity's mind the vessel of reason was filling up fast. The islet was not the lurid place his imagination had pictured; it was nondescript and ordinary. He started to walk back to the jetty, following the line of the shore.

He stumbled: that damned illness again! But was it? No, it was just that his foot had caught on a stone. Looking down, he saw that it was one of a small pile blocking a shallow hollow under a projecting slab. Something about it reversed the flow of the liquid in the jars. He bent down, with some difficulty, and pushed the fallen stone away.

At this point his compulsion to repeat his actions came into play. He began automatically to remove the others.

Joe Miners came up. 'What are you doing?' he enquired.

'I ... don't know. I think I may have found something.'

They could both see, behind the removed stones, a flash of dusty green. What was that? Why yes, a canvas bag.

'Leave this to me,' said Miners, getting excited.

Verity straightened up – with immense difficulty – and Joe poked one corner of the canvas aside, taking care not to disturb it too much.

Borland came labouring up. 'What have you got there?' he wheezed.

'Well you might ask, lad!' said Joe. Under the canvas they glimpsed a row of transparent plastic bags, all filled with a white powder.

That same evening the Young Peking Opera Company of Shanghai, with their star actor Yü Chen-Fei, performed in the Astor Theatre in Kowloon. Sharkey, doing penance for having compared Peking opera to the noise made by copulating cats on a pile of dustbin lids, had managed to get three tickets. The third was for Wilson Ho, but Wilson, summoned at the last moment by Lok Yuen to translate a letter from a French import-export company (the millionaire was not above getting something for nothing), had to cry off.

Mary was in consternation. 'What shall we do?' she wailed, waving the little cardboard rectangle, 'These things are precious as gold dust.'

'Couldn't we try Alec?' Sharkey suggested. Wrapped up in their own concerns, they had been neglecting him again.

So, after a quick bite in the flat, they drove to the end of Lyttleton Road and, having parked the car against the high retaining wall, walked along University Path in the gathering dusk.

Ah Fun opened the door to them rather circumspectly. 'Massa not in,' he said.

'Nonsense, Ah Fun,' said Mary gaily, 'there's a light in his bedroom.'

She pushed past the cook-boy carolling 'Alec! Where are you? We've come to take you to the Peking Opera.'

There was a commotion upstairs and Scrymgeour appeared on the landing, red-faced and with his hair – wonder of wonders! – uncombed. 'Just a sec,' he called. 'I'll put on a tie.'

In a moment he reappeared, followed, to their utter astonishment, by a good-looking young Chinese whose cheeks were also glowing. He seemed familiar but in the heat of the moment neither Sharkey nor Mary recognised him. Muttering 'I'm afraid I must go' he crossed the room and vanished out the front door.

'I've been giving him a history lesson,' drawled Scrymgeour.

So that's what they call it nowadays, thought Sharkey, but his new, considerate self said nothing. Mary, flapping her arms like a perplexed seal, said: 'We've a spare ticket for the Astor. We thought we'd take you along.'

'I'd adore that, Mary, but as it happens I'm going tomorrow.'

'That's torn it!' she wailed; somehow she hadn't envisaged a refusal.

'I'd willingly go twice but I've a lecture to prepare and term starts on Monday.'

Sharkey shrugged. 'We'd better buzz off then. Wouldn't want to miss Yü Chen-Fei.'

'Sell your ticket at the theatre,' suggested Scrymgeour. 'You might even make a profit.'

The door closed behind them. 'God, but we put our foot in it that time,' said Mary ruefully.

'I should have guessed. A man without a visible mistress must be getting it some other way.'

'Don't be crude.'

'He once said Rose was his cover. I thought he was joking.'

They sold the extra ticket without any difficulty. The purchaser was Julian Massingbird, in whom four months of Hong Kong had wrought a sea-change: he had dropped his mincing ways, bought an MG tourer and acquired an appetite for Chinese girls. He was sitting on the other side of Mary and, as they waited for the curtain to rise, looked around him imperiously, in quest of a victim.

The theatre was packed, mostly with Chinese families, children and all. They devoured potato crisps and chattered at the top of their voices. Among them, in an ankle-length wadded coat with toggle-fastenings instead of buttons, sat General K'ou. Where on earth had he found the money for a ticket? The answer was sitting in the seat next to him: Fergus O'Hanlon.

Sharkey settled down to watch the show. The company was performing a sampler of its repertory, three extracts from full-length plays. First there was a scene in which the poet Li Po, drunk and half asleep, is summoned by the Emperor to write a poem. He does so, but in a burlesque manner, humiliating the chief eunuch in the process.

There were roars of laughter at his sallies, most of which were beyond Sharkey's by now tolerable Mandarin. The part enabled him to display the laugh for which he was famous: a cross between a peacock's shriek and a turkey's gobble, somehow transposed into the world of music. It was greeted each time by staccato cries of 'Ho! Ho! Ho!' (good, good, good).

'Wonderful!' cried Mary over the din. Sharkey was put in mind of Johnson's dog, but had to agree.

In the second scene a concubine, slighted by the Emperor, got splendidly drunk, and in the third a young scholar, tricked into entering a princess's bedroom, wasn't put to death; instead the princess fell in love with him.

'Never happened to me,' commented Sharkey.

He pondered the nature of Chinese theatre. By western standards it was totally artificial, but once you accepted that fact you began to appreciate it. Take the leading lady in the play about the princess. Although actually played by a man, she was the Platonic essence of feminine beauty and elegance. She wore a magnificent white silk under-dress, with a cloak on top that was peach-coloured and patterned with flowers and scrolls in pastel green and lavender. Her face was a vivid white, with very red lips and very black eyebrows, like a living doll.

Her hand movements were exquisite; and to emphasise them she had two sets of silk sleeves that were too long for her arms. She would raise her forearms delicately, showing off their beauty and allowing the sleeves to ride up as far as her elbows; then, by a series of finely calculated movements, would let them work their way down again till the hands were covered. Then she would start again. Sharkey was put in mind of the use of the fan in Restoration comedy.

But she wasn't all elegance and beauty; the convention allowed for comedy too. When she reached one side of the stage she would kick her silk train aside with a little athletic skip that would have done credit to Oliver Hardy: a small masterpiece of cheeky elegance.

After the show Massingbird disappeared with a hoydenish Chinese girl he had picked up in the interval, and Sharkey and Mary sought out a little northern restaurant near the cinema, noted for its jiao-tse. As they were eating the succulent little bags of pasta from their bamboo sieve Mary said: 'We ought to go back to Alec's.'

'I'll be buggered if I do!' replied Sharkey, roaring with laughter at his own witticism.

'Enough of the filthy jokes. He's my oldest friend here – I've got to go back and make conversation as though nothing had happened.'

'Why are you always right?' grumbled Sharkey. 'Still, there might be a drink in it.'

So for the second time that evening they knocked at the door of the big house in University Path. This time Ah Fun showed them in without comment.

It was half past eleven, but Scrymgeour was still up. 'What brings you back?' he enquired.

'How's the lecture going?' Sharkey countered.

'Not bad.' He gave the 'a' the full Edinburgh treatment. 'Now you answer mine.'

'We thought we'd call in and tell you about the Peking Opera,' said Mary brightly.

'I suspect you're really looking for a drink.'

'Curses, foiled again,' said Sharkey.

'Ah Fun!'

Mary had a gin and tonic, Sharkey a beer (he was thirsty after the jiao-tse) and Scrymgeour himself a glass of neat Glenlivet. The Glenlivet, of course. After that they talked.

Sharkey expatiated on the artificiality of the Peking Opera. How the make-up transformed characters into types: the villains extremely villainous, the heroes wildly heroic, the heroines improbably beautiful. Everything was pushed to the limit of exaggeration. The stories too were fantastic: episodes from myth or legend, set in the distant past.

'Just like Shakespeare,' said Mary stoutly.

'Not altogether,' emended Scrymgeour, 'the difference being that the Bard treated his impossible situations in a realistic manner. Look at Viola.'

'I have a theory about that,' said Sharkey portentously.

'What's that?' asked Mary.

'Give me a moment. I'm just inventing it.' He drew breath. 'It's like this. Realism is a function of individualism. It crops up in societies where the individual is prized. In societies where he sinks back into the commonalty, like ancient China and Japan, art remains myth and fairytale. You need the first stirrings of bourgeois democracy to produce a Shakespeare.'

'You're a clever sod, Liam,' said Mary admiringly. 'I always said so. – But tell me this: why did it happen in England, not Italy or France, which were much more advanced than we were?'

'Methinks I am a prophet, new inspired. Between the door-post and the door, between the San Mig and the gin-and-tonic, I prophesy unto you: no man shall enjoy an individual relationship with another until he has an individual relationship with his God. In other words, put it down to the Reformation.'

'Trust an Ulsterman for that,' said Scrymgeour. 'You'll be attributing it to King Billy next.'

'No. This is pre-Billy. It's Luther and Zwingli and all those obstinate fellows who insisted on having free access to God and won free access to themselves. It was the first time that it had happened in the history of the world and it happened in Europe. The Chinese were oblivious of all that. They went serenely on their way, and their art got stuck in a groove.'

'Not only their art,' said Scrymgeour, whose historian's mettle was roused. 'Their whole development. Their admirable civil service, their enlightened education based on the classics, were light years ahead of us. And stayed that way as long as the world didn't change. But it did. The Renaissance came along – and that's much more important than your Reformation. It gave free access not to God, but to science, which is a different thing altogether.'

'I accept the emendation,' said Sharkey mildly.

'You could say that the Chinese backed the wrong horse. Its name was Stability. It enabled them to preserve art forms like painting and calligraphy with only minute changes through the centuries. There must have been great comfort for ordinary people in that. But the west backed the horse called Change (not the *Book of Changes*, ha-ha). Change brings insecurity, but it ushers in progress. And it is written that the insecure shall inherit the earth. Amen.'

They sat back sipping their drinks and feeling pleased with themselves. It was late and they were tired, but they had a sense of having made up their minds about something important.

Mary mused on the marvellous artefact of ancient China. It was her own barbarian ancestors who had trampled it underfoot and ripped up its silks, driving trains and tanks through a fabric that was the most cunning and elegant ever devised. 'I just wish we could have left it, somehow,' she sighed.

'Left what?'

'China of course. Left it to a Shangri-La existence outside time. With its scholars and emperors and concubines and warlords all dancing together in a sort of Parthenon frieze. We could organise tourist trips for the enlightened – no package tours of course; you'd have to pass an examination before being allowed to buy a ticket.'

Sharkey put his arm round her shoulders. 'The impossible dreams are the best ones,' he said.

'It would certainly be more attractive than a textile factory at Laichikok,' observed Scrymgeour.

'The trouble is, they have to go through the textile factory stage,' said Sharkey gloomily. 'They were Cathay, they are Hong Kong, they will be America. It's what they want, and the sad thing is that the rest of the world wants it too.'

Scrymgeour nodded. He had been playing absent-mindedly with a sort of ornament on a string. Now it fell to the ground.and lolloped across the floor to Sharkey's feet. 'What's this, Alec?' he said.

Mary took it from him. 'It looks like a chop – you know, a Chinese seal,' she said. 'Only it's elliptical, not round.'

'It belongs to my friend who was here earlier,' said Scrymgeour carelessly.

'Where have I seen him before?' wondered Sharkey.

'He's a clerk in one of the district offices. Name of Jeffrey Wing.'

'That's it!' said Mary and Sharkey simultaneously. 'He works for Nigel Verity in Gascoyne Road,' Sharkey added.

'I believe so,' drawled Scrymgeour as if the matter had no importance.

'I tell you what,' Sharkey proposed, 'I've got to go across to Kowloon tomorrow morning. If you like I'll drop it in with him.'

'Good idea. Thanks.'

Sharkey slipped the little irregular cylinder in his pocket and thought no more about it.

⌒

Verity's body still ached but his mind was at ease He had been freed from the thing he most feared, namely the prospect of being forced out of Hong Kong as a public failure, a disgraced man. While Borland and Miners were doing their odd little jig of triumph, like a pair of tipsy pachyderms, he had let himself gingerly down on to the slab of rock above the heroin and sat there feeling only relief; he was far too exhausted for celebration.

Now he would be able to do what he knew must be done, namely take medical advice. What if that did mean forced retirement? In his own mind his entire period of office was now vindicated, and it would soon become public knowledge: just as soon as somebody put in at the islet to collect the drugs and was apprehended by the plain-clothes team that would be waiting – complete with launch – from that very evening on.

Sitting now in his office at nine-thirty the following morning, having already telephoned the Queen Mary Hospital to confirm his appointment, he felt a weary satisfaction.

The buzzer went, announcing a visitor. It was Liam Sharkey. 'You're a rare visitor,' he said, smiling.

'True, Nigel. I was on my way to Kai Tak to do an interview and thought I'd drop in.'

'That was good of you.' Indeed it was; their relations had become almost cordial.

'As a matter of fact I'd hoped to see one of your chaps but I'm told he's not in yet. Name of Jeffrey Wing.'

'So they tell me. I must say it's not typical of him; he's usually most meticulous about his time-keeping. May I enquire what it's about?'

'Of course. I just wanted to bring him something he left at Alec Scrymgeour's house yesterday.'

Sharkey handed over a little brown paper bag (a coin-bag from the Chartered Bank evidently) into which Mary had put the chop, stood up and said: 'I'm afraid I can't stay. I'll be late for my victim.' And he left.

Verity, somewhat uneasily, weighed the little bag in the palm of his hand, then shook out what it contained on to his desk. To his surprise it was a chop – not a personal one, because Jeffrey didn't have one (he wasn't important enough for that) – but an elliptical one, which indicated that it belonged to an organisation. What organisation could the boy possibly belong to?

Looking at it more closely, Verity saw that its central field contained three characters, one above the other. The middle one was shing, or victory; he didn't recognise the other two. Above the top character there was an arrangement of vertical and horizontal strokes that could possibly denote a double door, and under the bottom one stood something resembling the character for the sun, out of which two scroll-like squiggles rose to frame the rest.

The sight of this arrangement made Verity's breathing come fast, and a void scooped itself out in his stomach. Because he knew now what in his folly he had been hiding from himself these last weeks, what Joe Miners had been discreetly trying to tell him. One final piece of self-knowledge was too deeply suppressed ever to come to the surface: namely that he had been in love with Jeffrey. But the rest sufficed to kill his peace of mind for good.

The seal belonged indeed to no private individual, but to the Cho Hai, or Grass Sandal, or messenger official, of a triad.

III

Mountains of Buns

Monday 7th May 1962 dawned warm and hazy. Dumbell Island glimmered up out of the *grisaille*, its huddle of buildings dark between the twin peaks, its many craft scattered like wood-chips on the slate-grey silk of the sea. A faint mistiness steamed up from it; the first transistors began to wail.

Men in shorts and singlets emerged from houses, hawked, vigorously applied throat-scrapers, gazed at the decorated streets and shrines and turned aside to the more mundane consideration of a noodle breakfast.

Presiding over the scene were the forty-foot-high bun mountains: three giant bobbins set up on the quayside inside a framework of scaffolding like a triple doorway. Cloth banners were the doorposts and lintels, a riot of Chinese lettering waved around by flags and pennants.

On Hong Kong Island, high up on the Peak, in a Stewart Terrace floating in a cloud that sent damp fingers even under your sheets, Verity lay awake, tormented by the prospect of his medical examination and the thought of the empty desk at Gascoyne Road where Jeffrey used to sit. Where was its occupant now?

At mid-levels, in Breezy Court, Liam Sharkey's alarm clock rang. He fumbled sleepily for the stop-button, and Mary buried her head in his shoulder. He slid out from under her; she sighed something and fell back into sleep.

In Shaukiwan General K'ou practised tai chi, or shadow-boxing as the Europeans called it, on the waste area behind his shack. His old limbs moved with hallucinating slowness.

And in various other locations soldiers, refugees, Taoist priests and islanders, criminals and policemen, prepared to play whatever role the day would assign them.

The sun rose, colour was born, and at a bound Dumbell Island, Hong Kong, southern China were their living, waking, cacophonous selves.

⌒

By eight o'clock Sharkey was driving the Hillman over Route Twisk to Sekong, looking down on the straggle of army cantonments facing him on the other side of the plain of Yuen Long – permanently flooded, it would seem, with rice paddies and fish ponds – to the vague blue of the hills beyond the Shum Chun river.

He had an appointment with Lieutenant David Pegg of the Lancers, a fair-haired, puzzled-looking young man whose face was constantly peeling in the sun.

He was handed a piece of paper. 'That's your pass,' said Pegg. 'We'll be in and out of the restricted area.'

'So they're still coming?' said Sharkey.

'Like bats out of hell. So many we don't know what to do with them. We put them in the Police Training Camp at Fanling but it's bursting at the seams.'

'Isn't there anywhere else?'

''Fraid not. But the police are going to set up a shuttle service of buses to run them back to the border. A bowl of rice and fish and off they'll go rejoicing.'

'Or not, as the case may be.'

'True enough. Some of them are so hungry they can't eat. Stomach shrunk, you know.'

Sharkey parked his car at the designated area, and Pegg and he joined a detail of soldiers under a Welsh sergeant called Jenkins; they had a jeep, a driver and a lorry with them. Pegg and Sharkey got into the back seat of the jeep and were driven down the Yuen Long-Fanling road, choked with traffic, past rice paddies and vegetable patches, between rows of dusty eucalyptus.

Tugged at by the breeze, they passed between the two golf-courses at Fanling. The larger, the so-called Eden course, was studded with emerald greens, golden-yellow bunkers and little hillocks planted with fir-trees and flowering shrubs. After that they turned left and drove straight to the border, stopping only at a checkpoint where Sharkey had to show his pass.

Between anonymous fields there ran what Sharkey took to be an irrigation dyke. 'That's the Shum Chun river,' said Pegg casually.

The border between communism and the western world! Sharkey whistled; he had never seen it before. On the other side lay China, arbitrary rule, starvation – and you could practically step across it. It was only six feet wide. 'But there's nobody about!' he said to Pegg.

'They come by night.' As if to confirm what he had said there was glint of sunlight from a clump of trees. 'Mobile searchlight,' he observed. 'It sweeps the area at night.'

They followed the road eastward for a couple of miles, passing a gang of coolies putting up a barbed wire fence, and stopped at a hamlet of concrete houses smelling strongly of pigs. A woman gave them a surly stare and two small boys who were dragging a broom handle in the dust pretending it was a horse ignored them.

'Not very friendly, are they?' said Sharkey.

'The woman's husband has just been arrested.'

'What for?'

'Assisting illegal immigrants. Not that the poor sod could do much else; they'd have smashed his house up.'

'Are you telling me that the locals get it in the neck from both sides?'

'I am.'

They continued east to the village of Shataukok on Starling Inlet, where the border reached the sea. It was a squalid fishing village with a police sub-station, an army post, an immigration hut and chow dogs scratching themselves for fleas. Junks filled the narrow creek between itself and a small island just offshore.

It was half in Hong Kong and half in China, with the frontier running down the main street. The difference between the two sides was palpable: to the south, neatly uniformed soldiers and police, spruced-up vehicles; on the Chinese side absolutely nothing. Their frontier post was unmanned; there wasn't a uniformed man to be seen. Occasional civilians ambled along, indifferent to the spectacle of British military might. Stray scraps of paper blew in the wind.

Sharkey was nonplussed. 'What do you make of it?' he asked Pegg.

'It's the same as yesterday.'

'I'm not going to get much copy out of it.' He was filing a long piece, entitled 'Refugee Diary', for Teddy Broome.

'It'll hot up later.'

A van drew up, bringing their lunch: a distressful concoction masquerading as soup, smelling of burnt leeks, in an airtight aluminium cylinder that looked like part of a spin-drier. When it was opened a nauseous aroma smote the air.

Sharkey and Pegg looked at each other simultaneously and said 'School dinners!' They burst out laughing.

'You weren't by any chance at Wellington?' asked Sharkey.

'I was indeed.'

'After me, then. I'm old enough to be your father.'

'Only if you were precocious.'

'I was precocious.' They laughed again.

'You'll do better tonight,' said Pegg. 'We've booked you a room at Fanling. The golfers know how to look after themselves.'

The Queen Mary Hospital, being an old building, had no air-conditioning. A ceiling fan chopped the air in a series of soundless thuds.

Dr O'Young, who was not Irish, smiled with peculiar intensity. 'Sit down, Mr Verity,' he said. 'Sit down.'

Verity propped his lower jaw on his fist to prevent it trembling and asked him: 'You have the results of the tests?'

'Yes.' The narrow gold rims of the doctor's spectacles set off his facial colour, which was nicotine brown.

'What are they?'

Dr O'Young gave a little giggle, by which Verity knew that the news was bad. 'Do you mind answering a few questions first?' he said.

He fumbled with a file on the desk in front of him. Verity knew that there was nothing in it that required confirmation; but doctors sometimes need time to deliver unpalatable truths.

'How is your tremor?'

'About the same. It comes and goes.'

'How many times would you say that your hand trembles in a second?'

Verity removed his hand from his jaw, which broke loose. 'You can see for yourself,' he said stiffly.

'About four times a second,' Dr O'Young calculated. 'Do you have a tremor in your hand and foot at the same time?'

'Occasionally.'

'Same side or different sides?'

'Same side.'

'Do your joints feel stiff?'

'They do. I told you so before.'

'Do you drop things?'

'All the time.'

'Are you constipated?'

This at least was a new question. He reflected: he was chronically prone to constipation in any case, but had it got worse? 'More than usual,' he said.

Dr O'Young had a final question which he did not need to ask. That mask-like face, that hard unblinking stare, said it all. He took a deep breath and said: 'I'm sorry to tell you that you have ... ' His pronunciation made it sound like Pak Hing Sung disease.

'Parkinson's?' echoed Verity, clasping his hands together to keep them still.

'Yes.'

'Well, that's it then.'

The doctor gave him a judicious look. 'These diseases sometimes act quite slowly,' he said.

'What diseases?'

'Progressive diseases.'

'You mean incurable diseases?'

'Progressive diseases, yes. And we have drugs, like atropine ... '

'What does it do?'

'It counteracts the muscular spasms.' He omitted to mention that it had been the standard, indeed the only, treatment of Parkinson's since Charcot's time, nearly a century before.

'I see,' said Verity. 'A palliative.'

Dr O'Young made no comment, but took a large gold-capped fountain pen from his inner pocket and wrote a prescription in green ink. Verity watched him, curiously detached: he felt that he might easily float away from this large diseased object that was his body. He took the proffered prescription.

'There's one other thing,' he said. 'What about my job?'

'You'll have to stop thinking about that. You need rest. Otherwise you'll start having accidents, falling over and so on.'

'In other words, things will get steadily worse.'

'We mustn't look on the dark side.' O'Young screwed the cap back on his pen and sat back.

Now that the worst had come Verity expected to feel
dreadful pain, to shriek and scream in despair. But that didn't
happen; it was as though his system, like a locomotive, had
shunted the diagnosis off into a siding. 'Well, that's it then,'
he repeated.

'I understand you are returning to England next month,'
said the doctor.

'Yes.'

'I wouldn't count on coming back.'

Now, at last, the real anguish came. Never again to see the
Three Mountains Festival, never again to dot the lion's eyes,
never again to be an Important European! 'When will my
superiors know about this?' he faltered.

Dr O'Young was either a humane man or a good guesser.
'Three, four days,' he replied. 'Maybe a week.'

Verity went slack with relief. 'Thank you for your
consideration,' he said and stood up to go.

'Don't forget your prescription.'

The doctor, a professional to his fingertips, watched him
walk out of the room. There was no doubt about it; his
condition had deteriorated in the quarter-hour he had been
with him. His walk was little better than a shuffle.

After the burnt leek soup Sharkey was driven down to the
Police Training Camp to see the detainees, most of whom
had been picked up during the night. 'They crossed the
Shum Chun river after dark and scattered among the
paddies,' said Pegg. 'My chaps were chasing them all night.'

The refugees were housed in two rows of wooden huts like coolie lines, behind the wire fence. About two hundred of them – men, women and children – were standing at the doorways or squatting on the ground; many of the women had the customary double burden, a child slung pick-a-back behind and another in front, inside.

'They'll be put on a lorry to Lo Wu sometime today,' said Pegg. 'They say the Chinese are too disorganised to punish them; I hope that's right. – Anyway some of them will probably be back tomorrow.'

Sharkey looked them over. Most Chinese looked small and underdeveloped compared with Europeans; that was the effect of generations of high feeding in the west. But these people were more than that; they were half-starved. They had hollow eyes and the skin was drawn tight over their cheek-bones. Yet what resilience they must have! They'd abandoned the familiar and set off for the capitalist hell (so their propaganda depicted it), braving death from their own side to do it.

They had accepted the consequences, whatever those might be, without a murmur. Sharkey marvelled. What European could stand even one tenth of the misery that these people took for normal? Truly, he reflected, we are the world's spoiled children.

☞

Verity left the hospital and made his slow way to his car. The concrete of the parking lot was too hot to touch. Well, let it burn, bite, maim.

Across the harbour, on the western horizon, the heat had drained the islands – his islands – of colour.

He sat behind the wheel without switching on the ignition. The PVC of the seat burned through his trousers to the skin underneath; the wheel scorched his fingers; he had forgotten to put a newspaper over it.

His emotions were confused and curiously blunted. But the predominant feeling was relief. The uncertainty was over. And he had not broken out in wild lamentation, nor torn his hair, nor lacerated his cheeks with his nails, as he had feared he might. He didn't even wish to. In fact he didn't want to do anything, merely sit here and let the sun melt away whatever was diseased in him. It was the only kind of voluptuousness left to him.

He thought of possible palliatives: non-medical ones. There were only two, drugs and alcohol. Drugs would be preferable, but what drugs were available to an Important European in white ducks? He couldn't chase the dragon with blue-nostrilled coolies. If he'd been his own grandfather the silent, courteous opium-houses of old China would have been open to him; but where could you find such places today?

So it would have to be alcohol. Suddenly, he had a passionate longing to be home, in England, in a country pub, one of those humid wombs where the smell of hops has impregnated even the wallpaper. Or in a wood-panelled snug with the central heating dribbling warm air against his calves.

That too was impossible, but at least his thoughts were sorted out for the moment: he needed a drink. But where?

He rejected the great mausoleum of the Hong Kong Club, with its turbaned fokis stationed against the wall like caryatids. It would have to be the Gloucester lounge. He drove down to central districts, to the three-storey car park beside the Star Ferry. The concrete had had a fresh coat of white paint, and there was a notice reading PLEASE PAY SHROFF BEFORE LEAVING. Young chaps just out from England didn't know what a shroff was; he found the colonial terminology vaguely consoling.

He got out of the car. A little green-and-white ferry-boat was sidling crabwise towards the landing-stage; it churned up muddy eddies that boiled against the wooden piles.

The Gloucester was three hundred yards away, inland. He took them slowly. Going up in the lift, he realised that he was hoping to see someone, someone who had been there on that fateful day when his troubles began: Liam Sharkey.

The place was empty, except for the Chinese barman polishing glasses behind his counter. Sharkey wasn't there.

He was up near the border, and Pegg was showing him some action. The detail of soldiers was working methodically through the little plain between the Shum Chun and the low hills of Sparrow Ridge. They'd been over the ground before, but knew that there must still be people hidden there, in clumps of bamboo, in farm outbuildings, in the young green rice itself.

The work was hard but exhilarating. They spent hours running along the bunds with the crop waist-high on either side or, where the sowing had been more recent, between flooded paddies full of water like mud soup, on the surface of which the sun's rays were refracted in unsteady rainbows.

It was blazing hot; sweat trickled in fat drops down the runnel of his back.

They caught a couple of teenagers in the green rice, and a bedraggled little family in a clump of trees: a man and his wife, together with his aunt and his mother. The older women had about three teeth between them and their faces were filthy. Mud on a young cheek, Sharkey realised, was healthy and could even be attractive; on skin that was fragile and old it shocked.

On Sparrow Ridge itself they caught a young man with high cheekbones that gave him an Aztec look. He was clearly an intellectual and told them more about the refugees from the Yim Tin commune whom border guards had fired on a few days before.

The strange thing was that many of these had drifted back again, having nowhere else to go. Nothing happened to them. By tacit agreement they reintegrated themselves into their community. No questions were asked; those with gunshot wounds were treated by the commune's medical staff. It was a peculiarly Chinese way of solving an insoluble problem.

But there was nothing for them to eat. People were scratching the ground for roots, or swallowing grass which they could not digest. So many left again, this young man among them. To his astonishment, he found the border posts deserted, so when night came he crawled under the strands of barbed wire, jumped the little river and was in the New Territories. He lay out on Sparrow Ridge all day, without food or drink. When the soldiers finally caught him they gave him a slice of bully and a swig of water from a bottle.

All the prisoners had the same tale of starvation to tell. Rations were down to a couple of catties of rice a week, with the occasional bit of dried fish if you were lucky. They didn't blame the authorities; this was just another instance of mother China being unkind to her children. She withheld rain till the soil cracked and crops withered; they had to eat the seed rice. Animals died, or were slaughtered for food. Even the absence of fertiliser wasn't attributed to the government; it was just bad luck.

Then relatives and friends started to trickle in from the cities, where conditions were even worse. Accommodation was found for them, but rations had to be cut even further. The private plots, a relatively productive source of food, began to fail as people lacked the time and energy to tend them. That was the situation when the luckless five hundred had set off from Yim Tin.

A rumour swept through the camp: the Chinese authorities were supposed to have issued three hundred thousand exit visas, to export at least part of their problem.

'Is it true?' asked Sharkey, wondering.

'No idea,' said Pegg, 'but does it matter? People believe it. We'll be snowed under tomorrow.'

On Dumbell island, in the early hours of the evening, three terrific images were carried on litters to a mat-shed shrine, ready to welcome the local gods the following morning. They were Shan Shang, the god of earth and mountain; To Te Kung, who reports on the behaviour of mortals; and Tai Sze Fung, the black-faced god of the Chinese hades. They arrived amid a great banging of gongs and a plangent braying of pipas.

At every house door little lanterns like paper concertinas had been suspended; each had a coolie hat on to keep the rain out, and a lit candle inside to show the spirits the way to the feast.

A group of Taoist priests, red-gowned and black-caped, came trotting along the street calling on the people to adopt a vegetarian diet in order to avert calamities in the year to come.

In the shrines of the gods little tables with bowls of sand had been set out. Middle-aged women stuck joss-sticks in them, knelt and prayed – for good catches, for freedom from typhoons? Nobody seemed to know, but pray they did, with matter-of-fact fervency, while drums and gongs and trumpets made their din and, close by in its own mat-shed, the Cantonese opera of the Brothers of the Pear Garden was in full flow.

A laughing, chattering public seemed hardly to be listening to the wails and crashes and falsetto shrieks of Chinese music; they observed with unconcern as a gust of wind blew one of the mats aside to reveal a Sung emperor in full make-up stubbing out a cigarette; he set the butt on a rickety bamboo table for later consumption, swept on stage and shrieked out his elaborate part.

Tuesday 8th May.

Pegg's detachment was assigned a one-mile stretch of the border near the headwaters of the Shum Chun. Sharkey had been roused at five-thirty. No time to shave or eat; he found himself in the field just before six in the morning.

The men were split up into small details, each consisting of two squaddies and an NCO. Sharkey joined one of these, in charge of a small rat-faced corporal called Wheeler. The two soldiers were Jock and Bert: Bert was the owner of a transistor the size of a cigarette packet which emitted a wail of such tinny plangency that you felt it was being etched on your eardrum.

As they were looking idly across the river the landscape on the other side suddenly sprouted human figures, dozens upon dozens of them, perhaps fifty yards apart, all moving independently but in the same direction: towards themselves.

'Christ! We'll never stop that lot,' said Jock.

'By the time we've nabbed one o' them the other bleeders will be past us,' said Bert in a semi-comprehensible Midlands accent.

'That's probably the idea,' said Sharkey.

But Corporal Wheeler was having nothing of this. 'Come on, you lot,' he ordered, 'give your arses a rest.'

They did their best to stop the refugees, but were overwhelmed. When one man jumped the little river and squeezed under the barbed wire a soldier would make a move towards him, only for two others to cross, twenty yards away on either side. Even if he managed to collar the first one the other two would be across the water and away. And he'd probably lose the first one too in the general confusion.

'Fuck this for a lark,' said Bert, looking behind him and seeing the landscape dotted with flying figures, all heading in the general direction of Hong Kong.

'Can we shoot at them?' asked Jock, with a hopeful gleam in his eye.

'Use your fucking loaf,' snapped Wheeler. 'Where the

hell's the back-up?' he wailed in exasperation. 'Where's the police? Where's the bloody Immigration?'

In the course of nearly three hours they had managed to capture only six people; perhaps a hundred had got through. Bert had to be detached to mount guard over the prisoners, which left only Wheeler and Jock to try to stem the tide. So Sharkey volunteered to help. An unofficial, unarmed soldier, he could do little but make shooing gestures, like a shepherd at his dog.

Just before nine a peeling and perspiring Pegg drove up in a jeep, with a lorry accompanying.

'Sorry, corporal,' he called to Wheeler, 'we're overrun everywhere. Just do what you can.' Then to Sharkey: 'I'm taking these prisoners back to Fanling. Care to come along?'

'Don't mind if I do. I've seen all there is to be seen here.' Wheeler looked at him with undisguised disgust, but he was past caring.

'By the way, I've organised a car and driver for you this afternoon,' said Pegg.

'What are you, a magician in your spare time?'

'Service with a smile,' grinned the other. 'Hop in.'

Sharkey obliged and they drove off in a cloud of New Territories dust.

☞

On Dumbell island the crowds were getting denser. People kept materialising out of the town's narrow alleys, and each arriving ferry from Hong Kong added to their number. It was

Day Two of the Three Mountains Festival, not the climax but an important part of the build-up to it.

At noon, before the images of the gods, the Run Five Places ceremony took place. Strings of firecrackers went off, twisting and jumping like demented snakes; then the running itself began.

It was real, not ritual, running. A group of Taoist priests came in with a rush. No contemplative calm here; they galloped along the streets with their coat tails flying and their skull-caps askew, to fetch up in front of the gods.

There was a deafening burst of drums and gongs. The priests chanted in a nasal whine, interceding with the spirits. Five small tables stood before the altars, at the four corners and centre of a square; on these were piled all sorts of objects, to be blessed: oranges, bowls of rice, pink-stamped buns like those on the giant towers. Also piles of children's shirts in cellophane wrappings, each with a special stamp on the inside of the collar; once blessed these would become lucky shirts and protect their wearers; the priests carried them around the tables in a pre-arranged sequence of movements.

All this lasted an interminable time, as more and more objects were placed on the tables. Long before the end the Europeans with their clicking cameras had drifted away, wondering where the religion was in all of this. In their culture there was an invisible wall between the sacred and the profane.

Sharkey spent the afternoon having himself driven round the Territories, taking notes. A car and driver gave one a marvellous sense of freedom, he found. Most of his scribblings were about unmemorable things; what stuck most in his mind was a series of casually-glimpsed snapshots for which he had no practical use: three soldiers of the Hong Kong Dog Company, with glossy Dobermann-Pinschers straining at the leash; marching Gurkhas, little square men with bow legs sturdy as tree-trunks; coolies unwinding a great bobbin of barbed wire; a famished figure rising from a covert and skimming the earth like a quail with a broken wing.

Once, beside the border itself, a young man crossed over and slipped under the barbed wire, no more than ten feet from a village woman washing her clothes in the stream. What must she make of him? Her face was expressionless but she must feel something: sympathy, resentment or what?

He got the probable answer half an hour later. He had been daydreaming and suddenly found the car halted by a crowd of shouting, gesticulating men surrounding a cluster of concrete huts near the railway line. Then he saw that there were actually two groups, one of them threatening the other. It didn't occur to him to be afraid. He walked into the middle of the crowd, calling 'What's the problem here? Can I help?'

He was immediately surrounded by the smaller group of men, clearly the owners of the huts. 'Help us, sir, help us!' they cried. 'They say they'll burn down our houses, but we don't have any food to give them.'

So that was what it was about. The larger group were refugees; crazed with hunger and preparing to wreak vengeance on these local peasants – and he had, in his folly, chosen to intervene.

Their anger now focussed on himself. With terrifying clarity he realised that there was every chance he would be dead within the next couple of minutes. And not only he; also his driver, who was sitting petrified at the wheel of the car, too disciplined to move. He would be responsible for another man's death.

And what about Mary? Whatever happened to the driver and himself would be quick, but what she would have to suffer would not. It might well last the rest of her life. He formulated an involuntary prayer to whatever deity might hold sway here: for Mary's sake let it not happen.

It was answered. As the hostile faces closed in on the driver and himself there came the sound of marching feet along the road; it was the detachment of Gurkhas he had passed half an hour before. The mob hesitated, then broke, then melted quickly away. Even a mainland Chinese knows what a Gurkha is.

The English officer at their head came up and asked, in a lah-di-dah voice: 'What's the problem here?'

'We were just about to be lynched.'

The officer shouted an order in Home Counties Kirkali, and the little brown men set off after the refugees. He turned back to Sharkey. 'Shouldn't get involved,' he said. 'This isn't a picnic, you know.'

Something about the man – his sublime self-assurance, his limited intelligence, the conviction that he was right in all circumstances – told Sharkey that this must be Annabel Letterby's husband.

He was still shaking with nerves, but the vision of Annabel's husband as an agent of destiny was so comic that he broke out into a croaking laugh.

The putative Letterby strode off after his men, saying

nothing. But his thoughts were easy enough to read: this little man was clearly out of his mind.

Sharkey sat down in the front seat of the car, beside the driver, and said: 'Sorry about that.'

'That's all right, sir.' He mopped his brow. 'Mind if I have a fag, sir?'

'Go ahead.'

They sat there for perhaps ten minutes, recovering. A train came clattering past, pulling cattle-trucks full of refugees towards Lo Wu and the frontier.

In the space behind where it had been a water-buffalo was drinking from a rice-paddy. The long sweep of the animal's horns was mirrored in the water, until its glistening snout touched the surface and the image was shattered.

At the Police Liaison Meeting, Deputy Commissioner Dashwood (he had been promoted in January) was in the chair, a fact which in Joe Miners's eyes did not bode well.

They were having a heated discussion about the heroin cache on Siu Kau Yi Chau. Borland of Narcotics had just explained how it had come about, giving Nigel Verity due credit. Joe sat in a meditative cloud of smoke.

'I don't care who claims the credit,' said Dashwood sourly. 'The point is: what are we going to do about it?'

Miners removed his briar from his mouth and said: 'Nothing.'

Borland, knowing how he enjoyed baiting people like Dashwood, made a quick qualification. 'Nothing immediate,' he said, 'but I've got a squad watching the place day and night. The moment anyone makes a move for the heroin we'll pick them up.'

'Nobody's likely to,' said Dashwood scornfully. 'This clerk – Verity's clerk, remember – has cut and run.'

'He's not the only man in the Twenty-One K,' observed Miners.

'Nevertheless a determined effort must be made to find him,' said Dashwood to Borland. 'He'll lead us to the others.'

'Can't say I agree,' said Miners.

'Why on earth not?'

'He should be left till he thinks the scent has gone cold. Then he'll make a move.'

'And how long might that be?'

'A month maybe. Or six weeks.'

'Are you prepared to tie up three shifts of men a day for that length of time?' asked Dashwood, turning to Borland accusingly.

'Well, I thought ... '

'Think again. In the present situation, with the colony overrun with refugees, every spare man is needed. So please take these chaps off the drugs watch and reassign them.'

'But we can't just leave the heroin there and hope for the best!' said Joe.

'We've no intention of doing so. I shall announce the find the day after tomorrow and take the stuff away. That will allow us to reallocate the men.'

'What about Wing?' queried Borland.

'You say he's on Dumbell,' declared the Deputy Commissioner, who had regarded the island as his personal fief ever since the praya killing. 'Very well. The island is flooded with extra constables for the festival. No reason why they shouldn't do a trawl for triad suspects tomorrow. They'll probably get Wing as well.'

It was as Joe had feared. Dashwood would take the credit for the drugs find and the search operation, and the Twenty-One K, though dealt a temporary blow, would lie low and fight another day.

'Next business,' said Dashwood.

Sharkey, once he'd got over the experience of the morning, had further memorable snapshots impressed on his mind. There was a labourer in a road-mending gang, for instance: only a coolie leaning on his spade, his white sweatshirt dappled with tar and a collapsed cigarette of his own rolling hanging from his lips. But the plasticity of his attitude made him a living statue.

Or again, there was the old man he had seen watering his vegetables, with a pair of wooden buckets hanging from a pole slung across his shoulders. Each bucket had a narrow pipe rising from it at an angle of forty-five degrees, like a section of tree with a branch growing out of it; as he moved the buckets glided along beside him. It was as though the volition was theirs; they were pulling him along between them.

What struck him about these pictures was their timelessness. Such sights would still be around when his own fretful little concerns had gone for good. Thank heaven (or thank Mary), it was a prospect he was now able to face.

A third impression had nothing timeless about it. A skinny

man of indeterminate age, one of half a dozen refugees being guarded by a British soldier, addressed him in uncertain but still comprehensible English.

'Please, sir,' he said, 'will you help me? I am a Hong Kong national.'

Sharkey stopped in his tracks. 'There's nothing I can do,' he said cautiously. 'I'm a newspaper reporter, not a soldier. But I can take a note of your name.'

'Wong Li Fan,' said the man.

Sharkey looked at him closely. Those protruding eyes, that tense expression – did they constitute a family resemblance? And then there was the third syllable of the name. He found his heart beating faster. 'I'll do what I can for you,' he said to the man in Cantonese.

''Fraid you mustn't talk to the prisoners, sir,' said the guarding soldier politely. He turned to the prisoner and, rather less politely: 'Shut up, you. You can do your talking to the police.'

Sharkey moved off. He couldn't be sure of course, but he would keep an eye open for Wong Li Fan.

On Dumbell, not far from the Pak Tai temple, two lions and an unspecified number of unicorns were waiting to have their eyes dotted.

It was five o'clock in the evening. The more splendid of the two animals was lying flat in the street, like a rug made from its own skin. The head – the one three-dimensional part – was a riot of black and white stripes with yellow and black plush balls sticking out from it on stalks. The face was baroque, merry and sinister. Two gold-circleted eyes lay in hollow sockets; two red lips gaped like a clam, the lower one being a hinged flap with a long red plush tongue attached.

To a clamour of gongs and drums a team of boys dressed in black velvet with white shirts raised this hieratic animal shoulder-high and advanced with it like a forty-foot caterpillar, making for the temple. The musicians followed: the drummer with his buffalo-hide instrument in a little cart, the gong-players carrying their metal discs and hammers like kitchen utensils.

They put this lion down on a broad stone platform before the temple door. Lion Number Two then arrived, accompanied by the same formalities. And unicorns came by the dozen; they were little more than sticks with horses' heads. A group of island notables arrived, and then, finally, the Distinguished Foreign Devil himself: a tall, grey-haired man haggard under his tan, known to some of them. He seemed to have some difficulty in walking.

He was given a long-handled paintbrush and a little pot of black paint. He dipped the brush in the paint, said in Cantonese 'May the coming season be prosperous and the people at peace' and moved the tip of the brush towards the great blind eye. His hands were visibly shaking; the first dot was smudged. But after that he got a grip on himself and managed well enough.

It was half past five before the job was finished. The island worthies clapped him on the back, the drums banged, the gongs clashed. The heraldic animals moved off, who knew where.

Verity, this task accomplished, made his way back to the government launch. He was escorted by the local notables, all laughing and joking. They were of course all members of his Rural Committee.

‎☞

Meanwhile Sharkey had been breaking the law. It was his first venture into crime; until then sin had sufficed. It was, he thought, unlikely to be repeated.

His wanderings in search of copy had led him back to the place where the six refugees were being held by the single British soldier. They were still there, and looking utterly fed up.

'You all right?' called Sharkey.

'They've bleedin' forgot me,' the squaddie complained. 'Talk about browned off!'

'Anything I can do?'

'Naw. I got my orders. Got to wait till the lorry comes.'

'Hold on a minute. We've just seen a lorry, broken down. Maybe it's yours.'

It was true; his driver, an otherwise taciturn man, confirmed it with a grunt. The vehicle in question had its rear left wheel in the ditch; it was lying by the roadside with one haunch down and its nose in the air, like a cow with a broken leg. A glum-looking driver was sitting beside it.

'Just my bleedin' luck,' said the squaddie. 'And these blighters getting shirty and all.'

'What's wrong with them?'

'They've took against the bloke wot speaks English, blowed if I know why.'

'That's strange. – Mind if I have a word with them?'

'OK by me.'

Sharkey addressed the refugees in Cantonese. 'What do you have against this man?' he asked, pointing to Wong who was sitting at a safe distance from the others.

'He's a class enemy.'

Sharkey laughed. 'You're in Hong Kong now. There are no class enemies here.' He thought: old attitudes die hard.

They weren't having that. They protested that the man was an enemy of the people, a running dog of capitalism. They objected to being held with such people.

In response Sharkey took Wong a little further away and asked him, in English, what this was all about.

'They're frightened of me because I speak English,' he said. 'They think I'll tell lies about them and get better treatment.'

Clearly Wong might be in danger, as Sharkey himself had been a few hours earlier. He'd have to do something about it. But what? He had no idea; he'd have to improvise.

He turned to the soldier. 'You know I'm a reporter. Do you mind if I try to get this man's story?'

'Go ahead, mate.'

'Come with me,' said Sharkey and led Wong over to his car. He'd noticed that the driver was a few yards away, having an unofficial cigarette. Besides, the bonnet might give some cover for what he intended to do.

He took his notepad and ballpoint from his pocket and asked Wong a few innocuous questions: where he came from, how he'd got across the border, what he'd had to eat, and so forth. Having written the answers down, he lowered his voice and said 'Fan Fan?'

The man started, and looked frightened.

'Don't worry. And pretend that nothing's happening.' He

cautiously took out his wallet and slid four ten-dollar bills from it, together with his business card, then slipped them into Wong's hand. 'Go to this place,' he whispered. The card, Hong Kong-fashion, had his name and address in Chinese characters on the reverse side.

Wong's eyes were on the verge of starting out of his head, but he had enough presence of mind to pocket the money and the card: whatever happened, the forty dollars would come in handy.

Sharkey's heart was thumping again; this crime business was turning out to be no joke. But the car-bonnet had performed its function; he was pretty sure nobody had seen what he had done. But his driver was treading out his cigarette butt on the tarmac; there was no valid reason for them to stay any longer. What on earth was he to do?

He looked over to where the squaddie was keeping watch over the Chinese, and the Chinese sitting morosely on the grass ...

Grass! Of course, that was it. In English grass nothing dangerous lurked, but it did in Hong Kong. He started walking casually towards the Chinese, then suddenly pulled his foot back and yelled: 'A snake!'

Not for nothing had he played Lady Macbeth in the Wellington school play of 1931. His performance was so convincing that the two British soldiers leapt instinctively backwards, the driver also jumping into the car and slamming the door. Wong's eyes popped. As for the other Chinese, they continued sitting there, understanding nothing.

'It was a banded krait,' said Sharkey, backing off towards the car himself. 'One bite and you're a goner.'

Suddenly his hand went to his mouth. 'Jesus, I've got to tell them!'

'Tell them what you bleedin' like!'

Sharkey called to the refugees in Cantonese: 'There's a snake in the grass beside you. Clear off, as fast as you can.'

All six of them, Wong included, leapt to their feet. Then, as the significance of Sharkey's second sentence sank in, they turned and ran, a little way along the road first, then plunging into a patchwork of little fields with beans growing up bamboo rods. Behind these a clump of eucalyptus offered tempting cover.

The squaddie, knowing that it was out of the question to fire on them, stamped up and down muttering 'I'll get a year's C.B. for this!'

Sharkey tried to reassure him. 'Don't worry,' he said, 'it was the snake's fault. I couldn't do anything else, could I?' Doing good clearly wasn't always as unproblematic as it looked.

Fifteen minutes later David Pegg drove up with a fresh lorry, which was now not needed. Sharkey told him about the snake and offered fulsome apologies.

'Take it easy, Owen,' said Pegg to the disconsolate squaddie. 'You're not to blame. I'll say so in my report.'

It was now nearly six o'clock, and the light was beginning to fail. Pegg joined Sharkey in the car to drive back to Fanling.

'Why don't you come along to the Camp?' he suggested to Sharkey. 'Some of the Chinese have been talking to the police. You could pick up a bagful of stories.'

'I've got to go to the golf club first and phone through my piece,' said Sharkey. 'Perhaps later.'

But he knew that he wouldn't go. He had all the material he needed for his story and had no intention of looking for any more.

Did that mean that he wasn't a good journalist? Probably, he thought, being honest with himself. The good journalist will face any discomfort to get a better story and he, Liam Sharkey, patently would not. Was he too old, or too tired, or didn't he care enough any more?

A little of all three. He straightened his back: it was time to face facts. Journalism was for the loner, the man outside looking in. It was a profession for the unsatisfied. Even in his loner days he wasn't solitary enough for it; he could get by, granted, but only where standards were low, as in Hong Kong.

And now he no longer wanted even that. He wasn't on the outside looking in. He was a fulfilled middle-aged man who had stumbled on a contentment he didn't know existed. All he wanted from life was to enjoy that in comfort.

While Sharkey was composing his article General K'ou was doing his evening tai chi exercises. He performed these on a little open space near his shack. There, in the grey of dawn and the glimmer of approaching night, he kept his muscles in trim and protected himself from tension, a sensation not unknown even to gentle old men with serene faces.

His performance was hallucinatory. He had over the years acquired the art of moving very slowly; it took him twenty minutes to go through the one hundred and eight forms – most men were unable to spin them out to beyond a quarter of an hour. Each form was a kung fu movement slowed to the point of inanition, so long-drawn-out that you could almost hear the muscles crack.

But the muscles didn't crack; the constant slow shift of weight saw to that, and the disposition of movements in opposing pairs created a sense of harmony. An arm would go forward as the bust went back; both arms would part as though drawing out a concertina.

Slowly swaying, slowly parrying imaginary blows (which were hallucinatingly slow themselves), General K'ou went through his repertoire. He performed Step Back and Repulse Monkey, he performed Needle at Sea Bottom, Fair Lady Works Shuttle, Carry Tiger To Mountain, White Snake Puts Out Tongue and Parting The Wild Horse's Mane.

In all of these his limbs described harmonious ellipses, his mind found rhythmical consolation for the destruction of culture all over his motherland, and the regiment of red-faced foreigners and money-grubbing jackasses in this remote corner where the indifferent tide of history had cast him up.

⁓

The following morning, Wednesday 9th May, Sharkey struggled out of sleep into an awareness that somebody was knocking, quietly but insistently, at his bedroom door. Beside him Mary gave a sudden snuffle and sat up, wide awake. 'What is it, Ah Yee?' she called.

He couldn't understand the amah's reply but she was clearly in a state of high excitement. Finally he made out the words 'He come, missee, he come.' That woke him up too.

He reached over to the handle of the door, which was on his side of the bed. 'Come in, Ah Yee,' he said. 'Don't be frightened.'

She refused, but peered enquiringly round the door. Her face was almost sinister with pleasure; the eyes bulged and there was a regular pulse in the neck muscles. Her limbs could hardly keep still. 'Massa, massa, Fan Fan come!' she cried.

'Good heavens,' said Mary. 'Why, that's wonderful!' Then to Sharkey, who was lying back, bathed in a sense of delightful ease: 'Get up at once! Put your dressing gown on.'

So, dressing gown-clad, they followed Ah Yee into the kitchen, where Mary became aware of a tall thin man in his late thirties, with his sister's eyes and a shock of bristly black hair.

'Here he is, missee!'

'I'm very glad to see you,' beamed Mary, while the man said hello in English to her, and by implication to Sharkey.

'He say thank you to massa,' vociferated Ah Yee.

'To massa?' Mary turned to Sharkey in surprise, but Sharkey wasn't explaining. He addressed Wong instead, in Cantonese. 'Glad you were able to make it.'

'Thanks to you, Sha Ki Shing San.'

'Did you have much difficulty?'

'Not really. Once we got away from that soldier I avoided the others and made my own way to Kowloon. I walked four hours, or maybe five. Then I found a bus that took me to the Star Ferry. I crossed the harbour. On this side it was getting late and I didn't know what bus to take, but I had enough money for a taxi. The man brought me straight here.' Under Ah Yee's imperious gaze he fumbled in his pocket and produced four ten-dollar bills. 'You take please,' he said.

Sharkey would have declined but Ah Yee, in strenuous English, demurred. 'You take now, massa,' she said. He took.

By now the full implications of what had happened had dawned on Mary. 'Liam,' she said, awe-stricken, 'did you do all this?'

'I just helped a little. The only real problem I had was in not knowing Mr Wong's family name. I wasn't aware that Ah Yee was a Wong. But after that it was plain sailing.' He turned to the amah. 'Please make it clear to your brother that he can stay here. For as long as he likes.'

Ah Yee shook her head vigorously. 'Fan Fan no need, massa. We got uncle, he live near here, Pokfulam. He go there, maybe get work.'

The two siblings discussed this possibility together in Cantonese. They were touching to look at, with their obvious affection for each other, their excitement, their bulging eyes (might not both have inherited a tendency to hyperactivity of the thyroid?).

Then Fan Fan said 'My sister is right, Sha Ki Shing San. I shall stay with my uncle and apply for an identity card. I used to have one but it was confiscated when I was in the commune.'

'You won't have any trouble getting one,' replied Sharkey. 'Once you reach the urban area the authorities stop chasing you. That prevents blackmail rackets against illegal immigrants.'

After elaborate farewells Sharkey and Mary returned to the bedroom, where she gave a kind of sobbing sniff and threw her arms round his neck. 'Oh Liam,' she said, 'you are wonderful!'

He told her the full story of what had happened,

whereupon she wept outright, kissed him and sobbed: 'You really are, you know. Perfectly wonderful.'

Breakfast was delayed by half an hour or so. As they lay together, slack-limbed, he said 'I've been thinking of this Carte du Tendre business. There ought to be a fourth Tendre, on a river of its own called Honest Affection. The intermediate stops would be Wary Esteem, Shared Suffering and Mutual Help. It's less high-falutin' than the others but it gets there in the end.'

She stroked his stomach. 'You're a wise old bugger, you know.'

'I wouldn't say so! I'm extremely un-wise. Because, you see, I've come to a decision. About journalism. I'm going to give it up. – I'm tired of battening on to other people's misfortunes; it's a nasty business at best. You know the university's offered me a full-time post more than once, provided I registered for a doctorate. It would be less well paid of course, but I'm thinking of taking the offer up.'

She hugged him wordlessly. 'What would your subject be?'

'How about the Carte du Tendre?'

They laughed together, and Sharkey said: 'What's the programme for today? As far as I remember, neither of us has lectures.'

'It's all fixed up. We're going to Dumbell with Alec and Wilson, to see the Three Mountains Festival. Wilson got us stand tickets through his uncle.'

'No rest for the wicked,' yawned Sharkey. But he was well pleased. He'd never seen the Festival, and everybody said it was something you had to see – once.

At 2.25 p.m. precisely, the day being warm and sunny, His
Excellency the Officer Administering the Government – the
Governor, Sir Roderick White, being on leave, was at that
precise instant sipping his breakfast coffee on the island of
Ischia – shook hands with the chairman of the Three
Mountains Festival Organising Committee, namely Mr Ng.
There was polite applause.

H.E. the OAG, in reality the Colonial Secretary, was an
approachable-looking man of fifty, with a florid face and red-
blond hair, wearing a grey lightweight suit. Ng too was
European-suited for the occasion; his gesticulations,
combined with the narrow cut of the trouser legs, made him
look like a stick-puppet.

The temporary stand was packed with people, including
Mary's party of four. She asked Alec after Rose: how was she?
Why was she not here?

'She's not required any more,' answered Scrymgeour with
his snarling smile.

'Oh.' Mary, disconcerted, looked at the crowd, standing in
respectful rows behind lines of policemen. Beyond that, on
the flat roofs of the praya houses, stood more spectators, their
heads sticking up above the low parapets like the corks of
champagne bottles.

Sharkey, looking down rather than up, saw Gus Donoghue
at one corner of the stand, speaking urgently into a
microphone wired to a green tape-recorder; he was recording
the event for Hong Kong Radio.

The Colonial Secretary, having shaken Ng's hand, moved
on to a queue of Chinese notables and government officials

awaiting their turn; each was allotted thirty seconds of the gubernatorial hand, plus accompanying conversation, before making his way back to his seat. Their shoes made a pleasant clatter as they climbed the wooden stairway of the stand.

Last among the officials were District Commissioner John Cairns and District Officer, Islands, Mr Nigel Verity. The acting governor spoke cordially to both before taking his own seat in a throne-like armchair at pavement level, where he gave a wave of the hand to signal that the procession might now begin.

There was a barked command and a thump of feet shifting from at-ease to attention. Donoghue's voice was heard to say: 'And first of all we have the Gurkha Pipe Band. These wonderful little men are the pride of the British Army ... '

His words were drowned by a drone and a skirl as the pipes were tuned. Then, to another command, the band struck up. The spectators looked at each other excitedly; they both delighted in and feared these formidable little men.

The Gurkhas were a symphony of black and white: black trousers and white cotton jackets, black boots and white spats, black leather cross-bandoliers and white insignia. The leader had a silver-topped stick as big as himself; shouting another command, he marched his men off at their rapid rate (one hundred and forty paces to the minute).

Under the musicians' fingers the high-pitched pipes became something swift and fey: wild, elfin instruments curiously muted as compared with the highland pipe. As they moved away Donoghue's voice could again be heard, talking very fast. Drops of sweat glistened on the nape of his neck.

Sharkey was struck by an odd fact. He leaned over to Alec.

'Don't you think there are rather a lot of policemen about?' he asked.

Scrymgeour ran his eye over the scene. 'Really?' he said. 'Counting coppers has never been my thing.'

'But look,' Sharkey urged. 'There are all those constables along the route. And a separate detachment by the stand – that sandy-haired man is the new Deputy Commissioner of Police, and I recognise Inspector Borland of Narcotics from a story I did recently. The little man with the pipe looks familiar – can't think of his name, though.'

Scrymgeour did look, and agreed. 'You would appear to be right. Homo flatfootensis is out in force.'

'Why on earth should that be?' said Mary with a hint of indignation. 'Everybody's behaving perfectly.'

Their main quarry, Jeffrey Wing, was having an uncomfortable time of it. He was indeed on Dumbell; having fled there precipitately on the morning after Sharkey and Mary visited Alec Scrymgeour's house and discovered him there.

Only when he was undressing that evening had he realised that he had lost the chop. It could only have been at University Path so, in consternation, he telephoned Alec. He got the engaged tone, and kept getting it all through the night. He didn't know that Scrymgeour was in the habit of leaving his phone off the hook so as not to be disturbed in his sleep.

At half past eight the following morning Jeffrey had to make a serious decision: would he go to University Path and beard Alec in his den? But what if, for some reason,

Scrymgeour was not there and the chop had got into someone else's hands? It was too risky.

Better to lie low for a day or two and await developments. He could always spin Verity some yarn about why he hadn't come in. He was sure to be believed. So he caught an early ferry to Dumbell and presented himself at the house of his mother's kit pai.

There he was relatively safe, being in roughly the same position as a Sicilian villager with mafia connections hiding from the police. Who he was and where he was hiding were open secrets; anyone might denounce him. But he would be protected by family and clan loyalty, and the fear inspired by the triad. If the worst came to the worst there was always his mother's friend's brother who grew vegetables on a small plot at the south end of the island; he could always hide in the tool shed there during daylight hours.

He had got wind of an increased police presence during the final day of the festival, and was hiding there now.

He wasn't enjoying it. The shed was cramped and smelly, but he had been stupid enough to lose the chop, and now was paying the price. In any case most of the police were due to be withdrawn by the end of the afternoon, when the procession ended, and the rest would surely not stay longer than midnight, when the bun towers had been scaled and everybody was going home.

But he must take care that such a thing never happened again. . .

The procession began with an elderly man carrying a banner – an ornate brocade banner, rectangular in shape, with red silk streamers floating round it like an opera cloak flung over a man's shoulders. Its purpose was to prepare the arrival of the four shrines of the Queen of Heaven located on Dumbell island.

And there they were! There was a storm of applause for them and the deities that followed them: the Goddess of Mercy, Kwan Kung, Hung Shing Tai Wong – some of them riding on little red stretchers, others on miniature temples with curved oriental roofs. One impressive little god, frowning in concentration, was carried in a black lacquered shrine with a red and gold baldaquin. The Queen of Heaven herself sat in a big red armchair under a fishnet awning.

'Aren't they marvellous!' cried Mary, open-mouthed.

'Fascinating,' drawled Scrymgeour.

'Why have I never seen this before?' wondered Sharkey.

Wilson Ho said nothing. He sat there, straight-backed and blinking.

Armies of musicians accompanied the gods, making a glorious din. One fellow beat on a pot-bellied buffalo hide drum carried by women in straw hats. Boys and girls in red and white robes and silk caps banged on cymbals. Fiddle players slouched along, their instruments resting on their thighs: little snakeskin sounding boxes the size of tin cans, strings on their long stems projecting at an angle of forty-five degrees to the body. Other children beat on unpolished brass gongs which hung from bamboo poles across their shoulders, counterweighted by cloth bags full of sand. Pipa players, pop-eyed men with bulging face muscles, extracted plangent shrieks from their clarinet-like instruments.

Mingled with the musicians were priests in black and

yellow robes using umbrellas as parasols, and a drift of white-clad children with pumpkin-shaped lanterns on long poles. Everything was in movement, multicoloured and exciting. As the tempo rose Sharkey and Mary found themselves almost longing for a pause.

Then, on cue, a pause came and they were able to draw breath.

There was movement in the stand. Some people seemed to be leaving, others arriving. Among the latter Lok Yuen and his doll-like wife had chosen this moment to make their entrance. The millionaire pushed his way through the police screen, greeting all and sundry. His head was studded with its customary glints of gold from teeth and glasses; inside an exquisite piece of suiting he moved like a boxer entering the ring.

'Hallo missus Load,' he called, catching sight of Mary. 'Hallo mista Shakee. Hallo Wilson, how you Freng?'

Scrymgeour, offended at not being recognised, made an ironic bow.

'Who's you flen?' Lok asked Mary amiably.

'Professor Scrymgeour,' replied Mary soothingly. 'You remember, the race meeting.'

'Oh yeah, now I lemem. Nice to see you, plofessa.' He shouldered his way to his seat in the front row, a few places from the Colonial Secretary, who could be heard congratulating Mrs Lok on her elegant appearance and making some financial joke with the millionaire himself.

Lok laughed mightily. 'I see you hear I make killing,' he cried.

At that point there was an unheralded addition to the programme. It was the lion which owed the dots on its eyes – one smudged, one not – to Verity. Verity himself was hardly aware of it. He was having one of his attacks; he could feel the burning of it in his knee joints and the rushing, as of rivers of fire, in his veins. The only remedy was to sit up as straight as he could and lock his eyes on to the line of roofs; as long as that didn't move he knew he was all right.

Meanwhile, to roars of pleasure, the lion danced in, shaking its hundreds of stripes and nodding its shaggy head. It pranced along to a cacophony of cymbals and firecrackers, its great hinged tongue lolling from its jaws. In spite of its stylised joyfulness Sharkey detected something sinister about it. But the Chinese crowd, which centuries of lions had not succeeded in tiring of the experience, welcomed it deliriously. The great beast responded by flinging its coils from side to side in a frenzy, then sinking to the ground and bowing to His Excellency. After that it got up and danced away.

◠

The man called Vanguard heard the applause and opened his eyes. He slept mostly during the day because his line of work consisted almost entirely of night shifts. He had perfected the art of cat-napping, and the slightest alteration to the background noise found him instantly wide-awake. He registered the fact that this was merely increased crowd-noise and closed his eyes again.

He was holed up in a kind of broom cupboard, not far from the praya, which had once been employed by the T'ung but had fallen into disuse. He slept under a battered table, behind a pile of rolled-up mats which hid him from sight. His sleeping place was no wider than his own body, draughty and uncomfortable (he lay on the bare boards), but he had been used to such conditions since he was a child.

Properly speaking, he didn't have a home. His few possessions were stashed away in a junk belonging to an acquaintance whom he could trust, his domicile shared out among three bolt-holes, one in his native Macau, one in mainland China and this place on Dumbell. He took care that no one got to know his name; especially in Hong Kong where the police service was relatively incorruptible.

He too had got wind of the fact that there were more police than usual on Dumbell today, but with every hour that passed he became more confident that he would not be caught. If by any chance they happened on this hideaway he could always get out by a hole in the floor which he kept covered with a tea-chest lid.

In a moment he was asleep.

The procession, which had disintegrated under the impact of the lion, started to reform. Gods in their litters, straw-hatted children carrying censers, gong-beaters – the whole heterogeneous collection was marshalled and prepared to move off.

Mary once more became conscious of comings and goings in the stand, this time more marked. Large Europeans (who looked like policemen) and spick-and-span Chinese (who did not) were moving along the rows of seats apologising for treading on people's toes, whispering something to selected men and escorting them away. A number of seats, many towards the front of the stand, were empty now, like the sockets of drawn teeth.

Mary murmured urgently to Scrymgeour: 'Alec, have you noticed? A lot of people seem to be going.'

'No great loss, my dear.'

But Mary was puzzled. 'People seem to be taking them away,' she said.

Sharkey, overhearing, realised what it was all about. 'They're being arrested,' he whispered.

'Arrested!'

'Shh. You'll disturb people.'

'Did you say something about people being arrested?' enquired Wilson. For once there was a tremor of emotion in his voice: could he possibly be alarmed?

Sharkey was formulating a cautious answer to that question when his voice was drowned out by a great roar of expectation from the crowd. The tableaux, the Three Mountains Festival's speciality, were coming.

In all the excitement it was impossible to think of arrests or anything else: this was Dumbell Island saluting its unique art-form, its passport to fame. Sharkey and Mary were caught up in it; the only comparison that Mary, a North Country lass, could make was with a Cup-winning football team being driven round its home city in an open bus, bathing in adulation.

The first tableau, according to the programme, illustrated the theme of idleness: Take It Easy, or Let Things Go. A huge stretcher, borne by eight men, carried a little boy with a black-painted moustache, representing a Chicago gangster; he held in his hand a revolver on which was balanced a fanwise pack of cards, out of which sprouted a whisky bottle.

Balanced precariously on the neck of the bottle was the gangster's moll, an enchanting moppet about as wicked as a cherub. A British child, Sharkey reflected, floating along in mid-air like that, would either have been terrified or hard-put to keep her face straight. But this little girl was concentrating on the task in hand with divine solemnity. Mary was moved by her; she thought: I shall always love these people.

The bearers set the tableau down before the dignitaries, who applauded. Then the next set of swaying figures replaced it. Then another, then another. Each attracted deafening applause; only when your ear had become attuned to it did you realise that it had gradations; some fortissimi were louder than others. Why that should be was a mystery.

By now it was the hottest part of the afternoon. Sun and excitement made the spectators half drunk. The whole procession became a multicoloured whirl from which scattered images emerged: girls in lavender dresses and blue sashes; ghosts with flour-daubed faces; a hen-pecked husband with a bench across his shoulders and his shrewish wife with a stick (she gave him an extra-hard thump as they passed His Excellency); stilt-walkers swaggering along blowing whistles. Only the occasional glimpse of a wrist-watch betrayed the fact that this was the twentieth century.

The Kingfisher and the Oyster put in their appearance, then the Monkey, poking about for the scriptures in the clothes of children by the roadside, who screamed with delight when he touched them.

High above the mêlée sailed the children of the tableaux: a courtier from Imperial China clad in blue and silver, a small girl cycling round and round the rim of a paper umbrella; a courtesan in a blue dress with a tiara of silver flowers, her face as white as flour but shading off into pink round the edges.

And what perilous assemblages they were mounted on! One on a lotus, another on a cockerel's wing. One on a gold-framed calendar standing on a pair of candles that grew out of a golden bowl, itself on a tray in a little girl's hand. Another on a hoop mounted on a tennis ball on a racquet carried by another little girl.

'Aren't you glad you came?' cried Mary, squeezing Sharkey's arm.

'Indeed. It's amazing.'

'The symbolism is sexual, of course,' drawled Scrymgeour.

'Nonsense,' exclaimed Mary.

'All flying is. Read your Freud.'

'Do you imagine these people have?' put in Sharkey.

'Sexual, my foot!' Mary protested. 'It's the spirit of life exorcising death. Isn't that what this festival is about?'

Sharkey agreed, but wondered whether there wasn't also a whiff of death about it – just to add spice.

Somebody threw open the rickety door of Sin Fung's hideaway with a clatter. For once his sleep had been too sound; he lay behind his rolls of matting, trying to gather his wits. Fortunately, his years on the run had taught him one valuable lesson: when you can't escape, freeze. He froze.

'Damn all here,' said a voice in Cantonese.

'We'll have to look just the same,' said a second.

They clearly belonged to Chinese constables.

'But there's nowhere to put anything. The place is full up.'

'We'll have to try. It's supposed to be a T'ung house.'

'All right.'

With much panting and swearing two sets of arms moved bamboo poles and banners, sacks of material that might be ceremonial clothes, even a crateful of china bowls and glasses, and piled them up on the stacked chairs and little tables that were the principal contents of the building.

'Like I said,' remarked the first voice, 'there's nothing here. It's been empty for years. Just look at the dust.'

Sin Fung, painfully holding his breath, was thankful that he had always used the hole in the floor for getting in and out.

'Hold on a minute,' said Voice Two. 'How about those rolls of matting – shouldn't we pull them out?'

'If you think so.'

The arms started heaving at the mats, but they were so heavy, and jammed so firmly behind the legs of the table, that they couldn't shift them.

'To hell with this!'

'Give them a kick for luck.'

A battery of blows from heavy police boots rained down on the matting. There was so much of it that Sin Fung felt nothing.

'Come on,' said Voice Two at last. 'We'll report it. Somebody else can deal with it.'

The boots now stamped on the floorboards and the door was slammed shut. Sin Fung, alone at last, expelled his breath in a great gasp. He was going to lose a good hiding place, but at least he was still a free man.

Wilson Ho looked uneasily across the stand, stood up and uttered a sound resembling the yelp of a Pekingese. It was a totally unexpected development, and Sharkey swivelled round in his seat to look at him.

Mary too was astonished and cried: 'What's wrong, Wilson?'

'They're taking him away!' The young man pointed to where a pair of European policemen were frog-marching a middle-aged Chinese with horn-rimmed glasses out of the stand.

'Who is it?' Mary asked urgently.

'My uncle, Mr Ho Man.'

'Not the man who got us the tickets?' drawled Scrymgeour, looking up. 'That's a bit thick.'

Something would have to be done. 'Come on, Wilson,' said Sharkey. 'I'm going down to protest.'

'I'm coming too,' said Mary decisively.

The three of them started picking their way past rounded backs and bony knees. 'Rather you than me,' said Scrymgeour. 'I'll stay and keep the seats.'

On the street unicorns were dancing, pipas wailing and the crowd cheering itself hoarse as they clumped their way down the wooden stairs and round behind the stand. They found themselves on a narrow strip of concrete between the stand and the harbour; it was occupied entirely by policemen, European and Chinese.

Sharkey and Mary pushed their way forward as though they were perfectly entitled to be there. They got away with it because they were Europeans, and Wilson – though attracting questioning looks – was tolerated because he was with them.

Inspector Borland, who had shown Sharkey the heroin factory on Route Twisk, was standing talking to the small man with the pipe whom he now recognised as Inspector Miners of Triads. The three of them went up to him.

Sharkey buttonholed Borland. 'Inspector,' he said firmly, 'can you please tell me why Mr Ho Man has been arrested?'

'I'm afraid not,' replied the big man, embarrassed but polite.

'Can you take us to him?'

'Afraid I can't do that either.' He pointed to a police launch which had just left the quayside. 'He's on that boat. Going back to Headquarters.'

'Arthur,' interposed the man with the pipe, 'there's no reason why we shouldn't tell these people. It'll all come out soon enough. This is an anti-narcotics operation. Involving triads.'

At this point Wilson drew himself up to his full height. 'I wish to make a statement,' he declared, gauche but oddly impressive.

'Oh yes?'

'Mr Ho Man is my uncle. He has nothing to do with drugs or triads.'

'I'm very glad to hear it,' said Borland impressively. 'In that case he'll be released straight away.'

Miners' reaction was more avuncular. He merely said: 'I believe you, lad.'

But Wilson was not mollified. 'You believe nothing,' he cried, 'otherwise you wouldn't have arrested him.'

Miners' pipe had gone out. He took it from his mouth and slid it into his breast pocket (Sharkey wondering the while whether he was in danger of bursting into flames). 'Listen, son,' he said, 'This is strictly off the record; if you say I told you I'll deny it. Understood?'

Wilson looked at him scornfully but said nothing. Miners proceeded: 'If you'd asked me a few weeks ago about your uncle and the other guys that opposed the Twenty-One K on Dumbell I'd have said they were T''ung members angry because their boat had been sunk. Now I know better – don't ask me how. They were honest men making an honest protest. – Of course they were intimidated later; people always are. They were told that their families – and that includes you – would suffer if they talked. It's an old story. Does it make things clear?'

'No,' said Wilson harshly. 'It explains nothing.'

Miners gave a rueful grin. 'You haven't understood,' he said. 'Not all my colleagues agree with me, and they're the ones who make the decisions. They're picking up everybody with triad connections, known or suspected, because of a drug seizure we've made. You'll hear all about it tomorrow.'

There was a pause. 'I do not believe you,' said Wilson unsteadily.

Sharkey was alarmed; there was something panicky and dangerous about the young man that reminded him of those coolies the papers were always talking about, who reach the end of their tether and lay about them with a chopper. He just hoped that wasn't the case with Wilson.

He was quickly disabused. Mary, wrung with pity, exclaimed: 'Oh Wilson, can't you just think things over for a bit – till tomorrow?' She held her arm out to put it round his shoulders, to act as a surrogate mother to him. His reaction was to start back as though a scorpion had stung him. 'Don't touch me!' he screamed. 'You are vile, unclean!'

Mary recoiled, devastated. Sharkey, suppressing his anger, put his arm round her and said, in as mild a voice as he could muster: 'That's not fair, Wilson. You owe Mary an apology.'

But the young man was not for apologising. He gave Sharkey a scornful look. 'Reactionary filth!' he exclaimed. 'You understand nothing. All you think of is sex. You disgust me.'

Miners and Borland slowly withdrew, realising that this was not their quarrel.

In Wilson the floodgates were open. 'Enemies of the people!' he cried. 'For years you have been pouring your decadent poison into me, your Eliot and Joyce and Yeats – the whole reactionary gang. Corrupters of youth, purveyors of filth, peddlers of false doctrine!'

'But Wilson ... ' began Mary. He brushed her aside.

'All literature is for the masses,' he declaimed. 'The political criterion goes before the artistic. Observe and depict from the standpoint of the proletariat. Shun uncritical borrowing from foreigners. Refresh your ideology by merging with the masses.'

'Mao, if I'm not mistaken,' said Sharkey.

'They say he's a good poet himself,' said Mary.

Wilson was incensed. 'Hold your tongue! How dare you speak of him? He would have cut his hand off if it had been capable only of writing beautiful trifles. – I would have cut it off for him.'

'Oh God,' wailed Mary. 'Is that what you've got from my lectures?'

'So you're a Maoist,' said Sharkey. 'Is that what it boils down to? And you an applicant for a position with the Lok Yuen organisation!'

Wilson flashed him a look filled with hatred. 'You poor fool! Can't you see that my plan was to subvert it from within? No? Then you weren't very intelligent. – I shall be denied that satisfaction now – but what does it matter? Men like Lok were made to be attacked frontally, destroyed, humiliated!'

'If that's your true belief then it's time for you and me to part company,' said Sharkey, holding out his hand.

'A bourgeois gesture,' sneered Wilson. 'Can you not be serious even now?'

Without a further word he pushed past Sharkey and Mary and, looking neither to left nor right, half-walked, half-ran to the end of the stand and into the crowd. He had taken Mao's advice seriously and merged with the masses.

'Oh Wilson, Wilson,' sniffed Mary, dabbing her eyes with her handkerchief. 'I feel so sorry for him. Now we'll never see him again.'

'I just hope he doesn't represent the future,' said Sharkey gloomily.

Alec Scrymgeour certainly didn't represent the future. 'Future?' he would have said, raising one eyebrow. 'What have I to do with the future? Anyway I've read all about it in Gibbon.'

He was watching the final tableau of the Three Mountains Festival procession, illustrating the theme Drug Addicts Are Self-Killers. It featured a small boy in a black coat and cap holding a long-stemmed opium pipe in his hand. On this, balanced at an angle of forty-five degrees, rested a second pipe with another boy sitting cross-legged on it; he was doleful of visage, his cheeks and eye-sockets made hollow with make-up.

As this was being applauded Sharkey and Mary appeared at the end of the stand and made their way up to him. 'You seem to have lost young Wilson,' he observed.

'We have that,' said Mary sadly. As the other spectators went clattering down the stairs past them Sharkey and she explained what had happened.

'Here's a howdy-do,' commented Scrymgeour. 'I never thought our seats would be transformed into musical chairs.' Privately he was unmoved; Wilson wasn't much of a loss – when had he ever made an interesting remark? Besides, he wasn't even good-looking.

'What shall we do now?' Sharkey asked.

'Oh, I'm taking the first ferry to Hong Kong.'

'Aren't you staying for the buns?'

'I think not. Ah Fun expects me home for dinner. I shall crack a bottle of claret and curl up with a good book.'

Extra ferries were waiting at the quayside; they accompanied Scrymgeour there and, when he had found a place on one of them, left him.

'Shouldn't we have gone too?' Sharkey wondered.

'No,' said Mary decisively. 'I'm staying to the bitter end.'

'All right then. But aren't you depressed about Wilson?'

'That's why I'm staying.'

They decided to go for a walk, as neither knew the island. Around them the crowd was dispersing: to eat a vegetarian meal, the last of the Festival, to wait for night to fall and the bun mountains to enjoy their orgiastic moment.

In the gathering dusk they wandered up the little path to Dumbell Peak. It was cool and quiet there; they had the white-painted houses and casuarina trees to themselves.

They sat on a bench near the summit and talked. Mostly about Wilson; they worried about what would happen to him if, as looked likely, he did go to China.

'How could he do it?' Sharkey said. 'With Fan Fan's example in front of him.'

'People don't seem to learn,' said Mary. 'We all start at scratch, as though nobody had ever learned a thing before us.'

'Perhaps that's the real meaning of eternal recurrence. We all make the same mistakes over and over again.' He had a vision of the human race: a multitude of dunce's caps, repeated ad infinitum.

On the path a tall, slow-moving figure appeared. It was Verity, who had been eating at the government bungalow and was now heading back to town.

Mary gave Sharkey a nudge. 'Look who's here.'

'Can we get away?'

'No chance. Anyway he's your old school friend. So talk to him.'

Verity kept doggedly on. When he saw them he tried, and failed, to straighten up.

'Hello, Nigel,' said Sharkey.

'Good evening, Liam. Good evening, Mrs Rhodes.'

'Mary, please.'

Sharkey examined him in the half-light: superficially a bronzed man with grey hair, but inside him there had been a land-slip; the skeleton had started to crumble, leaving the skin flaccid and deflated, like a punctured balloon.

'How are things with you?' he asked, foolishly.

'As a matter of fact I'm dying.'

Mary gasped, horror-stricken. 'Oh God, how awful!' she said.

'Not all at once, you understand,' Verity went on with an

odd, twisted smile. 'Little by little. I've got Parkinson's, you see.'

'Has it been diagnosed?' asked Sharkey, feverishly seeking a way out.

'Oh yes, it's official. – It's a curious sensation. You resent other people's good health. But weakly. You do everything weakly.' Then, abruptly changing the subject: 'I've come to the conclusion, Liam, that you were right and I was wrong.'

'About what?' asked Sharkey, surprised.

'About the choices we made. You chose the real, I chose the ideal. Look where it's got me.' He stared out into the twilight.

Sharkey thought: here at least I can bring him some comfort. 'You don't seem to realise,' he said, 'where reality brought me – to my knees. Only I was lucky; I found Mary. She gives me all the ideal I need, and that turns out to be the cure.'

He put his arm round her; she kissed his cheek in return.

Had Verity heard what he said? Did he understand it? Impossible to tell. He merely said: 'My mistake was to think that life was a foretaste of heaven. It's not. It's the waiting room to hell. And in hell all values are reversed – I believe you will find that in Milton.'

He bowed painfully to them and said: 'Perhaps we shall meet again at the bun-towers.'

And shuffled off unsteadily, moving downhill.

Deputy Commissioner Dashwood was sitting in the police

sub-station on Dumbell, with a glass of cold tea in front of him. He frowned in concentration.

He had still not picked up his principal suspect, although his men had combed the island. They had been round the south-west knob past Shui Hang and Kau Kung Tong; up the Peak; past the Salvation Army Children's Home and the Alliance Bible Seminary; north to the radar station with its little coral beach; and, of course, endlessly in and out of the tiny streets of the village itself.

They had searched houses, shops, restaurants, tin sheds. They had turned people out of their premises. They had shifted piles of goods and left them lying. They had arrested literally dozens of people. But there was no trace of Jeffrey Wing.

Yet Dashwood was convinced that he was on the island, somewhere. What was to be done? He frowned even harder and barked to the sergeant standing beside him: 'We'll search the whole place again.'

The sergeant, bored and weary but endlessly patient, transmitted the order.

⌒

Jeffrey Wing, determined to take no chances, stayed in the discomfort of his tool shed until darkness began to fall. The time passed without incident – most of the islanders were out watching the procession – apart from the clump of two pairs of boots about six o'clock.

Half an hour later he decided it would be safe to venture out. He met with a surprise. He was caught between the boots, which belonged to police constables, and the little village. What's more, the two policemen were moving systematically in his direction, searching as they went. He deduced that they formed part of a cordon closing in from the periphery.

It would be too much of a risk to try to slip through it; so, willy-nilly, he would be forced into the built-up area himself. But was that such a bad thing? Would he not be even safer to be lost among the crowd?

A thought came to him: perhaps it would be even better if he were mistaken for a performer. His mother's kit pai had, he knew, a musician's costume in green silk in her house; if he was quick he might contrive to get it away without being seen.

He broke into a run.

With darkness the ghosts came. They were invisible, of course; but you could feel their presence everywhere. They sailed majestically round the bun mountains, waiting to be fed.

Some said they were the souls of all living creatures eaten by the islanders during the past year, others that they were the spirits of murdered humans, the buns representing their severed heads. Most people believed both at the same time, because what was the point of making a distinction when you didn't make one between a ghost and yourself? Ghosts were just ghosts – and Dumbell ghosts at that: family members who lived not in the next street but in the next dimension.

themselves up on to the face of the towers; they had taken off their ceremonial costumes and were in shorts and singlets, with bags slung round their necks. They swarmed their way upwards, finding finger and toeholds in the gaps between the buns, as rapid and intense as ants.

Some filled their bags at lower levels and climbed down again; others, more ambitious, made for the summits, because the higher a bun's position the greater the luck it conferred.

The inevitable letting off of firecrackers began. In the midst of the cacophony stood Sharkey and Mary; they had eaten at a noodle stall, and whiled away the hours to midnight as best they could; now they were exhausted. But this noisy tumult acted on them like a shot in the arm, rousing them to a last spurt of energy. The anxiety of Wilson's disappearance was temporarily forgotten.

'Look, Liam!' cried Mary, her words more guessed at than heard.

A huge figure came swaying in, above the heads of the crowd. He looked more south Indian than Chinese, like a character from the Kathakali theatre: a fierce countenance painted black and red; green and gold armour; bangles on his arms; his left shin advanced at an angle of forty-five degrees to the body – his whole appearance spelled menace.

He was the god of the Chinese underworld, as profoundly equivocal as so many other things in the festival. The people surging round him might have been worshipping him or baying for his blood. And, embodiment of death as he undoubtedly was, did he not have a tiny effigy of the Goddess of Mercy enthroned on his forehead?

On the towers the young men were swarming higher and higher, hacking off buns and throwing them down to their friends below. Others were dislodged by the climbing feet. There was a mad scramble to get hold of these trophies; people crammed them in their pockets, others tried to steal them. It was a many-sided struggle for the luck-bringers, ending in a tangle of arms and legs.

Not far away a tall, bent European observed this with deep anguish: why, this was the valley of worms all over again! Was this the true expression of life: a writhing of worms in a corpse, like the dance of diseased cells in his own body?

As the buns came raining down, as Sharkey and Mary's last spurt of adrenalin began to fade, they tried to convey their feelings about the whole spectacle – was it a manifestation of life, or of death? Sharkey shouted 'Both!' Meaning that at a certain, fierce level of intensity life became as malevolent as death.

Mary could not have heard a word he said but, somehow, she understood. She flung her arms round him and he responded; they stood there, holding each other tight.

The crowd grinned at them: look at the crazy foreigners! But their mockery was good-natured; they slapped them on the back and shouted incomprehensible things at them in Cantonese.

Meanwhile Jeffrey Wing was dodging through the crowd, a hunted man. The silk costume had not been a good idea; he was the only person wearing one. He was jostled and shouted at; hands snatched at his silk jacket, trying to pull it off. Worst of all, the advancing police cordon had reached the praya and sealed it off. There was nowhere left to go.

He made a desperate, off-the-cuff resolution: safety sometimes lay in the most dangerous place, secrecy in the most exposed. He ran towards the bun mountains, skipping round people as he went.

Sharkey and Mary, their arms still round each other, elbowed their way through the crowd too. They were both exhausted and satiated by the experiences of the day; they could take nothing more in.

Sharkey jerked his free arm towards the quayside where the special ferries were moored; Mary nodded in mute agreement. It was time to return to Hong Kong and whatever life had in store for them.

On the middle tower a green-clad figure was climbing, higher and higher. Verity, staggering with exhaustion, tried to fix his eyes on it; maddeningly, they refused to stay in focus. Nevertheless, something about it reminded him of Jeffrey Wing.

Then it seemed to him that the figure was being attacked by other climbers who swung their fists at it, bent on thwarting it. Someone had told him – was it Joe Miners? – that rival triad gangs vied for the honour of bringing home the largest number of buns. He was filled with anxiety.

But the figure was tenacious; it climbed on, a green wriggling thing that made Verity shudder involuntarily.

At the top of the tower there was a blue and silver hexagonal crown. The green-clad one struggled up to it, only to find another man already there. This man's arm flashed in the harsh light; the green-clad one staggered backwards, lost his footing and began to fall.

He fell with hieratic slowness, rebounding from the convex bulge of the great corn-ear. At the same time the unknown force that for months had been pushing Verity forwards finally had its way. A moment after Jeffrey Wing had been transformed into a small green bundle spurting blood he pitched forward himself and lost consciousness.

Jack and Lilian Cairns found him and took him in charge. They got him on the second ferry to Hong Kong and saw him into hospital.

By then Sharkey and Mary had reached Breezy Court and fallen into bed. And, somewhere off the most northerly point of the island, a man with no longer glossy hair – his luck holding till the end – had been hauled aboard a junk heading for Macau.

Back on Dumbell, the chief priest declared the spirits reconciled, whereupon the islanders fell upon the god of the underworld and belaboured him with sticks. Not for them the despair of Verity or the intellectual subtleties of Sharkey and Mary.

When the god had been thoroughly hacked to pieces they set him on fire; his pyre made an orange splash against the dark.

At last the flames flickered out, and from their ashes everyday life was reborn. Men and women went about their usual business and, somewhere in America, a researcher in a laboratory worked on the properties of the hormone L-dopa.